# The Kingdom Come Series

Book One

Transgression

Olivia,

I HOPE YOU ENJOY THE BOOK AND HAVE A GREAT SUMMER! THANKS!!

# The Kingdom Come Series

Book One

by

## Brandy Ange

Printed in the United States of America

First Printing, 2017

ISBN 978-1-947992-00-9 (paperback)

Marturia Publications

www.brandyange.me

For Distribution Inquiries:
Itasca Books
Attn: Customer Service
5120 Cedar Lake Road
Minneapolis, Minnesota 55416

For Beth Kraft

# Acknowledgements

I would like to thank all of my friends and family who listened to endless hours of idea vomit. Huge thanks to those who sacrificed their time to give me feedback and a second pair of eyes, my sister Candice Ange, my dearest friend (and adoptive sister) Jo Beth Elliott, Alistair Crompton, Debbie Broyles, and Shari Stalls. A special shout out to those who encouraged me to push through doubt and self-criticism and finish the project, Teri Woolard, Mollee Holloman, my mom and dad, Debbie and Michael Calvino, and Christina Cison. The encouragement I received from classmates in college when I first started writing was invaluable. My heartfelt gratitude goes out to three specific teachers, professors, and role models I looked up to and who not only encouraged my writing, but who helped me to develop as a person, Beth Kraft, Bob Ebert, and Rafael Rodriguez, I couldn't have done any of this without you. I would also like to thank Phil Thomas for all of his artistic contributions as well as brainstorming conversations. Finally, a special shout out to Marshall Rushe, see you in Penance!

Praise and glory and wisdom
and thanks and honor and power
and strength be to our God
for ever and ever. Amen!

Revelation 12:7

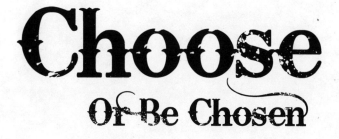

Choose

Or Be Chosen

# Prologue

"How you have fallen from Heaven,
Morning star, son of the dawn!"
Isaiah 14:12

The moon hung high in the sky, the color of parchment. A lazy cloud hovered before it, blurring the view of its bright edges, not unlike the bugs on the windshield of Shael's BMW. The people of Washington DC swarmed the city, like fireflies and mosquitos. The humidity that summer weighed down on the evening's meanderers. Anna's hair especially felt its effect.

"I step outside and it's as if there's been an explosion, and the only thing affected by that explosion is my head. I look like hell smacked me in the face."

Shael covered a wince with a laugh. Anna didn't notice, as she fussed with the passenger-side sun visor.

"And don't you try to tell me otherwise either, 'cause I can see for myself."

"Alright, I won't. You look terrible, horrific really-- If I'm being honest. I mean I've seen amputees--"

"Okay, I don't want your opinion." Anna said abandoning the mirror and flipping up the visor.

"Really?" Shael asked. "Because, it's just that it doesn't matter what you look like. You're the only senator in the country's history with an approval rating as high as yours... Despite that rat's nest of yours, the people love you." Shael grinned and turned at the stop light.

"Well, yeah, it's got to be for my brains because this," she pulled out a chunk of her expanded, frizzy, red curls, "isn't attractive. How far have we got to go?"

"Eight blocks."

Anna let out a groan. "I have to do something with this."

Shael's eyes didn't leave the road as he maneuvered through the city traffic toward the gala. He knew without looking that his wife was performing what he liked to call "Anna-magic" on her hair. By the time they reached the gala, she would look incredible and all the other women would look on with envy.

For Shael the gala invitation acted more as a mandate. He hated politics. Unfortunately, in Shael's line of work he couldn't escape them. As one of the Nephilim, you didn't get to choose your Charge-- they were chosen for you, and you protected them at all costs.

Shael, recognized as one of the best, had never lost a Charge. With that sort of track record, he usually found himself assigned to the most important of humans. Anna occupied a role of significance. Not just to Shael, but to the world. She endeavored to do great things-- Shael's duty was to keep her alive so she could do them.

Shael had never met anyone as positive as Anna. She loved everyone. Everyone loved her. He had fallen for her almost immediately. Even being an angel, Shael had never met anyone more passionate, more caring, more-- he hated admitting it-- Christ-like.

Sure enough, as he pulled up to the curb Anna sighed, "It'll have to do." Her hair was pulled back as tiny ringlets fell around her temples, drawing attention to her piercing eyes. She leaned back against her seat to unbuckle herself. "I hope she wasn't cursed with my hair." She smiled a weak dainty smile over at her husband.

Shael knew she meant Achaia, Anna hated leaving their baby-girl at home; she wanted to show her off to the world. Achaia had a fire, in place of her mother's gentleness, that was all Shael. He knew that was the Nephilim blood at work. But she already had a bushy little bundle of red curls atop her head, just like her mother.

"What are you talking about? With the way you look tonight, anyone would count it a blessing." Shael could still see a flicker of worry in Anna's eyes and smiled, "She'll be fine." He brushed his hand along her cheek. Her lips parted into a nervous grin. "You look great." He winked at her before opening his door to get out.

As if he had wiped away all of her worries, Anna shook her head and opened her own door as Shael stepped out into the street. He reached out his hand with the keys to the valet and stopped short, recognizing the familiar face, "Naphtali?"

"Shael." Naphtali was a tall broad shouldered man with maple skin. Though it had been hundreds of years, he still looked exactly as he had when he and Shael had fought together in Egypt.

"What are you doing here?" Shael asked recovering from his shock and cocking an eyebrow.

Naphtali was the Seraphim assigned as Shael's sort-of probation officer. He didn't usually show up just to shoot the breeze.

"He's stirring." The hint of a smile from before had vanished and his tone had turned serious. "Tonight, keep your eyes open. He's going to make a move." He looked grim.

Shael felt like a stone had dropped in his gut. "There's no way I'm going to let anything happen to her. I've got this under control."

Naphtali shook his head, looking at the ground. When he looked back up Shael could see the doubt in his eyes. "You were never supposed to fall for her." Naphtali gripped the door handle and swung himself up into the driver's seat. "I have a really bad feeling about this. Your judgement has been skewed ever since you married her. You're overconfident," he sounded frustrated, then sighed. "Humility friend." Naphtali spoke gently his pleading reminder.

"She is safe with me. I've never lost anyone." Shael said defensively, feeling as if Naphtali had smacked him in the face.

"Yeah, and do you want tonight to be your first?" Naphtali looked around. When he spoke again his voice softened as he leaned in, "This is a risky business. In order to save them you have to be willing to lose them. You're too emotionally invested if you ask me. You have to be willing to gamble to win--"

"You're trying to tell *me* how to win?" Shael's voice turned cold. His face shook in anger. He searched for the right words to convince his old friend, but came up empty. "She's waiting." He nodded toward Anna who was standing on the other side of the car, looking through the passenger window.

Naphtali looked Shael hard in the face before giving up hope and taking the keys from his hand. "Just expect the unexpected." He started the car.

"I always do." Shael's throat relaxed easing the tension in his voice.

Naphtali put a hand on Shael's chest, stopping him in his tracks. "Which is why when I say it to you, I mean expect the obvious." Naphtali dropped his hand, he had Shael's attention. "Maybe it's been a while, but he knows you. You're smart, but you're cocky. He can, and will, use both against you." Naphtali put the SUV into drive.

Shael, ignoring him, slammed the door and crossed to the sidewalk where he took his wife up toward the gala. The tranquilizing classical music flowing from inside waged war with his mood.

***

Anna wrapped her arm up into her husband's. The hardness in his face worried her. Although he smiled, she could see the lines of tension set in his jaw. "What's wrong?" she asked, giving his arm a slight squeeze.

"What? Nothing," Shael said, placing his free hand over hers on his arm. His brown eyes looked black.

"You've always been an awful liar. You would've never made it in politics." She beamed at her husband and tried to be pleased with the slight increase in his smile.

"It's a good thing you're the politician then." Even though he joked with her, there was still something unsettling about his tone.

"Are you sure you're alright?" This time she stopped walking altogether.

"I'm fine. I just hope he doesn't do anything stupid."

"The valet? I'm sure they wouldn't have hired him tonight if he was a bad driver." Anna's hope dissipated, all of her attempts just about wasted. She watched the tension set further into his jaw and spread to his forehead.

"Come on, we've got to get in there. Everyone is waiting for you." He tugged her gently toward the wide double doors leading into a ballroom.

Anna gave up, hoping maybe once he got to mingling with people he would forget about the valet. He always worried too much. He had a protective tendency toward everything they had.

Anna allowed him to lead her through the doorway and into

the ballroom where hundreds of people stood huddled in groups around tables, chatting politely and enjoying champagne.

"Ah! Anna!" a short, round man exclaimed with a tipsy joy, making his way over to her. "Anna, you look as lovely as ever. Doesn't she?" he said casting a bleary-eyed smile at Shael.

"Indeed. That's what I tell her every morning," Shael agreed. The tension in his jaw faded.

The man looked taken aback, a little confused. Sometimes Shael sounded sarcastic, even when serious, and he would never bother to explain himself to people.

"He really does," Anna confirmed. The man looked pleased once more.

"You know, you may very well be the luckiest bastard in the world. If I were twenty years younger..."

"Twenty years wouldn't be enough, Ira." Shael laughed, patting the old man on the shoulder.

The old man looked half serious and nodded his head. "You're probably right," he smiled. He stood a good foot and a half shorter than Shael, and a few inches shorter than Anna, but Anna found him adorable with his jovial disposition.

Ira was one of Anna's favorites. He had retired from politics, but still paid attention to everything, remaining full of good advice. Sometimes she'd take it, sometimes she wouldn't, but he always offered it whenever he came around.

"She's going to do great things, you know!" As one of the catering staff walked by with a tray of champagne, Ira snatched up another glass almost tipping over the rest.

"Oh, I know that better than anyone," Shael said putting an arm around Anna's shoulders. She leaned into it, happy to see that most of the tension had disappeared.

Her husband had astounding strength; sometimes it still surprised her to feel the muscles, like stone, under his skin. She always envied his confidence, and wished she could borrow some in her career.

Shael had a right to be confident; he held the prize for 'Most Beautiful Man' she had ever seen. When they had first met, Anna thought she had seen an angel. He towered over most men, and was far more fit, even then. He had brown hair with brown eyes, which sometimes held a hue of honey. His voice was low and soothing whenever she had needed calming down; but when he was angry, it was terrifying. He had never been that way with her, though-- only when he felt compelled to "defend her honor." He had an unwavering sense of chivalry.

"We should let her make the rounds; don't need to piss off a bunch of politicians by hogging her all night." Shael smiled down at the old man, a gentle and genuine smile. Anna knew that Ira meant a lot to Shael, too. He often suggested inviting him over for dinner, especially after Ira's wife Emily had passed. Shael always had compassion for him after that. She sometimes got the feeling that he could relate to loss better than most. He didn't like to talk about it, but Anna knew that Shael didn't have any family—at least none that came to their wedding. He only had one close friend, and he was a bit secretive and odd...

"Right. I should get on with the mingling," Anna said, giving Ira a hug and a kiss on the cheek.

"Don't get jealous now, sonny, but I think she's flirting." Ira laughed, the wrinkles in his face accentuated by his smile.

"Well, then I best take her away from you now! See ya later, Ira. It was good talking to you."

"Always a pleasure. More because of her than you." Ira

laughed again, winking at Shael.

"Oh, of course," Shael said as he turned to lead Anna to all the right people.

A lot of Anna's political success, she owed to introductions Shael had made, and she knew it. She did alright on her own, but it always seemed like Shael knew exactly who she needed to talk to and would even keep the conversation going in the right direction. Sometimes she thought she had married her guardian angel.

\*\*\*

The night felt as though it had the intentions of dragging on forever. Shael became more and more agitated with the small talk and niceties, especially being on guard the way the night called for. His eyes grew weary from constantly prowling the room, analyzing every person and the level of threat they posed.

Anna seemed like she had grown tired too. Her eyes looked heavier, and her smile less vibrant; her hair fell out of its up-do and into her face in less elegant ringlets. As the Vice President walked away after a polite but brief conversation, Anna leaned her head against Shael's chest.

"My head is killing me," She said, placing a couple fingertips on her right temple. "Do you think my approval rating would drop if we made an early exit?"

"I think you have some room to fudge," Shael said placing a gentle hand on her back, relieved that he wasn't the only one ready to leave.

They walked slowly to the door, mumbling polite goodbyes as they passed familiar faces. They stood close on the sidewalk, Anna leaning her fatigued body against Shael's as they waited for the car to be brought around. A lanky boy, who looked barely old enough to drive, returned with the car, handed them the keys and wished them a good evening. Shael wished him one as well and opened the door for his wife.

Getting in behind the wheel, Shael started the car. Before taking off, he looked over at Anna; she looked completely drained. "I think we're out of pain medicine at home. We need to stop at the drugstore on our way back." She leaned her head up against the window and closed her eyes.

"Alright," Shael reached over, resting his hand on Anna's leg, which she took hold of sleepily. He drove down the road in silence trying to give Anna's head a rest. It looked as though she had fallen asleep. Shael located an ATM across the street from a department store and pulled into the parking lot of a gas station. Anna's eyes fluttered. "Are we home?"

"No, just at the ATM." Shael got out of the car, put the card into the machine and typed in his PIN number. Just as he punched in the amount for withdraw, he heard a low grumbling sound. He looked around. It rumbled again, just as a faulty pipe would before a burst. He knew perfectly well, though, that the sound hadn't come from a pipe at all.

He listened closely letting his angelic senses take over. He stood perfectly still, his eyes darting around aggressively for the source of the sound, the creature growling. The sound came again, closer. Shael saw the reflective eyes just beyond the corner of the building. The store's closed sign dangled in the window, the only dim light filtering into the parking lot, but Shael could see just fine in the dark.

"Anna stay here, I'll be right back."

"What? Where are you going?" Anna asked, getting out of the car.

"I'll be right back. Just stay in the car," Shael said, following the demon behind the building.

\*\*\*

Anna watched her husband run behind the wall, wondering what in the world he could possibly be doing. He acted so strange sometimes. She walked over to the ATM to get the money out of the slot where it sat fluttering in the wind. She held the money in one hand and hit the return card button. As she tugged the card out of the slot, she felt something cold against her aching temple.

\*\*\*

Shael cornered the demon between the store and the dumpster. He pinned it to the brick with a kick to the gut, and drew a dagger out of the back of his belt. The creature began to choke. At least it sounded like someone choking, but in reality the beast was laughing.

Its black, snake-like face convulsed hysterically as the gurgling sound vibrated in its thick throat. Its eyes, small and beady in comparison to its body-- which was twice the size of Shael's-- filled with victory and euphoria. It didn't even put up a fight; Shael lunged forward and slit its massive throat. Instead of blood, the cement where they stood flooded with a boiling sticky substance, which soon turned to ashes and blew away. The demon had already won, and it knew it.

Shael ran back to the car. He noticed the open car door casting a faint glow along the pavement from the interior light. He ran around to the front of the ATM and found Anna standing white faced. She wasn't alone. The man behind her looked to be about forty, and perhaps homeless. He had a ragged beard and, from the looks of it, hadn't showered in weeks. He held a gun in his hand; shiny, black, and against Anna's head. "What is your name?" Shael asked, with more anger than fear. His reaction frightened Anna. She stood rigid, her eyes widening in disbelief.

The man's eyes, once a pale blue, turned black and his face contorted. Suddenly his teeth were tripled in number and grew razor sharp. The throat beyond appeared endless, like a black pit. His veins burst through his skin, dying his flesh purple, blue, and black. "We are Legion." The man spoke, but instead of the man's voice, it was the voice of a hundred speaking in unison in low raspy tones, dry and crackling.

Anna stiffened and made a move to get away, but was yanked back. The man buried his face into her, sniffing her neck and her hair, his nose formed from two slits in his face. Anna cried now, trembling with fear. Legion's vast mouth twitched up in a sadistic smile.

Shael lifted his dagger. Anna began to weep, tears pouring down her cheeks. She looked deep into her husband's eyes, pleading with him, confused. She didn't understand, that this is what God built him to do, that this is who he was. At that moment the man's face was his own again-- he looked scared, panicked.

"Gi-give me the money, lady," he said. His voice broke, confusion written clearly on his face.

Anna reached up her hand, horror taking hold of her. The man snatched the money from her. Once the money reached his hand his face contorted once more. Shael threw the dagger. It flew through the air with a whistle and dug itself into the man's neck. The gun fired.

The man's body went limp and fell. The face, now that of the demons', laughed as the body plunged toward the ground. Blood poured profusely from the man's neck. Then, the demonic face vanished, and the frightened face of the man was there screaming out in pain.

Shael looked down to Anna. She lay on the ground motionless. Blood twisted through her hair, interwoven rivers of red strewn across the pavement. Her eyes were closed, not tight, but relaxed against her cheeks, drenched with tears. The emptiness of her face told Shael he had failed.

Shael, with a knot in his heart, leaped over her to the man. He lay shaking all over, genuine tears streaming down his face. "Stay still," Shael said, placing a hand over the man's heart. "In the name of Jesus Christ, the son of the living God, I command you-- free this man!" Shael's voice, full of aggressive finality, penetrated the night, drowning out the man's cries.

The man screamed and his chest flew upward as what seemed like a mixture of black smoke and ash flew from his body into the air. The man's body slumped back down to the ground. A flock of nearby birds pecking on the ground was smothered by the ashes and flew straight up into the air and then into the windshield of an on-coming semi.

"I'm sorry, I'm so sorry! I'm sorry," The man cried over and over again, his voice beginning to gurgle in his blood.

"Shh," Shael said, holding the man close, hugging him. He felt the soreness growing in his own throat. "Shh, I forgive you. You're forgiven."

Shael held the man until his weeping ceased and his body grew still. Shael lay the man's body down on the ground, and his own tears began to wet his cheeks.

"I'm sorry," he wept as he crawled over to his wife.

Anna's bleeding had slowed, but red curls continued to fall out of their pins as Shael lifted her onto his lap. Her chest was covered in small beads of sweat from the heat of the evening, looking like tears on her pale skin. Shael's chest tightened. He felt like he was trying to swallow a boulder, which made it hard to breathe. He gasped.

"I'm sorry." He wept into her hair. "I was supposed to protect you; I was *meant* to protect you." He pushed her hair back away from her face, his hand coming away bloodied. She looked like she was sleeping, but the emptiness in her echoed of a deeper slumber; a final rest.

***

"Shael."

At first Shael didn't hear the voice calling his name. His eyes were shut so tight the tears could no longer flow from them.

"Shael," the voice that drew him back to consciousness was soft, coaxing. "Shael."

Shael finally opened his eyes and looked up to see Naphtali standing in front of him. "Naph, I..."

"She's gone, Shael. She's not here anymore." Naphtali came closer to inspect the body of the man. The body leaning against the tire of Shael's SUV was as limp and mutilated as the bodies of the bugs on the windshield.

"I couldn't save either of them." Shael had stopped crying altogether, but he could tell his stillness was more terrifying to Naphtali. Shael's voice had gone emotionless, the raspy hoarseness of sorrow fleeting. His monotone voice and expression told Naphtali that he now flogged himself internally.

"The past is the past. No use in feeling regret. Nothing can be done," Naphtali said walking back over to inspect Anna's body.

"Now, come on, we have to go. He has a new Charge in mind for you."

"So soon?" Shael looked down again at his wife. His voice came in almost a whisper. "I want to tell her I'm sorry."

"She knows."

"I want to tell her in person. I want to explain what I am. I want her to know."

"She knows."

"I want to see her."

"You know the rules. There are rules for a reason, Shael. You've broken enough; you see what happens!"

"What could happen now?!" Shael's voice cracked as if under immense pressure. "I want to see her!" Shael said more quietly, laying her body down softly and standing up with supernatural speed.

"I have neither the power, the authority, nor the desire to grant your request," Naphtali said with a chilling sternness.

"What about my daughter?" Shael asked his voice stern but soft.

"I'll relieve the baby sitter and watch over her while you're gone. Now go."

Shael looked at his friend with an ardent disdain before a pair of brilliant white wings expanded from his back with the sound of crunching bones.

The wings stretched out six feet on either side of him. Beautiful and fierce, the feathers were each a foot long and three inches wide. Shael looked down at his wife's body one last time, and with bitter tears in his eyes launched himself into the night sky.

\*\*\*

Naphtali looked down at Anna's body. He knelt next to her and prayed, then moved to pray over the body of the man. He stood silently, and with his back to their bodies, he too splayed out his wings and took off into the sky.

\*\*\*

Shael stood surrounded by bright white. As he waited, time stalled. It didn't seem to pass at all, but had been passing for far too long. It didn't race, like his mind. Nor did it stand still, like his heart.

It remained, relentless and pitiless.

But Shael had expected this torment. He busied himself thinking of what to say and how to approach the subject of seeing Anna. The prospect of petitioning someone who already knew your every argument, tear, laugh and cutting remark, washed over him with a sense of helplessness.

He knew nothing he could say would make a difference. Nothing he could do would have shock value. He simply hoped for mercy, for grace. Shael knew of God's abundance in both, but he also knew of God's justice.

Shael knew he didn't deserve God's compassion. God was jealous, and Shael had given himself to someone else, and was suffering the consequences. He had compromised God's will for humanity. Asking to see her implied, "I know I hurt you, and I was immensely stupid. It was all for this human, but can I see her even though that would break more of your rules and your heart?"

The clouded wall in front of Shael opened. A Seraphim, with a flaming sword and who was himself on fire, approached in slow, calculated steps. The flames flickering and reflecting off the clouds, turning all the white to gold.

Shael bowed low to the ground, also formed of clouds, as God entered through the opening after a second Seraphim.

Today, God appeared as a tall man wearing white robes, his skin changing colors in ever-shifting hues of black, white, olive, and maple, all at once and independently. His eyes in the same way were blue, green, brown, golden, black, and hazel. He was an astounding sight to behold. The eye could scarcely look at him without driving the mind mad. The mind would try to predict what change would occur next while still sitting in awe over the last, but would never be able to capture a single, stable image. Shael kept his eyes on the floor out of reverence and self-preservation.

When God spoke, no tone of voice existed, but an emotion itself filled the space between them. He didn't so much convey thoughts, but the thought itself traveled audibly between them. All of Shael's thoughts and emotions lay bare before The Lord.

Shael struggled within himself, helpless to hide a single one of them. "This feeling is too much!" Shael screamed aloud.

"But you can handle anything, can't you?" God thought. If there had been a tone, it would have been stern and fatherly.

"Not your burdens. No," Shael said weakly on his knees, where he had collapsed with his hands over his head. At once, the overwhelming senses all subsided into more of a dull ache or vague idea.

"Shael, I will not give you what you have come to ask." Finality filled the air.

"I understand," Shael said, removing his hands from over his head and placing them on the floor, standing himself up on all fours.

"It is hard for you to let her go. You feel that she still needs you." Again he just stated fact, no questions at all.

"Is she scared?"

"Perhaps a little confused." The tone that filled the room eased, becoming less stern and almost humorous, relaxed and father-like. Shael could feel God smiling.

"Father, please."

"Shael, no. Look, Son, I know you feel responsible for her, even more so because of the love that you have for her. But I can assure you, for thousands of years, millions of souls have entered Heaven, Hell, and Purgatory without your assistance."

Shael bowed his head even lower to show his submission to The Father's decision. It also conveyed his sorrow.

"I know your heart. I feel it. But you acted as a human, and thus, you must suffer as one. To love is to lose, and to feel that loss. That is the path you chose, the penalty you chose."

"I know."

"I know you do." The feeling of God's smile faded. Sorrow filled the room, an unbearable sorrow; more sorrow than Shael felt at losing Anna, a crushing sense of loss, and dread. "Your new Charge's name is..."

"No," Shael said with finality. "I'm done. I'm not losing another. I can't do this again. I won't." The sorrow deepened.

"I know," God said, if he had spoken with a voice it would have cracked. Tears fell to the clouded floor from Shael's face. Yet He went on, "You chose this penance, fought for it. It is your duty and destiny to protect, and-"

"No, I won't do it. I'm finished." Shael stood. As he did so, the sorrow nearly crushed him. He fell through the clouded floor, pushed out by the sheer force of agony. As he reached the air outside and the sun, he could no longer feel the crushing weight of God's pain, but his own anger, and with a pang of guilt he hurled himself downward.

\*\*\*

Shael stood among the rocks. Everything around him was frozen. His skin, so dry and cold, had begun to crack and bleed. His blood freezing on the surface of his skin. His lips were chapped, and they, too, were frozen over with blood. He had to keep his lips parted to keep them from freezing together.

He'd forgotten how cold it was here. The breath from his mouth rising like smoke to the stalactite strewn ceiling. Humans pictured Hell as a place of flames. When they told each other to "Burn in hell," they never imagined freezer burn. Shael knew better. He could feel his skin growing paler as his blood contracted inward to keep him warm, but it wasn't working.

"Shael! Well, I'd be lying if I said I wasn't surprised. But that's not really out of my character, is it?" Shael could almost hear the smile in his voice.

"Luc, I'd be lying if I said I was glad to see you." Shael tried to sound serious but with great difficulty since his jaw shook uncontrollably.

"Awe, come on, I haven't seen you in.... How long has it been?"

"Um... A few million years, give or take a hundred thousand or so." Shael smiled, his lips cracking open painfully.

Despite what he had become, Shael could still see his old friend hidden beneath Lucifer's disfigured body, once handsome and charming. He had blue eyes, brown hair, a fair build, and an angelic face. He still appeared well built, but his skin, now blistered and frost bitten, had turned black with frost bite. He was forever cursed, unable to die, unable to heal, pain stacked upon pain. Each injury and ailment a complement to the last. His clothes covered most of the disfigurement, but Shael knew that he wouldn't want to live inside that body. Always in pain, no comfort to be found.

"You look like Hell." Shael said, wincing.

Luc looked around, taking in all the ice in the room. It had a glistening deep blue hue, like his own frostbitten skin. He smiled. "We do resemble each other quite a bit, don't we?" Luc leaned absentmindedly against a block of ice, swishing his robes to adjust them again. He sat and crossed his legs, leaning on one arm. He looked flamboyant in the utmost sense, but only in mannerism, never in speech. He was charismatic despite his isolation. His hair had grown long and black. He wore it spiked out in all directions. The pants under his robe fit tight enough to see more than Shael wanted, and his skin glistened like melting ice. "Tell me, are you comfortable? Too hot? I can turn the AC on if you like. Ice cold lemonade?"

"I'm just fine. I won't be staying long." Shael rolled his eyes. If lying was Luc's first language, sarcasm was a close second.

Luc's face fell, disappointed; his expression genuine, depressed. His deep blue eyes darkened beneath long thick lashes, and stared at the floor. "Oh."

Shael felt bad, he couldn't imagine living like this. Your only company-- demons and enemies-- never a true friend.

"I thought you'd..."

"Died? No. Sorry to disappoint." Shael said harshly.

"Or changed your mind--" Luc smiled as he shrugged a shoulder, recovering from his vulnerability.

"Not quite, I still think you're a bleeding lunatic. I'll never know what I was thinking when I followed you."

His depression subsided, and he transformed back into his flamboyant and manipulative self. "Well then," he said perkily. "What can I do ya for?"

"I lost my Charge tonight."

"Idiot. Where'd you check before here? I doubt they wandered in by accident."

"She was killed. He won't let me see her; He's tried to give me a new Charge already. I'm not ready. I can't do it anymore."

"That senator was yours- oops. My bad." Luc shrugged with a smile. "It wasn't anything personal. The ginger was just in my way."

"Whatever. I know you were after me, you vengeful bastard." Shael tried to calm his temper, taking a deep breath before moving on. "That's not the point. I don't want to do it anymore. But I'm bound. This was my sentence."

"The only way to get out of it is to bind yourself to another." Luc's grin widened filling the bottom portion of his face. He stood up a little straighter with anticipation.

Shael looked down to the floor, his stomach sinking with his eyes. "I know. That's why I'm here." Luc laughed maliciously and jumped once with joy. "I want to sell you the angelic half of my soul. In exchange, I want to be a human, live a normal life. And when I die-"

"We have a slumber party that will last for eternity." Luc smiled childishly. "It'll be fun! What terms are you thinking?"

"My soul in exchange for a normal life. I get to raise my daughter. I don't want this life for her."

"And once she's an adult-"

"I'm all yours, and she lives a normal life, unbound. No ties to him or to you. But not until she's a woman."

"When she becomes a woman, I get you?"

"Yes. But not until then."

"Agreed."

Until now Shael hadn't thought it possible to get any colder, but nevertheless a chill went down his spine. Luc's smile, though beautiful, never comforted those who beheld it.

"I'd offer you a drink, but unfortunately I was kidding about the lemonade. I'm afraid all is frozen down here. Eternally thirsty."

"It's alright. I need to get going anyway. I guess I'll see you later," Shael said in a melancholy tone.

"Oh... right. You get to go back up there." Luc's face dropped, a vastness developed behind his eyes, a hopelessness you couldn't help but feel. "Well, I guess we'd better go ahead and shake on it so you can get back to your little girl."

"Yep," Shael said with as little emotion as possible, walking over to where Luc leaned nonchalantly against the ice.

He approached slowly, so many things rushing through his

mind all at once-- Anna's face, her hair, her smell, Achaia's cries, her tiny hands reaching up at him, Naphtali's warning glances. He reached his hand forward to meet Luc's. Their fingers brushed, the icy chill of Luc's fingertips shook Shael back to reality. He pulled back for a brief moment, looking deeply into Luc's eyes--

An overwhelming sorrow, like the kind of sorrow Shael had felt in the presence of God, filled the space between them. The sorrow here was melded with victory, an internal conflict. Luc's loneliness grappling something unrecognizable within his presence. What might have been love, lay more along the lines of self-pity for being alone. But they had been friends, he didn't want this fate for Shael, did he? How could he?

The sorrow remained for only a moment before the selfish victory won out. Luc plunged his hand forward into Shael's. As he did, all the air was squeezed from Shael's lungs. Every breath he tried to take in suffocated him with a stinging remorse. He felt his strength ripped from him. His heart shattered into a thousand pieces and his back split open as his wings were pulled from his body like white ashes. As Luc let go of his hand, Shael fell to the floor-- weak, human.

# New City

"Photos are the only way,
To hold on to what you knew,
Because the moments they show never change,
When the people in them do."
-Erin Hanson

The floor of the tiny two bedroom apartment was littered with packing boxes. Achaia and her father had become expert movers. They had moved thirty-six times since her thirteenth birthday. Now, Achaia sat on her unmade bed and stared at the mountains around her. She scanned the tops of the boxes which were labeled according to what they held.

More than half of the boxes would remain packed. There was no use in unpacking them, only to pack them again in a matter of weeks. She hadn't seen the contents of some of the boxes since their initial move from Washington. She sometimes wondered what they held; if it would be like Christmas when they finally did open them; and if the boxes made her and her father "hoarders".

Speaking of Christmas, Achaia and her father, Shael, had skipped it this year. They had spent the day finishing up their packing and paused for about ten minutes to drink a cup of hot cocoa together before going right back to work. Ho ho ho.

Her father had been in a rush this time. He said he wanted time to move into the apartment in NYC before the schools started back up from Christmas break; to give her a chance to get "settled". As if they ever settled...

Achaia lay back on her bed, exhausted. Her copper hair stretched across the bed in curly tendrils. Her blue-green eyes scanned the ceiling, drawn to the dust on the blades of her ceiling-fan. She let out a sigh as her stomach growled, pulling her out of her trance. She stood and stepped around the maze of boxes blockading the door with her heart set on food.

Down a short hallway, her father sat in the living room on an ottoman facing what used to be a fireplace, which was now bricked off. He had placed a number of pictures on one half of the mantle and sat hunched over a small box holding the rest of the family photographs, ninety-nine percent of them were of Achaia. The picture in his hand was the oldest of them all. Achaia knew which one it was—she had a copy of the same photo in her room. It was a study in contrasts. Her mother, fair skin and bright red hair, tucked under her father's dark arm. After the terrorist attacks, people had started to look at her father differently. An old woman had even asked Achaia if she was really Shael's daughter. Aside from the shape of her nose, and the set of her eyes, there wasn't much about Achaia to point to her Israeli heritage. She looked almost like a clone of her mother, who looked more Scottish. At least from what Achaia could tell from the photographs.

The one in her father's hand, however, was beaten, folded, tear-stained and worn. He did this every time they unpacked. His fists were clenched around the picture. His face, red and blemished, looked as though he'd been crying, though his cheeks were dry.

"Dad?" Achaia knew it'd be a minute before he noticed she was talking to him, so she took a few steps closer to move the process along.

Achaia hadn't known her mother, and though she'd missed out on having one growing up, now, at the age of sixteen, she had learned to deal. It's not that she didn't miss her mother, she did. Just not in the way girls who had once gotten to know their mothers did. She missed her mother, yes -- she just never mourned her. "Dad?"

"Oh! Yeah? Sorry, sweetie," her father said sitting up and looking in her direction. Though his mouth spoke to her, there was no sign that his mind was following suit.

"It's not your fault," she walked over and took the photo out of his hand and studied its tattered edges. "I'll never understand how you could forgive the guy who shot her, but you can't forgive yourself." Achaia sat down on the floor beside her dad, looking up at him, searching his face for any sign of comprehension.

"I don't know. Maybe I should stop saying 'you'll understand some day.' Maybe you never will. But I don't blame him. His -- state of mind-- the way he was, wasn't all his fault. I should have known better than to leave her alone." His voice was strong and steady, but his face was weak and aged.

"Dad, you had no way of knowing..." Achaia started. Talking about her mother was always an awkward and unproductive topic. At that moment her stomach rumbled, providing the perfect excuse for a change of topic.

24

"Pizza?" they said in unison, smiling at each other halfheartedly.

Shael stood up and walked over to the phone hung on the wall, the only thing in the room that could be easily located.

***

The tile floor felt cold even through Achaia's shoes, but not nearly as frigid as the expressions on the students' faces as they passed her by. She'd counted exactly one smile, the guidance counselor, and even hers seemed forced. Nobody liked coming back to school after Christmas break.

Pretty much every school smelled the same- every cafeteria, every gym, every library... She found her locker down a short hallway under a stairwell. It came pre-dented, and with the last resident's old lunch sack still in it. She hoped it was empty; judging by the smell of it though, she guessed not. She tossed the old sack in the garbage bin at the end of the hall.

No one seemed to have a locker in the little nook but her. She felt a little like Harry Potter, the only kid shoved under the stairs. She decided then and there to refer to the little hall as the dungeon. That, after all, is how the space felt—claustrophobic, dark, and abandoned. New York had been her father's idea. It was the one city she had been hoping not to end up in; it was crowded enough already. The students that passed the mouth to the dungeon and noticed her, looked at her like they agreed; there was no room for her here.

She opened the locker-door and started unpacking her book bag. Once empty, she hung the bag on a hook inside and took her schedule out to see which class she had first. *Geometry, gross*, she thought.

As she looked up from the piece of paper, she noticed a group of students had formed a few lockers down, at the mouth of the dungeon. So, she wasn't alone in this prison. The congregation was weird in that, unlike everyone else, they were wearing actual expressions on their faces.

There were five of them: three boys and two girls. Two of them had to be brother and sister. They were both thin and pale, with bright blue eyes that she could see from a distance, accentuated by their pitch-black hair. It had to be dyed, nobody had hair that dark. The boy actually looked happy to be there. The first girl, on the other hand, looked ten times more miserable than the rest of the students, but at least she was showing some form of emotion.

The students at this school were like mindless drones, listening to their phones and texting without even looking at each other except to scowl. Occasionally, a group of girls would pass by the end of the hall talking way too loudly. The second girl looked like she could join them. She looked like a model who'd fallen out of a preteen magazine. She was tall, thin, with light brown hair and brown eyes. She seemed chipper as well, smiling wider than Achaia had ever seen anyone smile. She'd never known a mouth could be so vast.

The girl laughed and flirted with the black-haired boy tugging on the arm of his sweatshirt, and giggling at every word he said. Achaia came to the conclusion that either he was hilarious, or the girl was really ditsy.

One of the boys looked younger than the rest, but he was the bulkiest in terms of muscle. He had dirty blond hair and green eyes. He looked like a surfer-skater punk. He held his books shoved haphazardly under his arm. They looked like they would fall and scatter at any moment, held in place only by his biceps; which flexed as he laughed along with the others. He looked like the kind of boy who wished he had an attitude problem, but in reality, was just too happy.

The last boy grabbed Achaia's attention more than the others,

26

mainly due to the fact that he was staring at her, not seeming to pay any attention to the black-haired boy's jokes. He didn't seem to be ashamed of the fact; instead he held eye contact without reservation. He was confident, and he had a right to be.

He was muscular for sure. He, too, had green eyes with a lighter shade of blond hair that was an intentionally-unkempt kind of shaggy. He was tan with freckles, and when he responded to his friends she could see his teeth were bright white, but not necessarily straight. He was flat out gorgeous. He was relaxed and reserved, more so than the rest of them. But something about him seemed restless. His eyes were captivating. They held onto hers with a magnetic appeal.

The group divided into two and headed off to their classes. The boy flashed a brilliant, crooked smile at her before breaking eye contact and heading down the hall away from her. Her stomach flipped in on itself as she realized that she had noticed him staring at her because she had been staring at him. It made sense, but somehow, she'd not put two and two together.

She bent down to grab her geometry book and tucked her schedule inside the front cover. She stumbled as she stood back to her feet before heading for the staircase. *Idiot. Awkward idiot.* She cursed to herself as she joined the swell of students climbing the stairs.

Achaia walked into the classroom as everyone else was taking their seats. She was finally starting to see people smiling and talking to each other about what they'd done over break. Achaia walked slowly over to the teacher. The tall, lanky woman greeted her with a smile. "You must be... Ah-chee-ah?" She reached out her hand. "Did I say your name right?"

*Not unless you were referring to a clay animal that has grass*

27

*growing from every orifice of its body*, she thought silently to herself. Achaia smiled reaching for her hand. "It's actually Ah-kay-ah."

"Oh, okay. Sorry, it's not a very common name."

"No. No, it's not." Her smile widened diplomatically. Her father said she got her diplomacy from her mother who had been in politics before she died. Apparently she had been heading for the presidency.

As the handshake ended, the woman turned to address the rest of the class. "Okay guys, listen up! We have a new student with us. Her name is Achaia, she's from..." The woman looked down at her inquiringly.

"Um...everywhere. My dad and I move around a lot," Achaia said with a weak smile.

"Oh, alright then. Um...you can take the seat next to Olivier. His name isn't too popular either, so you have something in common," the woman said softly, smiling. She pointed to the chair next to a boy who was rummaging around in his backpack.

As Achaia took her seat, the boy sat back up, putting his notebook down on his desk a little too noisily for her liking. *Just obnoxious.* She looked over, exasperated, and found that the younger, bulky, too-happy boy from the hallway was smirking at her.

"I'm Olivier." The boy said in a whisper, ignoring the teacher's lecturing and the notes on the board. She noticed that, unlike the other Brooklyn kids, he didn't have an accent. Any kind of accent--

"I know." Achaia's heart sped up involuntarily. "I mean, that's what she said your name was." Achaia said in a softer whisper, pointing toward the teacher with the eraser of her pencil. In that second she made a promise to herself to stare at her paper and at the board — nowhere else.

"Well it's nice to meet you," Olivier said holding out his hand to shake hers.

Achaia looked down at his hand, caught off guard. Are teenagers supposed to shake hands? She looked up for a second into his eyes, then looked back down at his hand. *This guy is serious.* She switched her pencil to her other hand and shook his hand quickly before turning back to her notes.

***

Out of the corner of her eye Achaia had watched Olivier practically stare at her through the entire class period. *What is it with these kids? Do they not pick up on social cues?* Then it occurred to her that he had maybe seen her staring match in the hallway and was not-so-subtly making fun of her. Or, maybe she had something on her face... Or, maybe she was just paranoid.

Achaia sighed as the bell rang. She hated the first day at a new school, the constant second guessing of herself. She closed her geometry book and pulled her schedule out again.

"So what class do you have next?" Olivier asked putting one foot on his chair and leaning in closer to her, looking over her shoulder. He smelled musky. In a strangely comfortable way. "Do you need help finding it?"

"Oh, um..." Achaia, taken off guard, fumbled around in her head with whether to accept or reject the offer.

"It's a pretty big school, and a little bit of a maze." He nodded down to her schedule to coax her on.

"I have French next, and yeah that'd be -- nice."

"Yellaina is in that class," he said smiling. "Do you need to stop back by your locker?"

"Yeah," Achaia said looking down to her single geometry notebook.

"Okay, I'll walk you. I think my locker is right down from

yours." A few girls in the row behind them looked at Achaia with complete disgust. *Obviously Olivier's attention is a hot commodity around here.* "Not that I just mysteriously know where your locker is, in some creepy mind-reader or stalker kind-of-way." He added a little too quickly. "I just, um, your hair is kind of hard to miss, and I'm pretty sure I saw you this morning."

"Right." Achaia nodded with a small laugh, comforted by the fact that she wasn't the only one who was coming across as a total weirdo.

They walked out of the classroom and toward the stairs. He was only a few inches taller than her, but he carried himself as if he were the tallest person on earth, even with his endearing awkwardness. He reminded her of someone. Olivier was quirky, but somehow he just oozed confidence. Her father's friend, Naphtali, was also like that.

Naphtali would come and visit them all the time. He traveled a lot with his job too, and no matter where they moved he always seemed to end up in their area at some point. It was kind of nice that her father had a friend he could keep in touch with despite all the moving.

If she was honest, Achaia envied that, though she supposed that Naphtali was her friend too. Sometimes her father would have to go out, and Naphtali would always offer to stay with her. He had a way of making it feel less like a baby sitter and more like a friend hanging out. He, too, was always sure of himself.

"So, what's your dad do?" Olivier asked, breaking the silence between them. It was as if he knew what she was thinking. "Why do you guys move so much?"

"Oh, well, he's a writer. So, depending on what he's writing about, and for who, we have to go there." Achaia fidgeted with the binding on her book, stopping only once they'd reached her locker.

"That's pretty cool. I guess you'd know a lot about a lot with that kind of job."

"Yeah, he's brilliant." Achaia thought of all the useless information her father would randomly heap out from time to time, about the most worthless places. Occasionally some of it was actually pretty interesting, but most of the time it wasn't. "He is working with some history professors at one of the universities here on a new textbook. He is kind of an Historian, it's a hobby. He writes a lot on anthropology."

She turned the lock and opened the door to her locker. Olivier leaned up against the locker next to hers, and she watched as girls passed by shooting her loathing glares. She tossed her geometry book in and looked around for her French notebook and text. "So do you know any French yet? Or is this your first class?"

"It's my first class." She said standing back up with her books, all of a sudden self-conscious about the lingering smell of the last occupant's rotten lunch. She shut the door curtly. "I couldn't even tell you what the words on the cover mean," Achaia said holding up the textbook. The cover had two unbelievably happy looking teenagers waving over-enthusiastically.

Olivier looked at the cover and laughed. "That is so, not realistic."

"Right!" Achaia laughed. "Have you been to France? Do you speak any French?" She asked as they started walking down the hall again.

"I have been to France, actually. That's a long story. But languages aren't really my gift either. What about sports? Do you like sports?" He asked eagerly.

"I don't know. We never stayed anywhere long enough for me

to join a team. I took karate when I was younger. I think I was pretty good, but then we moved. My dad wouldn't let me take it again. He said we couldn't afford it."

"Oh, that stinks. Well, I play soccer if you ever want to come out and watch me play. You know, when the season actually gets here." He nodded.

"Oh, well I don't know. Maybe."

Olivier laughed to himself, his green eyes shining, as they reached his locker. He had it opened before Achaia could have even processed that he was reaching for the door. He had his books exchanged just as quickly and with them under his arm, he walked on, toward the others who had formed his group before.

Olivier waved over to one of the girls.

The model-looking girl separated from the group and met them in the middle. "Olivier?" She cocked an eyebrow in way of asking for an introduction.

"This is Achaia." He gestured to her Vanna-White-style. "Achaia, this is Yellaina." He said pointing to the supermodel girl. "She's in your French class."

"Oh, sweet. It's nice to meet you." Achaia said. Now she was the one reaching out her hand. Yellaina smiled sweetly and took it lightly in her own.

"Bonjour! It's nice to meet you." Yellaina's voice was almost nauseatingly cheery, but it was hard to be annoyed by someone so nice. Unlike Olivier, Yellaina had a slight accent. She sounded almost Russian.

Achaia struggled with the conflict in her head for a moment. *To like her, or to hate her?* She'd never been one to hang out with preppy people.

"So we should probably head to French, huh?" Yellaina

pulled on Achaia's arm, tugging her away from Olivier and to their next class. Achaia followed along, throwing caution to the wind.

She hadn't made friends this quickly at any of her old schools, if she had made any at all. She decided to give the preppy girl a chance, wondering if Yellaina and Olivier's group of friends were foreign-exchange students and that's why they were being so nice to the new kid.

\*\*\*

"Have you taken a foreign language before?" Yellaina asked as they entered their French class.

"Nope, this is my first," Achaia said, looking for a seat near the back.

"You should sit next to me. We don't have assigned seats in this class." Yellaina walked up to the teacher and began conversing quite comfortably in French. Achaia wondered for a second if it was her first language; her accent sounded authentic. She laughed and the words trickled off her tongue like water off a wet leaf; natural, beautiful. She walked back over to where Achaia stood in awe. "You've come on a good day. We're learning the days of the week!" Yellaina sounded excited.

"It sounds as if you'd already know those. What are you doing in French One?" Achaia asked following Yellaina to two seats in the front row.

"Oh well, you have to take a foreign language to be on the college track," Yellaina said simply, as if Achaia should have already known since it was so obvious.

"Are you French?" Achaia asked rather bluntly.

"Oh no, pas du tout. I just think it's pretty. I pick up on languages pretty quickly. It's a gift." Yellaina said shrugging the hair away from her shoulder and pulling out her notebook with too much enthusiasm. "I'm from Moscow originally."

"That's awesome. Why did you move here?" Achaia asked, thankful that despite all the moving, she had at least stayed in the same country.

"My father. He moved here for work and made me come." Yellaina had a twinge of bitterness tainting her cheery tone. This made Achaia a little too happy, convinced that Yellaina might actually be a normal girl too.

"I can relate to that!" Achaia said opening her binder and copying the date in French from off the board.

"Yeah?" Yellaina asked. "Then we'll get along quite well, I think." She smiled brilliantly.

\*\*\*

Achaia walked home from the bus stop with her face scrunched against the wind. When she got to her door she unlocked it and walked inside. Shaking the moisture from her jacket. "Dad?" she called, hanging her jacket on the coat rack next to the door.

No answer. She walked quietly through the apartment, which took about a minute seeing as it was so small. With no sign of her dad anywhere, she perched herself on the couch, turned on the TV and propped her legs up on an unpacked box.

Achaia flipped through the channels idly for a few minutes before deciding there was nothing good on. She gave up hope, and left it on the history channel where two men were having a debate about the Bible. Two theologians argued over what some ancient people group called Nephilim were.

Half listening to the TV, half focused, she worked on her homework until the door opened. "Dad?" She set her notebooks down on the couch beside her, as the coated figure turned around. "Naphtali!" Achaia exclaimed leaping from the couch and bolting across the room to hug him.

"Hey kiddo. How are things at the new school?" Naphtali asked, giving her a quick squeeze and holding her at arm's length to get a good look at her. Normally it would have bothered a sixteen year old girl to be called kiddo, but when it came from Naphtali, it was endearing, especially with his mashed up accent from all the places he had lived.

"Pretty good, actually. I'm taking French." She smiled widely; she was pretty sure he had lived in France at one point. It'd been months since she'd seen Naphtali last. He had a cut across his left eye. "What happened?"

"Awe, nothing really. I had a disagreement with a sliding glass door."

Achaia raised an eyebrow and smirked with curiosity. "Did you have the disagreement or did Jack?"

"It's a story for another time. But I assure you, I wasn't drinking." He laughed. "Your dad asked me to come check on you. I ran into him downtown today. I figured I'd come by and make sure you ate some real food for dinner."

"Okay!" Achaia said skipping toward the kitchen, taking pots and pans out of the cabinets. She ripped open a cardboard box and started scrambling through boxes of macaroni and cheese.

"I was actually thinking of something a little more fresh," Naphtali said walking toward the kitchen bringing a bag out from behind his back.

"Is that -- fish?" Achaia asked, her eyes lighting up with excitement. She loved Naphtali's cooking, especially with fresh ingredients, which he always seemed to have. There was something exotic about the flavors he combined. "You know I love seafood."

"I do. And yes, it is, straight from Fulton's market." Naphtali smiled.

***

Naphtali cooked, Achaia did what she could to help, like passing him the salt shaker, and opening the refrigerator when his hands were full. The TV played in the background, the same argument about the Bible. Naphtali's ears would perk up every once in a while and he would laugh about whatever the men were saying and shake his head.

Achaia took a bite of okra and chewed happily. Life with her father was a series of frozen dinners, delivery pizza, and easy mac. She wondered if her mom had been able to cook, and if they would have had family dinners if she were alive.

"So, where have you been?"

"Cairo, and then to Iraq."

"Iraq? How was that?" Achaia didn't make a habit of watching the news, she was usually too busy packing or unpacking... But she knew enough about the turbulence in the Middle East to be surprised that Naphtali would take a trip there.

"It was a bit hostile," he nodded. Achaia took note, again, of the cut on his eyebrow.

"What were you doing there?"

"I had to meet a client. Urgent business, unavoidable." He shrugged a shoulder as if his stint in a war torn country were no big deal.

"Where's my dad?" Achaia asked looking at the clock behind her on the stove.

Naphtali's brow furrowed. "I was just wondering that myself."

# 2

# Secrets and Lies and Stars in the Skies

"Man is not what he thinks he is,
He is what he hides."
-André Malraux

Shael's breath went up before him in a cloud of steam. He hopped down from the fire escape and checked his watch. It was four in the morning. He had spent a majority of the day and, it would seem, most of the night setting up a perimeter around the new apartment. New York was crowded; much more crowded than most of the other cities in which they had taken refuge.

Shael knew he was taking a risk trying something new, but Luc had gotten too close too quickly in Tucson and Tampa. Shael was hoping that if he could clean up the area that they may be able to stay here longer.

Of course, it would be easier if he could just keep Achaia home. The regular routine of her leaving for school and coming home was too easy to track, and her hair made her easily spotted. Shael swallowed hard at the memory of Anna referring to her hair as a curse the last night he had spent with her. He had tried to talk Achaia into homeschooling, but she understandably continued to object. Shael hadn't made the bargain with Lucifer for his daughter to be a prisoner under house arrest. The whole point was for her to have as normal a life as possible.

Shael tugged the cuff of his sleeve down as he walked out of the alley and onto the main street, to cover the blood dripping down from a cut he had sustained from his last opponent. Even at this hour, there were people wandering the streets. He had hunted and set up surveillance systems he modified to specifically pick up demonic activity. He even developed an app for his phone that would alert him of anything out of the usual. He knew he needed to pace himself, and keep a low profile, so he hadn't tracked every demon he'd crossed. The last thing he needed was Luc catching his scent so soon because all the demons in Manhattan were dropping dead.

Something about New York didn't feel right. It felt heavy, and dark, and tainted somehow. Shael wasn't sure if it was the sheer number of people crammed into the city, or if he was being paranoid, but he didn't like it here. He couldn't move Achaia again, yet. As much as he didn't want to arouse Luc's attention, he didn't want Achaia to have cause to become suspicious, either. Shael huffed a sigh. He was tired of running, and hiding, and lying. Sometimes he thought it would be easier to just tell Achaia the truth, but the consequences of that were too severe. No. That wasn't an option.

Shael turned the corner onto Nineth Avenue and into the bar. It was darker inside than it was out, but Shael could see, sitting in one of the duct taped booths toward the back, a tall man with an angular face.

Shael slid into the seat across from him, not relishing the idea of actually touching anything in the establishment. He huffed to himself, thinking of the fact that the humans called this part of town Hell's Kitchen. "Don't ever let anyone say you Seraphim don't have a sense of humor. You picked a nice spot." Shael said, pulling his cuffs down again before letting only his forearms rest on the edge of the table with his hands clasped above the table's surface.

"I thought it would be fitting," the man said coolly. "You wanted to see me?"

"Zephaniah, I need help. This city is way too crowded, and it's completely infested with demons. I need reinforcements."

"You chose this place." Zephaniah said, his ice-blue eyes staring emotionlessly into Shael's.

Shael knew that Zephaniah wasn't just talking about the city, but Shael's current situation. "I did. But she didn't." Shael hated begging, but for Achaia's safety, he would stoop to just about anything. He hated that he couldn't protect her the way he should, that he was weak as a human. Shael's training was unparalleled, but he didn't have the speed or ability he once had.

"The Lord has already charged one with Achaia's safety." Zephaniah scooted toward the edge of his booth to leave. "But we can do nothing for you. You made your choice," he added, standing. "Achaia has a Guardian?" Shael said scooting out of his seat and standing in front of Zephaniah before he could leave.

"Yes." Zephaniah confirmed. "He was charged this past evening."

Shael breathed a sigh of relief. "Wait. Who is it?" Shael asked, panic beginning to blossom in his chest. He knew all the Nephilim, but there were only a select few who wouldn't begrudge having to protect the daughter of Shael ben Yahweh. Shael didn't want the Council knowing where he was, any more than he wanted Lucifer to know. He gave himself a mental rebuke for having made so many enemies over the millennia.

Without answering, Zephaniah side-stepped around Shael, and was gone. Shael hated Seraphim sometimes. Some of them were so self-righteous since the fall of the Nephilim. He glanced at his watch again, it was nearly five-thirty. As he left the bar, he wasn't as reassured as he had hoped he'd be. In fact he was more nervous, now. Depending on who was charged with Achaia's protection, her guardian could be more dangerous than Luc.

***

Achaia woke up the next morning in her bed, with no memory of how she'd gotten there. Her best guess being that she'd fallen asleep on the couch and Naphtali had carried her to her room.

*Naphtali...* Achaia stood, shakily at first. She walked from her room, running her fingers through her hair, the tips getting tangled in her curls. In the living room, a pillow and disheveled blanket lay on the couch. *Naphtali must have stayed the night.*

A movement at the counter startled her. "Dad?" Her father sat at the counter. The dark bags under his eyes told her he hadn't slept. "Where were you last night?"

"Oh, you're up," he said turning his attention toward her. He looked as if he'd been straining himself to hear something outside their walls, perhaps eaves-dropping on one of their neighbors.

Achaia casually meandered over to the window to look out. There was a man kissing his wife goodbye before getting into his car, some little kids jumping rope, and a cat on their fire escape. *Nothing out of the norm.*

"Are you alright?" Achaia asked, turning back around. Again, his attention was elsewhere. "Dad!"

"Huh? What?" He mumbled stirring in his seat; still when he looked at her, it was as if he wasn't really seeing her.

"Nothing, I guess. You're just acting strange, that's all. And where were you last night? We waited for hours..."

"Some stuff came up."

"Work?" Achaia attempted to pry deeper.

"Yeah." he looked back down at his newspaper, shrugging off any further conversation. It was easy to tell he wasn't reading it, but it was his way of letting her know that he didn't want to talk about it anymore. It was clear he wasn't going to give her any more information.

Achaia poured herself a bowl of cereal and ate in silence waiting for the mood to pass. He did this from time to time, mostly after something with work caused him to miss out on sleep. He was always weird, high strung and awkward when sleep deprived. It didn't normally last long though. Today, however, the mood wasn't passing. In fact, he was getting worse.

He stood from his stool at the counter and began pacing in front of the window, then by the door. He was on high alert for something.

"Are you waiting for someone?" Achaia had asked at one point; her question went unnoticed.

"Go get ready for school," was all he said.

"If you don't calm down, you're going to give me an anxiety attack." Achaia dropped her cereal bowl not so gently into the sink, making her father jump. She wasn't hiding the fact that she was over his attitude, as she fixed him with a defiant look before she turned and walked down the hall to her room.

***

Achaia got dressed for school quickly, ready to be out of the house. *Hopefully he'll be over whatever it is by the time I get home.* She scampered down the six flights of stairs and stopped in the coffee shop on the first floor for a latte before heading down the street to the bus stop. The couple of blocks walk, she spent lost in thought. She didn't even see Naphtali as she passed him on the sidewalk, walking towards her apartment.

***

Achaia struggled to find her geometry homework, and realized that she had left it loose in her bag. She slammed her book shut and slumped back in her chair. She didn't have enough time to go back to her locker for it before the class started.

"Hey, what's up?" Olivier asked, sitting beside her.

"I left my homework in my bag." Achaia huffed out her frustration. Unable to believe her absentmindedness.

"I'll get it," Olivier offered standing.

"Class starts in like, thirty seconds." Achaia said with a huffed laugh, dismissing the offer.

"I'm fast." Olivier was already halfway to the door before he finished speaking, and was out of sight just as quickly.

In hardly any time at all the bell rang, and Olivier was stepping inside the door, Achaia's homework in hand. He took his seat again next to her, not even short of breath.

"How did you—"

"I told you I'm fast," Olivier smiled. "And your locker is just down the stairs."

"I was going to say, 'know my locker combination.'"

"Oh," Olivier smirked, "well that is a completely different set of skills." He winked and handed her assignment over with a bow.

"My lady."

Achaia wanted to smile as she took the paper, but it wouldn't come.

"What's wrong?" Olivier's smile faded.

"Okay everyone!" Mrs. Welch interrupted. "Let's settle down and get started, shall we?"

Achaia winced in apology by way of an answer, and re-opened her text book as class began.

\*\*\*

Achaia was lost in thought staring at the space of wall behind Mrs. Welch's head when the bell rang and she realized she hadn't heard a single word the entire hour. Her book wasn't even open to the correct page.

"Achaia?"

Achaia blinked and looked up at Olivier who was waiting for her by the door.

"Are you coming?"

"Yeah," Achaia said shutting her book, and gathering up her things to join him. They left the room last, and melted into the flow of students crowding the stairwell.

"So, I'm assuming you didn't glean much from today's lesson." Olivier practically hopped down the first few stairs and looked back up at her. "Do you want to tackle the homework together tonight? I might be able to recap the highlights."

"There were highlights?" Achaia asked sarcastically. She had only caught every other word, as she was struggling to rearrange her hastily snatched up books under her arm while simultaneously descending the last few stairs. "Tonight?" She repeated, stopping.

"I mean unless you want to hand it in late, on purpose, really stick it to the man!" Olivier mocked, leaning against the stair rail at the bottom. Other students bumped passed them into the hall beyond.

"Oh, no. I mean, yeah. Homework. Tonight. Yes." Achaia nodded, finally looking back up from her juggling to meet his eye. She resumed her descent of the stairs. "I live above a coffee shop, it's pretty good. Do you want to meet there after dinner?"

"Sounds good," he said as they reached her locker. "Text me the address," he handed her a slip of paper before continuing down the hall to exchange his own books.

Achaia looked down at the paper, acknowledging in the back of her mind that it had been years since she'd actually had a friend to text. She opened her locker and exchanged her geometry things for her French books. When she looked back up, Olivier was once again surrounded by Yellaina and the others.

He had plenty of friends, it came easily to him, as naturally as breathing. Achaia had never been that comfortable with people. The only numbers she had in her phone were her father's, Naphtali's and the places in past cities where they had frequently called in take-out orders.

The black haired boy was smiling and saying something to the girl who looked like him. The taller blond boy, whom Achaia had accidentally stared at the day before, was listening to Yellaina talk animatedly about something.

Olivier met her eye and waved her over. Achaia felt a stone drop in her stomach. She'd never been so nervous to meet people before. She felt outnumbered, and for some reason a little insecure. In their own way, they were each pretty intimidating. Olivier smiled down at her, as she reached them.

"Guys," he interrupted each of their conversations. They fell silent and looked at her, Yellaina waved in greeting. "This is Achaia."

Everyone in the group smiled except for the black-haired girl. Her blue eyes narrowed, her plum colored lips spread thin across her face, and her nose twitched up on one side.

"This is my brother, Emile, and my sister, Amelia; they're twins." Olivier said gesturing to the pale black-haired boy and girl. "I know they don't look anything like me; I'm kind of the odd ball out." Olivier with his blond hair and tan skin, was quite a contrast to his siblings.

Achaia smiled and held out her hand to them. Emile took it smiling at her. She thought she'd melt under the weight of his eyes. "It's a pleasure to meet you," Achaia said softly.

"The pleasure is all mine." Emile spoke without any hint of irony.

Achaia had a hard time ripping her eyes away from him to greet Amelia. As she did, Amelia's expression was not at all welcoming. She looked as though she had an ardent disdain for Achaia's joining their group and walked away with a dramatic sigh.

"She doesn't really like new people. It's not you." Olivier said putting a hand on the small of her back. "This," he said using the hand on her back to turn her toward the final boy, "is Noland."

"Hi," Achaia said in a soft voice. *Noland* -- He'd been the one she was most anxious and most nervous to meet.

"Hi," he said with a crooked smile.

This time he reached his hand out first. She looked down at it for a moment before taking it. When she did, his hand shake was firm but gentle. His skin tone was like warm honey, dusted with dark freckles. He held her gaze steadily without any kind of reservation. Achaia was sure she didn't look nearly so confident.

"Welcome to New York." She noticed how low his voice was compared to Olivier's upbeat tone, and Emile's sweet lull.

"Thanks." She said, not actually sure of what he had said.

The bell rang, but Achaia didn't hear it.

"I guess we'd better be getting to French, huh?" Yellaina said pulling Achaia's arm, and thus pulling her from her trance. Noland seemed not to want to leave as well. Either that or he was making fun of her again. She couldn't decide. She cursed herself again for her awkwardness.

"It was nice meeting you," Achaia said, forcing her eyes away from Noland to Emile.

"You too," Emile said with a sweet smile as she walked away arm in arm with Yellaina. What was she to do; how were they all just so attractive? Achaia could hardly think as she walked to class.

*** 

Noland balled his hand up into a loose fist, rubbing his fingers with his thumb. His hand still tingling from her touch. *She is magnificent. She is like a porcelain doll.* He turned to walk down the hall to class with Emile by his side. She had seemed more interested in Emile-- He tried to brush aside the thought of how her hand had felt in his; tiny, but strong. Was she shy? Or Nervous? He wondered about her personality, what was she like?

Emile looked at him with a questioning, amused look on his face. "Come on dude, we're going be late for class," Emile said grabbing his arm and pulling him into the classroom.

"So, do you think she's yours?" Noland asked as casually as possible, tucking his books under his arm. He knew better than to think he could hide his true intentions from Emile, but he played casual out of habit, or perhaps his own necessity.

Emile laughed; of course he'd known what Noland was about to ask. "You know as well as I do that we don't know until it's time. I still don't understand why He works that way."

"Yeah, and how sometimes one knows before the other. That must be frustrating as hell," Noland said halfheartedly.

"Oh yeah! And dad says Hell is the most frustrating place he's ever been; second only to the rush hour line at Starbucks." Emile laughed as they took their seats.

"Still, it's different for you. You know what she was feeling, what everyone is feeling. You don't have to ask questions," Noland said taking his usual seat in the back row.

"I know what you're feeling-- flustered. But you know my rules, I don't talk about what other people are feeling without their permission." Emile leaned on his desk, straddling his books with his elbows. "Well, other people we *know*," he smiled mischievously, "I have no guilt in telling you that a third of the girls in this room *want* you right now." Emile chuckled to himself.

Noland smiled crookedly and cocked an eyebrow, "And the other two thirds?"

"Are wanting me."

\*\*\*

Achaia texted her father after her last class to see if he was going to be home. He had taken longer to text back than normal, but had finally responded in the affirmative.

As Achaia walked to the bus stop she was caught off guard by her doubt. She usually took her father at his word, but this time she wondered whether or not he would actually be there when she got home.

It occurred to her that she had never second guessed him before. She hadn't always agreed with her father. There were times she hated moving so often, and never being able to put down roots anywhere. But she had always believed him when he said it was necessary, and when he had said that he was sorry. Never before had she not believed him when he promised her something.

So when the doubt began to grow in her mind, it clouded her vision of everything else. She hardly remembered getting on the bus home. She didn't remember the ride, or the walk to the apartment building. All she knew was that when she stood at her front door to go in, she, for the first time, wasn't sure if he would be there waiting for her when she did.

As Achaia walked through the door, the first thing she noticed was the silence. "Dad?" All the lights in the apartment were off, and with the sun setting so early in winter, the apartment was already engulfed in darkness.

"Yeah?" He answered coming into the living room from down the hall.

Achaia breathed a sigh of relief. She hadn't liked the feeling of not knowing where he had been the night before. "Hey," she said taking her book bag off to remove her heavy coat.

"Hey," he said, taking a seat on the couch. "Sorry if I worried you last night."

"It's okay," Achaia said, now feeing silly for having made it a big deal.

"So, you want to bust out some homework before dinner? I'll make something."

"What? Mac and cheese?" Achaia asked smiling. Her father was a terrible cook.

"I'll have you know that I was going to make a frozen lasagna, complete with garlic bread."

"Which is also frozen—"

"Which is why you have plenty of time to knock out some homework before it's done." He stood and walked over to the freezer and took out the two packages. Achaia almost laughed at her former concern as she watched him read the heating directions on the back of the box.

\*\*\*

Shael had only burnt the lasagna a little. He had been distracted and not set the oven timer.

He knew he needed to go. He had a meeting with another Seraphim, a friend of Naphtali's, to take a second stab at adding more security to their perimeter. Shael didn't like how close Luc's demons had gotten the night before. He had spent the entire trip home leading them around in circles and toward the opposite end of town, but he had a sinking feeling in his stomach, that this time, he hadn't been able to lose them.

Ever since they had moved to New York, Shael had felt that he was being followed. He had hoped that the crowds would have been enough to hide them; but with the crowds, came ample opportunities for Luc to possess more spies. Everywhere he went he felt eyes crawling over him like spiders; spiders he couldn't swat away.

Then this morning, when he was almost home, the demon— it was no random demon; it was too easy to track, to kill. Shael had the sickening feeling that by killing it, he had somehow taken the bait and given away his location. Then he had caught a glimpse of his pursuers. He had stayed out rather than lead anything or anyone back to the apartment, back to Achaia.

Naphtali was late. Shael cracked his thumb in his fist, and then used it to crack the other knuckles on his hand; anxious habit. Achaia sat on the sofa with one of her text books open on her lap and an ear bud in one ear. "Hey, I have to go. But, dinner is ready."

Achaia looked up from her studies. "Where?" Her eyebrows knit together. He'd been gone a lot lately, he knew. She looked like her mother when she was displeased.

"I have to meet with one of the professors I'm writing with." Shael had never lied so much as he had in the last three years, or really since he sold the angelic half of his soul. But the only way to keep Achaia safe, was to make sure she never knew anything about angels or demons, or even God. If she knew, she'd have to choose a side; and that idea terrified Shael. "We're working with a tight deadline. They want the book by March. Look, I don't want you leaving the apartment while I'm gone. Okay?"

"What about just downstairs to the coffee shop?" Achaia asked. "I was going to go down there to finish homework."

"No, just—make some coffee up here. Don't go out."

"Dad, it's just right downstairs. It's in the same building."

"This is a dangerous city."

"As opposed to all the safe cities we've lived in? Dad please," Achaia said brushing his argument aside.

"No. Just stay in tonight. Naphtali will be here soon. Don't let anyone in. Don't even ask who it is. Just pretend you're not home."

"I wish I wasn't." Achaia said with a bitter twinge to her voice.

"Just don't let anyone in. Okay?"

"Then what is Naphtali supposed to do when he gets here? Set up camp in the hall?" She rolled her eyes and stood. She walked over to the kitchen and took the coffee and French press out of the cabinet.

"He has a key."

Shael could tell from behind Achaia, that she was rolling her eyes at him. "And aren't I old enough to not need a baby sitter? Or is he a warden now," Achaia said, setting the press down a little too hard and turning around.

"Achaia," Shael was out of arguments; out of fake explanations. He thought about telling her the truth. How would she react?

50

Would she even believe him? Would she be afraid? Shael shook the thought away. He didn't sell his soul so that she could live her life in fear, or in submission. He did it so that she could be free. And yet, she thought she was being held captive; that *he* was holding her captive. "I have to go," Shael said opening the door. "Eat," he said pointing to the lasagna on the stovetop.

"Whatever project you're working on, this time," Achaia started. Shael paused half way out the door as she finished, "I hate it." Shael sighed, continuing through the door, letting it click shut behind him.

***

Achaia looked at the French press, the steam rising from the hot coffee inside and reached in her back pocket for her phone to text Olivier.

CHANGE OF PLANS.
UNDER HOUSE ARREST.
HW @ MY PLACE?

YEAH WHAT #

7C

OTW

Achaia pulled two mugs down from the cabinet and poured herself one. She looked through the cabinets for some kind of desert, and pulled out an unopened package of ginger cookies. By the time she had plated the crackers, gotten her text books out and laid them across the counter, there was a knock on the door.

Achaia peeked through the peep hole and saw Oliver with his

messenger bag slapped across his chest. She opened the door to let him in. "Hey."

"Hey," he said taking the strap of his messenger bag off, and leaning the bag against one of the bar stools.

"I didn't know how you liked your coffee..." she said gesturing to the press.

"Cream and sugar." He said rounding the counter.

Achaia pulled the cream out of the fridge and pulled the container of sugar forward for him. As he prepared his coffee, Achaia took a seat on one of the barstools and opened her book to the page assigned. "Yeah— I have no clue how to do any of this."

"I suspected that." Olivier said chuckling as he blew on his coffee and took a sip. "What's up with the house arrest?"

Achaia shrugged. "He's acting weird."

"Your dad?" Olivier sat next to her and pulled out his books.

"Yeah," Achaia said writing her name and date at the top of her paper. "I mean he has his moments, but it's different this time. It's like he's on edge all the time. He just refuses to tell me anything." Achaia could feel a lump of frustration rising in her throat. "I kind of have a bad feeling that whatever he isn't telling me—it's bad."

"Maybe it's something with work," Olivier offered optimistically, opening his own book to the proper page.

"Maybe, but it doesn't feel like it." Achaia stopped herself. "So anyway," she said feeling ridiculous, it was probably nothing; some sort of mid-life crisis. "How do I do this? What are we even doing?"

"Proofs."

Achaia groaned. "Alright, teach away."

\*\*\*

A couple hours had passed, and still Naphtali had not shown up. Achaia and Olivier had finished their homework and were vegged out in front of the TV; Achaia slung across the sofa, and Olivier stretched out on the floor in front of her leaning against the couch.

A crime drama played on the screen but Achaia and Olivier came up with their own dialogue. It seemed that a man was murdered and his wife was the number one suspect, but in their version, they hadn't known they were brother and sister.

A bag of chips laid empty on the floor next to Olivier and two empty soda cans were littering the coffee table. Their laughter stopped as the knob clicked and turned apparently of its own accord. Naphtali entered, his back to them as he removed his jacket.

"Naphtali," Achaia said sitting up as he turned around. His eye was black from being hit by something. "What on earth?"

"You have company?" He cocked an eyebrow, which was swollen, apparently aware that her father had forbidden guests.

"Your eye." Achaia's stomach turned. She realized her father hadn't been the only one acting strange. "Let me guess, another sliding door?" Achaia accused.

Naphtali looked at Olivier, but didn't seem to be disturbed by his presence there.

"Achaia," Naphtali started.

"Is anyone ever going to tell me what going on? You're in on it with him, aren't you? Is he in some kind of trouble?" She asked, now standing. Olivier stood up next to her.

"Yes," Naphtali answered to her surprise.

"What?" Achaia asked, shocked.

"Yes he is. But it is not for me to tell you. He does not wish for me to speak of it." Achaia could tell that Naphtali wanted to talk. He didn't seem to appreciate being sworn to silence. She debated pushing him further.

"Maybe I should go," Olivier said, walking over to gather his things.

"Sorry, Olly."

"It's cool. I'll see you tomorrow." Olivier gave her an encouraging smile before shutting the door behind him.

Achaia turned on Naphtali. "You're really not going to tell me anything?" Achaia asked.

"Not yet. I can't."

"Where's my dad?" Achaia pleaded, hoping for an answer. Naphtali frowned apologetically, "I really wish I knew."

\*\*\*

It was a cold and windy night. The kind of cold you felt in your teeth. Shael pulled the collar of his trench coat up around his face, and shoved his hands in his pockets to keep his coat from blowing open and revealing the sword strapped to his belt. Tonight he would have to walk to the other end of town. He was stealthy, but he didn't feel like trying to sneak a sword onto the subway.

Shael's weapon of choice had always been the dagger. He never minded having to get close to his enemies to slay them. He preferred to make certain he had dispatched them properly, anyway. No matter how much Shael disliked someone, he wasn't a sadist, and he wasn't one to wish anyone to suffer. He generally ended his opponents cleanly and quickly, with honor and dignity. What few swords he did own, he rarely used. He kept them mostly for sentimental reasons. The one strapped to his hip would have been famous amongst humans, had anyone actually seen him use it.

Shael had been walking for too long, which in its monotony had made it easy for him to lose his focus to wandering thoughts. A chill running down his spine brought his senses back to what he was doing. But it was too late.

Shael was thrown off his feet, and into a dark alley. His brain was trying to play catch up and process what was happening when he was grabbed from behind by a pair of hands around his throat. Talons dug in through his collar. Shael felt warm droplets of blood dripping down his collarbone. He figured if the demon were going to kill him, he would have done it. He decided to stand still, and see how the scene unfolded. Luc probably had ordered them to bring Shael in alive.

Another demon rose up in front of Shael, blocking out the light from the main street. It was a massive silhouette. Shael couldn't make out any of the demon's features, only that it was about seven feet tall, had broad shoulders and long fingers that ended in pointed claws. The creature tilted its head to the side, appraising him. "I expected more from the great Shael ben Yahweh." Its voice was gravelly and hoarse. "Or have you lost your touch as well as your angelic abilities?" The demon laughed. He wasn't alone, multiple voices laughed with him. Shael, without being able to turn his head to count, guessed there were about four or five of them.

Shael's fingers inched toward the sword at his side, but his coat was in the way. There was nothing for it. He couldn't draw his weapon without notice. He would just have to do so swiftly. Bracing himself for the grip around his throat to tighten, Shael reached for his sword.

He drew it out in an arch, slicing the chest of the demon in front of him. As anticipated, the hands strangling Shael tightened. Shael choked, and watched little stars burst in front of his eyes. He grabbed his sword with both hands, and went as if to stab himself in the face, but aimed a few inches higher, praying that the demon behind him was as tall as the one now gripping at its bleeding chest.

More demons rounded on him, and descended like a pack

of wolves, hunting together. Shael felt them clawing at him. They grabbed his legs and his arms. He felt heat flash across his face, as a set of talons raked across his cheek. The cuts felt like miniature bonfires set ablaze all over his body. Like a thousand paper cuts, only wider.

Shael fell backwards. He hit the ground hard, with nothing to break the fall, and assumed that he had killed the demon that had been choking him from behind. Shael struggled to grip the sword. His hands were wet with blood and sweat, mostly his own, but some of it was black and sticky. He kicked up, hard. His foot connected with one of the demon's jaw bones. Shael felt the crunch of the broken jaw travel up his leg. Another one of demons bit down on his right arm. Shael screamed. With his left hand he drew a dagger from his belt and drove it into the side of the demon's head until his arm was released.

That was two down, one injured, and two more to go, Shael tallied. A demon on his left grabbed him by the throat and began to lift him. Shael, brought his arm with the sword down, slicing through the demon's wrist.

The demon hissed and spit as it drew back, clutching its stump with the other hand. "Two down, two injured, and one to go," Shael chanted in his head like a mantra, to keep from passing out. Human strength was hardly strength at all, Shael had found. His endurance was less than a quarter of what it once had been. But worst of all, was the aging. Shael felt sluggish, and cloudy in the brain. He was now on his feet, but his legs were shaking.

The last demon was facing Shael, circling him slowly. Shael felt a little like a bullfighter. "Oh come on. I don't have all night. You've already made me late." He spat impatiently.

The demon charged. It barreled forward into Shael's gut,

rugby-tackling him backward. Shael let out a grunt as the air was knocked out of him. However he couldn't help but laugh a little at how stupid a move this had been on the demon's part. Shael raised up the sword with both hands, holding his dagger against the hilt, and brought both of them down between the demon's shoulder blades. The demon's body rained down like ashes, and was carried away in the harsh wind.

Shael looked at the two writhing demons on the ground. They were gripping their stump and chest, respectively. "I have a message for Luc," he said glancing down at them. "Actually," Shael paused, looking back and forth between them, "one of you is super-fluous." Shael slung the sword and decapitated the demon that was now missing a hand. He turned back to the demon who had laughed at him before. "Is this about what you had expected?" Shael smiled.

"Cohen." The demon choked, spitting out blood. He was leaning against the wall of the alley, gripping his chest. "That's what you call yourself now, isn't it?"

Shael said nothing, but stared back steadily, not denying his chosen mortal name.

"Do you still think of yourself as a holy man? Even though you have no soul?" The demon laughed.

"You know what?" Shael said, clenching his jaw. "The message wasn't that important." Shael slung the sword out, almost lazily, slicing the demon's throat. The demon choked, not dying immediately. "I was just going to tell him to piss off," Shael shrugged. Then, he wiped his sword clean on his coat as the demon choked, one last time, and disintegrated into ash.

***

Shael limped into the park looking like he'd seen much better days. He was completely covered in blood, and was feeling a little lightheaded from the loss of it. He would have to seek out a healer. The mortal hospitals weren't equipped to treat demon venom, and his right forearm was already completely numb with it. The arm was convulsing as it tried in vain to fight the venom off. The infection was already setting in.

"Shael." A fair haired man, with bright keen eyes rose to meet him, as Shael nearly collapsed on a park bench.

"Jophiel," Shael collapsed on his left side, grasping his right. "Do you have any hyssop?"

Jophiel knelt beside Shael and pulled out a vial of oil. He began to pour it out and massage it into the bite on Shael's forearm, which was now swollen and irritated, and turning green. "Let me summon Raphael. He could heal you."

"No. I," Shael sucked in a breath, "I can't accept any more help from Heaven than what I am already about to request." The spasms in Shael's arm began to calm. Shael sat up, and Jophiel sat next to him looking concerned.

"You have risked much in coming here." Jophiel's voice was troubled. "They have tracked you easily. You are all but captured, and more will come. Let them take you, only don't lead them back to your daughter. I know that Naphtali loves her as his own. He will protect her. I know it." Shael could tell Jophiel took no joy out of giving this advice. Shael had always valued Jophiel's advice and regretted it the times he had chosen to ignore his wisdom.

"I came to ask for protection, but it appears that I am too late for that." Shael coughed. His injuries, in addition to the cold, were wearing on his human flesh. This body infuriated him in its near uselessness. "Accept this as a gift," Shael presented the sword to Jophiel. "In exchange for keeping an eye on Achaia and Naphtali for me."

"Elkana Ezer." Jophiel whispered, reaching out and taking the blade in his hands. "Forged from bronze, was it not? Before the creation of diemerilium."

"Bronze laced with emerald, tipped in diamond. The sword that slayed the Assyrians before reaching Judea." Shael smiled at Jophiel's reverence for a human possession.

"I couldn't," he said, handing the sword back to Shael.

"Then keep it safe," Shael countered, pushing the sword away, refusing to take it back.

Jophiel clutched the sword to his side. "Shalom Shael ben Yahweh."

"Peace, wholeness, and restoration—," Shael mused under his breath. The sentiment was one so commonly given, and yet so rarely received. Shael knew there would be no peace tonight, no wholeness as long as he lived, and there was no restoration in his eternity. Shael smiled sadly. "Go, brother. You've wasted enough time on a lost cause like me."

Jophiel stood, but clasped Shael's shoulder tightly. "No cause that breathes is ever lost."

# 3

## Farmacy

"Remember tonight,
For it is the beginning of always"
-Dante Aligheiri

The whole next day at school Achaia had a hard time concentrating. Since her father hadn't come home, she had even debated skipping school and waiting for him, in case he came home while she was out. But she was far enough behind in all of her classes, and didn't think she could risk missing a full day. In the end Naphtali had insisted on walking her to the bus stop and waiting with her until it came.

Even though she tried her best to follow along in geometry, she had been completely lost and made plans with Olivier to do their homework together again. When she arrived home she was pleased to find that her father was actually there, at least physically. He had deep dark circles beneath his eyes, and his skin was pale, like he hadn't been eating well enough. He had a bandage across his face, and told her he had cut himself, embarrassingly bad, while shaving. Achaia sat at the counter trying to get a head start on her French homework. Instead, she sat at the counter pretending to do her homework. In reality she was too distracted by her father's erratic behavior to focus. His act of normalcy had ended with 'How was your day?' She tapped her pencil on her text book as she attempted to read the second paragraph for the third time. An untouched mug of post-dinner hot chocolate sat in front of her. She glanced up at the steam rising from the smooth brown liquid. Her father was steaming too, she could feel it.

As she turned around she was caught off guard by the sight of her father standing in the center of the living room tapping his foot and wringing his hands. "Dad?"

Her father clenched his jaw, and swallowed hard. "Yeah?"

"You're acting really weird, again."

He rolled his eyes and looked at the floor, biting his lip. "I'm sorry we've been moving so much."

"Are we moving again? Is that what all this is about? We just got here!" Achaia said annoyed. He always acted a little anxious before telling her they were about to take off, but he'd never been this disturbed.

"I'm sorry sweetie." He took a seat on the ottoman in front of the sofa. "Do you like it here?"

"I don't know, dad. How well can you like a place after a week?" Achaia abandoned her books and turned backward on her stool. "I haven't even gotten a chance to see the Statue of Liberty."

"Okay, let's go!" Her father stood with a little too much enthusiasm.

"What is going on? Why do we have to leave again? Do you have a new assignment?"

Achaia watched as something dark passed behind her father's eyes, and the smile left his face. "There's so much you don't know. That you couldn't understand."

"Couldn't? How do you know if I am capable of it or not, if you don't give me the chance?" Achaia stood up and crossed the living room to the arm of the sofa. "What is it I can't understand?"

"It's not your fault. There are things I haven't ever taught you."

"How to do my own taxes? How to hotwire a car? Yeah there's a lot you haven't taught me. That doesn't mean I wouldn't understand it, if you did."

"You're better off not knowing some things Achaia. You don't need to know everything."

"Right, because ignorance is bliss? It might be," she granted, "but what you don't know *can* hurt you." Achaia realized that her posture mirrored her father's. Both stood with one leg cocked atop a tapping foot, and arms crossed; both were unwilling to yield. "Besides, if you didn't want to tell me, why bring it up?"

Shael sighed. "Because a part of me wonders if it wouldn't be better, easier if you knew. But the majority of me doesn't want to burden you with it. If I was going to tell you, I should have done it a long time ago."

"Better late than never."

"Can't you just trust me?" He asked exasperated. He looked at her as if seeing her for the first time as a miniature carbon copy of himself.

"That would require me to know you, and I'm not sure I do anymore." Achaia tried to unclench her jaw; it was starting to hurt.

Shael's face shook as if she had smacked him, but he said nothing.

"How do you expect me to trust you, when you obviously

can't trust me?" Achaia, realizing that neither of them would ever give in, went for the door and grabbed her coat. "I'm going to go explore this place before you drag me off to the next nowhere." She let the door slam behind her.

She ran down the stairs as fast as she could, lest he come after her. Once she reached the street she reached for her phone and texted Olivier.

HOW DO YOU FEEL ABOUT

SIGHTSEEING INSTEAD OF

HOMEWORK?

WAIT. NO GEOMETRY? :(

JK I'M IN.

CAN I BRING SOME PEOPLE?

SURE.

MEET YOU AT

BROOKLYN BRIDGE?

KK

\*\*\*

Achaia waited against the rail of the boardwalk that ran across the Brooklyn Bridge, gazing out over the water. She looked at the buildings across the glassy surface and wondered if life were simpler in Brooklyn; less chaotic outside of the city's heart... The wind was bitter cold against her face, her teeth were chattering, and she was beginning to regret her decision, when she heard her name called out behind her.

As she turned she saw Olivier walking briskly toward her. Noland and Emile lagged behind.

"Is everything okay?" Olivier asked as he reached her. To her surprise he reached out and hugged her in greeting. She hugged him back, feeling unsure.

"My dad wants to move again." She said quietly so that only he would hear.

Olivier frowned. "Already?"

She could tell he was disappointed, and not just for her.

She turned back against the rail and looked down into the water, then back out over it. Emile and Noland caught up to them and took up the rail on either side. She could smell Emile's cologne. It was musky and reminded her of Christmas, something spiced.

"So you want to go over there?" Olivier asked pointing across the bridge. Achaia looked up at him and back toward Brooklyn.

"What is there to do there?"

"Have you had dinner?"

Achaia nodded.

"Desert?" Olivier smiled.

Achaia shook her head.

"Farmacy?" Emile asked looking across to Noland.

"Yellaina is going to kill us for going without her." Olivier laughed. "Let's go. This is a part of New York you can't miss."

"What is it?" Achaia asked following them as they began to walk across the bridge.

***

Shael grabbed his coat and limped after Achaia. His hip twinged as he descended the seven flights of stairs. His whole body was sore and ached, even after Jophiel had taken Shael to a healer named Rebecca in SoHo.

He had spent the first part of the visit in an ice bath while Rebecca rummaged around in cabinets, collecting jars and vials of God-only-knew-what. Healing had never been Shael's forte. After the bath, Shael had been stripped down, lathered in a pleasant smelling sort of paste and wrapped like a mummy. He was told to lay down and rest, but he wasn't able to sleep.

Shael had watched the sun come up over the building tops outside thinking about what he was going to do. He wondered if it was time to stop running, to entrust Achaia to Naphtali's care, as Jophiel had suggested, and turn himself in. Shael really didn't think it was in him to surrender. Call it pride, or determination, Shael couldn't seriously consider it an option.

As the room filled fully with morning light, Rebecca came into his room with a mug of hot coffee and a bowl of fruit. Shael sat up and ate, gratefully, as she unwrapped his bandages. She had heated a combination of oils (Shael could smell that hyssop was among them) and massaged him before setting him in a hot salts bath.

By the time Shael had left Rebecca's, it was late afternoon. He was feeling significantly improved, but was still weak and sore.

As he reached the bottom of the stairs, he knew he'd already lost Achaia. She was young and quick, angry, and not injured.

Shael paused looking either way down the street to try and catch a glimpse of her bright red hair. He assumed she had pulled her hood up. *Smart girl*, he smiled. Achaia had so much of him in her, even without training. Sometimes he wondered what it would have been like to be able to train her up as a Guardian, to take pride in the achievement of her full potential. He shook the thought away. That was a future that was taken from them when her mother was killed. When Shael had sold his lot as a Nephilim.

He followed his gut and turned right. He prayed he could find her. Even if the demons were mostly focused on him, New York had enough human dangers to trigger Shael's protective fatherly instincts.

Shael had been tracking Achaia for about an hour when he

caught glimpses of glares in the crowd on the street. He knew he was being watched. He prayed Achaia was safe, but knew he needed to stop looking for her. He redirected his course away from wherever she might be, and away from the apartment in case she went home. Shael took off toward Tribeca instead, praying that Achaia was being smart, and that she wasn't alone.

***

After hearing about the Farmacy and Soda Fountain the whole trip over, Achaia was ready to dive in. Apparently the place was well worth the trip into Brooklyn. It didn't look like much from the outside, but as Noland held the door open and Achaia walked inside, she felt like she had stepped back into the fifties. The shop was composed of a long narrow room with shelves of goods lining the walls on the right and a long counter to the left.

She took a seat on one of the stools near the register and Olivier sat beside her. Emile and Noland each chose a stool and grabbed a laminated menu from beside the register.

"Grilled cheese? At a pharmacy?" Achaia smiled as she read through the offered items.

"It's the old school kind of pharmacy, not a drugstore. They have the best egg creams here." Olivier said nodding to the girl behind the counter that he would take one as his order. She seemed to recognize him. She smiled at Noland as she wrote Olivier's order.

Emile ordered a hot chocolate, and Noland a New Orleans Mead. Achaia knew it was cold out, but she couldn't resist the atmosphere. "I'll have a South Pole."

"A good choice." Noland smiled. The girl behind the counter frowned.

"You come here often?" Achaia asked Noland, as the girl put his sparkling soda down on the counter in front of him.

"Whenever we get the chance. It's a good place to come and unwind. Though our trainer would kill us if he knew how many milk shakes we drank a week." He laughed, looking across at Emile.

The girl set Achaia's drink down on a napkin. "Trainer? Like at a gym?" Achaia asked taking her first sip of her South Pole. "Oh my God!" Her eyes widened and she stared at her drink.

Noland smiled and Olivier playfully elbowed her arm. "I told you right!"

"That is so good." Achaia said taking another sip, getting a hint of the eggnog ice cream in with the mead. It was a strange combination, but it worked.

"Worth the rebellion?" Emile asked.

"Oh definitely." Achaia nodded and took a longer sip through her straw.

She felt like a little girl. As she sipped her float, she started to shiver but, she didn't care. It was the best float she had ever had.

As they walked back to the subway Achaia couldn't wipe the smile off her face. The Farmacy had done the trick.

"Better?" Emile asked, walking next to her.

"Much. Thanks for coming out, that place is awesome," she said as they descended the stairs.

"No problem, it was fun." They swiped their metro cards and waited on the platform.

Achaia felt sinking guilt in her stomach, knowing that when she got home she would probably be in trouble. If nothing else, her father would probably be worried sick by now. She tried to temper her guilt with anger. She was still mad at him.

The 2 train came to a halt and the doors opened to admit them. They rode most of the way in silence, save for Olivier joking about their homework.

"Yeah I have no clue how I'm going to get that done." Achaia's stomach flipped again, wallowing in the guilt of her expedition. She tried to convince herself that it had been needed, and worth it. "Granted, by tomorrow it may not matter." She frowned. "So where do you guys live?" Achaia asked, wondering if they would need to separate soon. Achaia hadn't traveled the city at night by herself yet, and the thought of the experience being thrust upon her made her nervous. What if she didn't find her way home?

"The Upper West Side." Olivier answered. He was looking down at his phone. "Have you checked your phone?" Olivier asked Emile more quietly. "Apparently Amelia has been trying to reach you, she's freaking out." Olivier snorted. "And apparently Jacob is going to kill me for not finishing my train— tutoring stint before I left." Olivier smiled.

"Tell her we are on our way back, and we'll be there in like forty-five minutes." Emile said softly.

The train came to a stop in Chelsea. "This is me." Achaia said nervously. Olivier waved, and Emile smiled and told her he'd enjoyed hanging out with her.

Achaia followed the crowd off the train, and started for the exit. She wasn't sure which corner she wanted to exit from. She looked back and forth between the staircases. A man running with a briefcase bumped into her knocking her off balance. She felt a hand on her back to steady her. She looked up and saw Noland. "Which way you headed?" He asked, looking at the departing crowds.

"Um, this way," she said following the largest crowd. He led her up the stairs with his hand still on her back. She wondered if he had little trust for her balance, or if it was a protective instinct.

When she got to the top of the stairs she looked around trying to get her bearings. She took out her phone but her battery had died. That explained why she wasn't getting repeated calls from her father.

"What's your address?" Noland asked her.

"Do you live around here?" She asked relieved not to be alone.

"No, but I was raised that a lady should be walked to her door after dark." He smiled.

Achaia told him her address and he turned and pointed behind them.

"It's that way." He said simply. He started walking and she followed. "I thought you might like some company. New York is an exciting place, but it can be intimidating at first. And not all neighborhoods are safe at night." Achaia noticed that he was fidgeting with his fingers. When he saw her recognition of the fact, he put his hands in his pockets.

"Yeah, I wasn't really sure I could find my way back. Everything looks different at night." Achaia admitted.

"It's a good thing I know my way around then." Noland smiled without looking at her.

"And that you were raised to walk me home." Achaia swallowed. "I mean, not me personally..."

Noland laughed. "You, as in, a general woman?"

"Exactly." Achaia cursed herself, and told herself to quit talking. "It's just, after a while, all the cities start to look the same. It's easy to forget where you are."

"Tell me about it." Noland huffed.

"Have you moved a lot too?" Achaia asked, glad to have found easy conversation.

"Um, well 'moved' a couple of times, but I have had to travel a lot."

"What for?" Achaia asked.

"Um," Noland thought for a minute. "Think of it as a study abroad kind of thing."

Achaia nodded. "So where are you from originally?"

"I grew up in Germany."

"You're German?" Achaia asked. "You don't have an accent."

"It slips sometimes." Noland smiled. "Anyway, I moved here to study when I was eleven."

"What about your parents?" Achaia asked.

Noland swallowed hard. "Well," he paused, "they died."

Achaia looked up to his eyes, but he kept them on the sidewalk ahead. "My mom's dead too," was the only thing she could think of to say.

"How old were you? Do you remember her?" Noland asked, stopping to look down at her.

"I was a baby. Sometimes I think I do. But, I'm not really sure what's real, and what I made up."

"I know what you mean. I was eleven when my parents died, but it still feels like so long ago. They weren't around much, so I'm not sure what I've created, to hold onto them, and what, or who they actually were."

Achaia looked steadily into Noland's eyes. He seemed surprised at himself.

"I've never told anyone that." He said, shocked.

Achaia smiled. "Your secret is safe with me."

Noland smiled sadly and continued walking down the street. He seemed to have caught himself off guard with his honesty. Achaia decided to give him some space. She had surprised herself as well. She'd never met anyone else who had lost their parents...

As nervous and awkward as Achaia felt around Noland, she

felt like she could breathe. She'd never been able to talk about losing her mom. Talking about her mother upset her father, and she had never had close enough friends that would understand.

Noland was hard to start a conversation with. She couldn't read him the way she could Olivier, but she felt somehow bonded to him. He was the only person she'd met who could, in that aspect, understand her.

They walked the last few blocks slipping between comfortable silence and awkward sighs. Achaia wondered if Noland was okay with the silence, or if he was trying to think of something to say.

Finally Achaia saw the familiar awning of the coffee shop. "Oh, this is me!" She said relieved.

"Are you good from here? Or do you have creepy stairs?" Noland asked.

She couldn't really tell from his tone whether or not he was joking.

"I think I've got it from here." Achaia answered. "But um, thanks for walking me back. And for—just—"

"You're welcome." Noland said smirking. "I'll see you tomorrow?"

"Yeah," Achaia said tucking a thumb into her pocket. "I'll see you tomorrow." Her breath rose in the air like steam. And it struck her, she might not see him tomorrow, or ever again.

She watched Noland walk away down the street. As she opened the door to the stairs, he turned back and smiled at her. She waved and smiled back as she walked inside. Her stomach flipped and she felt a bit like throwing up. Never before had she wanted so desperately to stay in a city.

Moving so often had been cumbersome, but she had never, with the exception of the first time, had to leave behind people she would miss. She found herself hoping her new friends wouldn't forget her once she was gone.

Achaia took her time going up the stairs, postponing the inevitable. When she opened the door to the apartment all of the lights were off. Achaia looked at the clock on the stove. It was almost midnight. She walked quietly to her room and plugged in her phone. When she turned it on, she had three missed calls from her dad. She had expected more. Achaia walked quietly to his bedroom door and peaked inside. He wasn't there. She hoped he wasn't out looking for her.

She dialed his number and waited for him to answer.

"Achaia?" He sounded worried, not angry.

"Dad."

"Where are you?" He asked.

"Home." She heard him breathe a sigh of relief.

"Look, I want you to lock the door, and keep all the lights off. Just go to bed. I'll be home soon."

As far as punishments went, 'keep the lights off and go to bed', wasn't exactly what Achaia had expected.

"Where are you?" Achaia asked.

"Close." There was a click.

"Dad?" The beep on the other end told her that he had hung up. Yet more strange behavior… she was no longer surprised. She changed clothes and decided to wake up early the next morning to finish her homework before school.

After crawling into bed, she set the alarm on her phone, and fell almost instantly asleep.

# 4

## Revelation

"I wonder how many people
I've looked at all my life
And never seen."
-John Steinbeck

School was going by fairly quickly; Achaia had seen Olivier in geometry and Yellaina in French, but had been too lost in thought to really talk to either of them.

She wasn't sure if her father had or hadn't come home the night before, but he hadn't been there that morning. Neither her father nor Naphtali were answering their phones. She knew she had made a mistake storming out the day before, and didn't want to make things worse by skipping school, too, but she wasn't mentally present at all. Her mind was with her father.

She'd spent minimal time in the halls and got to all her classes early. Conversations, if there had been any, were lost on her.

As Achaia walked from her third period Civics class back to her locker, a hand tapped her on the shoulder. Olivier.

"You okay there, Frenchy?"

"Frenchy?" Achaia replied with as much sarcasm as possible.

"Yeah, I figured you'd need a nick-name sooner or later. It was the first thing to come to mind." Olivier smiled innocently.

"Well, it could definitely be taken the wrong way. If you know what I mean."

"No, what do you mean?" Olivier asked, honest confusion written across his naïve face.

Achaia blushed. "I..."

"I'm just kidding, I know what you mean." Olivier laughed.

Achaia hit his arm lightly as they continued down the hall.

"But for real. Are you okay?" His face turned serious once again. "When do you have to move?"

"At this point I'm just hoping my dad hasn't moved without me." Achaia felt a spasm in her chest, like a butterfly trying to escape from beneath her ribs. Her breathing was shallow and uneven. Before she could stop herself, she started to spew everything out that she'd been thinking and feeling the entire morning. "I've hardly seen him since we moved here. He's been acting really strange, and jittery. Is that a word? He tries to keep me hostage almost. He is constantly getting Naphtali to come and watch me when he isn't home. And Naphtali is acting weird too. But he won't tell me anything. I never heard him come home, and he isn't answering his phone— and he seems to have disappeared off the face of the earth. I feel like I'm losing it!"

"Shhh— Hey," Olivier grabbed her in a hug.

Achaia felt a couple of tears escape, but wiped them away, and tried to go back to a casual tone. "Sorry." She sniffed and stepped back. "I think I may have been a little lost in my own world today."

"I'd say." He smiled, going along with her lighter tone. "You've been pretty out of it. I'm guesstimating you've ignored at least eight greetings." He smirked out of the side of his mouth. He reached down and wiped a stray tear off her cheek and led her down the hall toward his locker.

"Really? Eight? I'm so sorry. I didn't even realize I'd seen you that many times today." Achaia blushed leaning against the locker next to his. But of course by the time she'd done this he was done exchanging his books.

"Oh no, not just me." He shut his locker door. "I'd say about four of them were me, but Yellaina and Emile, too." He started off toward her locker.

"Oh, great. They probably think I'm the biggest jerk." As they reached her locker she fiddled anxiously with the lock. She fumbled with numbers in her head but had forgotten her combination.

"No, just mildly concerned, that's all. But, you're okay?" Olivier asked.

"Yeah," Achaia said in an 'of course' sort of tone. Giving up, she sighed and let her hands fall to her side before kicking the bottom of her locker. It dented. "Dang it!" She breathed, frustrated, and leaned her head against her locker.

"Well that was convincing." Olivier laughed and reached up with a hand to rub her back.

"Is the school going to charge me for that?" Achaia sighed looking at the basketball sized dent in the door. "I've screwed up enough in the last week... My dad, if he hasn't left me, is going to kill me."

Olivier leaned in closer to her. "No, they won't have to. But, you don't seem alright?"

"No." Achaia breathed in a defeated whisper. His hand felt good on her back, calming. She felt as though she'd known him for more than a week. He acted like he knew her, knew how to calm her. She turned around slowly, facing him.

"What happened?" he asked softly.

"I don't know. My dad has just been weird lately. Yesterday morning he was acting all paranoid. I don't think he came home the night before, he didn't come home last night either, and then..." Achaia took a deep breath. She felt a little off kilter confessing private family matters with a boy she hardly knew.

"What?"

"I don't even know. It's like he's acting like we're being watched."

"That is weird. Is he okay now?" Olivier stood back up straight, but the expression on his face remained calm.

"I don't know. He's done this before, but normally it doesn't last long. But he wasn't home when I left this morning. I don't know where he is."

"Hmm," Olivier's eyebrows were knit together in a contemplative huddle. He put in her locker combination, but she didn't think that was what he was deep in thought about.

Achaia exchanged her books slowly and turned back around to face Olivier again. "Sorry."

"What are you apologizing for?" he smirked, recovering from his serious expression. He bent down and punched the dent back out of the bottom of the door.

"You barely know me, and I'm spewing my guts to you." Achaia sighed tucking her books under her arm. "I swear my life is not usually this dramatic."

"Eh, it's whatever. Besides, it was at the very least entertaining watching you try to open your locker."

Achaia mustered up a laugh. "Okay, fair point."

*** 

"Achaia!"

Achaia looked up at the sound of her name. She had been contemplating whether or not the meat on her tray was to be trusted. Emile was sitting at a table across the room by himself.

"Hey," she said as she approached.

"Glad you're here," he said as she took a seat. "There aren't any cool people in this lunch."

Achaia smiled at the compliment. But couldn't help but wonder why he was sitting alone, when all the girls in the vicinity were staring at him. "I'm just glad I know someone in this lunch now."

Emile nodded. "So are you saying that I'm not cool, just the only person you know? That's alright if it's the case. You can settle for me." He smiled.

"Oh no, that just came out wrong." Achaia blushed.

"So how are you liking New York?" Emile changed the subject.

Achaia breathed a sigh of relief. "It seems pretty cool so far. Pretty chaotic. It's hard to tell if people ever actually stop and relax around here."

Emile laughed. "They do, just never at the same time." He took a sip of his water and looked across the table at her. She couldn't help but feel like she was being appraised. But she knew that's what you do when you meet someone new, you size them up; decide whether or not to like them.

Achaia had never wanted anyone to like her more. In this city more than any other, she felt her lack of friends. She wasn't ready to leave it yet. It was the first place they had moved that even showed the possibility for friendships. She was usually the solitary type, but something about Emile made her want to know him better. Maybe because he was beautiful, but it could have been something else as well...

"So where did you live before here?" He asked.

"Well before here, it was LA. Before that it was Nashville, Houston, Seattle, Tampa, Phoenix..."

"Wow, that's quite the repertoire. Why so many?"

"My dad writes for a living, and there's always a new project somewhere..."

"Which city was your favorite?" Emile asked looking up at her through his eyebrows as he leaned over his plate.

Achaia felt a little creepy for noticing that the blue lunch tray accentuated the hue of his eyes. It wasn't the most attractive accessory, but it worked. His eyes were the most piercing shade of blue she'd ever seen. They had a light pool-blue iris, with a darker navy band surrounding it. They reminded her of nautical maps where the shades of blue signified the depth of the waters.

"I'm not really sure, they were all so different." Achaia thought for a minute. "I loved LA for the coffee."

"I would have thought that would be Seattle?" Emile said, trying not to talk with his mouth full.

Achaia smiled at his attempt to cover his mouth as he chewed and spoke. "Seattle had great coffee; but LA has more coffee shops than any other city in the country. Some of those coffee shops had some pretty unique drinks." She picked around her plate for something that looked edible.

Emile nodded, attentive to every word.

Achaia went on, "I liked being outside in Phoenix and Tucson, it's a different atmosphere there. Houston and Nashville were fun. I hated Tampa. The whole time we lived there it felt like the vacation from hell. I was actually happy that time when my dad told me we were moving again." Achaia took a bite of pasta salad and just about spit it out, she made a mental note to pack a lunch the next day; if there was a next day.

"Olivier says you're moving again?" Emile frowned. "Any idea where you're heading next?"

Achaia shook her head. "What about you? Have you always lived in New York?" She asked, changing the subject to him.

"No, actually I was born in France, I lived there until I was twelve." Done with his meal, he fiddled with the cap of his water bottle.

"Olivier never mentioned that! Why did your family move to the US?" Achaia asked, risking a bite of green beans.

"Well, my mom and dad sent Amelia and me here for school. Olivier was driving them crazy without us, so they sent him not long after."

"They sent you to America for this?" Achaia said holding her arms out around her and grandly gesturing to the cafeteria at large.

Emile shrugged and nodded. "And— It's, I guess, a sort of extra-curricular program?"

"So, your parents didn't move? Who do you live with?"

"Our guardian, Yellaina's dad. I guess you could call him a sort of mentor. We do most of our learning outside of school." Emile said, though he was beginning to look a little more guarded.

"Well that explains why Yellaina is pretty much already fluent in French."

Emile nodded. "She spends more time studying than the rest of us." Emile smiled. Achaia found herself hoping that he wasn't dating her.

"Is she your girlfriend?" She asked cautiously.

Emile laughed. "No! She is definitely more like a sister to me than anything." His cheeks turned an adorable shade of pink. "I don't have a girlfriend."

"Gotcha, just wondering." She swallowed hard but tried to move along quickly. "So this program, is that the foreign exchange program Noland was talking about?"

"Yeah, He and Yellaina were kind of the first students here at the New York Academy. But we can travel to the different Academies to learn from instructors all over the world."

"Wow. That sounds expensive. Why would you still go to public school?"

"Socialization?" Emile shrugged. "The Academy is pretty small, and some Academies only have one student, at times. So we attend public schools so we can interact with local peers. It also helps with language emersion."

"Well, I'm officially jealous. How do you get into that program?" She asked, finally pushing her tray away and giving up on her lunch entirely.

"You basically have to be born into it. It's a network of families." Emile tried not to sound smug, but he also sounded like he didn't really want to talk about it anymore.

Achaia was saved from coming up with anything further to say by the bell ringing. "Well I've got to get to Bio."

"Yeah, I've got calculous next." He said collecting his things. Achaia stood, but when she went to grab her tray Emile had already stacked it onto his own. "I've got this, you go on. It was good talking to you." He smiled.

"You too, thanks for letting me sit with you."

"Letting you? *You* saved *me*, remember--" He winked at her and took her tray to the garbage and cleaning bins. Achaia smiled and left the cafeteria for class.

\*\*\*

Shael had been walking for hours around the city in circles. He was too weak and slow to lose the demons tracking him, and knew the time had come. He was going to be taken, whether he wanted to surrender or not.

He made his way back toward Chelsea, looking like a drunk man, the way he kept stumbling and falling over. He caught himself on a trash can and tried to catch his breath. His head was spinning, his stomach was empty, and he felt like he was about to pass out from the pain in his side and headache. Shael shuffled along to the subway to conserve his strength. He got off, and made his way back to the apartment, perfectly aware that he was being followed. He hoped and prayed Achaia had gone to school, and hadn't stayed home waiting for him.

He opened the door, and breathed a sigh of relief as the apartment appeared to be vacant. He shut the door and bolted it behind him. He guessed he only had minutes. He leaned heavily against the counter, scribbling a quick note. When they had lived in Washington, Shael had put extra protections around Ira's home, hoping to protect the old man from any harm. He wasn't granted a Guardian, but Shael knew how valuable his insight had been in Anna's life, and he wanted to insure he would be around for whoever rose up in her absence. Naphtali would know this, and hopefully take Achaia there tonight. Achaia would know Ira, they usually spent Thanksgiving with him, and he was like a grandfather to her. He was getting very old now, and Shael liked the idea of Achaia and Ira keeping each other company when he was gone.

Shael leaned against the hall wall, working his way into his bedroom to get the vial of hyssop Rebecca had given him. He rubbed it on the bite on his arm, and into the cuts on his side. He heard the doorknob shaking violently as someone tried to get in.

Shael tucked a dagger into his belt, and the hyssop into his pocket, and walked with all of his remaining strength boldly into the living room. The doorknob broke as the shaking became more violent. Shael vaguely heard mumbled voices from the other side. He leaned against the counter and waited. The door vibrated, and the surface of it began to shimmer with condensation. The droplets from the door joined together in the air before him, and shaped themselves into a translucent body, which solidified into a demon made of ice. It looked like a sculpture, but its mobility was not impaired by its frigid looking limbs. More demons followed him. They came through the front door, and the widow by the fire escape. Shael was surrounded by at least ten of the creatures.

"Greetings." Shael said, trying to look as if he were casually leaning against the counter, instead of relying on it.

"Shael." The first demon to enter spoke. His voice was high pitched and airy. "It is time to stop running and embrace your fate."

"You know what, I was thinking that myself, just this morning." Shael said casually.

"Then, you will come with us?" The demon asked surprised.

"Sure." Shael said, going to stand. His stomach twisted as he thought of the last time he had seen Achaia. He hadn't gotten to say goodbye, hadn't ever explained himself. Would she hate him? Would she be afraid? He was leaving her an orphan. His throat grew sore, as he tried to maintain his composure and not show weakness before the demons surrounding him. He wasn't ready to leave. In all the times he had imagined it, it had never been like this. In his mind, he had always had more time. "Why not?"

The demon nodded to the demon standing closest to Shael.

"Oh that's not necessary," Shael started, but the demon had already raised its clubbed icy fist. He brought it down on Shael's temple.

\*\*\*

At the end of the day Achaia looked down the hall to see if Olivier and the rest of them were standing there, but having left her last class a little late she'd missed them. She had somehow managed to push her father out of her mind and focus in her last few classes. But she was glad the day was over. A dark cloud was forming in the back of her mind at the thought of going home. Would her father be there?

"Hey," a voice came from behind her. She turned to see Emile walking towards her a few feet away.

"Oh, hey!" Achaia smiled sweetly as he stopped next to her at her locker. She adjusted her book bag on her shoulder.

"So, headed out?" he asked smiling. He had thin little wrinkles around his eyes when he smiled. And his forehead wrinkled up, too, with most of his facial expressions, which she found to be endearing about him.

"Yep." She smiled turning around to walk with him.

"So, any plans for this weekend?" he asked politely.

"Not really, other than repacking what I just unpacked. You?"

"Yeah, nothing really yet. I don't really make the plans. I just kind of go with them." He shrugged the strap of the messenger bag he wore over his left shoulder. He was wearing a black pea-coat but even through the thick material Achaia could tell he was built.

"Do you play sports?" She blurted out without thinking. "Sorry, that was random."

Emile chuckled. "No. No, that's more Olivier and Noland's

territory. Why do you ask?"

Achaia didn't answer; she just looked down at his arms.

"Oh," he smiled as they reached the doors to go outside. "Na, I just work out." He raised the collar of his jacket against the wind, squinting his eyes as it blew. "You're pretty fit looking too," he added, squinting down at her. "Do you play anything?"

"Oh," Achaia looked down at herself in her puffy white jacket. "Yeah, I don't know. I guess it's natural. I don't really work out or anything. In fact, with the way I eat, I deserve to be fat."

Emile laughed a hearty, throaty laugh. It sounded nice. "That's great." By this time they'd reached the buses. "Well, I guess I'll see you later?"

"Yeah, I hope so," Achaia said leaving him in a line outside of one bus as she walked to catch another.

***

The bus ride to Achaia's neighborhood was jerky at best. Every little annoyance was setting her teeth on edge; the cuffs on her jacket were itchy, and she was getting a rash around her wrist from scratching. The guy standing in the aisle next to her smelled like cigarettes and body odor, and the freshman girl across from her was listening to Taylor Swift too loudly in spite of using ear buds.

On top of it all, her stomach was growling incessantly too, since she'd given up on her lunch in the cafeteria. Her stop arrived about twenty minutes too late for her liking. She was sluggish getting off the bus, grateful for the chilly, yet fresh air. As her feet reached the sidewalk, she adjusted the strap of her bag on her shoulder and took a deep breath to try to settle her nerves. She opened her mouth wide to stretch out her jaw and started walking down the block.

She took off toward her apartment building at a brisk pace, her mind racing. Would her dad be home? She climbed the stairs in spurts, losing her breath occasionally. She wasn't as in-shape as she looked.

When she reached the door to her apartment she stopped a few feet short, noticing that the doorknob was hanging out of the door, leaving a hole which you could see through into the apartment. Achaia pushed against the door with her body. The door was still shut tight, the inside deadbolt was still fastened. Her first thought was that someone had tried to break in.

Achaia knocked loudly on the door. Her dad had to be home if it was locked from the inside. She felt a cold sting on her leg and looked down to see that something had dripped onto her pants. The doorknob was wet. *That's weird.* "Dad, are you home?" She knocked again, even more loudly. "Dad!"

"Shut up!" A voice called from down the hall, the voice of the cranky old lady from 7B.

"You shut up!" Achaia yelled back out of frustration.

"Oh, very nice," A calmer voice said from behind her, sounding half amused, half concerned.

Achaia turned to see Olivier standing in the hall, looking rather alert. His weight was distributed evenly between his feet, and his arms hung a little ways from his sides. "What are you...? How did you...?" Achaia stammered in confusion looking from his straight face to her door.

"I have something to tell you." He said taking a look behind him. Just then, Emile rounded the corner followed by Noland.

"What in the..." She started, stopping as Olivier put his hand on her hip, pushing her lightly aside to look through the hole in the door.

Emile grabbed her gently by the arm and pulled her closer to his side. "Just wait, we'll explain." Olivier stood up again and backed a couple feet away from the door.

"What is he going to...?" Achaia started as Noland came around and kicked down the door. "What are you thinking?" Achaia yelled. "I could have called the landlord, he could have gotten us in. My dad isn't going to get his deposit back now!"

"This way was faster." Noland said taking a few steps into the apartment. He looked around cautiously, and proceeded inside, checking each room for intruders. He stepped back out seemingly satisfied, and Emile moved forward, Achaia's arm still in his grasp.

When all four of them were inside Olivier set the door back into its frame and stood in front of the hole.

"People just don't do that in real life!" Achaia argued looking from the door to Noland with a very stern look. "What the hell do you think you're doing? Y'all are really starting to freak me out."

"I'm really sorry," Emile said sincerely. He had his arm around her now. With his hand on her arm, he began to rub up and down. It was soothing, despite her anger. "Let us explain."

She wiggled away from him and clung to the counter for support. Emile dropped his eyes to the floor with an abashed look on his face. Noland's mouth flinched in the direction of a smile before he and Olivier exchanged loaded glances.

Noland walked around the room and yanked something off the refrigerator. "He's gone," He exclaimed handing the note to Emile. "We're too late."

Achaia snatched it from him and read it. *It doesn't make any sense; why would he want me to go to Uncle Ira's? Where is he? Too late for what?*

There was a pounding on the door. "Let me in!"

"Naphtali!" Achaia called out as Olivier turned to open the door. Naphtali came in, shutting the door behind him. The hinges were barely hanging on and the trim was blown to bits around its edges.

"Shut up!" 7B yelled again from down the hall.

Naphtali rolled his eyes at the old woman, but his face was calm; how did he not think this sight strange?

"Thanks for coming. I knew you could get here before me." He spoke directly to Noland. "I got here as fast as I could."

*How do they know each other?* Achaia thought looking between the two of them.

"He's got him. Finally. He's been on the run for years. I never thought he'd make it this long." Everyone around her was nodding.

"Somebody owes me an explanation," Achaia said crossing her arms.

Naphtali looked her dead in the eyes but fidgeted with his hands.

"Okay, so maybe this would be easier if it weren't like an intervention," Olivier spoke up. "Come on, I'll explain everything."

"No, you won't either," Naphtali spoke up taking a few steps toward her. He was cautious, as though she would explode at any second. She knew she must look livid.

Reluctantly, Achaia followed Naphtali to her bedroom, which was still crowded with boxes. He led her over to her bed and sat her down. Sitting on a large packing box in front of her he smiled, but it was obvious he was thinking of what to say first; trying to be sensitive to the fact that she was feeling anxious enough as it was.

"So, what would you say, if I told you your dad is a supernatural being?"

"I'd say you're full of sh—"

"Or that you were one," he broke in.

Achaia stopped short, simply taken off guard by the ridiculousness of his statement. She stood to head for the door. "If you're not going to be serious…"

"Wait." Naphtali stood as she passed him and held on to her arm.

"What the hell is going on here? This isn't a great time for jokes." Achaia stepped back away from him. Tripping over a box, and landing hard on the floor, she brought her knees into her chest and wrapped her arms around them.

"Are you alright?" Naphtali asked, looking down at her. He had flinched forward, but had been unable to prevent her falling.

"What do you think?" She said bitterly. "What are you even talking about?" She choked back tears. She wasn't even sure why she was crying, maybe just out of frustration.

"Okay, okay," Naphtali sat on the floor next to her, putting his arm around her he held her closely.

"Please, don't touch me right now."

"Alright, let's just calm down for a second." He said holding up his hands as if she was holding a gun at him.

Achaia took a few deep breaths. After her breathing had fallen back into its normal rhythm, Naphtali scooted around on the floor to face her.

"Have you ever heard of Nephilim?"

"I don't know. What, like angels?" Achaia didn't even try to keep the bite of frustration out of her voice.

Naphtali nodded. "Kind of, yeah."

"I saw something about it on TV, once. Why?" Achaia asked furrowing her brow. She couldn't help but sound angry and sarcastic, even if she didn't mean to. This was all just too unbelievable. She fought the urge to look around for a prank show's hidden cameras, keeping her eyes glued to Naphtali's out of desperation and curiosity.

He was looking a little more optimistic with every second, which for some reason made her feel more comfortable. "Well, Nephilim used to be just angels. How much do you know about Satan? God? The Bible?"

"Not much. Dad didn't ever want to talk about it. He wouldn't ever let me go to church or anything," Achaia said rubbing her thumb back and forth on the knee of her jeans.

"That's not surprising. Okay, well, I'm sure you know *of* the Devil and God, right?"

Achaia nodded.

"Okay, well, Satan was banished from Heaven for wanting to be like God, trying to take his place, to make a long story short. There was a war, a battle; Satan had some of the angels on his side. They believed they were fighting for equality. I don't think many of them realized it was really just a mutiny, an attempt at a hostile take-over. When their battle was lost, they were all banished from the heavens, sent to a prison created especially for them, Hell. After they were banished, many of the angels repented. They realized what they had been led to believe was a lie.

"They pleaded with God. God was merciful on them, but He was also just. So, He let them out of Hell, but they could never return home, to Heaven. Their punishment, their penance, was to remain on Earth and to look over God's creation; to watch over humans, and to keep them safe because Satan would try to destroy them. He wants to use humans to hurt God as his revenge." Naphtali paused giving her mind a chance to process everything he was saying. "See, Lucifer always thought that God cared too much for humans, and that in His heart they were over the angels; he envied humans, hated them."

Achaia took a breath. She had been scratching her wrist out of nervous habit. In addition to her scratching on the bus, her wrist was now raw.

"Satan had a right hand man, his greatest warrior, and his best friend. He was the first to betray Lucifer when he learned of his true intentions, the real reason for all the fighting. He led the others to repentance, and petitioned God for their release. Achaia, that was your dad."

Achaia breathed in hard, and looked down to the floor, forgetting her burning wrist. "So, you're telling me that my father-- is Satan's evil henchman?"

"*Was*," Naphtali corrected, "and-- yes."

"Oh, my God." Achaia let her knees fall into Indian style, she leaned forward rubbing her face with her hands. "Have you lost your mind?"

"Your father was The Inquirer. He was the one who would be sent out to retrieve information, even if it meant torture. He's an amazing fighter. That's why he is called Shael. We don't have—normal names, in Heaven."

"My father is an angel?" Achaia cocked her eyebrow, staring at Naphtali in disbelief.

"Well, more specifically he's a Nephilim. There are different breeds of angels. Nephilim are kind of like-- supernatural chameleons. They are angels, but they take on the nature of whatever the most powerful thing is they are surrounded by. Nephilim in Heaven take on the nature of God, to an extent, but they could never be God, only representations of God. As such, they are among the highest and most powerful in Heaven. Nephilim, those being cursed to live on Earth, take on human nature. They look like humans, act like humans, but they are more than humans. You are more than human."

"But my mom?"

"Your mom was a human. You are half human, half Nephilim. As far as I know, the only hybrid."

"Hybrid—" Achaia mused. "And Satan?"

"Satan is even more dangerous. He has taken on the nature of demons."

Achaia shivered. Somehow finding out that Satan was real didn't faze her until she found out how close her connection to him was. "So, if this is all real, where is my dad?"

"Right, okay. So, your dad became a 'Guardian angel', if you will. He was the best of the best; he'd never lost a Charge. He knew Lucifer better than anyone, and knew how to combat him. But Lucifer knew him, too. He's been after him for millennia."

"Millennia? How old is my dad exactly?"

"Ageless. He is among the first The Lord created," Naphtali said simply.

Achaia looked down. It was amazing how all the years were coming together in her mind. All the years of not being allowed to talk about God, not watching cartoons where there was an angel on one shoulder and Satan on the other. Never hearing her dad say, 'what in the devil...' and watching him flinch every time she said 'oh my God.'

"So, what happened?" Achaia looked back up at Naphtali. He looked concerned. The wrinkles in his forehead created by his eyebrows gave him a look of curious disbelief. His eyes penetrating.

"Okay..." He looked away from her for a second to collect himself before going on. "Today, he found him."

"So, you're saying my dad is..."

"He's not dead. No, all the evidence would suggest he is alive. You don't have to be dead to enter Heaven, Hell or purgatory."

"Oh, thank God!"

"You should. Thank him, I mean." Naphtali smiled trying to

lighten the mood.

"Oh right, I guess he exists, too." Achaia tried to wrap her mind around everything he'd told her, but her brain hurt. "I can't think anymore." She sighed, rubbing her temples.

"I know it's a lot to take in." Naphtali stood and reached a hand down to her. Achaia looked up in disbelief.

"I still can't—I don't—" Achaia shook her head. "How can you expect me to believe any of this? I need proof."

Naphtali nodded. "That's reasonable. Are you sure you're ready?" He asked stepping a ways away from her.

"Does that really matter?" Achaia asked with the sarcasm leaking back into her voice.

"Fair enough." Naphtali smiled. He closed his eyes and spread his arms. Slowly his skin began to turn black and char. Flecks of his skin turned to ash and drifted into the air. Between the crevasses of burnt flesh, his veins began to burn red hot, catching his forearms and neck in fiery embers. Before long, he was burning. His hair was a mass of dancing flames, and there was a sword of fire in his hand. His eyes opened, revealing burning coals where his brown eyes had been.

Achaia scooted away as fast as she could. Staring on in amazement from against the wall. Even from there, she could feel the hair of her arms singed by the heat. "I believe you." She shouted in surprise.

Achaia blinked, and before her Naphtali stood as she had always known him. He was back in his jeans with a white t shirt and leather jacket. His dark skin no longer burning, but a honey brown. His black hair, no longer flames, but neatly cropped. And his kind brown eyes looking down on her with pride. "You handled that well."

"Yeah?" Achaia asked, still in shock.

"You didn't even scream." He said in a congratulatory tone.

"You— You were on fire." Achaia stammered.

"Naphtali ben Sariel, setting off fire alarms since 1890." He smiled, hoping for a laugh.

"You were born in 1890?" Achaia asked.

"No, that's when they invented the fire alarm. And my presence became a little more noticeable. I have to be careful nowadays."

"Right." Achaia said nodding. She tried to process the last hour, but her mind was a blank. She simply couldn't think anymore. "I— I just need—"

"I know, but we need to get you out of here." Naphtali said reaching his hand down to help her to her feet.

Achaia took his hand and stood. He hugged her for a moment. He was surprisingly cool to the touch. Achaia could feel the tears welling up in her eyes; she choked them back with difficulty. She tried in vain to steady her breathing, but she was hyperventilating.

*How could there have been so much I didn't know. How could he have kept so much from me? There have been so many lies— How am I supposed to figure out how to be...? What am I?*

\*\*\*

Noland paced back and forth, treading a path into the carpet in the living room. *What could be taking so long?* He thought anxiously, checking the time. "What? Did he start with the creation accounts? He doesn't have to tell her the whole story right now, just enough to get her to come with us. We need to leave." He looked down the hall way. "Or is she not taking it well?" Noland asked looking back to meet Emile's eyes.

Emile smiled at him weakly. "She's handling it extremely well," he said sitting down on a bar stool. "But yeah, we need to get going."

"I know. We're ready," Naphtali said coming down the hall followed by Achaia.

"Wait. Where are we going?" Achaia asked, looking only mildly confused. Her forehead wrinkled, her eyes vivid, bright. She looked up at Emile.

*Why does she always look to Emile?* Noland wondered. He shoved his hands in his pockets, unsure of why it bothered him so much. Her hair fell in bright curly ringlets down to her ribs, and he couldn't bring himself to believe that she could ever belong to Emile. *I'd always pictured someone darker for him.*

Emile looked back at her as he stood. "We need to get you out of here. It isn't safe."

"Well yeah." Achaia agreed with a sarcastic grin at Noland. "Especially since someone decided to kick in the locked door."

Noland held up his hands as if under fire. "Alright, I get it. Maybe a little rash?"

"A little?" Achaia looked over at the pile of splinters surrounding the welcome mat.

Noland just shook his head as if to say *what do you want from me?*

Noland watched as she lowered her eyes to the floor and shook her head. She was confused. That was understandable. But he knew they didn't have time for delay. If he was going to keep her safe, they needed to leave now. "Your dad isn't coming back here. There isn't any sense in waiting around for him. Until we can figure out what's going on, you're coming with us."

Achaia looked up, shredding him to pieces with her eyes.

*Maybe that was a little tactless.* He thought about adding something like 'it's too dangerous,' but Emile had already clarified as much. He made a mental note to work on his delivery and develop a filter.

"Fine, but can I at least have a minute to get a change of clothes?" Her voice was harsh and combative.

Noland smiled at her temper which seemed to just frustrate her further. He watched as she turned promptly on her heel and walked to her room shaking her head in angst. Glancing over, he realized Emile was looking at him with an amused grin and shaking his head.

"Good job bro." Emile laughed. "Ya know, impatience is understandable. I know you have her best interest in mind. But to her, you just look like an ass."

Olivier laughed. "You're good at a lot of things dude. But that wasn't your finest moment."

"Got it. Thanks." Noland said shortly.

***

Achaia could not understand her emotions. This was a lot to take in all at once, but did she really need to be snapping at people she hardly knew?

*Now they're going to think I'm some hotheaded....* She stopped herself, thinking back to Noland's tapping foot and annoyed tone. *But good grief! Who does he think he is? Commander and chief? Yes, Mr. President. Whatever you say, Mr. President.*

Opening her book bag she dumped all of her books onto the floor. She grabbed a few pairs of underwear, some thick socks, and some t-shirts and shoved them into the bag along with a second pair of jeans and a pair of pajama shorts. Slamming the drawer shut, angry with her own temper, she stomped off to the bathroom.

Achaia grabbed her toothbrush, toothpaste, and shampoo tossing them carelessly into the bag. She sat on the toilet for a moment and dropped her bag to the floor, holding her face in her hands. "Get a hold of yourself," she whispered. Just then she felt the weight of someone's stare. Looking up she saw Emile standing in the doorway.

"It's going to be okay. You know that, don't you? I'm going to see to it." He knelt down on the floor in front of her. Achaia just nodded. He cupped her cheek in his hand and tilted her chin to look at him. "I know this is a lot. But we really shouldn't be here." Achaia nodded again and stood up. Emile followed suit throwing her bag over his shoulder.

\*\*\*

As they left the apartment Achaia forced herself to not look back. Olivier trailed behind her, Emile beside her and they followed Noland and Naphtali who were in deep, hushed conversation.

Achaia was still annoyed with Noland. He walked with an air of self-confidence that was almost intrusive. *How arrogant can you be? You just get a kick out of flustering me. You're a jerk!* She silently berated him.

Emile chuckled next to her, pulling her out of her inner rant. "What?" she asked looking around as they exited the apartment building and made their way down the street to the subway.

"Nothing." He smiled and kept walking without so much as looking at her.

*Am I the butt of all jokes? Is this all just a prank? Why does everyone keep laughing at me?*

"It's okay. Emile just picks up on stuff that other people don't quite get," Olivier said from behind her, coming up to her left.

"Great. As if I don't feel out of the loop as it is." She sighed. Noland and Naphtali had already stopped at the entrance to the subway.

"Well, I'll meet up with you--" Naphtali was saying as they reached them. "Until then..." Naphtali just looked Noland hard in the face.

"I know. I'll take care of her," Noland answered his look with confidence, as if there was no chance of him ever screwing up. With one stiff nod Naphtali turned to walk the opposite direction down the street.

"Wait, where are you going?" Achaia called after him.

"I have something I need to do. You stay with them. They'll take care of you," he said with what she guessed was supposed to be a comforting smile.

Achaia ground her foot into the pavement. She had felt more comfortable with Naphtali there. Now, with him walking away, she didn't like the idea of staying with these people she hardly knew, being mocked. There was so much she still didn't know. She looked over at Noland who was watching her, impatiently. She could tell he was ready to take off.

It really didn't help that he had an obvious attitude problem.

# 5
# Diamonds Aren't a Girl's Best Friend

"Why not go out on a limb?
That's where the fruit is."
-Mark Twain

**R**eluctantly, she followed them down the stairs into the subway station. Emile kept a steady hand on her back. She wondered if it were there to comfort her, or to keep her from running away. She *had* thought about it, but Olivier was definitely faster than her, and she had nowhere to go.

They rode the train, sitting in silence, to the other end of town. They got off down the block from an old cathedral. Achaia had tried to ask where they were going, but none of them would answer, they just eyed the people around her, like they were all spies not to be trusted. She was beginning to think she was with a bunch of schizophrenic lunatics.

As they climbed the stairs out of the station it had started to sprinkle. The tiny drops of water hit her skin like bullets of ice.

They took off down the street toward the church. It looked out of place and molested with its Neo-Gothic architecture tainted by the modern metal handrails scaling its steps. Its door was painted a bright red, standing out from the cool stone that formed its walls. Most of the windows were stained glass, but there were a few that were plain and coated with cobwebs.

They walked in through the front door. There was some kind of service going on, but the others didn't seem to care or respect that. The people in the sanctuary, though, didn't seem to notice them, not even as they clamored up the stairs in the back of the room. They passed a few women upstairs who didn't look at them twice before they entered an office. There was a priest sitting behind the desk.

"Oh, hello." He sounded only mildly alarmed. He looked to be as old as the building and spoke with a mousy voice. "Here." He pushed his chair back and stood. He then proceeded to pick up his chair and move it over by the window.

"Thanks," Noland said walking over behind the desk and getting down to his knees. Achaia heard a loud creak followed by a thump before Noland's head reappeared above the desk. "Come on." He grunted before disappearing again.

Achaia sighed, he sounded agitated-- or was she just reading into his tone because that's how she felt. She wondered where there possibly was to 'come on' to, behind a desk. As she rounded the desk behind Olivier, however, she noticed that Noland wasn't there. There was a hole in the floor underneath the desk. Olivier smiled at her and dropped himself into it; it seemed to only be about three feet deep.

"It's very James Bond isn't it?" He wiggled his eyebrows at her as he knelt down and vanished into the dark, humming the Bond theme music.

Emile, who was standing behind her, offered her a hand and helped her down into the hole. Hitting her head on the desk on her way down, she swore. Achaia looked up to the priest apologetically; he just shrugged and smiled down at her. Emile patted her head with his other hand and chuckled.

"Follow Olivier. I'll be right behind you." Achaia knelt down. The tunnel was made of rotting wood and smelled moist and musky.

"Where does this lead?" She crawled forward, following the shadow in front of her created by the light seeping in through the floorboards above her head.

As expected, she didn't receive an answer. She was starting to feel claustrophobic in the two foot wide passageway before they reached another drop in the floor. The passage widened slightly where it dropped off, and Olivier maneuvered around to jump off the ledge, landing silently. He stood with his chest up to the edge when Achaia reached him, offering her both his hands. She slid down into his arms, landing with a dull thud at the top of a stairway.

They walked slowly and cautiously down the staircase, which creaked with each step they took. Achaia could feel the boards giving under her weight on each step and was convinced that one of the stairs was bound to give completely. Thankfully, they made it to the bottom without any of the stairs, or their bones, breaking.

Noland was there waiting for them, in what appeared to be a cellar of some sort. Only, instead of bottles of wine, an assortment of weaponry hung on the walls.

There was a variety of swords and daggers, crossbows and whips. There were also weapons Achaia didn't recognize or know the names of, but looked even more dangerous.

"Hey," Yellaina said from the corner, where she stood with a duffel bag in hand. She had been shoving weapons into it and looked way too perky to be in such a room.

At this point, Achaia was beginning to expect the ridiculous, and she wasn't at all surprised to see Yellaina and Amelia there.

"So we've got the passports, tickets, and all the arrangements taken care of. He's in the Vatican, so we shouldn't have a problem tracking him down." Amelia held her own duffel bag in one hand and raised a hand-full of boarding passes in the other.

"Passports? Vatican? Who?" Achaia asked in a squeakier voice than she had hoped for, frozen in place as she noticed a silvery sling-blade in the corner which looked almost as if it were made out of water. *The grim reaper shops here too,* she thought to herself. She took note that all of the weapons were made out of the watery looking metal.

Olivier answered her, "our... trainer, mentor if you will, is in the Vatican. But we need to talk to him to see what we should do with you," He stood next to her, rubbing her back reassuringly.

"What are these made of?" she asked more quietly, talking now only to Olivier.

"Oh," he said picking up a sword and twirling it around in one hand. "They are made out of diemerillium: a mixture of steel, silver, emerald, and diamond."

"Diamonds?" Achaia said studying the sword. It did have a greenish shimmer to it, so she could see the emerald. At first glance it looked like it was only silver and steel.

"Yeah. It's what gives it the watery look. Molten diamond. It's melted into the metal, and it also coats the blade. It's Heaven's adamantium. This stuff is the real deal, unbreakable."

"You're a comic fan?" Achaia smiled up at him.

"Yeah, I guess I can just relate to mutants, you know, with the spiritual gifts and all. Some of us pretty much are mutants."

"Spiritual gifts?" Achaia asked her voice growing quieter involuntarily.

"Yeah, you know. Like a gift God gives you. Something you're really good at, or do well."

"Naphtali left that part out, I guess." Achaia said looking around the room in awe. Her skin tingled here. Her fingers twitched, and every nerve in her body felt alive.

Olivier started loading up his own duffel bag that he grabbed from a bin by the stairs.

Achaia could feel herself starting to breathe in this room. Maybe this armory beneath a church convinced her a little more that this wasn't a joke. Why else would someone feel so comfortable next to a broadsword made out of a metal science didn't recognize?

Yellaina noticed Achaia looking at the broadsword and walked over. "Pretty, isn't it?"

Amelia huffed across the room, annoyed. "Yeah, diemerillium is a girl's best friend."

***

After a few minutes of silent weapon packing, Noland rounded everyone up to leave. Achaia remained silent and resolved within herself to just do as she was told, especially seeing as how they were now armed.

They left the church through a discarded rock in the side of the building, crawling out into the courtyard. Passersby looked on, some with amusement and some with confusion or alarm. Probably thinking they were a bunch of hoodlums vandalizing church property.

However, no one bothered to stop them or ask questions; so, the six of them crammed into a cab, bound for the airport.

\*\*\*

It was cold on the jet.

It was stunning to Achaia that a group of teenagers could stroll into an airport with duffel bags full of weaponry and load a private jet. It didn't inspire much confidence in airport security. Then again, they *were* angels, or Nephilim, she reminded herself. She supposed there was some sort of magic or miracle behind it all. Maybe they had a majestic deception super power, or some kind of Jesus mind trick.

Waiting for takeoff, Achaia was starting to feel the weight of her emotional stress in her eyelids. She took the blanket off the back of her seat (which looked more like an overstuffed armchair) and draped it around herself. "So this is what the people's church offerings pay for? Luxury jets?"

Noland smiled a sarcastic grin, but turned to speak to Emile instead of replying. Olivier patted her shoulder, giving it a slight squeeze as he passed her on the way to his seat.

Yellaina giggled before Amelia shot her a death glare. "What? It was funny!" She said lowly in her own defense. Amelia rolled her eyes.

Achaia closed her eyes and leaned her head against the back of her seat. She wanted nothing more than to sleep, but her mind was still racing.

She and her father were Nephilim. Satan for some reason had a particular interest in her father, and now, he had him. Lucifer would more than likely be coming for her next; at least she assumed that, due to the fuss about her safety. That seemed like a logical conclusion, even though it appeared that no one wanted to come out and say it.

It would make sense then, that she was now on a private

jet getting ready to hop on over to the Vatican to find a complete stranger who would be able to tell her what to do with her life. It was around this point that Achaia convinced herself that acceptance was better than understanding. At least it was if she was ever going to fall asleep.

The pilot got on the loud speaker, which on this plane wasn't so loud. The plane was driving slowly to its take off position, they were next in line for the air.

Achaia could hear the others conversing quietly but didn't feel compelled to strain her ears to hear. For the time being, she didn't want to know any more. She just wanted to work through what she did know… and to sleep.

She buckled her seatbelt and opened her eyes to pull down her window shade, for a second her eyes lingered on the moon outside her window. The day had ended, and so had life as she knew it. The beginning of something much darker and more complex was in the works. She slammed the screen shut along with her eyes and dozed off into an uneasy slumber.

***

"I don't want to wake her. She needs rest."

"But we'll be landing soon." Achaia could hear the near silent debate taking place about a foot away from her. Emile petitioning to let her sleep longer, and Noland insisting that she needed to wake up to be alert for landing.

Achaia was awake, but she was interested to see who would win the argument, so she lay with her eyes closed and tried to keep her breathing steady.

"She can sleep more at the hotel. She'll be fine. For now, she needs to be UP, UP, UP!" Noland chanted obnoxiously in her ear. Startled, Achaia shot up from her relaxed position and glared at him.

"Was that really necessary?" she seethed in the most menacing tone she could muster, which, to her surprise, was quite vicious.

"I'm not sure, but it was amusing," Noland said, smiling at her with his cocky grin.

Achaia exhaled, threw the blanket over her head to avoid looking at him, and leaned back against her seat.

"Nope, none of that," He said ripping the blanket, and her warmth, away from her. "We'll be landing soon."

"You say that like I care," Achaia said running her fingers through her hair and wiping away the sleep from her eyes.

"You should care, Frenchy." Olivier perked up from the seat across from her. "We get to have *Italiano* for dinner! Which actually might be more like breakfast... I'm not sure. The time change always gets me."

"Ah, maybe that's the problem. You haven't eaten have you?" Noland asked.

Achaia's stomach growled angrily. She hadn't had a real lunch, or dinner last night. That couldn't be helping her mood. "Nope."

"Here." Noland opened up his duffle bag as he buckled up for landing and tossed her a Snickers bar. "It's not much, but I hear it's a cure for hangry."

Achaia caught it and gave Noland a sarcastic smirk before turning back around in her chair and gratefully opening the wrapper.

The plane began its descent and eventually landed. After getting off the plane, they made their way through the sluggish customs line. *Apparently even God can't make this line move any faster,* Achaia thought bitterly as she hefted her book bag from one shoulder to the other, thinking back to the comfy arm chair on the plane.

*Back in New York it's four in the morning.* Achaia calculated and sighed. She glared at the back of Noland's head. He didn't even need to know she was doing it; it was just cathartic to do. Noland dragged his duffel bag behind him by the shoulder strap, occasionally kicking it forward with his foot when the line would move more than one person.

After what seemed like ages, a middle-aged man with a thick mustache at a desk gestured for Noland to come forward. "And her. She is with you?" The man asked.

"Her?" Noland repeated looking behind him as if he had forgotten she was there. "Oh, yeah. We're together."

"God, you say that like we're *together*—" Achaia said under her breath to him, disgusted. She had a tendency to be cranky when sleep deprived, but her current mood surprised even her. They moved forward and stood before the man, handing him the papers they filled out on the plane.

"And in the bags?" The man asked.

"Oh, well she's got clothes, makeup, you know *girl stuff*." Noland gave the man an awkward look. Achaia raised her eyebrows and glared at him.

The man forced a half smile.

*Obviously I'm not the only one with a short temper*, Achaia thought bitingly.

"And in your bag?" The man asked.

"Oh, I've just got clothes, a pair of sneakers..."

"And an extra box of tampons. Ya know just in case I run out. He's such a sweet pea!" Achaia said with the widest smile she could muster. Noland's face went red.

"You may go," The man said, ready to be rid of them, his face turning a rosy shade of pink.

"Tampons?" Noland growled furiously as they walked forward toward the exit.

"Sneakers?" Achaia mocked, kicking the bag full of weapons. Noland snatched it up, out of her foot's range.

"So does this 'God guy'" Achaia said making air quotes, "condone lying? I always heard he was a moral being."

"He may be, I however can find exceptions and am willing to—" Noland was cut short on his threat by the appearance of Emile with a glare on his face. Instead, he huffed a sigh and shot Achaia a look of his own out of the corner of his eye.

She silently congratulated herself on getting under his skin.

After everyone had met outside they loaded themselves again into a taxi. Yellaina spoke to the driver in perfect Italian, giving him the name of a hotel. Achaia looked at Yellaina, astonishment evident on her face. "How many languages do you speak?"

"All of them," Yellaina stated simply. "It's my gift."

"Oh, right." *That makes a lot of sense,* Achaia added to herself sarcastically. She nodded and tried to maneuver herself around to look out the window. Olivier's elbow was in her ribs and her leg draped over one of Emile's.

The city was beautiful. It was hard for her to process that the buildings she was admiring were older than the country she was raised in. Which inspired a new thought... how old were the people she was with? *Did Nephilim age the same as humans? Did they die?* Her father had potentially never been born...

Emile rubbed her arm, and she felt his calm rush through her. She wondered how he always knew when she needed it. She guessed he just figured she needed it all the time. In that, he would have been fairly right.

The cab driver pulled up to a curb outside of a tall, skinny building that Achaia took to be the hotel. They pushed and shoved their way out of the back seat while Noland tossed their bags from the trunk into a pile where they crowded the sidewalk.

Yellaina went inside to check into their rooms and get keys. The rest of them entered, soon after, through a narrow door that looked more like it should have been for employees only. They met Yellaina in the lobby, which was more along the lines of a maze of three small rooms.

The group walked through one of the rooms to find a narrow staircase hidden behind a half wall with a sculpture of a naked man on it. Achaia averted her eyes and tried to focus on the staircase; she could feel her cheeks flush.

"I knew it was only a matter of time before they sculpted a shrine for me," Olivier joked in an attempt to lighten the awkwardness that had fallen over them.

Yellaina giggled to herself and the guys smirked, but Achaia was too rigid. Amelia, who was directly in front of her going up the stairs, seemed to have not heard the comment, or she just didn't think it was that funny.

Achaia wished she could see Amelia's face, and wondered if Amelia was always this unhappy or if it was just because she had joined their group. She then wondered what she could have done to piss her off so badly.

As they reached the top of the stairs, they entered a slightly wider hallway. They followed Yellaina slowly down the hall, checking the numbers on all the doors. Olivier, who had been behind her on the stairs, tripped when he underestimated the uneven top step. He fell, dropping his bags as he slid on his hands and knees on the carpet.

"Olivier!" Amelia called out a little too loudly, clasping her hands together and bending forward. Gritting her teeth together, she went on in a hushed scorn, "watch where you're going." With that being said, she limped down the hallway trying to stay off of one of her ankles.

Achaia reached down to help him up, meeting his eyes with utter confusion.

"Later," he grunted getting to his feet, walking quite normally down the hall next to her.

"You alright?" She asked.

"I'm fine," he assured her.

They caught up with the others who were fighting a battle with an ancient door knob and lock. Noland, getting impatient, lightly pushed Yellaina aside and got the lock on his first attempt.

They all managed to fit into the room, Yellaina and Amelia collapsing on one bed while Emile fell onto the other. Olivier and Achaia fell to the floor and let their bags pile into their laps. Noland, as the last one standing, looked to Yellaina. "Tell me you got us more than one room."

Amelia then, also, looked to Yellaina.

"I thought they'd be bigger," she shrugged with an apologetic look on her face. Everyone moaned and grunted, pushing their bags away from themselves.

Noland stood, still staring at her disbelievingly.

"Just kidding; I got three."

Sighs of relief mixed with exclamations of appeasement tangled together in the air. "Okay, give me my key. I'm going to bed." Amelia reached out her hand as she stood up. She couldn't have appeared more eager to get out of the room. Achaia wondered if it could really be just her, or if she just hated people in general.

"Me too. I'm wiped," Olivier said standing to his feet heavily. His entire body seemed as if it were about to fall through the floor as he followed his sister from the room.

Achaia hadn't noticed how tired everyone else was.

"We need to find Jacob. Now," Noland ordered, looking to Yellaina.

"I know," she sighed.

"Who is Yah-cub?" Achaia asked looking up to Noland. It was time she addressed him politely and put this disdain behind them.

"Our mentor," He answered shortly.

Achaia was beginning to notice that Nephilim get cranky when they're tired too.

\*\*\*

Achaia had moved to the bed where Yellaina and Amelia had been laying. For a few moments Emile lay on the other bed in silence. Achaia had thought he'd fallen asleep when she looked over to see him staring at the ceiling, wide awake. He turned to face her, feeling the weight of her stare. Rolling onto his side, his stomach growled.

She rolled over too, placing her hand to her face and sitting up on her elbow. "I'm hungry, too," she smiled fighting an inner battle over which was more important, sleep or food.

"Want to go grab a bite?" Emile asked sitting up fully, grabbing one of the discarded room keys at the foot of the bed.

"Yeah, that sounds really good." Achaia sat up and pulled her shirt back down from where it had ridden up over her jeans. "Where should we go?"

"I say we find a little pizzeria. You can't go to Italy and not eat some pizza." He smiled as he stood.

\*\*\*

Emile locked the door behind them as they left and led her

down the hall. They exited the hotel onto a cobble-stone street. It was about time for lunch. People, just as colorful as the buildings, were everywhere. Down every street they walked, Achaia could smell bread baking, along with espresso and car exhaust. Her stomach rumbled, and Emile smiled. "I know, it smells good."

They turned onto a less populated street and found a tiny restaurant with a couple of tables outside. Emile opened the door for her.

As she entered, she noticed the place was virtually empty. With the exception of one other table occupied by a middle-aged couple, they had the place to themselves. They must have beat the rush.

They took their seats, and a waiter appeared bringing them a basket of bread and a pitcher of water. Emile ordered the pizza in a combination of English and Italian. As the waiter left, he smiled at her. "I don't think Yellaina understands how cool it is to have her gift."

Achaia laughed, but after taking a sip of her water her face fell. Once again her mind was bombarding her with thoughts. She found it hard to smile with everything on her mind.

"What's up?" Emile asked, looking at her through a hole he was picking in a piece of bread.

"There's just so much I still don't know or understand. I feel like I don't have the luxury of giving myself time to process." Achaia shrugged. She was trying to keep up. She attempted to stay analytical, rather than emotional. She had to approach the situation logically, otherwise she might lose her mind.

"Okay, so what are you trying to process that you feel like you don't understand?" Emile asked, leaning forward against the table.

"Well, I guess this spiritual gifts thing. Everyone has one?

Or is that a Nephilim trait? How many different kinds of angels are there?"

"Well there are several breeds of angels. Just like we have races on earth, and the lines get blurred occasionally. It's the same with angels. Some other breeds have something like spiritual gifts, but it is typically a Nephilim trait. All Nephilim have them, some more than one." Emile smiled.

Achaia nodded. "Okay—"

"Next?"

Achaia thought for a moment. "How do you all know Naphtali?"

"Ah," Emile smiled and leaned back against his chair. "Naphtali is a Seraphim. The Seraphim are ranked just under the Nephilim in Heaven. So, when most of the Nephilim were exiled, the Seraphim became the ones God called on to do his bidding, namely to keep an eye on the Nephilim. They are something like—" Emile thought for a minute, "parole officers, and messengers. They deliver orders from God. Give us the name of our Charges… that sort of thing." Emile took a sip of water. "As for Naphtali, he was your father's close friend, and they had a very close working relationship as well. So when the Nephilim wanted to keep a close eye on your dad, they reached out to Naphtali. He is the one who requested that we keep an eye on you when things started going south with Luc."

"He asked you to watch me? Do all Nephilim call Satan, Luc?"

"God has a special interest in keeping you safe. We were the best for the job, since we could blend into the human school."

Achaia nodded. "So you're my body guard?"

Emile laughed. "Something like that, yes. And as for Lucifer; most Nephilim have known him forever, literally. The rest of us,"

Emile's eyes went dark, "I will not honor him with a title. The most disrespectful thing you can do as a Nephilim is dishonor someone's name. To refer to him as Luc, is a dishonor, a slap in the face. Every time we say it. Nick names, and pet names are only for those you are closest to, with Nephilim. It's an intimate thing for us."

*Speaking of disrespectful*, Achaia thought, "is Noland your leader?"

The waiter arrived with a pizza, and placed it on the table between them. Achaia cut a slice and pulled it onto her plate.

"Yes. Nephilim are ranked according to birthright." Emile explained as he cut his slice. "Nephilim don't reproduce often. In fact it's only happened a few times since they were exiled here. Every few centuries the human population grows beyond our reach. In order to fulfill our purpose in protecting them, we will grow with the population. From each generation, the first born is a leader. Noland was the first born."

Achaia nodded. "So," she swallowed, not knowing if she should ask her next question. She thought about keeping it to herself but curiosity won out. "Noland's parents—died."

Emile nodded, looking grave.

"Nephilim can die? How do angels die?"

"There's a lot we don't know about that, actually. You see, until Noland's parents, we didn't even know we could die."

Achaia swallowed hard. At least as a human you expected your parents to die at some point. She couldn't imagine being under the impression that there was no death for you, for your parents, and to have them taken from you.

"We aren't like humans. We weren't offered salvation. We didn't think we needed it. We have no certainty, no idea what happens to us, should we— perish." Emile looked down at his pizza. He seemed to have to force himself to eat.

"Have any others—"

Emile shook his head. "Noland's parents are the only ones to have ever been killed."

Achaia couldn't even begin to try to process how that must feel. "Is that why he is so…"

"Controlling?" Emile finished. He had chosen a nicer word than what she would have.

Achaia nodded.

"Noland thinks that if he is strong enough, calculated enough, he can save everyone. That if he is prepared, no one else has to die."

"That's a lot of pressure." Achaia noticed.

"He has a very strong sense of responsibility." Emile acknowledged. "Humans have free will, we have mandates. Noland doesn't have an option. We don't have the luxury of failure. If we fail, someone stays possessed, oppressed, or worse—"

Achaia swallowed hard, losing her appetite. "That's—"

"A lot to live up to?" Emile raised his eyebrows. "That's why we have gifts. God equips us to be able to live up to those expectations."

"Real life super heroes?" Achaia smiled, trying to lighten the mood.

Emile laughed and nodded. "Something like that."

Trying to keep things light, Achaia decided to go back to another subject. "So you said that the different breeds of Angels sometimes mix—"

"Not often. Only under special circumstances."

Achaia felt her face crinkle in confusion. "Why?"

The waiter returned and Emile paid for the pizza. They left the restaurant and took off down the street toward the hotel.

"You've probably heard people say God has a plan?"

Achaia nodded, mostly old women, but she supposed they still counted as people.

"Well, it's true." They rounded the corner onto a more crowded street where people were headed home for a siesta. "He has a plan for literally everything. Now, that plan doesn't always happen because He's given us freedom of choice, and humans, free will. Humans have more of a say in the matter. But when it comes to us, his will is sometimes a bit more *defined* than it is for humans. Have you heard of soulmates?"

"Oh my goodness, are you seriously going to tell me that you believe in that stuff?" Achaia searched his eyes with disbelief, finding no hint of irony.

"I'm not telling you *I believe* it. I'm telling you it's *true*. Everyone has one. Even humans. It's just that humans have become so numerous that they rarely ever meet their soul-mate. It's possible to live a perfectly happy life with someone else, but it will never reach the full potential of what God had in mind for them.

"For Nephilim, though, it's a little more, strict. Not that we mind... Our emotions are controlled by it. God has a Nephilim in mind for each Nephilim. His way to keep us pure, if you will. To keep from breeding out the angelic blood. Nephilim are the top ranking species in heaven. To interbreed with Seraphim or Cherubim would weaken our bloodline. And to breed with humans is very strictly forbidden."

"So I guess a half human, half Nephilim is pretty rare?" Achaia asked.

"You're the only hybrid." Emile answered.

Achaia swallowed. So not only did she not really understand what she was, but no one else really would either.

Emile kept talking. "For us, love happens on God's terms. When He thinks the time is right. You could spend your entire life with your soul-mate and never know. Or you could know and not feel anything towards them. Sometimes one knows before the other." Emile paused, just looking into her eyes. "But the feelings never fully take hold of both people until God is ready for them to be together." They reached the hotel door, he opened it for her and followed her in.

Achaia could feel the blood rising in her cheeks and cursed herself for blushing. "So you could know you're going to spend the rest of your life with someone and still not have feelings for them yet?" she asked, turning to look at him before continuing up the stairs.

Emile smiled and nodded. "Exactly." He followed her up the staircase passing Olivier's shrine with a smirk. "You're catching on quick."

Achaia's mind was racing. She looked Emile hard in his smiling face as they reached the top of the steps. She wouldn't mind 'soul mates' being real if she ended up with someone like him. He had an angular face, and bright blue eyes, his black hair darting out from his white skin, he was beautiful. But she couldn't help but think Emile would look better with someone darker.

Achaia realized after a few minutes that she had been staring at him, and turned her eyes to her hands. She was twirling her fingers around in her long red hair. "I don't know—it's just a lot to take in. I think I'm in shock or something." Achaia tried to grin as she continued walking down the hall to the room.

"You are," Emile said factually.

Achaia's eyes snapped up to his again.

"I mean nobody goes through what you went through yesterday—processes as much information, and goes un-fazed. You're in shock." Emile smiled sweetly and unlocked the door. He turned to face her and reached down, putting his arms around her. It was a light hug but comforting as he rubbed her arm up and down and hummed in her ear. "I think you need sleep," he said quietly after a few moments.

Even though she hadn't been tired at all while they were talking, the sweet melody of the tune he hummed had burdened her eyes. As she walked into the room, she was fighting to keep them open. Laying down on top of the covers, within seconds, she fell asleep.

***

Shael was cold. Really cold. He didn't want to open his eyes. He didn't want the realization of where he was to wash over him. He just wanted to pretend for a few more minutes that he was still in his apartment. Still in the place where he lived with his daughter. But he had to face reality eventually. Shael did open his eyes. He squinted them against the bright white reflecting off the ice surrounding him.

Head spinning, Shael slowly sat up. His head throbbed, and he raised a hand to the lump that had grown up on his temple.

"Bastards." Shael mumbled, pulling his fingers away. He looked around and realized he was in a room, not a cell. That was a surprise. Shael was laying on a hard bed of ice, it was covered in layers of furs, and blankets. There were numerous pillows stacked against the ice wall that acted as a headboard. Fur rugs were scattered across the floor, and the room was lit from the ice itself, and whatever light was in the room reflected from surface to surface. Wherever the light originated, Shael could not say.

Shael stood and walked over to a bureau chiseled from the ice wall. The ice above it was clear and polished, his reflection in it stared back at him. He looked old and worn. He hardly recognized the weak man in the ice. His eyes were hollow and hopeless, his face was sunken and pallid. Shael pulled the vial of hyssop from his pocket, and rubbed the oil into his arm again, and his side.

He walked over to the door to check if it was locked; it wasn't. He opened it, and glanced outside. The hall beyond was empty. He could hear voices echoing down the corridor from somewhere beyond the curve in the ice. He shut the door, and hoped he would be left alone. He returned to the bed, and sat down, thinking about Achaia. He wondered how long he had been out, if Naphtali had gotten his message, if Achaia knew yet, that she was alone—

No. She wasn't alone, Shael told himself. Naphtali would look after her, Ira was like family. He hadn't left his daughter alone. She would be taken care of. She would grow up, get married, and have a family. She would live her life. There would be sadness, but she would be free. She would make her own choices, chose her own path, and live. Really, truly, live. Shael's sacrifice would not be for nothing. At least, Shael hoped...

***

Achaia had been asleep for about an hour when the door creaked open quietly. "Shh." She heard Yellaina whisper. "They're asleep."

"Dude, wake up." It was Noland's voice that spoke softly now, waking Emile up from the bed next to hers.

"What time is it?" Achaia asked drearily lifting her head from her pillow.

"Time for bed," Emile mumbled rising to his feet. He ran a hand over her hair as he walked passed to leave the room.

"Amen," Noland said following Emile as he left the room for their own.

"It's five in the afternoon," Yellaina yawned.

The door shut lightly behind the boys, but even so, the sound was startling to Achaia's ears. "How was your day?" Yellaina asked gently, opening her bag to change into her night clothes.

"Oh, it was good. Emile explained some more to me about Nephilim," Achaia said getting out of bed realizing now she was still in her jeans. "I should probably change too."

"Yeah, it'd be more comfortable." Achaia could hear the smile in Yellaina's voice. Was she always sweet to everyone? "What did he explain to you?" she asked pulling out a pair of pajama pants with pink and green stripes.

"Well," Achaia started, unzipping her own bag. Both were having trouble locating different articles of clothing in the dim light, but neither of them wanted to turn on the lights. Achaia waited for a moment for her eyes to further adjust. She fumbled through all the shades of gray in her bag for her shorts. Why did she have so much gray? "He explained about the birth ranking system you have." Achaia pulled out a gray t-shirt.

"We have," Yellaina corrected.

"Right." Achaia said, shaking her head. She had almost forgotten that she wasn't just learning about them, but about her own history, her own people. "He told me about Noland's parents."

"What?" Yellaina sounded shocked. "He shouldn't have done that."

"What?" Achaia asked.

"It's just, that—it's a really sensitive subject. Noland never talks about it."

"Noland had told me. Emile just explained about it being," Achaia struggled for the right word, "uncommon?"

"Noland told you?" Yellaina sounded even more surprised.

"Yeah, I just asked Emile what had happened—"

"I hope he was at least tactful about it. I can't really imagine him not being. I'm sure he wouldn't have mentioned it if he didn't think you could handle it." Yellaina took a deep breath. "The Nephilim don't like it spoken of."

"Well, he was great." Achaia said, finally finding her shorts. "Respectful. He didn't give any details, just ya know—"

Yellaina had changed into a black sports bra and a spaghetti strap, and was climbing into her bed. Achaia took her jeans off and threw them over the back of the desk chair.

"Did he tell you about anything else to do with Nephilim?" Yellaina was sitting up against the backboard of her bed staring into the dark.

Achaia slipped into her shorts. "Oh yeah, he told me about soulmates..." Achaia smiled a little as she said it. She could use some girl bonding time. It didn't look like that was going to happen with Amelia, and boys were usually a good starting point.

"Oh really?" Yellaina sounded more chipper as well. "What do you think of it? You know, not having a choice?"

"Ya know, I thought it would be upsetting, but it's actually kind of a relief to tell you the truth. Now I don't really have to worry about boys." Achaia smiled to herself.

"Oh my gosh! I know, right?" Yellaina was all about boy talk apparently. Achaia laughed a little to herself at Yellaina's enthusiasm.

"So Emile said sometimes you *know* and don't feel it yet. And sometimes one *knows* before the other?" Achaia laid into her bed and rolled onto her side propping her head against the backboard.

"Oh yeah, that's right. Like me and Olivier. We know. But right now—we couldn't care less." Yellaina chuckled as she said it.

Achaia tried to mask her surprise. She'd never even really

seen the two of them talk to each other, or show any kind of favor at all.

"Like right now, I think he's a good looking guy, and he's fun and all, but I don't even like him. But one day I'm just going to wake up and be like, 'Oh my goodness, marry me now!'" She laughed some more. Her laugh was soothing. It was nice to hear after the day Achaia had had. It felt good to wind down with a conversation that somewhat resembled normal.

Achaia laughed too. "What does it feel like to know? Is it like a feeling, or are you really sure? Could you be wrong?"

"It's more of a knowing than a feeling. It's not really emotional at all, not yet anyway. I kind of hope he gets there first," she added giggling. "But no, there is no room for doubt. When you know... you *know*."

"What about Emile and the others?" Achaia asked.

"Oh, as far as I know Emile and Noland don't have anyone yet. But the guys kind of like to keep it to themselves. The only reason I know Olivier's is 'cause he's mine. And as for Amelia, I don't think she'll ever have one. And if she does, I don't think it will ever happen."

"Is she that anti-social?" Achaia let out without thinking first. "Oh, crap. I mean, she really doesn't seem to be a people person."

Yellaina laughed and nodded understandingly. "She's not. She doesn't like to let people in. She's got a lot of boundaries, but she has her reasons for them. She's a great person, and she cares about people a lot. She just prefers to do it from a distance," Yellaina said yawning.

"Oh well, I guess that makes sense. I thought she hated me— Does she hate me?" Achaia asked laying down, feeling the conversation and herself dwindling.

"She doesn't hate you. She doesn't know you. She might not want to. But she will."

"So Nephilim never date?" Achaia asked.

Yellaina yawned. "No need," her voice trailed off.

"Right—Goodnight." Achaia whispered in the darkened direction of Yellaina's bed.

"Night." She heard her voice respond from the darkness.

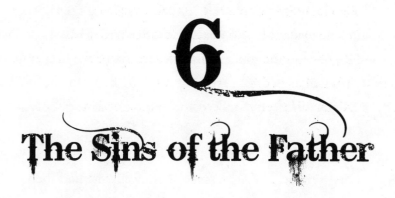

# 6
# The Sins of the Father

"Hold your head high
And keep those fists down."
-Harper Lee,
To Kill a Mocking Bird

Achaia woke up early the next morning, feeling like she may have actually gotten too much sleep. She got up and dressed in the bathroom so as not to wake Yellaina, who laid still in her bed, breathing steadily.

Achaia had just brushed her teeth and opened the door only to see Noland preparing to knock. "I beat you to it this time." She said squeezing out of the room passed him, and closing the door quietly.

Noland looked at her quizzically.

"Waking me up," Achaia said softly, nodding her head to the side casually.

"Oh," Noland said catching on. He hadn't moved to let her pass, but still stood close to her.

Achaia took a couple of steps back, noticing the lack of personal space between them. "I was going to see if they have breakfast." She nodded toward the stairs behind her that led down to the lobby.

"They do," he said, gesturing with his hand for her to lead the way. "I actually need to talk to you." He started as they began the descent down the stairs.

Achaia sighed, and braced herself. Conversations that started off with that sentence never seemed to go well. She had the instant feeling of being in trouble that manifested in a knot in her stomach. "About what?"

"I was given orders last night, by the council, to bring you in." He said bluntly.

"Am I under arrest?" Achaia asked confused. "You said that like a police officer." She turned to face him as she reached the bottom of the stairs.

"Unfortunately, not far from it." Noland said frowning. "I mean, you're not under arrest. But the Nephilim will of course be investigating what has happened with your father. As a witness, they need to know what you know." He walked toward one of the small rooms that composed the lobby aread.

"So you take me into the precinct, and I tell my story to a couple of guys with note pads?" Achaia shrugged, following him. "Sure, if they will help me find my dad. I'll do anything."

"More like a couple hundred guys..." Noland looked sideways at her.

Achaia stopped walking, she felt every nerve in her being, halt. "Like on trial? In front of a bunch of people?" Achaia lost her appetite and felt like she was about to vomit.

"Before the entire Nephilim council." Noland said. Achaia was surprised by the nervousness in his voice. "That's why I wanted to talk to you before the others woke up. Achaia, I need to warn you."

An elderly couple walked past, and Noland pulled her over to the side against the wall. She was shaking. "I don't understand."

"Achaia, I need to explain something to you." Noland looked worried.

Achaia's breathing was heavy, she felt like she was on the verge of a panic attack.

"Follow me." Noland led her through the lobbies, pausing to grab a couple of croissants and a bottle of some orange drink. He led her to a courtyard out the back door and sat her down on a stone wall that ran around the perimeter. "First, I need you to breathe, okay? This is important."

Achaia nodded. Frustrated with herself. "Drink this." He said opening the bottle and handing it to her.

She took a sip and was surprised that it was carbonated. She had thought it was regular orange juice. She felt the bubbles loosen up her tense chest. She looked up at him again, ready to listen.

"You're not a suspect or anything, okay. They just need to know what you know, so they can try to find your dad. But I don't want you to be caught off guard in there. Because of," Noland seemed to be looking for the right words, "a lot of things that happened… a lot of Nephilim don't like your dad." Noland paused. "Actually, they kind of hate him. They really don't trust him." He seemed to have given up on his search for tact.

"Thanks." Achaia said sharply.

"Hey, I didn't say me." Noland said defensively. "It's just a truth. But because of that, a lot of them aren't going to trust you."

Achaia nodded. That made sense. They didn't know her.

"And Achaia, you're the only half-blooded Nephilim with human parentage. We don't know what this means—" Noland handed her one of the croissants. "Nephilim abide by a code, not entirely by choice. We don't have free will like humans, we have more like—room to fudge." He explained. "But you're half human," He cocked an eyebrow. "We're not sure where that leaves you. Chances are, you have more freedom than we do, and to the Nephilim, that might make you seem—"

"Untrustworthy?" Achaia guessed.

"Dangerous." Noland said looking down at her. "Don't be surprised if they verbally attack your father. But I want you to brace yourself for what they might try to say about you."

"Why would they…?"

"They *really* hate your father." Noland looked sad. "Some people are all too quick to forget greatness in the midst of mistake." His sadness deepened. Achaia got the feeling he wasn't just referring to *her* father anymore.

"What do I do?" Achaia asked. "I don't think I can—"

"Just try to keep calm. You haven't done anything wrong. You barely know anything. Best case scenario they will write you off as inconsequential. You'll be free to go."

"Inconsequential?" Achaia's eyebrows furrowed. "That's the best case scenario?"

Noland frowned. "Not that you are—" He fidgeted with the knee of his jeans.

Achaia was starting to get cold. "What's the worst case scenario?"

Noland looked at her, noticing her shaking. "Don't worry about that, now." He said standing. "Come on, you're cold. They have hot chocolate inside." He reached down a hand to help her to her feet. She noticed that though he only wore a light jacket, he wasn't shaking. When she took his hand, it was warm.

As soon as she stood, she dropped his hand and followed him inside. "When do we leave?"

"As soon as you can be ready." Noland frowned. "I'll go wake the others."

"Just do it nicely." Achaia looked up at him over where she prepared her hot chocolate.

"I'll do my best." Noland smirked.

\*\*\*

The cab ride to the Vatican wasn't long enough. All too soon, Emile was helping Achaia out of the cab. She stood on the curb and looked up at the great stone wall that surrounded the ancient sacred place. A queue of tourists lined the pavement, waiting for entry.

Noland led her to a hallway beyond a door at which she wouldn't have looked twice. He explained that this was where Nephilim gathered, their headquarters. She looked around. It was average looking, nothing supernatural or exciting, no portals to the beyond—though she hadn't really known what she had expected.

After the others were led by some sort of official down a short hallway to the main entrance to the meeting room, Noland stood behind a closed door with Achaia. "You're going to be okay."

Achaia nodded, and tried to swallow the frog in her throat.

The door before them opened. A dark skinned man with broad shoulders and a surly disposition stood in the doorway. Achaia had to lean her head back to look at the man's face. She had never met anyone so tall. "Bring her." He said in a low voice that rumbled through her chest, nodding to Noland.

The room was long and cold, cave-like. It reminded her of an indoor coliseum. There was a chair set in the middle of the room, the only place that seemed intentionally lit. In front of the chair was a sort of podium with a panel of people sitting on it. The rest of the room was stadium seating, with stone bannisters separating her from the people who sat in them. The seats went farther into the dark than her eyes could see.

Achaia stopped and stared at the massive crowd around her. Noland reached forward from behind her and grabbed hold of her hand, giving it a tight squeeze.

The massive man then led Noland to his seat in the front row next to the door they had entered through. The man, then, stood in front of the door as if to keep her from running away through it. He crossed his arms and shooed her forward with one hand.

Noland had said she wasn't in trouble, but Achaia couldn't help feeling like she was a criminal on trial, and that the tall man was the world's largest bailiff. She walked forward leaving him, and everything she thought she had known and understood, behind her.

Whatever she had thought or expected, this wasn't it. The room was bigger, and there were more Nephilim than she had ever imagined. The sinking feeling in the pit of her stomach was threatening to consume her. She remembered that the people filling the seats before her had once been an army that had fought together. When she looked into the faces of those on the podium in front of her, she could see it. The faces of warriors. She wasn't sure if it was just her paranoia, but there was a blood thirstiness to the look in their eyes. Especially the man in the front.

Achaia sat down and glanced back behind her at Noland. He gave her an encouraging nod. She noticed that Olivier and the others were seated a few rows behind him. When she looked up at the panel before her, the front man spoke.

"Achaia Connolly Cohen, here known as Achaia bat Shael,"

he said in a low voice that carried. For some reason she thought of how dogs often reacted to low voices, and when you punished a dog you used your lowest possible voice to make it pay attention, to make sure it knew it had done something wrong. The man's voice shook her, though it was calm, like he was using his voice to make her feel like she had done something unspeakable. "I am Joash ben Yahweh."

Achaia cringed and waited for him to proceed.

"You are the daughter of Shael Cohen formerly Shael ben Yahweh?" he asked.

"Yes," Achaia said in almost a whisper, her voice failing. She cleared her throat. "Yes," she said more strongly. She found herself wishing she had someone, anyone, next to her. She had never felt so alone or exposed. She felt the weight of every eye in the room laying on her.

"And your mother?"

"Anna-Maria Connolly." Achaia said loudly, so as to be heard. She sounded small in her own ears.

"The *human*." The man added with disgust.

Achaia wanted to roll her eyes, but thought it unwise, instead she nodded.

"Do you have any knowledge as to the whereabouts of your father?" The man asked leaning forward to get a better look at her.

"No." The man cocked an eyebrow in suspicion. "Sir," she added, not knowing what else he could have been waiting for. She was getting the feeling this man was not easy to appease.

"Recount your experience of the days leading up to the disappearance."

Achaia wrung her hands, telling a room full of strangers about the arguments she'd had with her father, about how he had looked as if he hadn't slept or eaten in days. She felt violated being forced to share such personal information about the only family she had left. As she finished, the man before her just nodded.

"And he never mentioned where he was going?" The man said.

"He never mentioned *that* he was going. He didn't leave me," Achaia said angrily. "He was taken." She fixed her stare on the man as though she could force him to believe her with the sheer force of her will.

"So you think," The man said.

Achaia swallowed hard. She could feel her cheeks burning.

"Shael *Cohen*," He said their last name with a curl of disgust on his lips, "was the Lord's bounty hunter. *Who* do you suggest could have overpowered him, to take him?" The man sounded as if he were laughing at the idea. "Your father annihilated armies completely alone. Yet, you propose he was kidnaped." The man shook his head.

"But he wasn't—"

"Strong? Smart? *Trained*?" The man looked outraged. "There is not a man alive that could apprehend Shael Cohen if he didn't wish to be. Or he would have been imprisoned centuries ago for his *treachery*."

"Treachery? My father didn't betray you, he defended you! He pulled you out of Hell—"

"That was the mercy of God, not your father."

"Because he sought penance for you!"

"*Penance*? You call this penance? This is torture!" The man shouted before he was able to catch himself.

The crowd around them looked stunned.

"Forever cursed to protect the ones we *stooped* to envy—" The sadness in his voice would have earned Achaia's sympathy, had he not earned her hatred first.

"But Shael's history of abandonment tendencies speaks against him in this instance."

"Tendencies?" Achaia asked, outraged. "My father has never, nor would he ever, abandon me!"

"Shows how little you know him." The man stood and leaned over the stone bolster separating them and glared down at her. "He made his deal to leave you when you were an infant." The man said harshly.

"Deal?" Achaia asked.

"I see your father has been just as forthcoming with you as he once was with us." The man smirked maliciously. "Your father sold his soul to Lucifer when your mortal mother died."

Achaia felt as if she had been smacked in the face.

"For all I know, he is plotting something. He has allied himself with Lucifer once again, and they are planning something."

"My father is not working with Satan!" Achaia yelled. She felt ridiculous voicing the sentence. It was not one she had ever thought she'd need to make. It felt unnatural, as did the entire situation around her.

"What do you think it means for him to sell him his soul? Why else would he do that?" The man stood rigid.

"How should I know? I didn't even know Lucifer existed until yesterday! That any of this," Achaia stretched out her arms gesturing frantically around her, "existed, until *yes-ter-day!*"

"So you say," he said coldly. "And how are we to trust that you have not been left in our care to feed him information?"

"This is what you call care?" Achaia asked sharply.

"Check yourself girl."

"Check *yourself!*" Achaia shouted, standing. "You drag me

in here, presuming to know me. You know nothing about me!" She found herself pointing at the man, as if she could bruise him from fifteen feet below where he stood. "You may have history with my father, and granted I don't know much about that-- I have faith in the man I know. He's everything I have." Tears were welling up in her eyes, and her throat hurt from holding back tears as she collapsed back into her seat. She could not allow herself to cry in front of these people.

"Yes," The man's voice was low and rough. "Pity it isn't much."

"That is ENOUGH." Noland yelled from behind her.

The entire room seemed to gasp. Achaia turned to look at him, and saw that he was not only on his feet, he was rounding the bannister, and pushing the world's tallest man aside to approach the podium.

"This is not your affair Noland Amsel. You have no right to speak. Take your seat."

"She is in *my* Charge." He said gesturing at himself angrily. "I am the *only* one who has a right." Noland had reached her. He clutched the back of her chair to the point of his knuckles turning white. Noland shot a glare around the room as if daring someone, anyone to argue against him.

"You don't want to do this, son," the man said sternly.

Achaia's eyes were on the man, but she felt the heat radiating from Noland, her chair becoming uncomfortably warm. "I am Noland ben Nathaniel. The tongues of men could never accurately express the gratitude I feel, that I am *not your 'son'*. As a sign of respect, you *will* refer to me by my name." Noland's voice was hoarse with rage. Whispers spread through the crowd. "I am a Nephilim leader and your equal. This *interrogation* is over." Noland lifted Achaia to her feet and led her over to where he had been sitting.

The room broke out into murmurs. "Amsel," the man started in rebuke.

Noland sat her in what had been his seat.

"The Lord himself has charged me with the protection of Achaia bat Shael. Do you thus accuse God of harboring fugitives?" Noland glared at Joash, who was finally stunned into silence. "I ask the other leaders of the Nephilim; with the present information, how are we to proceed?" Noland spoke over the man and looked to the people sitting in the rows behind him.

They leaned in, and conversed with each other. A long moment passed. Achaia realized that she had forgotten to breathe.

A man stood, who looked surprisingly like Emile. "The girl is to be taken to the safe house in Russia until we can obtain any more information about Shael ben Yahweh's whereabouts."

"Amen," the crowd chanted in unison.

Noland nodded curtly and spread out a hand gesturing for Achaia to exit ahead of him. She watched him shoot one last angry glare at Joash as the door closed.

Noland stormed across to the windows on the other side of the hall and looked out over the city. "That was wildly insensitive and inappropriate." Noland said in way of an apology. "I had hoped they would have shown more decorum."

"Decorum?" Achaia asked. "You think I expected decorum?" Her voice cracked.

Noland turned to look at her.

"Humans may not be supernatural, or divinely ordained, but when a father goes missing, they generally show *compassion*. Here I'm met with contempt. Is this what your God looks like?" The tears were flowing from Achaia's eyes now. She hated crying in front of Noland, but she couldn't hold them back any longer.

"No," Noland said sadly, shaking his head. He took a step toward her. "That behavior was not an accurate depiction at all, of *our* God." Noland closed the space between them. He raised a hand as if to touch her face, but lowered it again. "Achaia, the way he has just treated you is unacceptable. I knew there were still residual feelings about your father, but for him to…" His hands were balled into fists.

"Thank you," Achaia paused, at a loss for words, "for stopping him…"

"Achaia!" Yellaina called out behind her. A crowd of people was now working its way into the hall. As she reached her, Yellaina wrapped her arms around her protectively in a hug. She was a few inches taller than Achaia. Achaia wondered if this is what it would have felt like to have an older sister.

"We need to get her out of here, now." Emile said urgently. He wasn't looking too good himself, Achaia noticed. His eyes were wide and wild.

Noland nodded, and took her by the arm, nearly dragging her down the hallways. Achaia could hear the shouts growing louder behind them.

"Noland!" Achaia said. "My legs aren't as long as yours." She had been nearly running to keep up with him, and her arm was sore. He released her arm, but kept walking briskly toward the exit. He practically shoved her into the cab when they reached the street.

Achaia looked back up and saw the crowd following them out. Noland pushed Yellaina in after her and slapped the roof of the car for the driver to take off as he slammed the door shut. Out of the back window she watched as Noland and Emile turned to face the crowd, then the cab rounded a corner.

"I don't understand what just happened." Achaia said wiping the wet from her face.

Yellaina frowned. "They had no right to attack you like that. I've never seen Noland so mad. And he has never claimed equality with the elders." Yellaina looked down.

"What does that mean?" Achaia asked.

"He basically just announced, very angrily, that he is ready to step up and lead." Yellaina sighed. "But how are you feeling? I can't believe brother Joash attacked you like that!"

"Noland warned me that might happen." Achaia said.

"Yes, we knew there was a chance they wouldn't trust you because of your father, but to blatantly call you a spy for Lucifer! To insinuate that your father doesn't regard you as being of value. I could smack Elder Joash." Achaia noticed that Yellaina had gone slightly red in the face. "Of course I'd be locked up for about a hundred or so years for that, but it would be worth it!"

"A hundred years?" Achaia asked.

"We are immortal Achaia." Achaia blinked. Of course. It made sense. How else could her father have been alive for thousands, potentially millions of years. But it had never registered with her that she, herself, was immortal.

"Is it true that my dad sold his soul? When I was a baby?" Achaia swallowed. "That my whole life, he's been planning to leave me?"

Yellaina looked sad. "I don't think anyone can really answer that but him." She grabbed Achaia's hand. "I've heard so many versions of what happened, but only from people who weren't there. That's what you have to keep in mind. Every Nephilim in that room has preconceived notions of what your dad is like. They make up what they think his motivations were. Whether they hate him or idolize him, those stories are going to be inaccurate. None of those people were there."

Achaia nodded.

"And as far as I know, none of them have given him even a hint of a chance to explain."

"Is that supposed to make me feel better?" Achaia snorted.

"No, but it's true. Most of the Nephilim have had a long time to hold on to this grudge and let it fester in their hearts. Some of them don't even seem to have hearts left. What they had to begin with boiled away in resentment."

"So glad I get to be the manifestation of everything they hate. My dad, humans, all rolled up into one *ignorant* little package." Tears were streaming again out of Achaia's frustration.

"Achaia, have you ever seen a bomb?" Yellaina asked.

"What? No! Why?" Achaia asked taken aback by the randomness of Yellaina's question. The cab driver was now staring at the two of them in his rear-view mirror.

"They usually come in pretty small packages. But you treat them gingerly unless you want it to blow up. Sometimes I think these Nephilim could learn from new age weaponry."

"Are you calling *me* a bomb?" Achaia cocked an eyebrow.

"I'm telling you, you're a force to be reckoned with. Whether they know it or not, whether *you* know it or not. You're not a helpless little girl or an 'ignorant little package'. You're a bomb. When you go off, you'll reshape *everything* we thought we knew."

\*\*\*

"I was wondering when you were going to join the party," Luc said jovially as Shael entered a great room with vaulted ceilings held up by massive columns.

"Greetings," Shael said morosely.

"Oh, come now." Luc smiled. There was a crow sitting on one of his shoulders. He was wearing a pair of black pants, and a long silver tunic over them.

Shael was reminded of another time, when that was the common dress. Lucifer's hair shimmered, black with a slight natural curl. The contrast was flattering. His blue eyes were dark and stormy, a sure sign Shael needed to take warning. "No need for bitterness today. Today is a day for celebration! It is a reunion after all!"

Shael slumped down into a chair covered in fine lush fabrics, but he could still feel the ice beneath them. "Of course. Pardon me." Shael bowed his head in apology and waved a hand in half-hearted reverence.

"I have planned quite the soirée," Luc beamed, waving Shael's apology aside. "There is, of course, to be a feast. You are hungry I presume?" Shael confirmed with a nod. "Then blood games, and we will finish the night off with some debauchery!" Luc walked over to a bar and poured two glasses of something honey colored. "There is some proof that God is good, in that liquor doesn't freeze. I guess he still loves me a little?" Luc joked, handing one of the glasses to Shael.

Shael threw it back, feeling the burn down his throat, and was himself a little grateful for liquor.

Luc made a reproving "tsk tsk" sound. "You didn't even wait for the toast!" He took Shael's glass and refilled it, then handed it back to him.

Shael lifted his glass in placating expectation.

"To the Nephilim council!" Luc cheered.

Shael didn't catch himself in time to hide his surprise. "The council?"

"A little birdy has informed me that they have taken in your Achaia, and that somebody has finally told her the truth." Luc grinned malevolently. "It's about time someone did, if you ask me."

Shael felt like he'd been punched in the stomach. "You're lying." He lowered his glass to the arm of his chair.

Luc looked offended, though it wasn't in earnest. "Actually, for once, I am not."

Shael was flabbergasted, the drink in his hand forgotten. How had this happened? Where was Naphtali?

"I wonder how much of their hatred she will inherit." Luc said taking his drink, and refilling his own glass. "What will those human-hating traditionalists do with that," Luc paused, grimacing, "...*abomination*." He threw back another shot. "You know," he said looking over at Shael, who felt nauseous. "I've always been rather fond of abominations. We could always invite her here!" Luc's face lit up, as if this were a new idea.

Shael knew the truth. "No," he said outright. "If you or your demons lay a finger on my daughter—"

"Relax." Luc raised a hand to silence Shael. "It was only a suggestion."

Tension spread through Shael's chest. He could see the storm brewing behind Luc's eyes. Lucifer's insatiable appetite for winning would not be satisfied with Shael, alone. Shael's stomach flipped in on itself. He knew Achaia wasn't safe; not from the council, and not from Luc, and Shael was the one who had opened the door wide for them both.

***

Achaia sat on her bed at the hotel, trying to process what all had just happened. She was in some sort of twisted witness protection program, where she was somehow also a suspect of something, and more like a prisoner than a witness. What she was guilty of, she still wasn't sure. Existing?

Achaia hadn't spoken since she got out of the cab. Yellaina had gone down the hall to Amelia and Olivier's room to await Emile and Noland's return. Achaia appreciated the privacy, but she still had questions. Questions she didn't want to ask Yellaina; questions she wasn't sure Yellaina could answer.

Laying back, she closed her eyes. She could still see the crowd in the stadium-like room. She pictured the gladiators and lions of the coliseum and cringed. She heard the tap on the door just before it opened. Emile peeked his head inside. "Hey."

"Hey," she said waving him in.

"Holding up?" He sat on the foot of her bed.

"I guess." She shrugged, sitting up to sit with her legs criss-crossed, facing him. "What just happened?" She asked rhetorically, dazed.

"Well, that didn't really go the way we'd hoped." Emile frowned. "I think Jacob had hoped they would be a little more open minded."

Achaia cocked an eyebrow. "Yeah, that would've been nice."

Emile smiled sympathetically, putting a hand on her knee and squeezing it lightly. "I know, from where you sat, it looked bad." Achaia gaped at him.

"Okay, it *was* bad." Emile cocked his eyebrows and nodded. "But, you couldn't see the Nephilim in the stands. I think a lot of them believed you." He looked hopeful. "At least they wanted to." He rubbed her knee comfortingly. "Not all of them hold your father's sins against you."

"Ah, the silver lining." Achaia said sarcastically.

Emile took one of her hands out of her lap and held it. "You may not see it now, but you will before the end." Emile smiled, looking her in the eye.

His eyes were a deep blue that looked almost purple. They matched the area beneath them that looked bruised from exhaustion.

"That sounds hopefully ominous." Achaia smiled, squeezing his hand back.

"You'll learn soon enough Achaia. That's all the future really is." He looked down at their hands. Where he rubbed the back of her hand with his thumb.

The door opened again and Noland stepped through. He took a look at Emile, which seemed to serve as a silent conversation between the two. Then he took note of their hands, clasped on Achaia's lap.

"So, we have the afternoon. We leave in the morning." He said shortly.

"For Russia?" Achaia asked, sitting up a little straighter. Emile's thumb stopped moving, and his hand eased its grip on hers.

Noland nodded waving what looked like plane tickets.

"You know, when I imagined backpacking through Europe, this isn't really what I had in mind." Achaia tried to keep her voice casual, but disappointment was evident.

Emile grinned sympathetically and gave her hand one final squeeze before letting it go and turning around to fully face the door.

"Can we join the party?" Olivier arrived in the doorway, Amelia and Yellaina behind him.

"Come on in." Achaia said sitting up.

"How about you come on out?" Olivier smiled. "From what I hear, we have the afternoon." He looked at Noland, whose jaw tightened. "Come on. When is she going to be in Italy again? Let's do the tourist thing!"

Achaia wasn't sure if she felt up to sightseeing, but if the alternative was sitting in this room replaying the morning over in her head, she'd opt for the distraction.

"At least the Trevi," Emile gave her an encouraging smile.

Noland shook his head from side to side. "Our first priority is protecting Achaia, not tossing coins in a fountain."

"We don't even know for sure if Luc is after her!" Olivier interjected.

"Yeah, well better safe than sorry," Noland said. "And at the very least, there is a city full of Nephilim who would be less than pleased to see her gallivanting around town like she's on holiday."

"Come on! You can't deny the girl the Trevi! Be human, man!" Olivier joked to lighten the mood that Noland had a habit of making rather bleak. He winked at Achaia, and Yellaina giggled. Emile cracked a grin, staring Noland down.

Noland frowned, his brow furrowed. He was outnumbered. "Sorry, not sorry. Not human…" he said, stone faced. Achaia wondered if that had been his idea of a joke, or if he was being serious. She sat silently, trying to predict if Noland would crack.

Finally Noland broke eye-contact with Emile and looked over at Achaia. She met his gaze with a blank stare. She knew the decision was his, and she wasn't sure there was anything she could say or do to persuade him if his mind was made up. He closed his eyes and sighed. "Fine, for a few hours," he decreed.

Yellaina clapped her hands together with a little jump of excitement. She rambled off something in Italian that no one else understood, and Noland rolled his eyes.

"Okay, ground rules." Noland began, warranting a heavy sigh out of Olivier. "For all we know Luc is out there with his sights on Achaia. We have to assume the worst. Be on your guard, stick together."

"Yeah, yeah, yeah." Olivier said waving a dismissive hand. "So, where to, first? The Coliseum?"

Achaia glanced at Emile whose smile wavered. "I think I'll skip the Coliseum actually," She winced.

"She probably feels like she's seen that one already," Emile said frowning.

"The Trevi then!" Olivier decided.

Achaia raised her eyebrows in agreement and nodded. "Yeah. And," she smirked. "Can we stop somewhere for gelato?"

"It's thirty-something degrees outside." Noland said in disbelief.

Achaia shrugged.

"When in Roma!" Yellaina smiled.

\*\*\*

The cab driver dropped them off on the side of the road next to a low half wall. Achaia looked around she saw buildings and alley ways, but no big fountain. "Maybe the driver didn't understand?"

"No, the Trevi is just off in its own little square. We'll have to walk from here." Emile smiled down at her. He swept his hand forward, and led her with his other hand on her back.

Achaia pulled her coat a little tighter. Out in the open, the breeze was still cold. She followed the others down a crowded little side street that, at first, looked like an alley-way with cars parked in random places. Not far into the street she noticed there were little shops along the sidewalk, even a gelato shop. "Can we go in there?" Achaia asked Emile.

Noland shook his head in disbelief.

"You can't go to Italy and not try gelato." Emile defended her. "Come on," he said leading her into the shop with the hand that was still along her back. Yellaina and Olivier followed while Amelia stood outside with Noland, both looking sullen.

Olivier and Yellaina split a lemon flavored gelato, it was both of their favorite. But Achaia was too in shock looking around at all the flavors.

Under a glass counter there were at least thirty flavors. For some reason she had been expecting vanilla, chocolate, or strawberry. "Is he always such a stick in the mud?" Achaia asked looking out the window. "They make a good pair." She added laughing at the nearly identical body language of Noland and Amelia impatiently tapping their feet outside.

"Are you kidding? The world wouldn't survive their union." Emile laughed. "They would kill each other and take everyone else with them."

"Will you split one with me?" Achaia asked looking from the case up at Emile.

"Sure, what flavor do you want?" He asked leaning over the glass with her.

"What's your favorite?" Achaia asked, still overwhelmed by the options.

"I've always been a mango man myself, but the mint chocolate chip isn't bad either."

"Both sound good to me." Achaia said scanning the top of the counter for a sample spoon.

"One scoop of each then?" Emile suggested.

"Sure."

Emile ordered the gelato and got a big paper bowl from the lady behind the counter. There was one large scoop of mango and one large scoop of mint chocolate chip next to it. The two melted together to make a muddy looking slide. "I think we should eat it before it melts, I don't think they'd be as good together." The two of them sat down at a table with Olivier and Yellaina, Achaia could see Amelia and Noland standing just outside the window. He looked more annoyed than before, and turned his back to them, apparently watching the people on the street.

Achaia and Emile made a mess of splitting their gelato, and by the end were both wearing a fair amount. They wiped their coats with napkins and made their way out of the shop laughing with Olivier and Yellaina. Emile had been right, both flavors were good, but not so much together.

"Finally." Noland said as they caught up with him at the corner of the street. Achaia couldn't help but notice that he seemed more than annoyed, he seemed downright agitated.

*What is the big deal?* She thought to herself.

Emile looked concerned as he caught hold of Noland's eye. "Here." He said taking a coin out of his pocket and handing it to Achaia, "go make a wish." Achaia realizing that he wanted to be left alone with Noland, took the coin and headed to the fountain with the others.

***

Emile knew he needed to tread carefully, Noland was more than pissed. "Hey, I know what you're feeling, but I don't understand why." Emile said softly as Noland stood with his arms tightly crossed over his chest.

"Are you sure you don't?" Noland said, his jaw tightening.

"I have a few suspicions-- I can only read your emotions, not your mind." Emile said defensively. "I can't tell why you feel what you feel. So if you have a problem with me, I need you to spit it out." Emile thought it best to be blunt. When Noland said nothing he went on. "From what I can feel, you are angry about us not following your lead. You wanted to stay at the hotel, we wanted to sightsee—" Noland rolled his eyes.

Emile knew he hadn't hit the nail yet, so he kept going. "You're not used to us not doing what you want, and Achaia never seems to do what you want. She drives you a little nuts."

Noland laughed, a frustrated sounding scoff.

"But also, knowing you," Emile continued, "I have to think that's not what has you so mad, and not what has you so mad at *me*."

"I'd say you're right." Noland mumbled. "About that last part."

"Okay, so my observations would tell me that you are jealous whenever I am around Achaia, but from what I feel from you, you don't *know* anything so I don't understand why you are angry."

"Neither do I," Noland said a little louder.

"I thought I was getting some frustration in there, but I thought it was at me." Emile said looking around the square, neither of them seemed to want to look at each other.

"No, I just--" Noland broke off. The two of them watched silently as Achaia tossed her coin in the fountain. She turned smiling at Oliver, talking cheerfully.

"Curiosity," Emile mused, "you want to know what she wished for--"

Noland looked at him, his green eyes guarded.

Emile was used to Noland confiding in him... Emile took a deep breath and felt a stone drop in his stomach. He knew that humans fought about this stuff all the time. He had always thought it was silly, but he knew how it felt for them. Now he was feeling it for himself. It sucked. "Bros before hoes... That's what they say right?"

Noland flinched at the word *hoes*. Clearly Emile's casual tone wasn't easing the tension.

"Well until either of us *know* anything, don't let this be a *thing*. Okay?" Emile said getting a little frustrated himself. Emile walked down the stairs toward the fountain where Achaia sat on the wall looking into the water.

Achaia stared at her coin, laying amongst the rest and wondered how many of the other wishes had come true. Would hers be among the successful coins, or would hers be a disgrace amongst the ranks.

"Hey." Emile had appeared next to her on the wall of the fountain.

"I really needed a wish today," she said looking up at him, smiling. "Thanks." His eyes were brighter than the water in the fountain, more fluid, but somehow just now they were clouded. "Did you and Noland fight?"

"Only a little," Emile smiled dryly.

"I'm making everyone's life miserable, I'm really sorry to cause so much trouble. I mean you guys are missing school and everything just to lug me around."

"Missing school? Achaia, please don't tell me that after everything you've learned about us, that you actually think we go to human schools--" Emile frowned. "And even if we did, it is a pleasure to be out of that place. If that is what they call an education, then the human race needs more help than we Nephilim can give." He smiled down at the water.

Achaia laughed "My dad always wanted to home school me, but I wouldn't let him--"

"I hope you know that none of us think of you as any kind of burden or inconvenience." Emile grabbed her hand, giving it a comforting squeeze.

"None of you?" Achaia turned and looked up where Noland stood, again with his back to them. "He can't even stand to look at me."

"That's not you, it's him. Okay?" Emile smiled weakly. Achaia nodded.

Achaia knew that logically none of this was her fault. She hadn't known who or what her father was. She hadn't chosen to be a Nephilim. She hadn't asked for their help or their protection. Yet, so much of their time and effort was being dedicated to her. Not just protection from who, or *what*, had taken her father, but now also from their own people... It almost made her feel worse. She hadn't chosen to become a burden to so many others, it's just what she was. How had everything in her life gotten so out of her control?

***

Emile could feel the weight Achaia was carrying like an elephant sitting on his chest. They were still sitting on the edge of the fountain talking. The others had begun walking around chatting with merchant gypsies and looking at touristy souvenirs, except for Noland who stood with his back leaning against one of the stone walls near the street from which they had come.

Emile could feel the tension rising up from him like steam, even from that distance, he was on edge. Emile could feel the crowd around him too. His chest fluttering with excitement, stress, annoyance...

In a crowd this size it was difficult to tell what was coming from who, if he didn't know them personally. Then one emotion cut through the rest. He huffed a deep breath out of his nose as it hit him, rage.

Emile looked away from Achaia, scanning the crowd. He squeezed her hand tightly, and tried to meet Noland's eye. But Noland was actively avoiding it. He was studiously watching Amelia.

Emile felt his eyes burn, and shut them tight as he tried to focus on the source of the rage. It was getting closer.

"Are you okay?" Achaia was asking.

"Something is wrong," Emile tried to calm himself, but the rage was consuming. He opened his eyes again and scanned the crowd. His eyes burned white hot. Then he saw him. A man on a mission, moving too fast to just be in a hurry, cutting through a tour group.

The man wore a cap that covered his face, but he looked up, and right at them. Emile saw the man's eyes, and stood up and in front of Achaia. The man's eyes were black like tar, and the blood vessels surrounding that portion of his face seemed to be carrying ink instead of blood, making his eyes look bruised. The look in his eye was so empty— inhuman.

Emile looked frantically back at Noland, but he still wasn't paying attention. "Olivier!" Emile called.

Olivier, who stood a few yards away with Yellaina looked up immediately. Following Emile's gaze, he nodded. Moving so quickly Emile couldn't tell what direction he had taken, Olivier vanished.

As Emile looked back to the man, coming through the crowd, he saw Oliver appear behind him. He matched his stride, and tailed him as he approached.

"Emile?" Achaia asked, putting a hand on his arm.

"Demon." He said lowly. "Stay behind me."

"Where?" Achaia sounded and felt calmer than Emile had expected.

"Two O'clock."

When Olivier had taken off, Yellaina alerted Amelia and the two were making their way toward Emile and Achaia. Noland had finally noticed as well, and was coming in behind Olivier and the possessed man.

Just as the man made it to Emile, bearing teeth that were too numerous for a human mouth and sharpened like needles, they had him surrounded. They closed in forming a tightened cocoon around him, Olivier blocking the crowd's view.

As the man reached out to grab Emile, Olivier, as quick as a viper pulled his dagger out of its sheath and slit the man's throat. Emile heard Achaia's gasp, as she squeezed his arm. He turned around as the man disappeared into ash, he was beyond saving.

Emile took Achaia's face in his hands. Her eyes were wide in horror. "He wasn't a man anymore. I couldn't sense anything human in him," he said.

Achaia didn't look like she was actually hearing him. "He just—"

"Disappeared?"

"Slit his throat." Achaia said staring disbelievingly into Emile's eyes. "Olly—"

"Achaia, look at me. I need you to hear me, and comprehend what I'm saying." Emile spoke lowly, so none of the passerby could hear.

Achaia shook her head in his hands, then looked back up at him with focused attention. She was utilizing every ounce of self-control she had. "Okay, I'm listening."

"There are two types of demonic procession. Voluntary, and involuntary. When demons take control of a victim, the person fights it. Most times the person thinks they are going insane, they seek help… When it's voluntary, a form of demonic or satanic worship, the person volunteers their body. They give up any and all rights to it. This guy, you saw that, his eyes were black?"

"Yeah," Achaia said nodding.

"You saw the area around the eyes, where the blood vessels looked black?"

She nodded again.

"That was the spread of the demonic infection if you will. It had taken over his blood, his life source. The man was becoming a demon. He couldn't be saved."

"At all?"

"If there was anything human left in him, his body would have laid here as the demons fled, he disappeared like a demon, because he essentially had become one."

Achaia nodded. "Okay."

Emile could feel Noland's anxiety levels rising. "Noland was right, we shouldn't have come out."

"Well at least we know for sure, now." Noland said, coming to Emile's side. "Lucifer is definitely after her."

Olivier nodded solemnly. "Yeah, we should be getting back."

"We leave first thing tomorrow." Noland didn't leave any room for debate or arguing. "And we aren't making any stops on the way."

# 7

# Walking in a Winter Wonderland

"The woods are lovely,

Dark and deep.

But I have promises to keep.

And miles to go before I sleep,

And miles to go before I sleep."

-Robert Frost

A ray of light shone through the shutters on the windows with a lustrous intensity turning the backs of Achaia's eye lids a bright orange. Achaia's body had been ready to be up hours before but having forced herself back to sleep, she was being woken up in the middle of a sleep cycle.

"Come on! Get up! We have a plane to catch."

*Noland,* Achaia thought a series of evil thoughts in his direction.

Noland, Emile, Olivier and Amelia were all standing at the foot of their beds as Yellaina and Achaia's eyes fluttered open with hostile glares.

"I hope you don't wake up that way every morning." Olivier said stepping forward. "I'd hate to see you look at me like that, first thing, for the rest of my life." Olivier joked sitting on the foot of Yellaina's bed.

Yellaina's glare instantly broke as she cracked a smile. Everyone looked shocked by his comment. Yellaina was smiling with more than her lips, her eyes were bright as well.

"Now that look on the other hand, I can handle." Olivier smiled.

Noland made a choking sound in his throat. "Okay can we get to the plane, please?" He interjected sounding as annoyed as usual. "At least they have barf bags." He added under his breath turning to leave the room.

*Is he incapable of being happy for anyone else?* Achaia was in a foul mood with him already, not a good sign for the rest of, what was sure to be, a long day.

"Good grief, just give us a minute." Achaia threw off her covers and sat up. "To be fair, I wasn't even told we had to wake up so early today." She stood and stretched her neck and shoulders which were stiff from the stress of the day before.

She hadn't slept very well. She could feel the stiffness of her bed-head from the restless tossing and turning, sure that it looked as bad as it felt falling over her shoulders.

"Oh, right. Well you passed out almost as soon as we got back, so…" Noland shrugged. Achaia glared at him. She couldn't tell if he was being sincere or sarcastic.

"Just get out so I can change." She demanded, moving to the foot of her bed in a power stance. Morning grumpiness woven through her words.

Noland chuckled to himself a little, but didn't move.

"NOW." Achaia said moving toward him shooing him with her arms. She grabbed Emile on her way to the door and tossed him out as well. "Okay Romeo, you too." She said snapping her fingers at Olivier, who was still sitting on Yellaina's bed, and pointing toward the door like an airport marshal.

"Oh right. Sorry." He stood up with a bashful grin. Making his way for the door, he turned his eyes down as he passed her.

Achaia shut the door behind him, and turned to grab her bag on the floor.

"He really gets to you doesn't he?" Yellaina asked with a grin on her perfect lip-stick-model lips.

*Who looks that good in the morning?* Achaia thought amazed. "Who?" she asked aloud, perfectly calm as she exchanged her shorts for her toothbrush and jeans.

"Noland." Amelia said, sounding annoyed at Achaia for not following what, was apparently, quite obvious.

"Oh, yeah. Is he always so— arrogant?" Achaia said, ignoring Amelia's tone. "He's just so..."

"Hott?" Yellaina added sitting up straight in her bed.

"I was going to say irritating…" Achaia shrugged "But I mean, yeah, I guess at first." She squinted remembering the first time she had seen him. How her nerves had all seemed so bare. "Now..." She shrugged again, trying to shake off the memory. "How could I ever be attracted to someone so obnoxious?" Achaia almost yelled as she zipped up her jeans.

"I've just never seen anyone get so worked up over someone

they didn't like. Maybe it's a human thing..." Yellaina got up out of bed and started getting dressed herself. "You have to admit though, he is super attractive."

"I gueff. In an infuryaing way. Whiff, I 'ont ike a aww." Achaia said with her toothbrush in her mouth.

"I didn't really catch that," Yellaina smiled. "But, whatever you said, I'm pretty sure it was just denial anyway." Her smile widened as Achaia groaned with frustration, and Amelia rolled her eyes.

"It thought you said Nephilim didn't date." Achaia said spitting out her toothpaste.

"Nephilim don't." Yellaina said.

"But your *human* is showing," Amelia smirked.

\*\*\*

After getting dressed and taking advantage of the breakfast provided by the hotel, they made their way back to the airport.

They sat in the terminal waiting for their flight for over four hours. Yellaina went to talk to someone about what had been taking so long. Hungry and cranky, Noland was getting on Achaia's nerves more than ever. "So this is why we were in such a rush to get here..." Achaia said looking around unenthused. "I see why you were so desperate to leave."

"Yeah, yeah, yeah. You know what? I'm an angel not a fortune teller." Noland snapped back. He was tired too. She could tell from the bags under his eyes, that it was taking a toll on his mood. The two of them, both hungry and tired, were not a good combination.

Yellaina walked back over to them with a look of dejection strewn across her face. "There is a lot of snow over the Alps, they've postponed all their flights."

Noland sat up straight, now he was awake with frustration.

"Private jet or not, we don't have a say in the matter." Yellaina said. "We can't use the runway."

"We really need to get out of here. We need to get *her* out of here. This place is so crowded..." Olivier started anxiously.

"But safe. With airport security... The worst thing that could happen to her is that she'll be pick-pocketed." Emile said calmly. He seemed to be the only calm one in the room, he also appeared to be the most exhausted.

Achaia looked at him with concern. He crossed over to her row from his seat across from them and sat down next to her. "You don't look so good." She said examining his face.

"I hate airports. I try not to stay in them for very long. It's never a good idea for me." He slouched in his chair and tried to close his eyes, but was unsuccessful.

"So talk. Distract yourself. What's up?" Achaia smiled at him in an attempt to change the subject.

"Well we have to keep you on the move, so Luc doesn't find you. Our flight's late, we're in a place completely crowded with people, most of which are overly emotional, freaking out about something. And for you, and for me, this is bad." Emile sighed.

She'd never seen him in a bad mood, but this was as close as she'd gotten. She didn't like seeing him unhappy.

"Yeah," Achaia agreed, "other than that?" she added enthusiastically cheery, smiling wide.

Emile laughed, it was a pathetic sounding laugh but a laugh none the less.

***

Noland hadn't realized that his leg had been shaking so violently that he'd been vibrating the whole row of chairs connected to his own, until his duffel bag fell off of the seat next to him. He was anxious, sure, but why so agitated? He looked up across from him once more to Emile practically leaning on Achaia's shoulder. They weren't actually touching, but he might as well just go ahead and lay on her.

Noland stood abruptly and stomped away from the rest who were staring at him as if he were an armed gunman. Well, when put that way, he was armed, so the look made sense. But he didn't care. He calmed himself down and relaxed his face.

As he approached, the girl at the computer smiled crookedly. He'd gotten her attention. He smiled back and her cheeks flushed. "Hey." He said in a silky sweet almost nervous sounding voice.

"Hi," she said back with a weak smile and an Italian accent, trying to make eye contact, but unable to keep it. She was cute enough. She had long brown hair, an average build, and had a clear olive complexion.

"I was just wondering," he started, leaning against the counter in front of her. His hair was unkempt and he knew he looked tired, but maybe if he played it sweet she'd take pity on him at least. He made sure to speak mostly with his eyes. Their bright green reflecting the fluorescence of the overhead lights, sparkling.

"We had a private flight arranged for today. It was supposed to leave three hours ago. And, well..." Noland tried his best to look honest, "normally I wouldn't mind the delay, but we need to get to Moscow. My friend," He said nodding toward Emile. He really was starting to not look so good. He was now leaning fully on Achaia's shoulder. "He is supposed to be having surgery tonight. We really need to get there. This is the only doctor we've found who can perform this kind of surgery and he doesn't have anything else available until two months from now. And well..." He said looking back over again. "I don't think he has that long..."

"Oh no!" The girl said. Her eyes were wide and she had a

look of genuine concern on her face. "I'll see what I can do to get it authorized. It's just all the snow. It's not safe right now."

"I know. But like I said, normally I wouldn't care, it's just...." He looked over at Emile again.

"You're right, he really doesn't look good. What does he have?" She asked picking up the phone and dialing for assistance.

Noland struggled for only a second realizing that she was distracted by the phone and that her English wasn't good, so he threw out the first thing that came to his mind. "He has a disease called" He coughed and lowered his voice, "Consecotaleophobia." He squinted his face and shook his head knowing it was a terrible lie, luckily she wasn't looking at him or listening anymore as someone had answered her call. Noland stood up straight, and sighed. He began to pace as he listened to the girl's conversation.

"Yeah," she said nodding, her attention fixed on the phone. She rattled off something in Italian, which Noland didn't follow, paused, then said, "*Gratsi*." She looked back up to him with a semi-confused look on her face. "Oh that's awful."

"Yeah. It really is. He's only seventeen."

The girl now looked as if she was about to cry. He figured he'd done enough damage.

"Okay, well I'll just go wait with him. Thanks for all of your help." Noland walked back over to the group who were all looking rather worn.

"What was all of that about?" Yellaina asked. Amelia looked at him with scorn. Achaia didn't pay attention to him at all, she was too distracted by Emile's state.

Olivier smiled at him mischievously. "You got bored and needed a flirt?"

Noland smiled. "Nothing," he said looking at Yellaina. His

tone was smug, but he was trying not to laugh. Olivier knew him well enough to know what was going on.

A man arrived at the desk and Noland watched as she pleaded with him and pointed in their direction. After a minute or two the man left and the girl came over. "We have an emergency pilot who is willing to make the flight. If you'll follow me."

"Thank you so much." Noland said looking again sincere.

Everyone grabbed their bags and followed the girl, throwing Noland sideways glances.

"How did you do it?" Olivier asked.

"I told her that Emile had a deadly disease and the only doctor who could save his life was in Moscow, and he didn't have much time left." Olivier laughed.

"Oh yeah? And what ails me?" Emile smiled coming up next to him.

"Oh my friend you are dying from Consecotaleophobia." Noland smirked.

"Dude, that's the fear of chopsticks!" Emile whispered trying not to laugh.

"I know... It was the first thing that came to mind." Noland whispered.

Achaia giggled behind him. It was the brightest sound he'd heard in a week.

"That's great." Achaia said trying to keep her giggles under control. The combination of being tired and stressed had apparently resulted in an uncontrollable burst of laughter.

\*\*\*

Achaia tried hard to stop laughing but she couldn't. When they reached the plane and the girl turned around Achaia buried her face in her hands. It looked as if she were sobbing. To convince the girl that this was the case, Noland put his arm around her. "Shh, he's going to be okay. We're going to get there." He whispered loudly in Achaia's ear. "Thank you so much again for all your help," he said to the girl, as they passed her to load the plane.

"No problem. I hope he gets the help he needs." She said looking at Achaia with great concern, then to Emile.

"Oh he needs so much," Olivier laughed under his breath ahead of them.

Achaia followed Noland onto the plane. "You could have toned it down a little. She felt awful!" Emile whispered.

When they had all boarded, and the doors were closed, they all burst out into laughter. Even Amelia.

*So she does know how to smile.* Achaia thought, stopping her own laughter in mild surprise.

Amelia was pretty when she smiled, *really* pretty. Achaia wondered why she was so angry all the time.

They were all buckled and still smiling with the occasional giggle as the plane took off into the clear sky. Achaia leaned, once again, into the cushioned chair, shut her eyes, and fell asleep.

***

*Achaia was in the city again, only this time her and her dad's apartment was red. Everything in it was white. She looked in all of the rooms for her dad, but couldn't find him. When she opened the front door to go outside, there was no floor. There was nothing. It was empty, not black, not blue, not white, but nothing. There was a searing pain in her back and the apartment began to shake. No, not the apartment... the plane.*

Achaia opened her eyes. Everyone was quiet, the turbulence was the worst Achaia had ever experienced.

Noland's face was serious, and white. Emile had his eyes shut tight, Amelia looked horrified. Yellaina was crying silently, and Olivier was praying.

Achaia looked around again and noticed that in their different ways, they were all praying. Achaia's stomach dropped and Yellaina screamed, as the plane fell hundreds of feet. The turbulence rattling them all in their seats. Achaia's seat belt was cutting into her hip bones as she jostled.

Then the plane shot downward again. This time it didn't stop.

Everyone was screaming; instructions, exclamations, each other's names and wails of fear. There was a series of loud crashes, abrupt stopping, being jerked around, and pain... lots of pain.

Then there was nothing.

*** 

"You can think of this as an initiation ceremony." Luc explained. He had led Shael down a tunnel and into a darker room with a cage in the center, and rows upon rows of demons in stands. "The blood games establish your rank here in Hell." He opened up the door to the cage, and gestured for Shael to enter. "You'll be fighting Ragnar tonight. If you win, you can work your way up and challenge from there." Luc smiled encouragingly.

Shael looked at his demonic opponent. He was a huge lump of a beast, with hulking muscular shoulders. His skin was dry and gray, lending him a look of stone. In fact, if you didn't look at his face, you might think he was just a boulder. On the plus side, he looked rather dim witted, and Shael hoped his bulk would mean he was slow. On the down side, Shael still hadn't fully healed from his alley brawl with the five demon stooges. He felt the adrenaline course through him, waking up his muscles.

Shael shook out his arms as he entered the ring. Chaos rose in the stands as demons stood, and hissed, and cheered. Ragnar looked a little confused as he looked at Shael. He looked to Luc, as a dog looked to its owner for permission, when told to do something it knew was wrong. Luc nodded at him, then rolled his eyes as he locked the door of the cage.

Luc went up to a throne-like seat in the stands. From there, his voice echoed throughout the room when he spoke, as it would if he used a microphone. "Let the fight commence!"

Demons cheered. Shael blocked out the noise, focusing on his opponent. He saw Ragnar's left foot step, just before he jabbed. Shael ducked, missing the blow by an inch. Ragnar was slower than Shael, but not as slow as Shael had hoped. However, Ragnar was easy to read. His strikes were foretold by tells and were obvious. He wasn't a particularly skilled fighter, just a heavy one.

Shael lunged forward, sliding on his knees, slicing out with his dagger at Ragnar's hamstrings. Ragnar stumbled forward, tripping, but his skin was thick and tough. Shael checked his blade, there wasn't even any blood on it. "Damn," Shael said looking up at the massive figure that was Ragnar, shaking his head.

Shael ran forward. Springing up from a kick to Ragnar's hip, Shael launched himself onto the demon's shoulders reaching around to slit his throat. The spectating demons all hissed. Yet again, his blade came away clean. Ragnar reached up, and grabbed Shael by the leg, dangling him upside down. The demons laughed with mirth.

Shael sat up as Ragnar swung with his opposite hand and missed. Shael rolled his eyes. This fight was becoming tedious. Shael stared up at the hand holding him, and to the caged roof above it. If he could just…

Shael swung himself back and forth, Ragnar looked at him confused. In frustration, he shook Shael violently. However, this afforded Shael an opportunity to grab at the caged ceiling. He held tight, and as Ragnar's hand shook downward, Shael did not go with it. He swung himself as if on monkey bars above Ragnar's head. The demons were in uproar, some laughed at him, some jeered, and some stared on in confusion. Shael swung as Ragnar advanced, releasing himself into a summersault. He came down with his full force, jamming his feet unto the top of Ragnar's head. The demon swayed for a moment, and collapsed unconscious.

The demons all hissed. Lucifer smiled, though Shael was sure he had seen a frown of disappointment, just before he beamed his congratulations. "We have a winner!" Luc strutted down the steps and into the ring, thrusting Shael's arm into the air. "Shael ben Yahweh advances!" The demons moaned their disapproval, but fell silent at a reproving glare from Lucifer. Some of them cheered halfheartedly. But most of them just stared on in disbelief, unable to comprehend that they were to accept a fallen angel amongst their ranks.

***

The smoke that rose up from the ground where the plane had crashed didn't get far before it was swept away by the wind. The small fire that had started had already been put out by the snow.

The blizzard was so thick that Noland could hardly see the plane, though he could see the nose had been obliterated. The pilot couldn't have made it. The fire of guilt lit in his stomach, he pushed it down, smothering it with priority.

Noland looked down checking himself over, he felt fine, nothing was hurt, but he knew why...

Emile standing next to him was wide eyed and alert, though he was tired, and drained. "Amelia!" He tried to yell, but it came out as a hoarse cry, drowned in his throat before it ever even reached the howling wind.

Noland felt bad for him, but felt worse for Amelia. Looking

around, he could see Yellaina on the ground, Olivier helping her to her feet. Amelia lay unconscious a few yards away, Emile rushed toward her. But where was Achaia?

"Achaia!" Noland called out.

Once he checked Amelia for a pulse, Emile joined Noland in the search. Finding nothing in his proximity, Emile joined Noland in searching the surrounding area.

Olivier rubbed Yellaina's arm and began searching as well. Yellaina made her way over to tend to Amelia.

Each of the guys took off in different directions searching around the plane, calling Achaia's name.

*Where is she?* Noland thought, nearing panic. "Achaia!" Noland could hear his voice growing angrier, but he wasn't mad, he was scared. *Where is she? Tell me I haven't lost her,* he pleaded.

"Over here!" Emile called from the other side of the plane. "She's still inside!" Emile was pulling at a section of wall. Through the window Noland could see Achaia laying inside.

"Is she...?" Noland started, his whole body going still and numb. He couldn't bring himself to finish the question. "Watch out," Noland said, searching for a place for his hands to hold onto the fuselage.

Emile stepped back out of the way. Noland grasped the side and pulled it out and up, tearing it away from the rest of the plane. The metal screamed under the abuse. He pushed it away from himself, throwing it to the side, and climbed into the plane.

\*\*\*

Achaia heard a great tearing sound and flinched away from it. She tried to call out for help, but all she could muster was a moan. Her head hurt and she couldn't bring herself to open her eyes. It had all happened so fast. She wondered, in amazement, how she was alive.

"Kaya? Oh thank God!" She could hear a voice. She felt a hand run down her face, wiping the hair away, rubbing her cheek. "Thank God." The voice said again.

Her head was lifted up and tucked into something hard and warm, a chest. Achaia struggled to make her eyes open. Through squinted, bruised feeling eyes, she could see blue, a shirt. There was a hand under her head supporting it, she was grateful. She didn't think she could hold it up herself.

As the blue pulled away from her she looked up to find a face. *Noland?*

His dirty blond hair was drenched, blood running through it onto his forehead, and into his eyes. His green eyes, were blood shot, wet, and searching hers. His arms were hard and strong and gave her a safe feeling. Her head throbbed. She couldn't keep her eyes open anymore. She closed them and let the dark take her.

***

Emile stood shivering outside the plane. He could feel Noland's fear, relief, and worry.

Noland emerged from the plane with Achaia in his arms. "We need to grab as much as we can and take it with us. There has to be shelter around here somewhere." Noland juggled Achaia up to his chest and held her close against the wind, turning her face into him, like a child.

They walked around to the other side of the plane where Olivier and Yellaina sat next to Amelia trying to wake her up.

Their bags were scattered across the area. Emile walked around throwing straps over his shoulders, collecting them all. Amongst the rubble he found a box of plane crackers. He grabbed it and tucked it into Achaia's book bag which was only half-full.

When he rejoined the group, Noland took some of the bags from Emile and had him pack them on his back. Achaia stirred in his arms.

"Olivier why don't you go have a look around and see if you can't find shelter." Emile suggested. He felt Olivier's sense of purpose and urgency as he took off into the snow running.

Emile bent down and lifted Amelia into his own arms.

Noland picked a direction and started walking. Olivier met them a few minutes later. "There is an old cabin about a couple miles ahead, that way." He told them, pointing left, not even out of breath.

"I can't carry her that long." Emile said struggling to keep Amelia from falling out of his numb arms to the ground.

"Here, we'll take turns." Olivier reached out his arms, and took his sister from her twin.

Emile shook out his arms and looked around. How were they going to make sure they were going in the right direction? Everywhere he looked all he could see was snow, swirling around them. This blizzard was strong, there was no sign of it letting up anytime soon. He could feel everyone else's hopelessness. It was times like this that Emile was grateful for Noland's stubborn endurance and refusal to give up. It was refreshing in the midst of everyone else's distress.

"Olivier you lead the way." Noland commanded in a low steady voice. Emile envied him sometimes for his spiritual gifts. Not only did he get two, but they were two that Emile wouldn't mind having himself.

Emile's jaw chattered and he tried to grab the book bag straps sliding down his shoulder with his cold, wet, hands. Even as his fingers grasped the strap, he couldn't feel it in his hand. That couldn't be a good sign.

Olivier did as he was told and walked ahead of the group. They walked for what felt like an hour, but since they were headed against the wind now, they hadn't gone far.

"It's your turn" Olivier said falling back and passing Amelia off to Emile.

Emile struggled to hold her up, he had lost all feeling in his legs and arms. They went on though. Emile now had to breathe through his mouth, his nose had started running and now was covered with tiny icicles.

He looked over to Noland, who was wet, but still looked as he did on the plane, no icicles, nothing. Same for Achaia, she was warm and safe against his chest. Warmed by the heat radiating from within him.

They carried on for what seemed like forever, until time stood still. Emile had no feeling of time coming or going, or even of its existing at all. He had begun to walk with his eyes shut tight, against the wind, and because he was simply exhausted.

"There it is!" Olivier yelled from about twenty feet in front of him. His voice flew on the wind, but there was no use in responding, Emile knew Olivier wouldn't be able to hear him. Somehow, with an end in sight, walking became ten times harder. He was walking but the cabin didn't seem to be getting any closer. In every step he could feel the weight of his own body and Amelia's.

"Olivier!" Emile tried to yell. But his voice came out as a harsh sounding moan.

Noland rushed over to him and adjusted Achaia over one of his shoulders and took Amelia out of Emile's arms, laying her over his other shoulder.

Olivier and Yellaina reached the cabin and tried to get in. The snow was piling up on the steps and porch. Olivier, moving quickly cleared a path to the door in the time it would have taken most people to grab a shovel. Noland made it up to the porch ahead of Emile and handed Amelia over to Olivier. He let Achaia slide down his chest again into his arms, and held onto her tightly as he kicked open the door.

As they walked inside, Olivier hit the light switch but nothing happened. "It was worth a shot." Olivier said juggling Amelia in his arms.

With everyone inside Emile turned around and shut the door. It was a small cabin for sure, even small for a one room cabin, and it was full of junk. To his right, there was a set of small bunk beds. To his left, a slightly larger bed, that Emile guessed was *supposed* to be big enough for two people. There was a fire place in the center of the side wall behind him, by the door.

Noland walked over to the larger bed and laid Achaia down gently. Emile had never seen Noland be that gentle with anyone before. He could feel Noland's tenderness.

***

Achaia opened her eyes. Noland stood over her.

"Hey." He spoke softly. She'd never heard him use that tone before.

*Near death experiences really get to people,* she thought to herself. "Hey." She tried to smile but it hurt. Her lips split, she could taste the iron of her blood in her mouth.

"How do you feel?" He asked softly sitting down next to her.

"Cold." She said attempting to sit up. The room started spinning like the tilt-a-whirl ride at the county fare.

"Whoa!" He said, taking her gently by the shoulders. "Slowly." His hands were firm but gentle all at the same time; his eyes bright and warmhearted. He rubbed her arms and shoulders. "Yeah, I bet you're cold. We're all wet. We're going to start a fire..."

"Amelia?" Achaia asked, noticing the body next to her own. Amelia lay unconscious, face pale in the cold.

"We'll explain later. Right now we need to dry the clothes. Even the bags are soaked through. We had to walk over a mile in a blizzard to get here."

"Over a mile in a blizzard? How—"

"I carried you," he said simply. "We need to get out of these wet clothes and dry them before we all get hypothermia."

Achaia blushed but nodded. "Hey," she put a hand on his forearm to stop him as he stood. "Thank you."

Noland smiled his welcome, and helped her to her feet slowly.

The others were all looking around the cabin. "I found some rope!" Olivier exclaimed. "We can use this to make a clothes line."

"Good stuff," Emile concurred. "Noland... Fire?"

"Yeah, I'm on it." Noland walked over to the fireplace which was itself filling with snow. He took a few logs from the pile next to the door and stacked them inside. He then leaned down in front of the logs and worked for a second, and there was a fire.

"How did you do that?" Achaia asked. "That should have been impossible, those logs are wet and there's snow in it."

"I have my ways." Noland smirked. "It's one of my spiritual gifts."

"Oh yeah. I forgot about those." It felt weird being nice to him, but it felt good. *He is cute,* she thought to herself with surprise, taking in the warm glow of his skin. His eyebrow had a gash through it, but it gave him the look of an action hero— She concluded she had obviously hit her head.

"Get out of those wet clothes, all of you." Emile ordered, himself taking off his dripping wet t-shirt. The room went quiet, save for the sound of wringing out wet t-shirts, and stumbling out of wet jeans.

Noland grabbed at the bottom seam of his t-shirt and pulled it up over his head revealing a perfectly sculpted stomach and chest. Achaia swallowed hard and looked away as he unbuttoned his pants. Her cheeks burned, as she turned her back on him. Behind her was Olivier. She turned around again and Emile was pulling his feet out of the legs of his pants.

Yellaina stood over in the corner, undressing in the dark. There were no corners left for Achaia to hide in, nor a way to get to one without passing one of the boys. Achaia closed her eyes and moved her hair all to one side, stepping at least around the head-board of the bed. Then grabbing the bottom seam of her own shirt, she pulled it up over her head.

When she opened her eyes, Emile was hanging the rope, No-land was tending to the fire, and Olivier was making the top bunk of the bunk beds. Emile looked like he was having a hard time tying the knot.

Achaia wrung her shirt out and took off her jeans with difficulty. She was glad no one was looking. She ungracefully hopped and tripped trying to pull her leg from the suction-cupped tight wet pants. Then she stood, not knowing what came next in a navy bra and bright orange underwear, so much for discrete....

She stared down at her feet, feeling the blood rising in her cheeks. She wished she could melt between the wide set floorboards. She yanked and pulled at the blanket under Amelia, but to no avail. So, she squatted down behind the headboard and waited to see what they were all going to do next.

\*\*\*

Noland melted the snow and added a couple more logs to the now growing fire. Emile hung the rope across the room, in front of the fire, for the clothes to dry on.

Liking his success after the fourth log Noland stood and turned around. Crouching, not altogether hidden, behind the log headboard of the bed to his left, the only person he could see lit by the fire, was Achaia. She was pale, the fire seemed to dance off her skin throughout the rest of the room. Her red hair hung in soaked ringlets over her shoulders, looking almost brown. It struck him how small she was.

He watched as she folded her clothes over her arm and stood to bring them to the clothes line. Then, there was a sharp pain on the back of his head. His attention snapped back to, and he looked over to see Emile drawing back his hand. "Dude, what was that for?" Noland whispered.

"Do you really want me to answer that?" Emile whispered back looking him dead in the eye.

"It was a rhetorical question." Noland said glancing quickly back over to Achaia to see if she had noticed the conversation. She hadn't.

Everyone came over then to hang their clothes on the rope except Amelia who was still passed out on the bed. Noland noticed Emile was shaking all over, looking overwhelmed.

"Okay that's it!" Emile yelled after a minute. "That is *it*!"

Everyone froze and looked at him with shock and confusion written across their faces. Noland couldn't help but laugh.

He watched Emile walk over to the wall where the knot had been tied in the rope and untie it. The clothes all fell to the floor as he drug the rope across the room and tied it to the mantel piece above the fireplace. He then proceeded to walk over to the other side of the room to the second knot. He untied it and walked across the cabin to the wall farthest from the fire. Tying the rope to a deer head hung on the wall.

"From now on this side of the room," Emile yelled gesturing to the side with the bunk beds, "is Germany. This side," he yelled pointing to the side with the larger bed, "is France. I'm building a blockade! "

Everyone looked at him like he was crazy.

"From now on, no one crosses the boarder. Not until everyone puts some clothes on! Girls get over there," He said gesturing to France. "Noland go over there," He said gesturing to Germany. "*Way* over there," he added under his breath. "Germany, France," he yelled again reminding everyone of their place.

Noland ducked under the rope to stand in front of the bunk bed, where Olivier had perched himself on the top. Olivier smiled up over the clothes line at Achaia, "Night Frenchy." He said mock-seductively, winking at her.

"Frenchy?" Noland asked.

"Nick name." Olivier said.

Noland watched Achaia blush, and rolled his eyes.

Once the clothes were hung between the countries, no one could see anyone else as long as they were standing. They explored their respective sides of the cabin finding things like pots, pans, and blankets, but no food.

Yellaina wrapped Amelia up in a thick blanket and Achaia and Noland made beds for themselves on the floor.

It was a good thing they'd broken the lock to the cedar chest at the foot of the bed, it had been full of quilts, pretty well taken care of. The other boys each got one, and chose a bunk. Yellaina took two and crawled into bed next to Amelia.

Testing out their beds on the floor, and getting down below clothes-line level, Noland and Achaia realized their beds were only about a foot away from each other. Noland chuckled a little to himself. "You better not snore."

Achaia looked mocked offended for about a second. "I don't. But I know you do. I could hear you all the way down the hall last night."

"Ah," Noland said holding up a finger. "That wasn't me. That was Olivier." Noland laughed.

"What? No!" Olivier objected throwing a black clod of something at Noland's head which splashed as it made contact-- his dirty wet socks.

Noland rubbed the back of his head where they had hit, and picked up the socks and threw them in the fire.

"Dude!" Olivier yelled.

"Have I taught you nothing?" Noland asked. "You never just throw your weapon at your opponent."

Emile rolled his eyes. "Everything is a lesson opportunity."

***

Wrapped in blankets sitting on their beds or floors, respectively, Yellaina, Achaia, Noland, Emile, and Olivier sat up to talk. "Life sure has gotten exciting since you guys entered the picture," Achaia agreed as she laughed off a joke Olivier had made. They were each enjoying a bag of plane crackers for their dinner. Though the crackers weren't much, they worked miracles on their aching stomachs.

"Oh yeah," Emile started, "we never actually explained our spiritual gifts to you."

"Right. How do they work?" Achaia asked chewing on her last cracker, sad there wasn't more. She was still hungry. She tried to ignore the rumble in her stomach by focusing instead on Emile as he spoke.

"Well everyone gets one," he started.

"Or more than one," Yellaina added.

"Right, or more than one. It's something God gives you to help you fight. Something good for spiritual warfare. For some people it's a physical skill, for others it's not so much physical as it is mental or emotional. Some people's gifts help them, and some were meant to help other people." Emile tried to explain.

"Okay. So, how do you know what it is? When do you get it?" Achaia asked.

"Well, you're born with it. I don't know I guess you just figure it out eventually." Olivier shrugged.

"I don't think I have one." Achaia looked down feeling, yet again, left out. She couldn't think of anything she was particularly good at; nothing she was better at than anyone else. She couldn't think of anything weird or abnormal about herself, either. She was just an average girl. "Maybe since my mom was human, I don't get one?"

"Maybe you just haven't been put in the right circumstances yet. You'll figure it out. But you have one, for sure. You're Nephilim." Olivier assured her.

"What's yours?" She asked looking at Noland.

"Oh great," He sighed, "are we going to start playing one of those get to know you games? 'Okay let's go around the room and everyone say your name, your age, where you're from, and your spiritual gift.'" Noland said with mock enthusiasm.

Everyone laughed.

"Naw," he went on still chuckling a little. "I have two, the first one being fire. I can control it, create it, I am it. It burns in me. I think it's the root of my second one, which is strength and endurance." He knocked on the frame of the bunk bed to signal to Emile that he was next.

"Okay, so mine might not be as macho..." Emile started.

Olivier and Noland chuckled.

"I'm empathetic. I feel other people's emotions. I know what everyone is feeling. Which is why I hate airports. Way too much going on. People coming, people going, people missing flights...way too much emotion in a place like that. Second worst place in the world, next to high school."

"So you know what I'm feeling... all the time?" Achaia asked blushing again.

Emile nodded.

"Oh great. Thanks for the heads up."

Emile smiled weakly and mischievously all at once before tapping the upper bunk with his fist.

"Oh, my go?" Olivier asked looking down. "Yeah, I'm fast. I got speed."

"I kind of guessed yours." Achaia laughed.

"You're telling me I blew my cover?" He mocked being shocked and appalled.

"You always moved so fast at your locker."

"Yeah, I struggle with restraint." He smiled, then gestured to Yellaina that it was her turn.

"Okay right, and you know mine. Linguistics. I can speak every language, spoken or otherwise," She said signing everything she was saying.

"Interpretative dance?" Achaia asked jokingly.

Noland snorted. "Please explain that to me, it's a mystery."

Yellaina laughed. "I wish I could!"

"Now that one would be handy!" Achaia laughed. "Actually, they all sound handy." Achaia observed looking around the room at all of them.

"That's kind of the point. But, not all of them are a blessing." Yellaina said sounding mournful.

"What do you mean?"

"Not every gift is given for the benefit of the one who possesses it. In fact, some are more like curses." Yellaina explained.

"I don't understand."

"Amelia." Noland interjected.

"She feels other people's pain. Physical pain." Emile went on, "We're twins. I got the emotional side, she got the physical side. She feels other people's pain. Only hers isn't for everyone. Her gift is based upon how much she cares about the person. When she feels their pain, they may bleed, but she suffers."

"Which is why you were all fine after the crash. She felt it for you. Because — she loves you." Achaia realized now that though they were all bumped and bruised none of them were so much as even limping. She put her hand to her side under the blanket and felt a whelp forming on her rib. Amelia didn't know her. She couldn't have felt her pain. After bringing her attention to it, her rib grew sore. "That's awful." Achaia pressed on her bruised side and felt the ache. She couldn't imagine what it would be like to feel that much more pain for four other people in addition to her own. No wonder she hadn't woken up yet.

"Well hey, I think that's enough talk for one night." Yellaina said yawning.

"She's right, we have to hunt tomorrow to try and find some real food. All we have are plane crackers for breakfast." Noland added lying down on his mound of quilts. "We're going to be here a while. This storm isn't going anywhere anytime soon."

Everyone chanted goodnight and laid down in their beds. Achaia laid down with her back to Noland, trying to avoid awkward eye contact. He however didn't seem fazed by the idea and laid down facing her.

*** 

Achaia woke up in the middle of the night shivering. The fire had burned down and was a mere flicker of a flame. She curled in on herself trying to warm up against her own body heat, but even her arms and legs were cold to the touch. She could feel the draft coming in from the gaps between the floorboards.

Half-awake, half-asleep, she felt her covers yanked from where she had tucked them under her. The air that rushed in was freezing. She shook even more violently. The floor creaked the tiniest bit as Noland moved across it. He tossed his blanket over hers and slid in behind her. She stiffened in surprise, but his body was warm, really warm. He wrapped his arms around her waist and buried his face in her neck, his mouth resting gently on her bare shoulder. Her entire body warmed in seconds. She shivered a little more and sighed as she fell back asleep.

# 8

## Into the Wood

"Meet me at midnight
In the forest
Of my dreams.
We'll make a fire
And count the stars
That shimmer
Above the trees."

-Christy Ann Martine

Achaia woke up to the wind howling and hissing while it was still dark outside. She felt as if she'd been asleep for hours; her body, well rested, warm and grateful.

Opening her eyes, she saw a muscular forearm draped over her waist. She jerked awake, startled. The arm flinched squeezing her tighter for a moment before pulling away from her.

"Are you okay?" Noland whispered in her ear.

"What —Why...?" Achaia was speechless.

"I'm sorry." Noland took his arm away from her and quickly backed away. "I woke up and you were shivering. You were so cold — your lips were blue and I..."

"No, it's okay. I just..." Achaia stopped whispering and rolled over to face him.

His eyes were bright despite the darkness of the room. She found it hard to look directly at him. It was like looking into the sun. She wanted to touch him. His skin was so warm. He was so beautiful.

Woah! It's just early, she thought. She tried to shake the thoughts out of her head. "I just..." Her eyes flicked up to where Emile lay sleeping.

"Right. I got it." He whispered pulling farther away from her back to his makeshift bed on the floor. "Germany and France, right?" He smiled.

"Thank you." She mouthed silently, smiling, before rolling back over and trying to fall back asleep. She missed his warmth. She was already shivering again.

\*\*\*

Noland lay awake for a while watching Achaia breathe. It was a few long minutes before her breathing settled, telling him that she was asleep. Finally, he sighed and rolled over to fall back asleep himself.

Why did he feel like this? Whatever this was? It wasn't a knowing... but it was a liking. This wasn't supposed to happen to Nephilim. Especially not when the girl was potentially set aside for your best friend. "Stupid!" Noland let out in a frustrated yet nearly silent whisper. Gripping his face in his hands. It's a good thing Emile is asleep, he thought to himself. If he felt him beating himself up so much there was no telling what he'd say.

"She's not mine." Emile whispered looking down on him from the bottom bunk.

"Dude!" Noland said in a loud whisper, jumping up into a sitting position. "Warn a guy before you do something like that. Jeez!"

"I'm sorry dude, but that feeling is awful and I want it gone. It woke me up." Emile said looking down on him with pity. "As far as I know, she's not mine."

"But the two of you are..."

"She's been on an emotional roller coaster. She needed some calming down. I needed some calming down. It comes with the territory. She might be mine, but as far as I know, she's not. Stop worrying about it. Just let it play out. Now go back to sleep. We haven't slept enough in the last couple days." Emile sounded concerned but grumpy.

Even when the guy was downright pissed he couldn't be inconsiderate. When he was mean to someone else, it was like being mean to himself. He still felt the pain. He actually had to treat others the way he wanted to be treated. That made him one of Noland's favorite people.

"Okay, I'm sorry." Noland said jokingly, then laid back down and closed his eyes.

***

Naphtali stood in a room of clouds, facing a man who was not quite his equal in stature. Where Naphtali was tall and dark, and possessed of brute strength, the man before him was fair and slight of build. However his ferocity was of wit. "Why will not you tell me of Shael ben Yahweh's whereabouts? You must, of course, possess the knowledge, you who possess nearly all knowledge."

"Flattery will not suit you here Naphtali. Do I not know your motives? That you would seek to save the traitor!" Tabbris was rigid.

"He chose his fate, and sealed it with his own will."

"His will was broken. He had just lost his wife!" Naphtali could no longer hide his frustration. He couldn't find a single soul in Heaven willing to help him.

"He spurned Heaven itself!" Tabbris spat.

"What would you have done if Amorriah was ripped from you?" Naphtali asked.

Tabbris fell silent. It appeared he had never once taken the time to view the situation from Shael's point of view.

"Shael's heart was broken open, and the darkness creeped into the void. Do not even the purest of hearts struggle to spurn shadows?" Naphtali's voice was soft. "Shael may have rejected redemption through penance, but not justice. Where is your mercy? Are you not amongst those closest to the Lord's heart? Shael's time has not yet come. Will you not help me establish justice, and remind Satan of his place, that the Lord, not he, is ruler still?"

Tabbris stepped back, humbled and silent. He looked unsure for a moment, and when he spoke his voice was uneven. "You seek to beguile me with manipulation."

Naphtali sighed. "Not at all brother. I would have you see truth. I would have you cease to view life itself through a narrow lens!" Naphtali knew immediately that he had said the wrong thing.

Tabbris' face hardened. "You think you know better than I!" His face shook in anger. "That you are privy to knowledge that I possess not?"

"Perhaps only that of pride, and its pitfalls." Naphtali said, knowing he would not get the help he had hoped for. "Rest assured, I will find Shael. I will discover how to reach him, and I will pluck him from Hell itself. And when that feat is accomplished, it will have been without any aid from you. And in the books of life, there will be no mention of you in the telling of it."

"You would enter Hell for that traitor?" Tabbris asked, completely at a loss for comprehension.

"Yes. Because I call him friend." Naphtali said. With that, he released his wings, and departed into the clouds.

\*\*\*

When Achaia woke again, the sun had been up for a while, but no one else. Moving as quietly as possible, she stumbled over to where her clothes hung on the line and searched them with her hands to see if any of them were dry. She pulled on a pair of frozen damp jeans and a mostly dry t-shirt. With her blanket still wrapped around her she moved cautiously across the room to sit in front of the fire, which at this point was more like smoldering ashes.

She sat, a hump of quilt, alone in silence staring into the fireplace. The windows were packed with snow to the point, she couldn't see out of them. It was nice to be able to just think, to process.

Her father was friends with Satan, there was more to her mother's death than she ever imagined, and she was a Nephilim. Either she was still in shock, or she just didn't care about anything as much as one would expect to...

Before her, the ashes she was staring at began to glow and come alive again. A flame burst forth, stopping only inches away from her face. She jumped backward, bumping into something hard. There was a grunt, and then she fell backward to the floor.

"Oh sorry." Noland apologized from underneath her. "I was starting the fire back up."

"I didn't realize anyone else was awake." Achaia said struggling to pick herself up off of him and back to her knees. Noland grabbed her arms firmly; holding her still for a moment, steadying her, before placing her back up into a kneeling position before the fire.

"I wasn't," he said coolly crawling forward to sit next to her. "Until somebody drug a blanket across my face," he said in a grumpy tone, though he spoke with a smile.

"Sorry." It was cold enough that her breath was like smoke in the air, and here he sat in just his boxer briefs on the cold wood floorboards. Oh to be your own fireplace... She envied him in her mind. Then she realized she was staring at him, a boy, in his underwear.

She looked back up to the flames that danced around in circles, embracing each other, destroying each other, dominating one another and merging together. The warmth they provided was nothing in comparison to Noland's arms. The fire that burned within him was ten times as fierce. He burned with love, passion, anger, loathing... emotion. It was evident in his eyes.

"You sleep well?" He asked looking from the fire to her, at least what he could see of her from beneath her bundle.

"Yeah, really well. Thanks. You?" She asked politely. Secretly, she wondered if he'd been looking for a specific answer, an answer to a different question or if she was just reading too much into things.

He sat for a moment, longer than what would have been considered socially acceptable, and looked her in the eyes. "Mmm," he wore a mock-pensive expression, "probably the best I've slept in a long time."

"Oh, good." Achaia said looking away quickly. He had a way of making her nervous and uncomfortable.

"I'm thinking I should wake everyone else up. We need to find some food." Noland said standing up and grabbing a pair of his jeans from the line.

Achaia looked up just as he was pulling them up to his waist and zipping them. She blushed and looked away for a second before looking back up at him. His skin was a warm honey brown, and coated in dark black freckles. He looked like he was glowing.

"Yeah. That's probably a good idea." She agreed scooting closer to the fire to thaw out her own jeans.

"Okay!" He said loudly, but not as obnoxiously as he had when he'd woken her up at the hotel. "We need to get up and get going." Achaia didn't turn around but she could hear the other's stirring.

"Going?" Yellaina mumbled from beneath her mountain of quilts. "I don't want to move."

"Yeah we need to figure out what we're going to do next. But first we need food. Which means," Achaia could hear Noland grab the squeaky rail of the upper bunk. "We're going hunting."

Achaia turned to see Noland tousle Olivier's hair.

"So let's WAKE UP!" He yelled loudly, his tone piercing in the otherwise quiet room. Even Achaia was annoyed and she'd been up for a while.

"Too loud. Too early." Emile mumbled from under his blankets. "Stop making everyone hate you." Then, pulling the blanket from over his face he, cocked and eyebrow. "Unless you're looking for me to punch you in the jaw? In which case, proceed." Emile said in the foulest tone Achaia had ever heard him use. Noland laughed at the thought.

\*\*\*

Slowly but surely everyone woke up, except for Amelia who was still lying unconscious bundled in quilts. After everyone was dressed they broke open the box of plane crackers of which everyone was granted one pack. Emile was set on rationing them out just in case hunting didn't go well.

As they ate Noland discussed a plan. "Okay so two of us will go hunting. Olivier, you'll come with me. Yellaina, you stay here with Amelia, keep her warm, maybe move her closer to the fire for the day. Emile, you and Achaia scout the perimeter for humans, see if there are any around. If there are demons around, we want to know about it."

They all nodded in agreement. Olivier tore open his duffel bag and took out a few choice weapons before helping Yellaina move Amelia closer to the fire.

Emile looked over at Achaia and stood, "You ready for this?" He picked up his own duffel and took out a few weapons for himself.

"What are those for?" Achaia asked confused.

"Well, where there's humans, there are demons. If there are demons, we'll be needing these." He explained tucking knives and daggers into hidden places under his clothes.

"Oh right." Achaia agreed sarcastically. "That makes sense."

Emile smiled and tossed her jacket, from the line, over to her. "Let's go."

Achaia put her jacket on and followed Emile out into the bitter air. She pulled her jacket around her more snuggly but still the wind seeped through, chilling her to the bone. Emile popped the collar of his jacket around his neck and headed for the trees.

The trees were laden heavily with snow. Icicles hung from the branches like frozen wind chimes. If the forest had been a photograph in a calendar it would have been ideal for January. Being in the picture was frigid, mind numbingly cold.

Achaia already couldn't feel her toes, but she forced herself to keep walking, begrudgingly following Emile into the wood.

They walked in silence out of the clearing, save for the crunching of snow beneath their steps. Once they were among the trees the wind was whipped every which way, until there was hardly any wind at all. It was strangely quiet in the woods.

After walking a ways they reached a clearing. Achaia watched as Emile stopped in the center of it and turned to face her, his expression strange, alarming.

\*\*\*

Olivier followed Noland around to the back of the cabin and into the forest. They strained their ears to hear. The wind was still too loud so they headed deeper into the woods where the wind would be blocked by the trees.

After a few minutes of trudging as quietly as possible, they stopped again. The wind was nonexistent here. The air was still, silent. They strained their ears once again to listen.

Olivier, watching Noland's face, noticed his mouth was twitching with anticipation; he looked like an animal himself. Finally, Olivier heard it, the faintest sound of crunching snow and the snap of a tiny twig.

Noland's head whipped around. In the distance, he could see it too, a buck.

\*\*\*

"What is it? Humans?" Achaia asked, trying to read Emile's expression and failing. His eyes were alive, angry almost. It was hard for her to tell, but his eyes looked gray as opposed to their usual blue.

"No." He said coolly. "There are no humans around, I would have felt them by now." He looked down at the ground for a moment. Achaia watched him closely. Even though she could not feel his emotions she could tell he was struggling within himself.

"Okay, you can't say anything to anyone. Okay?" His voice was strained.

Achaia nodded but wasn't sure if she could agree. She searched his face deeper for any hint of where he was going with this, but came up empty.

"Promise me." He demanded.

"I promise." Achaia spat out quickly, her voice was shaky, not from the cold but from confusion and fear. She'd never seen him like this before.

"What I want to do, I'm not allowed to do. It's completely up to you. But I want you to be able to defend yourself." He stopped, breathing hard. "It's against the law for me to train you. But I feel that to leave you without a basic knowledge of our warfare would hurt you."

Achaia could only nod.

"I want you to understand that I am breaking the law, but it's that important, Achaia, for you to be able to defend yourself—we're up against…You must meet me halfway. I need you to try."

"Okay." Achaia's voice was soft, but she knew that he didn't need to hear her to feel her agreement. Achaia remembered what it had felt like to sit before the Nephilim, she wouldn't wish a trial on Emile. Especially, not a trial for helping her. She hated the risk, but she knew she needed all the help she could get.

***

Noland looked back to Olivier, nodding for him to make his move. If the buck were closer Noland would be the better one to take him down, but with him being so far away, Olivier would be the only one who could catch him after they made their presence known. Olivier took a step forward, a twig beneath the snow snapped. Noland threw a sharp glance at him, Olivier shook his head with frustration and concentration, moving still closer.

The deer looked around, nervously it took a few steps, then forgot the sound. Olivier crept closer again, he moved a few feet before another twig broke. This time it was louder and the buck took off into the woods.

Olivier took off running, ripping off his winter jacket and his shirt. With the sound of crunching bones, large white wings sprung from his back. With them he pushed against the still air, gaining on the animal. Within a few seconds he had caught up with the deer. He struggled to free the dagger from his jeans. He flew next to the deer. The buck, too confused to try turning, only ran faster. Olivier put the dagger to its throat...

***

"Okay," Emile seemed to relax a little bit. He smiled weakly. "Now, angels have their own art-form when it comes to battle. We have our own laws. We have our own techniques.

"When there are only two angels fighting, we duel. This can be used to settle disagreements, or there can be stakes. Now, the rules for dueling are simple: No subs, meaning no one outside the match can join in the fight. No unseen weapons, be upfront about your weapons of choice, each participant gets two. No shape-shifting, or other extra-angelic powers can be used. And last but not least, third blood wins, fourth blood forfeits."

"What does that mean?" Achaia asked, her face growing pale.

"This is an honor fight. It means whoever draws blood three times first, wins. If you draw blood four times, you're a blood thirsty bastard and you forfeit. To the death or otherwise, third blood first, wins.

"Now we're not going to duel, but I'm going to attack you, I want you to defend yourself. I just want to see what you're working with."

Achaia nodded, they stood for a moment in silence before Emile smiled. He moved slowly rotating around her in circles, getting closer and closer to her.

Achaia's heart was hammering against her rib cage, like an animal trying to break loose.

Emile drew a dagger from somewhere on his person so quickly, Achaia had no idea how it had gotten into his hand.

Achaia's heart began to race, she could feel the cold of her sweat against the breeze. Emile moved so fast, she wondered if he didn't share Olivier's gift. She tried to recall any of the karate she had learned, but came up blank.

Emile rushed her, and she dodged to the side. Her mind seemed to slow down, taking in every movement, every breath, and every twitch of his face. She closed her eyes for a second and felt the air move across her face, heard the snow in front of her crunch. She almost wondered if she was hearing her own heartbeat, or if it was Emile's.

Opening her eyes, she grabbed his arm just as he swung at her. She twisted it around behind his back.

With his other arm Emile attempted to stab at her with the dagger. Achaia popped the shoulder to the arm she held out of its socket.

Emile screamed in pain and tried harder to stab her.

Achaia grabbed the hand with the dagger in it and twisted the wrist until he let go. Before the dagger could even hit the ground, she snatched it out of the air. She pushed Emile forward until he fell onto the ground looking up at her from his back. In a flash she was kneeling on the ground next to him holding the dagger at his throat.

Emile swallowed hard. "Well done." He said breathlessly. "Maybe I was wrong to think you defenseless." He chuckled.

Achaia, as if snapping out of a trance, leaped back away from him and threw the dagger far away from her. "I'm so sorry. I don't even know what happened."

"It's okay," Emile said crawling toward her on the snow. "It's a lot of instinct for us. When we go into battle, it becomes second nature. But you picked up on that rather quickly. I might even think that it was..." A look of realization crossed his face. He stood slowly to his feet in front of her.

"What?" Achaia asked anxiously. "What?"

"Well, Achaia," He started, popping his shoulder back into place with a sharp breath. "I think we might have found your spiritual gift."

\*\*\*

Shael sat on the edge of his bed with his shirt off, rubbing hyssop oil over his cuts and his demon bite.

"That looks like it was a good one!" Luc said, leaning against Shael's ice dresser. Shael had added to his injuries with each fight in the blood games. He had been fighting lower level demons, none of which were very smart, but all of which were massive.

"Yeah, you have some interesting creatures in your cohort," Shael said, grabbing a fresh shirt that Luc had laid out for him. It was hardly Shael's taste. The shirt was black silk and collared. Shael hated dress clothes. He preferred linens or cotton. Clothes that were easy to move and fight in.

"I forget how much has changed since we last called each other friend." Luc was staring into the reflection on the floor between two fur rugs. The light danced up from it, and other spots like it, making the room look like it was under water. "Tell me," he said looking up at Shael, as he buttoned the shirt given to him, "what is new with you?"

"Like you haven't been keeping tabs on me for hundreds of years? You already know everything about me." Shael said, letting his hands fall to his sides, gripping the edge of the bed. Luc frowned, and appeared to be deep in thought. Shael, looking at him, could almost remember the angel who had been so dear to him in Heaven. "What's new with you?" Shael asked, pityingly.

"Ah well, you know, mayhem, murder, deceit, seduction, and on the weekends I hang out with Benny. He's an incubus," Luc smiled, recovering from his thoughtfulness with sarcasm. "Tell me," he said excitedly, "do you ever hear from Lailah?"

At the sound of her name, Shael felt like he had been punched in the stomach and immediately felt like he was going to throw up. He hadn't heard or spoken her name in a million years or more, not since he fell and they'd been parted forever. "No."

"Shame. Now she was a real beauty. Don't get me wrong, your senator was cute, but Lailah," Luc whistled, "she was the Cherub's arrow!"

Shael desperately wanted to shift the subject away from his soulmate. "What of your heart? Do you ever hear from your Hilmya?"

Luc's face blanched. "You mean after you turned her against me?" he asked bitterly. "She used to come down for the occasional tryst. Until she got pregnant. Then I guess she realized it wasn't the greatest idea." Luc spat.

"You have a child?" Shael asked shocked.

"I have an adolescent." Luc nodded. "About the same age as your Achaia."

"And Hilmya—"

"Forbids contact. Yes." Luc looked genuinely put out by this. Shael couldn't help but wonder if there was still perhaps the shred of a heart left in him after all. "I did not lose everything, it was taken from me." Luc said sadly. "Why did you do it?" Luc looked deeply into Shael's eyes.

Shael flinched as if he'd actually been slapped. "Me?"

"You fought with me, as brothers. Then not only did I lose my fight for justice, I lost my army, my wife… and it was my own best friend, my brother who turned them from me. What made you hate me? What was it that hardened your heart toward me?" Luc's blue eyes looked like the sea before a hurricane.

"Your lies. Your deceit." Shael answered truthfully. "You beguiled and used us for your own purposes. We trusted you. You broke that trust. You turned our hearts against you, it was not my doing," Shael said, not without compassion.

"I have not seen the face of my own child, because you plotted to take Hilmya from me. You could not even leave me my wife. My family."

"Hilmya made her own decision."

"Only after you suggested it!" Luc wiped his arm across the top of Shael's dresser, smashing its contents to the side. When he turned around, Shael could see thousands of years of heartache turned to bitterness in his eyes.

Shael didn't flinch at the violent outburst, only sighed sadly. "You blame me for the crop you reap, but you are the one who planted it."

"Don't forget, you helped me sow the seed." Luc looked venomous. "You have taken my child from me. I will take yours. You will spend eternity knowing her fate was your fault."

Shael stood, but Luc stormed out of the room, slamming the ice door behind him, causing the ice to crack with spider web like fractures throughout.

\*\*\*

Back at the cabin, Emile and Achaia stood in front of the fire, thawing their frozen legs and fingers. Yellaina sat on the bed next to Amelia who was still asleep. Emile was glad, seeing as how his shoulder was dislocated about an hour before.

"I took the pots we found and washed them." Yellaina was saying cheerily. "For when Noland and Olivier get back with food. I hope they find something."

"Sweet, and I'm sure they will." Emile smiled, turning around and seeing the stack of dishes at the other end of the room. There were spoons and pots, and camping plates and cutlery. "She hasn't stirred at all, has she?" He asked looking over at Amelia.

Yellaina frowned and shook her head.

The door opened letting in a gust of cold air, but otherwise the cabin was fairly warm thanks to the fire. Oliver walked into the room and shut the door tightly behind him. "Noland is cleaning it up outside, dinner will be in soon." He shook the snow off his jacket and took it off, hanging it on a hook by the door.

"What did you find?" Yellaina asked standing and bringing the dishes over to the fire.

"A buck." Oliver stated in a matter of fact tone. "Six pointer too."

"Wow." Achaia laughed. "Could you sound any more hick?"

"Yeah, laugh now, but you'll be glad when you're eating it!" Olivier pointed at her.

Noland came inside with his arms full of meat. "Olivier, go get rid of the rest of it, take it as far as possible. If the wolves smell it they'll be all over us." Oliver with a disappointed sigh put his coat back on and went outside.

Noland divided the meat up into the pots Yellaina had washed. "I found some spices and stuff too. I'm not sure if they're any good, but it's better than plain meat." Yellaina said pulling some dusty bottles off the shelf above where the pots had come from. "We've got pepper, salt, and garlic.... everything else looks pretty sketchy."

"That'll do." Noland smiled taking the jars from her hand and opening them. He rubbed the meat down with the seasonings and placed the pots over the fire. In another pot he tore the meat apart with a small knife and threw the little chunks of meat back into the pot. He dumped seasonings into the pot and took the pot outside. When he came back inside the pot was nearly overflowing with snow. He put the pot over the fire next to the first one. He turned the meat in the first pot over, and the snow in the second pot began to melt. He shook the second pot, mixing the seasonings and meat into the water.

Olivier came back saying he took the carcass a few miles away and dumped it in the woods. By the time he returned there was stew and garlic venison ready for eating. Venison wasn't Emile's favorite, but it was exceedingly better than plane crackers. It was nice to eat something hot.

"So," Noland started looking up from his bowl of stew to Emile. "Did you find anything today?"

"Nope, no humans around, at least not for miles. I couldn't feel any." Emile said simply.

When Noland had looked away satisfied, Emile risked a glance at Achaia, a stern warning in his eyes for her to remain silent. She nodded she understood, and Emile took a deep breath.

"The cabin warmed up nicely today." Yellaina stated after a moment or two of silence. "I didn't even feel like I needed my jacket. I vote we don't open the door unless it's absolutely necessary."

"Agreed." Achaia consented quickly.

"I'll third that motion." Olivier said with a mouth full of meat.

"Alright, no leaving unless it's to patrol, or hunt. Emile and Achaia are on patrol, every morning, and Olivier and I will hunt whenever we run out of food." Noland decided.

"You talk like we're going to be here a while." Yellaina complained, Emile could feel her pang of disappointment.

"Well, until this weather stops, I don't see how we're going to get out of here without freezing to death. We're here until further notice," Noland stated bluntly. "When God provides the weather for us to come up with another plan, we will... Until then, maybe he's giving us the cover to lay low for a little while."

Yellaina sunk back against the wall next to the fire where she sat, cuddled up with her stew. Emile knew that she disliked being stuck here more than everyone else. Yellaina didn't care for the cold.

\*\*\*

They finished eating with little conversation. Achaia, even without Emile's talents, could deduce that everyone was tired. After dinner, they poured the left overs all into one pot and put the other pot next to the door to be washed out in the morning.

It was already getting dark outside and with no electricity the cabin was devoid of light save for the light from the fire. Achaia and Noland remade their piles on the floor for beds, and Yellaina covered Amelia up with an extra blanket.

Olivier was already passed out in his bunk with his arm hanging over the rail before the rest of them had gotten into their beds. Achaia supposed he had a right; he had probably run after the deer pretty hard. He didn't have Noland's strength. She guessed something like that would have taken a lot out of him. Luckily, with the looks of the left overs and what was left buried and frozen in the snow outside, he wouldn't need to hunt for a few more days at least.

Achaia lay down on her make-shift bed and covered herself with a couple of quilts. It was much warmer tonight than the night before had been. She rolled over on her side facing away from Noland to reduce awkwardness and shut her eyes.

She thought back to how powerful she felt when she had defended herself. She had moved so fast... She thought about when she was a child and had taken karate, she had been great before her father stopped her. She wondered if maybe he had realized early on that it was her spiritual gift; if he wanted to keep that from her, to hide the fact that she was different, that she was Nephilim.

***

Noland lay on his back for some time, listening to everyone else's breathing. One by one, each of the others' breathing slowed and steadied as they each fell asleep. His own breathing was harder than everyone else; sounding, in comparison, as if he had just run a marathon.

Noland tried shutting his eyes, but they preferred to be open. They scanned the wood boards that made up the ceiling, plaited with cobwebs and dust. The fire danced at his feet. The reflection of the flames on the webs diverted his eyes from sleep.

His mind grew weary but found it impossible to slow down to rest. He tried to scan his brain for the cause, until his mind found the burden impossible to bear anymore. He closed his eyes, finally able to succumb to the exhaustion.

# 9

# Forces of Flight

"She wasn't doing a thing I could see,
except standing there leaning on the balcony
railing, holding the universe together."
-J.D.Salinger

Achaia could hear birds chirping outside. She opened her eyes to alarming hues of yellow coming through the window. The sun was significantly brighter than it had been the past week.

She lay in her bundle of blankets warm, snug, and content. She closed her eyes once again and breathed softly. A hand shook her shoulder, beckoning her to open her eyes. Emile stood above her dressed and ready to go.

Achaia sighed and stood to her feet unstable at first. She put on her coat, an extra pair of socks, a beanie, and her shoes and walked out into the chill air. It was warmer than it had been, too, thanks to the sun. There were still clouds in the sky, but not snow clouds. She followed Emile into the woods as had become their custom.

Over the last week Achaia had learned about some of the different weapons, and some basic defense maneuvers. Emile had proven to be a patient teacher, but it was almost unnecessary since Achaia was picking up on everything so quickly. Emile often joked that soon she would be teaching him new moves.

Achaia knew he was joking because as much as she had learned, she was still only learning defensive basics, and the names of weapons, not how to use them. She could now defend herself from someone with a dagger, a knife, or a small blade. But there were still swords, crossbows, regular bows and arrows, and numerous different weapons she still didn't know; all of which were made out of the mysterious liquefied diamond-like metal, diemerillium.

As they reached the clearing, which had become their usual spot, Emile dropped his duffel bag to the ground with an alarming thud. "Okay. So, before we begin do you have any questions about anything we've gone over so far?" Emile unzipped the bag and pulled out a crossbow. "If not, I'm going to teach you how to dodge arrows today."

"Actually, I do. Not about something we've gone over, but something we didn't." Achaia began. She thought back to the week before, when he had first brought her there. "So the first day we came out here, before you attacked me... your eyes... they looked gray...."

"Well I wasn't in full battle mind set." He loaded an arrow into the crossbow. "You remember I told you your instinct takes over?" Achaia nodded.

"Well by instinct, I mean your angelic half. It's almost a different body within your body. Nephilim are chameleons, shape shifters. We take on the appearance of humans, but this isn't our natural body. Our angelic nature is a body that is faster, and stronger, with quicker reflexes and a steadier mind. When that nature, or our spiritual body, becomes more dominant, our eyes change color. It depends on your spiritual gift. When I am in full battle mode, my spiritual body's eyes are white; signifying a blank slate, I am in full control of my power, not only can I feel my opponent's emotions, but one day I will be able to control them. I'm not that far in my training yet, but I'll get there one day." Emile smiled.

"That is awesome! So, do mine change color?" Achaia asked eagerly. She felt childlike, as if she were asking if her superhero costume came with a cape.

Emile gave her a look that was as if he were saying 'oh yeah!' with his eyes as he nodded.

"Well, what color?" Achaia asked eagerly.

"Red." He said pulling the crossbow up and pointing it at her.

Achaia smiled, and wished she had a mirror. "Wait! One more thing." Achaia said putting her hand up to stop him from shooting.

"Okay..." Emile lowered the bow.

"You said you were breaking a lot of rules and laws to teach me all of this."

Emile nodded.

"Well—why? Why is it so important that I should know, now? Why can't it wait until we have permission? I could train with the rest of you." Achaia lowered her hand to her side and studied Emile's face. Times like this she wished she had his power, to know what he was feeling—thinking.

"Okay, well for starters, desperate times call for desperate measures. If Luc is after you, which, after the Trevi, I think it's pretty safe to say he is, we need to be as prepared as possible. His spies are everywhere; anywhere there are humans, there are demons. If something major happens and we can't be there to defend you, you need to be able to defend yourself, at least to an extent.

"I'm not trying to teach you everything, or really train you, but enough to keep you from dying. I believe it is necessary." Emile stood for a moment studying her face.

After a moment she felt satisfied with his answer and resolved within herself to train hard.

At that moment he raised the bow and aimed it at her heart. "I want you to dodge the arrow. Don't think, just react."

Achaia pulled a dagger from her coat and prepared herself, slowing everything with her mind. The arrow was released and flew toward her at a lightning fast speed, but to her it seemed to crawl. As it reached her, when it was a few inches away from her chest she raised her arm and sliced the arrow with her dagger. The shards fell to the ground, nothing more than splinters at her feet.

"WHAT THE HELL ARE YOU DOING?" The yell came from behind her. Noland strode towards them with heavy, calculated steps.

Achaia dropped the dagger with a dull thump into the snow. She stood up straight and then turned her eyes to the ground. She felt like she was about to be rebuked by her father.

Emile stood frozen. "I'm teaching her basic defense maneuvers."

"Basic?" Noland was outraged. His face was glowing against the cool air. "Since when do demons shoot crossbows at sixteen year old girls? These are battle tactics. They are sacred, and you are not designated to teach them. Not to mention, *we're* here. Why would she need to know any of this?"

"We can't defend her all the time, Noland!" Emile took a step forward, not just keeping his ground, but meeting Noland in frustration. "What if something happens? What if we aren't there? What if we can't get to her?" Emile was yelling now too.

A gun shot sounded in the distance, some hunters deep within the woods, it seemed to snap Achaia back into reality.

Noland and Emile hadn't even heard it. They were too busy yelling at each other. Achaia had never seen the two of them fight like this. She hated feeling like the root of the problem. She hadn't known that Noland would be so against her training. But Emile was breaking the law—it was a big deal. It was her fault he felt like he needed to...

"She doesn't know our culture, our lifestyle."

"And if she gets killed she never will!"

"She wasn't raised a Nephilim! She's not one of us!" Noland screamed.

A rock dropped in Achaia's stomach.

Emile stared blankly at Noland. Noland's face was hard, angry but otherwise emotionless.

Achaia's brain was a whirlwind of chaotic thoughts. A tornado of information. She was a burden to him, an inconvenience, nothing more. He didn't want her there—

Before she knew what she was doing she was running, as hard as she could across the clearing. If he wanted her gone, she'd be gone. She made it into the trees and yanked off her jacket, she could feel it holding her back.

Another gunshot sounded, it was closer this time. She heard footsteps behind her, chasing her.

"Achaia stop!" Noland yelled from behind her, he was catching up to her, there was no denying he was faster.

Achaia pushed harder, she'd never run like this before.

"Achaia stop!" He was still getting closer, he'd catch her at any second. Achaia's heart leaped. She pushed harder, desperate to get away from *him*, from *everyone*, from *everything*.

Out of nowhere there was a cracking in her back, the sound of bones breaking, and she heard herself yell out. It felt like her back was breaking, but instead of it being painful it felt good, like releasing an unyielding pressure, and then, she was in the air.

"Achaia NO!" Noland yelled from behind her.

She heard the difference in the distance; he'd fallen back. She flew upward, reaching the tops of the trees. A dark cloud of shadows formed on her right in the branches. At first Achaia had thought they were birds, but they were too large to be birds. They barreled toward her like a wave. She raised her arms to shield her face as they collided into her.

The creatures were small but muscular, they had faces with twisted sadistic features. Their hands were small and tipped with claws like razor blades. They reminded her, unpleasantly, of the flying monkeys in *The Wizard of Oz* that had terrified her as a child. Only the shadows were worse. They weren't comical in their special effects shrewdness. Her back slammed into branches, slicing her face, and her arms. The shadows slashed at her, cutting through her clothes, ripping open her skin.

Her ears were flooded with dark whispers that sounded like things you couldn't see moving in a dark room. Slithering sounding hisses, and creaking laughs, like rusty hinges. They were thick in her ears, a deafening hum. Her mind began to feel like a haunted house, full of invisible terrors.

She couldn't hear Noland yelling her name. All she could hear was the darkness they whispered; things she had thought herself a thousand times, things she knew to be true: She was a burden, an outlier, unwanted, worthless, unloved… an abomination. Her father wanted to leave her, chose to, he didn't want to be found. She was going to fail, they were going to kill her, rip her to pieces. She was weak… ignorant, superfluous.

She thought of her dagger she'd dropped in the snow. She fought back, kicking, clawing, punching, they drew back but there were more of them. She hit more branches, her wings getting caught in their twigs, she dropped a few feet, flew higher, she had no idea which way was up. All she could see were the shadows. She screamed in fear and frustration. She tried to beat her wings, to take her higher, but nothing happened. Then she was falling.

Achaia landed on her gut, bent over a tree branch, the wind knocked out of her. A cluster of the shadows yanked on her legs, causing her to lose her balance, she slipped off the branch, slamming her face against it as she fell. Her back cracked against another branch as she hurdled toward the ground in an uncontrolled summersault, slamming into branches, and shadows as she went.

Then, there were arms around her yanking her what felt like up. She pushed against her captor screaming.

"Stop, Achaia. Stop!"

The shadows swarmed thicker than ever as they cleared the trees like a dense thundercloud, blocking out the sun. She was carried higher. The demons clasped and cut, like lightning striking her arms and face.

Achaia kicked out at them. She was falling again.

Achaia was dizzy with disorientation. She squeezed her eyes shut. She wasn't falling. She was. She was falling up. Her stomach turned. There was light.

She opened her eyes and realized that Noland was holding her tight, pulling her into him. He flew upward. They were way above the trees yet he kept going. The shadows were still in pursuit. Achaia tried to focus on something, anything, but her mind could not slow down.

She closed her eyes again, pinching them tight. She buried her burning face into his neck as the bitter air tore into her cuts. Then they stopped. Achaia looked back, the shadows were retreating.

It was freezing, Noland let her go and put her on her feet. Achaia looked down, there was no ground, only white. Only droplets of rain. Achaia grabbed on to Noland's arm with an intense grip. "What the..." Achaia began. Noland grabbed hold of her waist to steady her. "Are we on a—cloud?"

"Your powers of observation are amazing." Noland said dryly. "Demons can't come this close to heaven." He was holding her close, examining her face. She could feel the droplets of blood cascading down her brow.

She released his arm, and looked over his shoulder at his massive wings, beautiful large white feathers that seemed to be coated in silver shone in the unobstructed sunlight.

"WINGS?" She yelled, pushing him hard in the chest. "We have WINGS?" Her temper was showing, but she didn't do a thing to shut it down. "And you didn't tell me?" She grabbed at the cloud and was pleasantly surprised to collect a dense chunk of it which she threw at Noland. It splashed against him like a big wet cotton ball.

"It never came up!" Noland said backing away from her.

Achaia advanced, punching his chest, and slapping his arms, which he held over his head as he ducked away. "WINGS!" she yelled. Stopping and staring at him incredulously. Noland continued backing to the edge of the cloud. "You MAKE it come up!" She advanced again.

"Okay!" Noland held still, grabbing at her wrists, and stood back up straight. "Okay." He said catching her second wrist, and holding her arms down. "I should have told you!"

"Hell yeah, you—" Achaia glanced quickly around her. "Heck yeah, you should have told me!" She corrected herself, but her voice had lost most of its anger.

Noland chuckled. "Did you just check around to make sure no one heard you say 'Hell' this close to Heaven?"

Achaia looked at his straight face. There was no denying it. "*Yes*? Yes, I did."

"You just checked *a cloud* for eavesdroppers?" Noland was cracking up laughing. He hunched over and held his stomach.

Achaia had never heard him laugh like that before. He had a hearty laugh that came from the diaphragm. It was a strong happy sound that seemed out of place coming from him.

"Seriously?" Achaia said, again looking around. More out of habit, embarrassed.

"That was so worth the trip." Noland laughed looking up at her.

"We almost died!" Achaia yelled, staring at him in disbelief.

"So," Noland tried to catch his breath, "worth it."

"You're ridiculous." Achaia shook her head, but couldn't help but to chuckle, herself.

Noland's eyes shot up, there was a loud rumbling that shook them. He grabbed onto her tightly and dove, with her, into the side of the cloud that billowed up next to them. He landed on top of her in the cloud and pinned her still.

Achaia was too stunned to resist, she felt as if she were frozen into a cube of ice cold Jello. Not even Noland was enough warmth for her inside the forest of frigid droplets.

After the tremors ceased Noland pulled her slowly from the heavy fluffy droplets to stand once more *on* the cloud. Soaked, and freezing Achaia felt like a drowned rat.

"What is wrong with you?" She pushed him away as hard as she could, but he barely moved. Her teeth were chattering too much for him to take her seriously.

"Could you imagine being on a plane, looking out your window and seeing a couple of teenagers standing on a cloud? We're trying to keep a low profile—" he explained. "Your lips are purple," he said, taking his jacket off. He grabbed hold of her waist. Achaia slapped his arms away from her.

"Don't touch me!" Achaia fussed, though her teeth were still chattering too much for it to sound intimidating.

"Stop me." Noland challenged, grabbing a hold of her waist and pulling her into him. He wrapped his arms around her, covering her with his jacket as she pushed off of his stomach and chest trying to pry herself away. He squeezed tighter, resting his head on hers. Achaia gave up, and gave into the warmth.

***

"You're so stupid, sometimes." Noland laughed.

"Shut up." He felt Achaia's jaw chattering against his chest as she attempted in her tiny way to sound fierce. Noland smiled.

He focused on radiating his warmth outward, feeling as if he were hugging a glacier. She was so cold; her skin was blue, and her lips were purple. He couldn't even see the blood vessels of her face. She looked like a corpse.

He looked down at the blood still flowing from her forehead to remind himself that she was alive. He clung to her desperately, pressing himself against her, trying to warm her.

Suddenly, his heart felt heavier, swollen, full. There was a knot in his stomach, and something in his chest fought, like it was trying to break out.

Achaia grabbed onto his waist, gripping his t-shirt, shaking. Noland squeezed tighter. He couldn't lose her. He'd almost lost her. Then he realized, he needed her, he wanted her.

He knew...

\*\*\*

Achaia was starting to feel her limbs again when Noland jerked away from her. "Come on, we have to go. You're going to freeze to death up here."

*Not with you here*, she thought to herself, but she nodded in agreement forgetting that she was ever mad.

He grabbed hold of her again; lighter this time as if he were trying not to touch her at all. He flew toward the ground at an alarming speed.

Achaia's stomach performed an Olympic floor routine as he abruptly leveled out before landing. Roller coasters had nothing on this guy!

As soon as they were on the ground he released her. He tossed his coat around her shoulders again, and walked forward. They'd landed in front of the cabin and without a word he marched inside.

Emile stood just inside the door, apparently having just arrived back himself. He too, was soaking wet, and wearing a dumbfounded expression. "Where did you go? I looked everywhere, I couldn't find which cloud you were...." Emile cut off. He stared deep into Noland's eyes and stopped talking. His expression changed from dumbfounded, to shock, to concern, and back to shock. Then his eyes turned to Achaia. The shock widened as Noland crossed the room, revealing Achaia, who had been hidden behind him.

"What is going on? *What* happened to her?" Yellaina demanded, running over to Achaia and wrapping her arms around her.

She drew back to examine Achaia's face and pulled her closer to the fire. Yellaina practically pushed Achaia to the floor to sit before grabbing a quilt and wrapping her in it. "Olivier—"

"Here," Olivier tossed an old metal first aid box to her before she could even finish her sentence.

Yellaina sat on the floor across from Achaia and opened the box. She pulled out some cotton balls and dabbed them in alcohol. "This is going to burn..." She said softly reaching her hand up to Achaia's brow. Achaia nodded. Yellaina brushed the cotton across her forehead, clearing away all the blood, setting Achaia's cuts on fire. "No one answered my question." Yellaina said more sharply directing her statement to Emile and Noland. She sounded like an angry mother. Not that Achaia really knew what that sounded like until now. She promised herself she would never make Yellaina angry.

Noland was sitting in the corner alone facing the wall, not moving, and remained silent.

Emile looked back and forth between everyone in the room. "I'm sorry, just give me a minute. There's a lot going on for me to process right now. Could everyone just try to not be so freaked out for a second?" Emile's eyes were wide, his expression pained. He took a few deep breaths before starting his side of the story. "Okay, well, there were some hunters in the woods. Achaia had her first demonic attack, and Noland took her up into the clouds to get her away from them. There were a lot. They did a number on her. They came out of nowhere." Emile finished, breathing hard. He turned quickly on his heel anticipating Noland's words before he said them.

"They didn't come out of nowhere, there were hunters in the woods. There were gunshots, we were just too busy fighting to heed the warning—" His voice was cold as ice, full of disdain. Then without another word Noland stood and crossed the room in three steps slamming the door behind him as he left.

"What was *that*?" Yellaina nearly yelled.

"He thinks it...." Emile muttered turning to the door and leaving himself.

"He shouldn't... It's my fault." Achaia mumbled looking down at her bruised and beaten hands.

***

Shael paced the corridor. He was hoping Luc had taken some time to calm down. The thought of Luc refocusing his efforts on Achaia made Shael sick. She had no idea what she was up against. She had no idea how the spiritual world worked, how wars were waged, or won. She had no allies, save for Naphtali. God-only-knew who her Guardian was, but would they be dedicated enough to face a full frontal assault from Hell itself? Shael doubted it.

Shael swallowed hard. He desperately wanted to know where Achaia was, who she was with, what she was doing. Who had been the one to explain to her what she was? The council? How had they done it? Was she taking it well? Did she hate him?

Shael thought of Anna, when she had died, he had wanted so badly to explain to her what he was. He hadn't been allowed. And yet, he had still wasted sixteen years of chances to not repeat that mistake with Achaia, and at a greater risk. He failed the test.

Shael entered the grand room with the vaulted ceilings which Luc used as his parlor. Luc was stretched out on one of the ice sofas. He didn't look up as Shael walked in, but ignored him. Shael approached the bar, and poured two glasses of scotch. The smell of it was strong. Shael could already feel the alcohol in his mind before even taking a sip. He set one glass on the armrest behind Luc's head, without speaking, then moved to sit on the opposite sofa.

"I want to hate you." Luc said, ignoring his scotch. "I'm good at hating."

Shael sat silently, not wanting to interrupt.

"But it is so much worse than hate that I envy you." Luc sat up, and took his glass and stared into it. "I've wanted to rip everything you possess away from you. If not to make it mine, then to taint it and make it like me; to make you watch. To make you understand what it's like," Luc paused to sip his scotch, "to be forsaken." He pressed his lips together, licking the scotch off of them.

Shael sat silently, letting Luc's words meet him like the tide on the beach, washing against him, before being pulled back out. Calm Luc was more chilling than Luc in a fit of rage. He was far more calculating, and exact with his blows. But Shael wouldn't drown in Luc's despair. He refused. He had denied his own chance for redemption, but he still had hope for his daughter, hope for the world. God's plan didn't end here. Shael, would cling to that truth. And while he froze in Hell, he trusted God's will would thrive. And so, Shael was not without hope. He would fight God's war from within Hell itself.

"I want to see your face when I tear out your heart. To prove to you that you are a coward. *You* could not look into my eyes as you betrayed me. You didn't meet my soul with yours to look into its shattered depths as you robbed it. But *I will*. I will prove I am stronger than you. I will meet you face to face, eye to eye, and soul to soul as I scrape out everything you ever cared about and bathe it in ashes, dry it out, and rot it from the inside. And when I end you, I will wipe you away like the residue that smoke leaves on glass. And you will be gone from me, forever, brother." Luc downed the rest of his glass and set it gently on the floor in front of him as he looked up into Shael's eyes.

Shael believed that Luc meant it. But he knew Luc, sometimes in ways which Luc didn't even know himself. Luc thought he was cold, and strong. But he was passionate, and scared. He was bitter because he was sensitive, and jealous because he was insecure.

"You talk a mean fight, but you and I both know you will never end me as long as you can torture me. You will not remove me from your sight, as long as I can stave off your loneliness. Demons are no company for a prince. You need me more than you despise me. You desire me more than you envy me. Such it has always been, and such it will always be, *brother.*" Shael said throwing back his own drink, and setting his glass down across from Luc's. "A never ending game of chess, isn't it? Between us?"

Luc's lips spread into a thin evil grin. "Indeed." His blue eyes were dark like storm clouds, looking almost gray. His pale face shimmered like a window pane in the rain. "This will be our most dangerous game yet." His voice came out in a growl like thunder. "Larger plots than the ones I have for you have been set into motion, now that you are out of my way to prevent them. The fun is just getting started."

***

Emile shut the door tightly behind him. Noland stood at the end of the porch, hunched over the rail. "She could have died today. It's my fault," Noland breathed without looking back at Emile. He kept his eyes glued down to the ground. "Isn't it?"

"Technically..." Emile started. "I guess, if we trace it back far enough, it's Lucifer's fault. If it weren't for him we wouldn't be here, demons wouldn't be here... Everything would be honky dory." He chuckled at his own cleverness. He chuckled alone.

He took a place next to Noland at the rail and watched as he blinked at the snow. His bare arms shone in the sun. He was fuming. Emile had never seen him this upset. He couldn't tell if it was anger, passion, distress, or what it was. It was all of them. "Something else happened, didn't it?" Emile asked, leaning his back against the rail, taking his eyes off of Noland to relieve some of the pressure he was feeling.

"Yeah," Noland said, and he did feel less pressured. One emotion in particular came to the surface enough for Emile to be able to pick it out amongst the rest. He furrowed his brow.

"Why are you so sad about it?" Emile asked. "I mean I'm assuming you figured it out today, that she's *yours*. I thought that would make you happy."

"It's just..." Noland stopped. "I don't know, I'll sound like a jerk and an idiot—"

"What you don't think she's pretty enough?" Emile asked, prodding for more clues.

"What? No! I mean, I think she's absolutely beautiful. That's not the problem at all. She's just so delicate looking, and she wasn't raised like us. She doesn't know what all is out there after her. Her defenses are nowhere near where they should be. What if she gets hurt? What if I can't protect her? What if she gets..."

"Okay, first of all, she's not going to get killed. We won't give Luc the chance. Secondly, if you'd just let her, she is more than capable of defending herself. I didn't get the chance to tell you, but that's her gift." Emile smiled weakly, trying to determine which of Noland's emotions would be brought to the surface by this new information.

"I don't want her fighting. Someone who's delegated to train should be the one to teach her. What if you teach her wrong?" Noland wasn't angry, but he was worried.

"I don't think it really matters if I teach her, or if I screw up. It's more like I point her in the right direction and she picks it up by instinct. She's actually incredible. Give her another week or two and I don't think I'd even stand a chance against her." Emile tried to be cautious about his approach, he didn't want this to end in another fight. He was trying to comfort him, not make him more upset. It was hard, though. Noland didn't even know how he felt. Emile was having a hard time trying to pick out which emotions to run with, and which ones were refusing to be left behind.

"No. I want to wait for Jacob. I don't want to make any mistakes, if they could have permanent effects." Noland was decisive sounding, but his emotions didn't comply. His face, which was firm and controlled, fell. "She could have died today," he spoke in a near whisper, his eyes falling back down to the snow.

***

Achaia winced as Yellaina pulled the last cotton ball away. Her whole face was on fire. Blood still trickled from the gash on her forehead. Yellaina taped bandages to the larger, deeper, cuts but left the smaller cuts and scrapes bare.

"That looks a lot better. But you still look like Hell." She said closing the first aid box.

Olivier, who was sitting next to her, examined Achaia's face. "How did you get away?" He sounded grateful, though stunned.

"Noland. He grabbed me and took me up into the clouds." She answered.

"Oh, so you know about the wings now then..." Oliver said half to her, half to himself. "You have them too, ya know," he added more cheerfully.

"I know, I found that out today when I was— trying to get away." Achaia decided it was best not to tell them about the fight. Emile or Noland would tell them if they wanted to.

"So did you try to fly?" Olivier asked eagerly.

"I did fly," Achaia said, trying to reciprocate his cheerfulness.

"What?" Yellaina and Olivier asked in unison.

"Yeah, I flew— ya know until the demons tackled me into the tree branches, then Noland grabbed me."

"Wow! It's just..." Yellaina started, trying hard not to sound like she didn't believe her.

"We're kind of like birds, it usually takes a while to get it. Being pushed off a cliff or building usually helps." Olivier explained. "We learn better in dire situations."

"Well," Achaia started. "I was trying to get away from a few dozen demons, of which I've never been subjected to before."

"Ah, yeah. That's true. I guess they would be pretty creepy the first time you see them," Yellaina agreed.

"Yeah, I don't remember the first demon I saw. They've been around for as long as I can remember. I'm pretty sure one tried to kill me right after I was born. I was too fast for him though."

"That, and your dad killed it. I've heard the story," Yellaina laughed.

Olivier liked to make himself sound as impressive as possible; the others rarely let it happen.

"So where are your parents?" Achaia asked.

"Oh well, my mom is in China, she's protecting some diplomats over there while some negotiations take place. She is actually a Cherubim," Yellaina said simply. "And my dad is in the Vatican."

"And my mom is in England for the United Nations. Politicians are the most popular Charges. Dad was in the Vatican, but should be back in England by now. They still live in France though," Olivier explained.

"How long are they there for?" Achaia asked, glad to have the subject changed from her to them.

"I have no clue. I probably see my mom every few years or so, we talk every few months," Yellaina explained nonchalantly.

"Yeah, my parents aren't really around much either. Once you get to a certain age, you start training. When you get to that point, your parents take kind of a back seat, and you focus on what your trainer tells you to do. We have a... longer life span than humans, and we understand the afterlife so we don't really feel the need to spend a lot of time with our parents here. Right now, we have a job," Olivier clarified.

There was a stirring across the room. Amelia groaned, Yellaina shot up off of the floor and ran over to her. "Amelia?"

"Where am I?" Amelia asked in a muted mumble.

"The plane crashed. We're in an old hunting cabin... How do you feel? Can you sit up?" As Amelia struggled to sit up, Olivier ran outside to tell Emile and Noland that she had awoken.

Yellaina brought a bowl of stew over from inside the fireplace where everyone's bowls sat warming. "Here, try to eat something."

Amelia nibbled down a spoonful of stew and Emile dashed through the door. "You're awake!" He exclaimed with a wide smile.

"Hey there stranger, I thought you'd never wake up." Noland said in a gruff sarcastic voice entering behind him.

He seemed happy, but Achaia could tell he was hiding something. What could it be? His disdain for the fact that she was there? That she was messing up everything? That she was some stupid little human who wanted to be more? Or didn't want to be more, but was stuck between two worlds that didn't seem to want her? With everyone distracted by Amelia being awake, Achaia took the opportunity to sneak out onto the porch alone.

***

Achaia sat on the step and stared at the snow. If he didn't want her here, why not just let her go? She hated the feeling that she was holding everyone else back, annoying everyone with her idiotic questions. She didn't ask to be here! What was she supposed to do to make them happy? Staying apparently didn't do it... *Why won't they just let me leave?* She thought, digging her fingernails into the palms of her hands and cracking her knuckles. Was she outraged? Or just an outcast? Did it even make a difference?

The door cracked behind her, Emile stepped out onto the porch. "I know you want to be alone, so I'm just going to say this and then leave you to it. You are one of us. And not only do we want you here, but we'll need you here before too long. Don't worry about Noland or what he said. He didn't mean it, he's just thinking about a lot of stuff right now." Emile finished talking and walked back inside shutting the door tight behind him.

Achaia knew he was right, because he could feel everyone else's emotions, it just didn't feel like he was right, *right now*. Maybe the past couple of weeks were just starting to catch up with her?

The shock was wearing off, and right now, she felt like she just needed to cry. Tears rose up, warm at first in her eyes before spilling over, and freezing on her cheeks. Her face turned red and splotchy, and her eyes burned with saline. It felt good to cry, like a pressure was being lifted from her chest. She cried until her body was numb, and she could barely stand up again as the sun went down behind the trees.

When she went back inside everyone else was in their beds with their eyes closed, if not asleep. She lay down on her makeshift bed slowly and quietly, and folding in on herself, hugged her knees gently. As she closed her eyes to sleep, a few more silent tears found their way down her cheeks and across her face to her pillow.

# A Sick Sense

"What good are wings
Without the courage to fly?"
-Atticus

Noland watched as the black cloud of smoke and whispers scattered into the wind like a blur of ashes, a mound in the snow left in their wake. Noland went forward to investigate. He went forward, through the snow, slowly, sword in hand and eyes peeled for their return.

The closer he got, the faster his mind raced, and his steps quickened. Throwing his sword to the ground he broke into a sprint. Slipping through the glacial mush, he nearly slid right into her. Her red hair vibrant against the pale white snow and her fair skin.

She moved. Her face turned toward him. Her lips parted as if she were trying to speak, but no sound came from them.

Noland watched as her blue-green eyes fluttered and closed. Her head fell weakly to the side. She was gone.

*Noland shot up from his sleep in a cold sweat, his heart pounding. He stared ahead, into the darkness. The fire had gone out.*

*"Noland?" A quiet whisper came from his right. Achaia, her voice sounded meek and mousy. She was scared.*

*Noland turned to face her, but he knew that she could not see him without the fire. With a wave of his hand the fire was revived, casting light and shadow across their faces. Upon seeing him, Achaia looked even more horrified.*

*"Noland. It's alright, it was just a dream." She placed her hand along his face. It was cool, gentle. She crawled closer to him, and with her other hand she covered his heart. "It was just a dream." She whispered into his ear, her lips tickling the side of his face. Finding their way down to his mouth.*

Noland shot up, awake.

\*\*\*

Achaia sat paralyzed. "Noland?" She asked into the darkness, her voice just below a whisper. She'd heard Noland moaning in his sleep, which woke her.

After she had woken up, she'd felt him moving around in his sleep. He must have been having a nightmare. She'd tried to shake him awake, it didn't work, but apparently after a moment of watching him, something in his dream had finally done it. He sat straight up, breathing heavily.

"Noland? Are you alright?" She whispered.

Just then the fire came back to life with a roaring vengeance. Achaia cringed away from it in alarm. Then she looked up to Noland, finally able to see his face. She moved back away from him with even more shock. An initial strike of horror took hold of her, before she was able to remember what Emile had told her.

Noland's eyes were flames themselves. Yellow, orange, and

red flames flickering, with deep black pupils. "Achaia." He spoke softly moving toward her on his hands and knees, silently.

Despite herself, she moved farther away from him. He shut his eyes, looking down, and shook his head. He was trying to calm himself down, flip natures. When he opened his eyes again, they were their usual green.

He continued to crawl toward her on the floor. Achaia's back was pressed against Yellaina's bed. She had nowhere else to go. She looked up at him in wide-eyed disbelief. Emile's white eyes were nothing compared to Noland's blazing irises.

For some reason she found herself unable to move. Noland made his way to her and sat on the floor next to her, right up against her, and wrapped his arms around her. He'd never done this awake before, unless the threat of hypothermia was knocking on her door. She was stunned, and still could not make herself move.

"I..." She didn't know what to say.

"I'm sorry. I didn't mean to scare you. Sometimes I have pretty violent dreams."

\*\*\*

Achaia was shaking in his arms, he had no idea what to say to her. He knew that he was probably the cause of her shaking, but he couldn't let her go. Instead he held her tighter, rubbing her arm, her back. He felt like he could wrap his arms around her twice.

"I tried to wake you..." She whispered into his ear, finally laying into him. "I was scared, I couldn't see... And then..."

"My eyes can be pretty scary sometimes, I'm sorry." He leaned back, pulling her onto him a little.

\*\*\*

Achaia sat for a while, comforted by his arms, like when her father held her when she'd wake up from a bad dream. Only she wasn't the one who had the nightmare... and this wasn't how her father held her.

Achaia looked down. She sat on Noland's lap, wrapped up in his arms, folded into him. His skin glistened with his sweat. She sat up and away from him, his arms loosening around her, his hands falling to her waist. She noticed that her own arms had been draped around his neck and that her hands now rested on his broad and muscular shoulders.

"I'm sorry!" He said moving frantically away from her. "I was just... you looked so scared." He looked up to Emile. Achaia did too.

"No I'm sorry. I just... It's okay. We were both a little freaked out, and not really awake. It's okay." She looked at him with a mixture of sympathy and confusion.

"Yeah, right." Noland said quietly looking away from her to the floor. "I'm just going to go back to sleep." He mumbled, it seemed more to himself than to her.

***

Noland laid down and faced away from her for the first time since they'd slept on the floor in the cabin. He could feel, without seeing himself, that he looked dejected. How had he screwed things up so royally? He began to pray to God silently. *God, is it possible to mess up your plan? I... Just give me the strength to do my job, God. Give me focus, Father, to stop getting distracted. Please, give me focus.* Noland closed his eyes, but he could not slow down his mind. When his eyes were closed he could still see Achaia laying there in the snow, her eyes closed, never to be opened again...

***

Noland looked toward the window, the sky was a dark shade of blue. The sun would be rising within the hour. He had failed in his attempts to fall back asleep. He sat up and huffed a sigh. Frustration, the feeling of not being able to breathe, poured over him. He decided to go outside for some fresh air, figuring that time alone would best be sought before everyone else woke up.

He sat on the porch. The birds sang a jovial tune, as the shade of blue that painted the sky lightened. He could feel that he was a contradiction to the scene painted around him. The fog of his breath was denser than the smoke of a cigar. He melted the snow around him.

*Calm down.* He repeated the command in his head, but he was unable to heed his own thoughts. He looked up to the forest line, where he could see the sun peeking through the trees. There was a creak behind him as the door opened slowly.

"Hey." Olivier's voice was shaky in the cold. Noland turned, and returned the greeting with a nod. He made eye contact for only a second before looking away. Olivier shut the door quietly behind him.

\*\*\*

Olivier walked forward and sat next to Noland on the stairs. He risked a glance at him, but knew better than to gawk at him while he was in a mood. Olivier couldn't get a read on him. It was times like this he wished he were more like his brother. Emile never had to guess. Noland looked angry, but not really fed up with anyone in particular; it was more of a tortured look. "What's up?"

Noland didn't answer. Nor did he show any sign that he had even heard him. He was distant, far away in his thoughts. Olivier looked away embarrassed, not that there was anyone else around to see him being ignored. He had known better than to ask.

Noland was the strong silent type, and Olivier was the yipping pup; at least that's how he'd always felt. No matter how hard he tried, he was always the young one, too little to do this, not old enough to understand that... He'd looked up to Noland for years, and was still so far away from being anything like him.

"I screwed up." Noland said in a low growl.

Olivier's head snapped toward him. Noland had *spoken*. To *him*... Sure they'd known each other forever, but Emile was always his confidant. "What are you talking about?"

"She almost died because of me." His face fell even further, Olivier had thought it would have been impossible.

"Dude, you saved her. Noland, you saved her life!"

"If it weren't for me, if I hadn't been, distracted, she never would have needed saving." His throat sounded as if it had gone raw.

"Distracted?" Olivier's voice was soft, like an adult comforting a child, though he'd managed to not sound condescending.

Noland sat for a moment staring into the woods, thinking. Olivier could practically see the wheels turning behind his vibrant green eyes.

"Never mind—"

Olivier looked down, defeated.

"Is Emile up?"

Olivier's heart sank. He'd thought they'd been making progress, Noland had been opening up... Olivier stood slowly with the realization that he and Noland would never be equals. They would remain how they'd always been, role model, and child; at least in Noland's mind. "I don't think so," Olivier said in a near whisper as he sulked back to the door and opened it quietly.

"Hey Olivier," Noland said as if it were an afterthought.

Olivier turned around.

"Thanks," and without even waiting for a reply, Noland turned back to his trees.

Olivier opened his mouth and shut it again realizing Noland

didn't care whether or not he said 'you're welcome'. The thanks was no more than a pat on the pup's head. *Run along now Skip*, Olivier thought to himself continuing inside and shutting the door.

\*\*\*

Shael sat watching the blood games, and the demons in the crowd around him. The greed and euphoria that filled their eyes at the sight of blood drawn, the way they licked their lips passed pointed teeth, it was as if ecstasy were achieved in admiring mutilation. Truly, the ongoing scrimmage was a bloody one. Shael could smell it from his seat. The front few rows were splattered with it, cheering on the victor, as he ripped his opponents arm from its shoulder socket.

Shael shifted his gaze to Luc, seated a few rows higher than Shael and on the other side of the arena. Luc's expression was guarded. He was watching the fight, but Shael could tell he wasn't enjoying it, his thoughts were elsewhere. He leaned over to the demon next to him and whispered something. The demon looked at him surprised, then stood and left. Luc looked up and met Shael's eye. One of his eyebrows twitched up in a silent gesture somewhere between recognition and challenge. The corner of his mouth followed in a knowing smirk.

The atmosphere between them had remained tense. They had hardly spoken through more than glances. Shael had silently pledged to himself to take in as much of Hell as he could. He sought to learn how things were done. He was going to master the protocols, and figure out how to wage war here. For now, he was studying the culture of Hell. What were its strengths, its weaknesses? Which were its weakest warriors, and its strongest? He explored its nooks and found its hiding places, sketching a blueprint of the place in his mind. He kept his eyes open for both opportunities and threats.

From what he picked up in listening to conversations between demons, he was somewhere between the third and sixth circles that made up the spiraling cone that formed the pit that was Hell. It was composed, it appeared, entirely of ice, a catacomb of caverns and tunnels. Though Shael had not yet been able to exit whichever circle he was in, he had put together choppy pictures of the others based on what he overheard. Some of the descriptions actually made him glad of where he found himself, as opposed to their rumored horrors.

Luc stood, and edged through the demons, heading out the way his companion had left. Shael stood, and cut through the crowd in his own stand, sneaking around behind it, to follow around the way Luc had gone. Shael stayed beneath the stands, sneaking from set to set, regretting the view the times he looked upward to check if anyone had taken notice of him. The feet over his head stomped, and cheers rose like screams, making Shael's blood curl. He pressed on, until he reached the set of stands Luc had been sitting in.

Behind the rows of seats, there was an archway exiting into the catacombs. Shael walked light-footedly toward it, and peeked around. The corridor tunnel beyond was dark and empty. Shael listened closely for any voices coming from either end, but couldn't hear anything over the shouts of the crowd. Shael took a wild guess and went left. He tiptoed along until finally he did hear a voice, Luc's voice. He was speaking quietly. There were two other voices as well, and when they spoke they were much louder and more excited. "Is it our turn?"

"Let us prove ourselves Master."

"We are capable."

"Yes," Luc said sounding exasperated. "Take your brothers, all you rage demons. Oppress those world leaders with the most weaponry. Whisper into their hearts until they start the next world war. I want to see nation war against nation. I want humans to be their own pathetic downfall. You are only to inspire them to seek the darkness in their own hearts. Their nature itself will do the falling," Luc paused. "Do you hear me? Don't get carried away. I want God to look down and see his *precious* creation eating itself alive."

"Yes, Master," one of the demons said excitedly.

"Let the others possess and oppress who they will, I hardly care." Luc sounded bored at the thought. "And if any of you should find Achaia bat Shael," Luc paused.

Shael swallowed hard in frustration. It appeared that Luc had made some sort of hand gesture that Shael could not see, but the demons snickered. Shael turned, and as quickly and quietly as he could, ran back down the corridor to the stadium before Luc could catch him eavesdropping.

Shael prayed those Guardians protecting the world's leaders were paying attention. Oppression was far less obvious than possession. Recognizing it was an art.

\*\*\*

Noland decided to go for a run to clear his mind. He found no use dwelling on the past, or on things that he had no control over. He jogged through the snow. It was a long time before he felt the burn in his calves and he gradually began to slow down until, finally, he could do nothing but walk. He could barely do that much.

He passed by trees eaten alive by moss. His mind could relax out here. No one to judge him, no one to rely on him. He felt the pressure lift from his shoulders and sat with his back against a tree.

"How did I become a leader?" Noland asked out loud, as if he expected God to answer audibly. He thought back to how Olivier had looked at him on the porch. He looked up to him. He was shocked to think there was something that Noland couldn't handle. "He thinks I'm invincible. That's a lot to live up to."

Noland felt a calm wash over him.

"I knew you were listening." Noland smiled. The sun seemed to shine brighter but Noland knew he was just giving it more recognition. "I promise, your efforts aren't wasted on me. I just don't know why..." Noland sighed.

He shut his eyes for a moment, just listening. Listening to the birds, the wind through the trees, the crunching of the snow... A sense of urgency rushed through Noland. He opened his eyes and saw a hunter ten feet in front of him, holding a gun at him. His eyes were black... The gun fired.

\*\*\*

Achaia sat by the fire munching on the last bag of plane crackers, lost in thought.

"Hey." A voice spoke right next to her.

Achaia looked up startled to find that it was Amelia looking down at her.

"Mind if I sit with you?" Amelia's voice was nice, not filled with disdain at all, as it had been before.

"Sure," Achaia said out of surprise, at a loss for any other response.

"I wanted to apologize for the way I've been treating you." She tried a smile, a pathetic attempt. Achaia could tell this was hard for her.

"They told me about your gift. I guess I don't really blame you at all. I probably would have locked myself in a room alone and refused to talk to anyone if I were you. I think it's really brave that you make an attempt at still living a normal life."

"Brave? Or Stupid? It's not without sacrifice," Amelia said looking down.

"I know..." Achaia agreed looking into the flames. She had

a feeling growing in the pit of her stomach that something wasn't right.

"Oh no, not like that. I mean sure. It comes with the territory. It's just that I guess my gift gets the best of me and I tend to alienate people. The scary thing is that a lot of the time I don't really care. Does that make me a monster?"

"No. I think it's just your human showing." Achaia smiled.

Amelia chuckled and nodded her agreement. They sat in silence for a few minutes eating and warming their hands.

Achaia without knowing why kept growing more and more anxious. "What's wrong?" Emile asked.

Amelia looked at her. "Yeah, you're really pale. Are you okay?"

"Something isn't right..." Achaia stood.

All of a sudden Emile looked horrified.

"You feel that?" Achaia asked looking at him.

Emile turned to Olivier. His voice was sharp. "Where's Noland?"

\*\*\*

Noland ducked just as the bullet tore a path into the tree behind where his head had been.

Trying to scramble up, his feet kept slipping on the snow. He settled for side-ways motion, crawling behind the tree; where he was finally able to stand. He risked a peek around the tree trunk only to be met with another bullet. It missed him by less than an inch.

He could feel blood trickling down his face where the debris from the first shot had clipped him. If he could get close enough, he could knock the guy out. But how was he supposed to get closer to a possessed guy with a gun? He peeked around again.

He hadn't heard footsteps, he couldn't tell where the man

was. Another shot fired.

Noland ducked back behind the tree again. The tree vibrated as the bullet lodged in the tree behind Noland's head. Noland strained his ears, listening for the crunching of the snow, as the man walked.

"Can the little Nephilim come out and play?" An inhuman voice taunted.

"Put the gun down and we'll talk about it." Noland replied, straining to listen to any movement from behind.

"What fun would that be?"

Noland heard tinkering sounds; the demon was reloading. Noland took the opportunity to bolt out from behind the tree. The man was still some distance away. Noland knew he couldn't reach him before he finished reloading, he wasn't as fast as Olivier, so he ran in the opposite direction.

The possessed man raised the gun again, and Noland dodged behind another tree.

"What are you doing out here alone in the woods?" The demon asked. "You're a young Nephilim. Where are your mommy and daddy?" The demon laughed.

Noland felt a fire ignite in his chest. When he exhaled, smoke issued with his breath. Noland took the risk and ran out from behind the tree. The gun fired.

He ran from tree to tree, advancing on the demon. The possessed hunter shot at Noland, tree bark flying like woodland shrapnel all around him as he sprinted.

Noland paused behind a tree as he got closer, and well within the hunter's range to get a clean shot. He waited for the demon to move, hoping he would come closer, so that Noland stood a chance at reaching him before the demon could stop him. But the demon was just far enough away to be able to easily shoot Noland before he could get to him.

"HEY!" A voice called from behind the shooter.

"Achaia no!" Emile's voice cried out.

Noland stepped out from behind the tree to see Achaia followed by Emile. She marched toward the shooter, her face livid.

*What is she doing!* Noland panicked. The shooter looked confused for a second, then raised his gun again. By this time, it was in Achaia's reach. She raised an arm and knocked the gun out of the hunter's hands and grabbed him by the throat.

The hunter, instead of looking surprised or alarmed, looked back with confusion, his pupil-less eyes scanning her face. He spoke with a gravelly voice, "I thought I helped kill you sixteen years ago." Achaia knit her eyebrows in comprehension, and looked deep into his black eyes. "*Get out*," she spat through clenched teeth. Her voice was harsh, cold, demanding. Noland had never heard her speak with such authority.

The man's body hemorrhaged in her hand, and collapsed, unconscious, to the ground.

Next to the body stood a rage demon. Five and a half feet tall, its body looked like that of a wolf. Its legs were scaled over with talons on its feet. The face was scaled as well, with lion-like jaws, but hawk-like, unforgiving, eyes. Achaia stood face to face with the creature, ten yards from Noland.

The demon had a snarl that echoed in Noland's chest. He ached with fear for Achaia. She'd never fought a demon like this before. The demon's teeth dripped with something that melted the snow where it landed and caused it to steam.

Emile was frozen in horror, and Noland found that he was having a hard time making his legs work as well. They both just watched as the demon and Achaia stood staring into each other's eyes. Black, to red.

"I think you have me confused with my mother." Achaia said venomously. "What is your name?"

"We were Legion then. We were recently unbound and released. I am Lussa," the demon sneered. "You look just like her."

Achaia didn't even appear tempted to back down. Noland stared in fascination as much as in fear. "What do you want?" she asked shortly.

"I've already found it," he answered in a voice that sounded more like the pounding of a heart. "I hardly expected to stumble across *you* in a forest. I was just having a bit of fun. My master will be pleased. And your only *protection*, little baby Nephilim… How convenient." He laughed, a shuddering laugh that sounded like a smoker's cough. He turned on his back legs, and broke into a run.

Noland's heart raced. They couldn't let him get away. He would come back with reinforcements. Noland knew he and the others were only lightly armed. There was no way they would be able to hold off a hoard of rage demons, not for long.

Achaia was already sprinting after Lussa, running like an Olympian toward the vault. Noland ran through the trees and into the clearing after them. He pushed off the last tree he passed, launching himself into the air. As he watched, Achaia spread her wings, and in a mixture of flight and jumping she land on Lussa's back. She clung to his fur, riding him like a horse.

"Achaia!" Noland yelled pushing harder against the wind. Lussa, in a fit of frustration was bucking like a bull, trying to dislodge Achaia from his back.

Noland had nearly reached them when Achaia grabbed Lussa by his top jaw as he roared, and twisted. Noland heard the snap of the bones as she broke his jaw. Achaia slid from Lussa's back, letting her wings catch her on the wind, and flew backwards. She pulled his head back with her, by the jaw still clutched in her fist, and yanked it down.

The abrupt change of direction against his momentum, broke his neck and separated his head from his body with a loud crack, and the sound of shredding muscle.

Lussa's body twitched as black pus poured from his lower jaw and neck, where it had once connected to his face. As Achaia straddled Lussa's steaming remains, they disintegrated before their eyes. His head alone remained in her hand, a spoil of war.

She dropped the trophy to the ground and it rolled away from her, the hand that had held it shaking, and bloodied.

"Kaya—" Noland said catching up to her.

She turned to face him as he approached. Her eyes were no longer red, they were back to being their lovely combination of blue and green. She was shaking.

"I..."

"Shh... you were amazing!" He grabbed her hands as he reached her and held them to stop their shaking.

"What the...?" Olivier said as he, Amelia and Yellaina emerged from the trees onto the scene.

"Achaia killed her first demon." Emile said proudly. He had followed them into the clearing and was standing behind Noland.

"Awesome! Way to go Frenchy!" Olivier exclaimed walking out to congratulate her, punting Lussa's head like a soccer ball.

"With her bare hands." Emile added.

Olivier stopped in his tracks, eyes widening "Whoa." Amelia and Yellaina looked on with pure amazement.

"You did very well." Noland said softly, smiling and bringing her attention back to himself.

***

Achaia stood frozen, letting Noland's warmth trickle into her via their clasped hands. What had she done? And how had she done it?

*This whole two bodies in one thing is insane,* she thought. She looked up to Noland's eyes to see that they were still flames. This didn't scare her as it had before. In fact, it seemed kind of normal. "What now?" She asked softly.

"Now we go back to the cabin to figure out what comes next. And we bandage up that hand." He said leading her toward the others. As they walked he dropped her hands by her side. "We need to get out of these woods."

The rest nodded and agreed and they all walked back to the cabin. "He's definitely found us." Olivier clarified.

"Nothing gets past you!" Emile laughed.

"Shut up!" Olivier punched Emile's shoulder lightly. "What did I miss? I want all the gory details."

"After you get that hunter back to wherever he came from." Emile said, in a fatherly tone.

***

"That is awesome, Frenchy!" Olivier exclaimed as they stalked up the porch steps. "I mean, you ripped off its freaking head with your bare hands! Is your gift strength do you think? Like Noland." He stopped on the porch and looked at them thinking of the possibility.

"I don't think so. I'm not as strong as him." Achaia shook her head. "It was more about the momentum and the leverage."

"It was more than that too." Emile added with a glance at Achaia and Noland. He was playing it off as if these were all new theories. "Her eyes were red. I think her gift might be battle. Warfare in general. I think she's just a great fighter. I mean— think about who her father was."

Emile felt a pang of guilt as he felt his stomach drop. He knew he had upset Achaia.

"Is," Olivier corrected. "Who her father *is*." Olivier opened the door and they all filed in.

"Was that his gift? Battle? I knew he was a great fighter, but was that his gift? Before he—?" Achaia asked as they all took seats around the fire.

"We don't really know. Our parents don't like to talk about him. Your dad wasn't exactly social. Not with other Nephilim I mean. His best friend, Naphtali, is a Seraphim. Other than that... He didn't really associate himself with anyone that reminded him of Satan. And after your mom, anyone who reminded him of God. I don't know how he and Naphtali remained friends after he became human." Emile shrugged off his jacket.

"And how was it I was able to sense that the demon was in the woods with Noland?" She asked. Still looking at Emile.

Emile glanced at Noland. Yellaina and Amelia looked at each other with slight smiles. "I don't know. I think that's enough for now," Emile said. "There's a lot about Nephilim you don't understand yet. I think we'll leave today's lesson at that." He smiled at her and went to sit on his bed.

"Yeah," Noland started with a small cough. "Right now we need to decide what comes next."

Yellaina smiled. "I think that since Achaia has her wings, and the demons obviously know she's here, we need to move."

"Moscow is probably thinking we've gone AWOL." Emile said.

"We have." Olivier clarified again.

"Not intentionally." Noland corrected.

"Flying sounds great, but there's no way she'll make it to Russia. She's not that strong yet..." Olivier added. "At least not flying wise." He smiled at her again "Rambo."

"And she's injured," Amelia said pointing at all the cuts spread across Achaia's visible body.

"I think we should fly to Paris, and catch a plane to Moscow. Paris is crowded enough for now, we can layover there. But we should leave tonight." Noland said decisively.

"Under the cover of darkness—," Olivier added in his best 'epic-movie-voice'.

"You're such a nerd," Achaia laughed. "I'm glad we're friends." She said smiling.

Olivier smiled widely at her, patting her leg, happy to finally have another nerd in the group. Emile was happy his brother had someone else his age, with similar interests, he'd always felt bad for Olivier being left out for so long.

Yellaina looked down, Emile could feel her disappointment. He knew she didn't want to fly at night in the cold. He wasn't really looking forward to it either. But he *was* looking forward to a warm hotel room, an actual bed, and real food.

They all stood and moved about the cabin, packing everything back into their book bags. Yellaina returned the pots and pans to the shelf and Amelia worked with Achaia folding the blankets back and putting them into the cedar chest.

When everything was put back the way it had been, and dark had begun to fall, they cloaked themselves with jackets, grabbed their bags and walked outside into the star-strewn night.

# City of Angels

"Those who have the privilege to know
have the duty to act."

-Albert Einstein

Standing in the snow outside the cabin preparing to leave, Achaia realized just how cold it was. She knew it would only get colder the higher they went into the clouds. She moaned to herself.

"Here," Noland said reaching his hand out for her bag. "Trust me, they get heavy after a while."

Achaia handed over her bag, and he threw the strap over his shoulder.

"Everyone ready?" Emile asked, securing the bags that he wore himself. Everyone either grunted or nodded, and Emile took off into the sky. Olivier and Amelia followed and then Noland, Yellaina and Achaia.

They flew in a "V" formation like a flock of geese. Achaia had a hard time flying at first since she was shivering so violently. She felt the frigid wind sift through the feathers of her wings, just as it cut through the roots of her hair. Flying was like running, it took her a while to find her rhythm. Every time she drew her wings up, she felt like she was falling a little. Every downward beat of her wings was a fight against gravity. The faster they flew, the more momentum was on her side, the easier it became.

Noland broke out of formation and went up the "V" on his side, touching each person's arm once, warming them. Yellaina was going blue in the lips before Noland grabbed a hold of her arm for a few seconds. Achaia was last in line. Noland fell back, flying next to her. He grabbed a hold of her hand and rubbed the inside of it with his fingers. Heat surged through her entire body. A heat that would last a while. Her palm began to sweat and Noland let go, flying back to his spot in the formation.

As the trees began to thin, Emile stopped for them to rest in the tree tops. They stood on branches in a cluster of trees at the border of the forest, in near silence. The only sounds were the rustling of the wind through the branches, and everyone trying to catch their breath.

Achaia was sore in her back where she had cracked it falling with the shadows. She was also sore from her entire body weight pulling on her wing joints every time she beat her wings. Her face felt like ice, and her cuts all stung. After they had all had some water, and a minute to breathe, they were off again.

After a while Achaia started to see little lights below them and realized they were city lights. They blurred as the rushing wind caused her eyes to water. They looked like tiny stars.

The wind in her ears was deafening. She'd gone mentally and

physically numb in her exhaustion save for her sides and abdominals hurt from trying to hold a plank position, breathe, and fly all at the same time. She was cramping badly and her breathing was becoming shallow and short.

As they started their descent, she couldn't even feel her wings. As far as she knew someone else was keeping her up in the sky. She was tired and beginning to lose her breath entirely when Noland went through the "V" one more time to warm everyone.

When he got to her he grabbed hold of her wrist as everyone began to land. She was glad he did. He landed before her, holding her arm. Her legs had forgotten how to stand and she stumbled into Noland as they reached the street. She would have fallen over if it weren't for him holding her. She also appreciated being wrapped in warmth.

They had landed in a back alley somewhere in Paris. Achaia guessed they were in the Red Light District by the looks of things. They walked toward the main street, passing bright green garbage bins and a few stray rats. Once they reached the main street, they stopped.

"Okay, I say we find food, then a hotel." Emile suggested.

Noland released Achaia's wrist, where he had still been warming her. "Sounds good to me," Noland agreed patting his stomach. "I'm starving... Well not literally but..."

"We get it." Achaia smiled. "So right or left?"

"I say right," Yellaina piped up. "There's more lights down that way. Maybe there are some restaurants."

"In Paris lights don't always mean food, Yellaina," Noland laughed. As they came into the light of the street He looked down at Achaia's face. "While we're out you should probably find a local healer, see if you can't get some provisions." Noland spoke to Yellaina, but his face studied Achaia's, and one of his fingers slid along the cuts on her cheek.

Yellaina grimaced. Apparently Achaia looked as bad as she felt. "I can do that."

They took off to the right toward the lights. They came up on a girl who was probably only a year or two older than Achaia. She wore a tiny leather mini skirt, and a shiny red halter top with knee high black leather boots. She was leaning against the wall with a cigarette.

*Oh my God, is that a—* Achaia started thinking to herself. She looked the part, except for her demeanor. The girl slumped against the building and didn't even try to look at Noland, Emile, or Olivier. As they got closer Achaia noticed a tear gliding down her pale cheek. "Hold up," Emile raised one of his hands for them to stop behind him. "Yellaina you wanna help me out with this one?" Yellaina nodded and stepped forward. Together they approached the girl.

\*\*\*

"*Bonjour.*" Emile started, getting the girl's attention. He looked to Yellaina. The girl looked up and tried to smile seductively at Emile. But she could not stop her crying.

Yellaina approached the girl and spouted off in rapid French, asking her what was wrong and if she was okay.

The girl's face dropped once more and she eyed Yellaina suspiciously.

Emile smiled at her sympathetically and told her that it was okay, that they were here to listen.

The girl cocked an eyebrow. It was obviously something she didn't hear every day. It was natural for her to be wary of them. "*Je m'appelle Emile.*" He held out a hand to the girl, "*C'est mon pleasure.*" He then gestured to Yellaina, "*tel est mon ami Yellaina.*"

The girl smiled at them, but didn't take Emile's hand. "*Je m'appelle Anastasie.*"

Emile smiled and let the hand drop back down to his side. He told her that they noticed she looked upset as they were walking by and just wondered if there was anything they could do, that they would really love to help.

Anastasie started with the immediate, that she was cold, and tired. That it was late, but she wasn't allowed to go home yet. She looked down in shame and explained what they had already surmised, that she was in fact a prostitute, but that she hadn't wanted to be. That this had never been her plan. Before long, Anastasie was spewing her guts to Yellaina and Emile. As she spoke, even more quickly, Emile found it hard to tell when one word had ended and another began. But she started to weep.

Emile could feel the depression demon working in Anastasie all the more because they were there. He had felt this demon before, he recognized it. The oppressor was a demon named Ania, the bringer of grief and trouble. She was desperate to hold on to Anastasie.

Emile took a deep breath, feeling Ania's presence as if buried in his own chest, making him feel heavy with worthlessness. It was hard to breathe. It took everything in Emile not to break down, himself.

Hearing Anastasie's story, and feeling the weight of it on her heart, Emile struggled. He knew Ania wasn't going down without a fight. But swords and bows were no good against this kind of demon. This was the kind you had to fight inside.

\*\*\*

"What's going on?" Achaia asked Amelia who was standing closest to her.

"Well, she's oppressed by a depression demon. Emile is trying to talk her out of it." Amelia explained.

"He's going to perform an exor..."

"No." Amelia shook her head. "See, there is demon possession and..."

"Oppression." Noland butted in. "It's not controlling her, like the hunter in the woods. It's not really in her. More like over her, influencing her. There is nothing in her to be brought out, so we can't kill it. The only person who can kill it is her. She has to conquer it within herself."

Amelia was looking at Noland funny. Achaia couldn't tell if she was offended he had cut her off, or just amused. Maybe even a combination of the two.

"So Emile is trying to make her happy?" Achaia asked simply.

"Yeah— You could put it that way. He is trying to give her *hope*," Noland explained.

Achaia turned back around to watch Emile and Yellaina work.

***

As Anastasie vented, Emile could feel the depression opening up and subsiding. He was encouraged by how much it helped, just to let her vent. Girls were funny creatures. He could feel the weight blowing away like a mist. When she stopped talking, she looked exhausted.

Anastasie had told them about how she felt worthless, like no one could ever love her because of what she was. How people only ever wanted her for her body, but no one really cared to get to know her. Her parents were dead, and when they died she had no money, no other family. She was forced into the business by one of her father's old friends. She had really had it rough. Ania had a wide open door into Anastasie's life.

After listening to her story, Yellaina was upset, too. Emile smiled sadly. Yellaina was getting a little taste of what it felt like to be him. "Yellaina, I need you to calm down. I can't stand feeling both of you hurt."

Yellaina nodded. She turned to Anastasie and invited her to come and get some dinner with them, and talk some more.

Anastasie was a little confused, but agreed. Emile felt a strike of fear, as she looked around. Emile knew that whoever she worked for would have eyes on her.

"*C'est d'accord Anastasie.*" He assured her, looking around himself. "*Vous êtes en sécurité maintenant.*"

She smiled weakly. He could tell she wanted to trust them, but she was anxious. She told them they could call her Ana, and led them down the street to an Asian restaurant that was still open.

Emile sat down at a small table with her and Yellaina while the others sat at the table behind him, to give them space. The waiter came and took their orders, and brought their drinks.

Ana went on with her story, explaining how things had gotten so out of control, and how afraid she was of her father's friend.

Emile could feel some of the pressure coming off of her shoulders as she spoke. There was a freedom to be found in saying things out loud, and Emile wondered if Ana had ever let herself talk to anyone about what all she had been through, in her short life. She finished by telling them that she supposed she understood why no one had ever offered to help her. She knew no one could love her. Because of what she'd become.

Emile looked into her eyes, deeply. He told her, in French, that she was worthy of love. Ana looked at him in disbelief. She held his gaze and tears started to pour out of her eyes.

Emile could feel her inner battle. Wanting to believe, but not being able to.

Yellaina chimed in, assuring her that she was beautiful, inside and out. She told her about there being a God who loved her, more than she ever knew. She told her that he was a powerful king, and that she was like a princess. Of how he was a true father, not like her father's friend. As Yellaina finished, Ana looked down.

Emile reached over and lifted her head up to look at him again. "He loved *you* enough to die for you, even when you were living this way. And he'd do it again. Not everyone out there is like your father's friend, or the men you've met. There are people out there like your parents. *Good* people, *loving* people."

Ana's eyes began to tear up again. Emile didn't remove his hand from her chin but continued to hold it.

The girl spoke softly, "People like *you*."

Emile nodded. He took his hand back away from her face. He looked up to the counter as the waiter came back with their food and saw a sign above the register. "Yellaina look."

Yellaina looked up and smiled. "Help wanted," Yellaina spoke to Ana and pointed at the sign.

Ana stared at it for a while. She turned back to them, looking for affirmation.

Emile nodded his encouragement, that if she wanted to, she should go. Then, with a huge smile, she strode proudly up to the register to talk to the manager. She came back with a sheet of paper and a pen, and started filling in her information, a huge grin on her face the entire time.

Emile smiled and picked up his chopsticks to dig in to his noodle bowl. But a hand laid itself over Emile's. Emile looked down in surprise and back up at Noland in confusion. Noland took the chopsticks out of his hand. "We both know what those do to you, man." He said in a hushed groan, so as not to interrupt Ana.

Olivier, who sat across from Noland was snorting, trying to hold in his laugh so the girl wouldn't notice. Achaia's face was pink also, with held in laughter.

"I've got your back bro." Noland smiled, handing Emile a fork.

Emile shook his head and turned back around, watching Ana fill out her application.

***

Achaia watched as the girl went from crying, to joyfully filling out an application. "It's amazing— how did he do it?" She asked more to herself.

"He simply let her know how much she was worth." Noland answered, turning back around and watching Achaia's face.

*How many times do people run into angels and not even know it? They could be anyone...* Achaia thought to herself in awe. *I am one. Everyone who's met me, ran into an angel and didn't even know it— And what good did it do? Nothing.* Achaia pondered somberly all the missed opportunities. Emile glanced at her, over his shoulder, with a small smile. Achaia's mouth twitched up in the corner, as Emile turned his attention back to the girls at his table.

She was surprised by how vividly she remembered the faces of each person she'd had an opportunity to help; she'd never noticed before. *It's my job to protect these people. To help them.* Achaia felt a rush of feeling wash over her, a sense of purpose as she ate her noodles. She smiled to herself as she ate and promised herself that she'd never miss an opportunity to save again.

***

When they were all finished eating and talking, they said goodbye to Ana, who was already having an impromptu interview with the manager of the restaurant, and continued in their search for a hotel. They found a cheap one not far down the street. Achaia mused for a moment; it was just down the street from Mulin Rouge. Amelia and Yellaina had stayed down in the lobby to inquire about the nearest laundromat before going in search of a local healer, while Achaia followed the others up the stairs to their rooms. She opened her door and felt a comforting wave of interior heat wash over her. Emile, Olivier and Noland opened the door to the room next to hers, and disappeared inside.

Achaia dropped her bag at the door and flung herself onto the bed by the window. It felt amazing after sleeping on a hard wood floor for two weeks. She closed her eyes, and had just started to drift off when there was a knock on her door.

Achaia sat up reluctantly, shaking off the drowsiness as she opened the door. "Hey?"

"Can I come in?" Noland asked.

"Sure," Achaia said, walking back over to her bed and sitting down. "What's up?"

Noland shut the door and followed her into the room, his authoritarian air disintegrating as he came closer. He sat down on the second bed facing her. "Hey." He looked pensive for a moment as he thought of what to say next.

Achaia felt her stomach do a little summersault and she fiddled with her hands in her lap.

"Um, our room is right next door. If anything happens—"

"Yell?" Achaia smiled.

Noland smiled and shrugged.

Achaia kicked off her shoes, hoping her feet didn't smell and tucked them up under her.

"Also, about Moscow—," Noland sounded more serious.

"Please tell me this isn't going to be like the council all over again," Achaia frowned.

"I don't know. It could be, it could be better, it could be worse," Noland said honestly.

"Well, that pretty much covers every possible scenario, so yeah…," Achaia shrugged, nodding.

Noland smiled with a chuckle, then his face fell. "The truth is, all of that will depend on one person. The Guardian of that safe house. We will meet him before we are even granted entry. He has authority in that place and will let us know what he expects of us when we arrive."

"Why do you make that sound so ominous?" Achaia asked, hugging her knees to her chest.

"Because I really don't know what to expect this time," Noland admitted.

Achaia stared down at her knees. She had a hole in the knee of her pants that hadn't been there a week ago. She picked at it. There were a lot of new holes in her life, she thought. As if sensing her downward spiral, Noland moved to the bed next to her. Achaia let her knees fall to either side indian-style, her left leg resting on Noland's, and looked up at him. He was close to her. Very close, she thought.

"In all likelihood, we will be assigned rooms, and the rest of us will receive our training as usual. I don't know how much of it you'll be included in…but hopefully, you'll start your Nephilim education." Noland smiled. He raised a tentative hand to her shoulder and patted it in awkward encouragement.

Achaia swallowed. Noland lowered his hand.

"I thought you'd be happy, about *that* at least." Noland frowned and scooted a little further away.

"I am." Achaia assured him. Thinking that her having feelings must freak him out, as she watched him scoot ever so slightly further down the edge of the bed. "I'm just a little nervous. What if I'm not any good?"

Noland didn't respond, he just stared at her in disbelief.

Achaia cursed herself for opening up. He wasn't Olivier or Emile, he wasn't the guy you talk to about *feelings*. "Oh, whatever, I doubt you want to listen to all of this. I'll just talk to Emile about it later." Achaia said blushing a little. "I'm sure you have better things to do with your night."

"I—," Noland paused for a second then stood.

"You're leaving?" Achaia asked, surprising herself. Did she really want him to stay? Or was his leaving just abrupt?

"I'm sorry," he said. "I know I'm not the best person to sympathize."

"I didn't mean—" Achaia started, but she didn't really know what she had meant, if it hadn't been that he wasn't sympathetic.

"I know. It's not really my gift." Noland tried to smirk, but it came as more of a wince. "I'm the 'suffer in silence' type." He rolled his eyes at himself.

Achaia desperately wondered what he was thinking.

"If you ever need someone to just sit in the ashes with you—" Noland's voice was low and quiet.

Achaia *felt* her eyebrows raise in surprise, more than she told them to do so. Noland looked down, his face pink.

"I can be a good *listener*." Noland said bashfully. "I just don't always know what to *say*." He swallowed, looking back up again. "But I am better with silence." He sighed heavily and rolled his eyes again. "I just mean—"

"If I ever want company in the pain, instead of a pep talk, I know where to go," Achaia said. Her heart felt like smiling. It felt like a beautiful, but sad, flower had bloomed in her chest. Her face however, remained still.

Noland nodded and went to leave. As he stood in the partially opened doorway, he looked back and into her eyes. "I really am sorry, for everything that's happened." Then he left. The door almost shut behind him, when Amelia and Yellaina arrived.

Achaia laid back on her bed. Yellaina looked her over as she came in. "How are you feeling?" She came over and dropped an armful of bottles and jars on Achaia's bed.

"What's all that?" Achaia asked. None of them appeared to be labeled.

"Salves, oils, salts, balms, ointments, things to heal you. Nephilim heal pretty quickly, but our healing abilities are amplified by certain herbs and such." Yellaina sat down on the edge of the bed. "Take off your shirt."

"What?"

"I need to see all your wounds," Yellaina said impatiently.

"I'll leave if I'm making you nervous." Amelia made fun of Achaia, as she opened the door to the hallway. She left, and Achaia removed her shirt, and jeans. She sat on the bed in a sports bra and her underwear acutely aware of how long it had been since she'd had an actual shower.

"Those demons did a number on you." She said uncorking a vial of some oil. "This is hyssop. It will make sure none of these get infected or anything. It will also help to soothe." Yellaina rubbed the oil over Achaia's face and arms.

"How do you know what each of these are, they aren't labeled." Achaia said picking up a tub of some sort of paste.

"You may have noticed I'm not much of a fighter." Yellaina

smiled.

Achaia nodded.

"I'm studying to become a healer, not training to become a Guardian."

"That makes sense." Achaia said, wincing as Yellaina applied some sort of green gunk to the gash on her head, where her face had slammed into the tree branch. She put the same paste on Achaia's hand where she had grabbed Lussa by his teeth. Yellaina wrapped her hand, and went into the bathroom. Achaia could hear her turn the tap to draw a bath.

When she followed her into the bathroom, Yellaina was pouring stuff from several of the jars into the hot water.

"Soak in there, drink lots of water, and go straight to bed," Yellaina said in a mothering tone, handing her a bottle of water.

"Yes ma'am." Achaia smiled.

Yellaina walked out the door, and went to close it behind her. "We'll just be next door, discussing the plan for tomorrow."

"That's nice," Achaia said bluntly. "Y'all go do that. I'm excited about this bath!"

Yellaina smiled.

"Hey," Achaia called. "Thanks."

Yellaina smiled again. "Just don't get your head or hand wet." She said pointing to the spots that had gotten the gunk. Then she shut the door and was gone.

As Achaia ran the bathwater, she thought of her dad. She wondered where he was, if he was okay, if he was scared, if he was worried about her—

Then, she wondered what Lucifer was like. Her dad had been his best friend, did they pal around? Or was Lucifer a malicious demon-thing that would eat her dad for dinner? She wondered if Lucifer looked human, or if he was some sort of creature... She knew how sick *people* could be. How would Satan torture his enemies?

She resolved within herself to find him, and bring him back. She had no idea where to start looking, or how to save him, if she did find him. As she added the hotel shampoo to the running water, she pushed thoughts of her father from her mind, again; this was becoming a bit of a habit for her.

As the tub filled, and she shut off the tap, she noticed for the first time how quiet her room was. Achaia sat relishing the heat, and the electricity; she scrubbed her hair and under her fingernails and slowly started to feel truly clean for the first time in weeks.

*\*\**

Shael lay on his bed, staring at the reflections of light on the ice ceiling above him, feeling a little like he was frozen into a gigantic fish tank; the world's most depressing aquarium exhibit. The reflections danced on the surface of the ice, twisting, and flickering.

No matter how many layers of blankets Shael had piled on top of himself, there was no warmth to be found. The chill here was bone deep. He watched his breath rise like smoke, and distracted himself by plotting his course of action. He hoped if he thought long and hard enough he would exhaust himself into sleep.

He hadn't gotten a single good night's rest since he had arrived. He had never before been so exhausted. It took a toll on his mood, his mindset, his ability to think. In his dazed state, he felt he almost understood Luc. The living conditions (if you could call them that) in Hell, would drive anyone to desperate measures, if not insanity.

Shael had an edge that Luc did not, though. He had chosen this. He had been the power that had placed himself here. He would not grow bitter or desperate; instead, he would use his position. He hadn't initially sold his soul to Luc to gain placement behind enemy lines, but if Shael could be of use while stuck here for eternity, he would make it his mission to be as useful as possible.

Shael knew that in order to do that, he would need to gain entry into Luc's inner circle. He would have to climb the ranks, and earn Luc's trust; not that Luc really *trusted* anyone…

That would be step one, Shael thought; he would fight his way up the ranks. In the meantime, he would remind Luc of the way they had been, carefree, radical, and reckless. Lucifer may be the father of lies, but Shael was no novice at manipulation. He would curb Luc's anger, make him enjoy his company again… Shael would learn his plans and do everything he could to foil them from within. "If You can hear me here, give me strength." Shael prayed.

Shael knew he had to make Luc believe he had lost hope, and embraced Hell. He turned onto his side, shutting his eyes against the cold, against the dancing reflections, against the threat of there always being a tomorrow here. He sighed at how easy it would be to fake losing hope, because he was barely holding onto it. But Shael knew that as long as he had purpose, as long as he could strive toward love in spite of hate, he could keep grasping at straws. He could hold out. He sighed. Whether an answer to his prayer, or his body finally giving in, Shael fell asleep. He slept restlessly, and had many nightmares, but he slept.

\*\*\*

Noland stood watching the news. Emile and Amelia were sitting at the foot of one of the beds with their mouths open as they watched. Yellaina sat on the floor with tears in her eyes, leaning against Olivier's legs, who looked like a stone statue. While they had been isolated in their cabin in the woods, the rest of Europe had become a war zone. There had been terrorist attacks in almost every

249

country. Paris, especially, had been hit hard, and the back lash was ugly.

As it turned out, it had been an act of God their plane hadn't made it to Paris to land the day it was supposed to. The airport had been the scene of multiple bomb detonations. The terminal building itself had nearly been reduced to rubble.

"So we're not flying to Moscow." Emile said shutting off the TV. Noland could tell by the shallowness of his cheeks that he had had enough.

"It's getting worse, isn't it?" Olivier asked. "Do you think this is it?"

"Mom and dad said the council has lost more Charges over the last month than we have in the last decade. It's not getting any better." Emile looked grim. "It's a sobering reminder of how short life is for them." Emile said, nodding toward the outside, to humans.

"Not always just for them." Noland reminded him.

"Right. Of course." Emile nodded. "Sorry."

Noland waved the apology aside. "No, Olivier, I don't think this is it. I think this is just the beginning."

It was easy for most Nephilim to think of Humans as an "us" and "them"— Noland was the only Nephilim who could really relate to loss the way humans experienced it. Emile could feel his pain now. But he hadn't been there when Noland's parents had died. He never felt that shock, disbelief, denial, and the pain of realization. He could feel the scar, but he never had to see the fresh wound.

"So how are we going to get to Moscow?" Yellaina asked.

"Security is going to be heightened now. People are going to be too nervous to travel, but this might actually give us an advantage. The humans are going to have their eyes peeled, and extra precautions are going to be taken by all major transit lines. Flying is obviously out, so it'll have to be the train." Noland looked around the room. Everyone was watching him, and nodding. They looked at him like his word was law. Their lives were in his hands, as well as Achaia's.

"You locked your door, right?" he said in a low voice to Yellaina.

"Yes, she's safe. No one saw us come in, save for the concierge." She smiled at him reassuringly.

"As for tomorrow," Noland went on, "the train for Moscow doesn't usually leave until later in the evening. So in the morning, we need to take care of some necessities."

"We got directions to the nearest laundromat," Amelia said. "It's not far from here."

"We can wash what we've got, that isn't basically destroyed from the last couple of weeks, but we'll need to buy warmer clothes for Russia. Those layers are too thin," he said looking around at what each of them was wearing. Most of their clothes were worn thin, and had holes in them.

"Yellaina and Amelia, you'll go and get the winter clothes. Emile and Olivier, you'll go get the train tickets and do a preliminary sweep of the station. See if anything looks suspicious. Achaia and I will go wash what is salvageable. We'll meet at Le Saint Régis for lunch, then we'll refresh our weapons before going to the station." Noland looked to Emile. "I'd say get a four-berth share for us, and a two-berth share for you and Amelia. I know you two probably need a break from company." Amelia smiled with a sigh, and Emile nodded in appreciation.

"Alright, for now, get some showers and some rest. Tomorrow, you can sleep in a little. The train that runs to Moscow won't leave until almost seven tomorrow night. We've got time."

Yellaina clapped her hands with excitement, Amelia mumbled something sarcastic under her breath, and Olivier and Emile smiled with relief. As the girls left for their own room, Olivier called first shower, and Noland collapsed onto the bed across from Emile's.

"You looked like you had something else on your mind when you first walked in," Emile said, turning to face him completely.

Noland shook away his thoughts about the next day. He knew Emile was talking about Noland's bafflement when he had come back from Achaia's room. "You know that empathy that comes and goes when you *know*?" he asked staring up at the ceiling.

Emile nodded. "That's how we found you in the woods when that hunter was possessed. Achaia knew you were in danger."

"But if she doesn't *know*—" Noland cocked his head to the side. "Why is she getting the side effects if she *doesn't* know? Unless-" Noland's eyes widened, and he sat up, looking at Emile. "*Does she know?*"

"No she doesn't." Emile smiled as Noland's face relaxed back to angst. "I don't know, I mean, her mom was human. She has human blood. Maybe she just writes it off as conflicting emotions." Emile pulled off his shoes, and laid down on his side, propping his head up on his arm. "Maybe she gets more of a say in it than you do." Emile wondered aloud.

"Olivier told Yellaina before she knew. Do you think I should tell Achaia?" Noland asked. He didn't know what he wanted Emile to say. He was so torn himself, he just wanted someone else to decide. He wanted to be with her, at least to an extent. The emotions hadn't really come in to full play yet. But, he didn't want to talk to her about it either. That would be awkward. Nephilim weren't supposed to have to talk about their feelings. Noland took off his shoes too, and leaned back against the headboard of his bed.

"I don't know man, it's up to you." Emile was having one of his 'Figure it out on your own, my young padawan,' moments, which always annoyed Noland.

"If God wanted her to know, she'd know—," Noland decided. "I'm just gunna leave it for now, I think." Noland pulled at the hem of his shirt, pulling it off over his head. He tossed the shirt to the floor, and slid down, laying on his back staring at the ceiling again.

Emile slid under his covers, and was silent. Noland thought about Achaia, she had almost opened up to him, but Noland sucked at talking to people about worries or anxiety. He was a plow-through-it sort of person with himself, and felt like most people probably took that as cold and heartless.

"Am I hard to talk to?" Noland asked.

"What?" Emile asked.

"Do I suck with people?" Noland turned his head to the side, Emile's face was thoughtful. It helped having a best friend that knew your every emotion and could interpret your words accordingly. Noland wondered if he took that for granted, and if everyone else only saw half of what he was trying to convey.

"I don't think you're the warm and fuzzy kind of person that people can easily chat with, no," Emile said finally. "But I think that the people who know you, know what to expect from you."

"And what is that?" Noland huffed, disappointed.

"Steady."

"What?" Noland gave Emile a squinted quizzical look.

"You're steady. You're not an emotional rollercoaster, and you don't fly off the handle. You're just calm, and when necessary determined. It's reassuring in times of distress to have someone like you around," Emile assured him. "Even if you aren't super compassionate."

"And what about people who don't know me?" Noland asked, wondering about Achaia. They were still getting to that point.

"It could go two ways." Emile nodded. "You're probably really intimidating," Emile listed.

Noland huffed, that wasn't good. "Or what?"

"Or they probably think you're a douche." Emile smirked.

Noland sighed. "Thanks."

"I'm here for you brother."

\*\*\*

Achaia was already asleep when Yellaina and Amelia came quietly back into the room. "She looks so young," Amelia said, leaning over Achaia, whose breathing was soft and steady.

"Oh hush." Yellaina whispered ushering Amelia away from her, so she wouldn't wake her. Yellaina looked down. Achaia was so small. She was relatively short and petite. If you didn't look at her face, you might think she was a child under the covers. But her face was mature. Her jaw line was tight and sharp. Her nose was thin and rounded. And her eyebrows were rather severe looking for her to be so young. "I think she looks like a little warrior," Yellaina smiled.

"Yeah, like one of those little Army men toys," Amelia smirked.

"You can joke. You're trained!" Yellaina whispered grabbing her shower bag. "She's already capable of more than I could ever dream of."

Amelia smiled sadly. "Your gifts just lay elsewhere."

"I know," Yellaina said with a weak smile. "But I think she's fierce. That's why God painted her hair red." Yellaina stared down at the red curls crowding Achaia's face. "That's a warning. This one isn't to be tampered with. Just you watch."

"Yeah, okay," Amelia laughed, "Go take your shower."

# 12

# Eye of the Beholder

"It takes a great deal of courage
to see the world in all its tainted glory,
and still to love it."

-Oscar Wilde

Achaia's eyes shot open. A crippling crick in her neck hindered her from sitting up too fast. She had dreamt that she was late for school. After glancing around the hotel room, she remembered that school was no longer a top priority.

She slumped back into her bed and attempted to slow her heart back down. The sun came through the window, warming her skin. She stood slowly, a little dizzy, and pulled back the blinds. The street below looked pretty average, significantly less impressive than it had the night before. It was a busy city street, crowded with vendors and pedestrians, but the night before it had seemed magical.

She ran her fingers through her hair. As she did, she tugged her head down and pulled out a chunk of curls.

"Owe." She looked at the hair in her hands, she must have slept pretty restlessly. She walked over to the desk where she left her brush, and sat in the chair. She watched herself in the mirror as she combed.

She barely recognized herself. A new sternness lined her face. She reminded herself of her father. Her freckles no longer made her look childish, but they accentuated the angels of her jaw and cheek bones, along with all her cuts and scrapes. Her eyes were piercing in her reflection. Her skin seemed to glow, which seemed strange with all the cold.

She hadn't thought about it, but she hadn't seen herself in weeks. She put her brush down on the desk again and looked at her hands. Her fingers were long and skinny like a pianist, and undeniably strong. She stood and lifted the hem of her shirt; she had abs! Her arms had toned as well...

She felt like she was having a Tobey Maguire-Spider-Man moment. All the training with Emile had transformed her. Achaia looked down at herself. *This is who you are now.*

She glanced at the clock, and noticed with surprise that it was after nine, and Noland hadn't come to wake them up.

Achaia quietly unzipped her bag and grabbed her toothbrush, and headed into the bathroom. After brushing her teeth, Achaia put on a pair of jeans and a plain fitted gray v-neck t-shirt. She scrunched her hair in her hands with some water, accentuating her curls. Looking in the mirror again she knew who she looked like-- her mother. For the first time in her life she truly wished she had her to talk to. She wished she had a mother to tell her this change was okay.

Someone knocked lightly at the door. Achaia crossed the

room and answered it to see Noland standing in the hall.

"Are the others awake?" He asked quietly.

"Not yet." Achaia looked back over her shoulder at the mounds under the blankets, breathing steadily.

"Want to grab breakfast?" He asked in an almost whisper, so as not to wake the others.

"Yeah," Achaia said grabbing a room key off the desk, and closing the door silently behind her.

The two walked on tip toe down the hall, as if they were still trying not to wake anyone up. Either that, or they both felt like they had to walk on egg shells with each other. "I was surprised you let us sleep in." Achaia said finally as they reached the staircase.

"I thought everyone could use it, and the train doesn't leave until almost seven tonight," he said gesturing for her to go ahead of him down the stairs.

"So we're taking the train?" Achaia asked.

"Yeah. We are going to split up and run some errands first, and then we'll meet up for lunch before heading to the station."

"How long of a train ride is it to Moscow from here?" Achaia asked as they reached the lobby. Noland led the way to a room off of the main check-in area, where a table had been laid out with coffee and pastries.

"We should get there mid-morning on Sunday."

"Sunday? It's Friday." Achaia said shocked. "I thought everything in Europe was close."

"Trains make stops, Achaia," Noland said with the tone of it having been the most obvious thing in the world.

"I know they make stops. But if we flew we'd be there in a few hours," Achaia said with a twinge of attitude which dissipated when she saw a shadow pass over Noland's expression. "What?"

"We can't take a plane," he said shaking his head.

"Because of what happened in the Alps?"

Noland nodded. "Turns out that was God saving us from something worse." Noland grabbed a plate and a croissant.

"Worse?" Achaia asked feeling her stomach flip.

He lowered his voice as he poured himself a cup of coffee. "The Paris airport was attacked by terrorists. The place is rubble. The train is pretty much the only way we can go."

"What?" Achaia asked shocked. The hand holding her plate dropped to the table with a loud clank. She startled at her own noise. "Sorry," she said looking at Noland, who had flinched at the sound, as well. "Terrorists?"

"They bombed it, several bombs went off simultaneously."

"But how? What about airport security?"

"Chances are, Luc had several people on the inside, demons," Noland shrugged. "The humans never saw it coming. With all the security since terrorism has been on the rise, people expect such public places to be safe. I'm hoping that after this, that might actually be true." Noland chose a table for them and sat down. "Emile talked to his parents last night. They said the Nephilim in the East have lost more charges than ever, and that Europe is becoming just as bad. They haven't heard anything from the Institutions in the Americas in a week. It's just static."

"What do they think is going on?" Achaia asked, pinching her croissant into pieces, without actually eating any of it.

"The council? I haven't heard anything official. I'll have to wait and talk to the head of the Moscow safe house to be sure." Noland took a sip of his coffee which was steaming hot. He didn't flinch.

"Are you worried?" Achaia asked.

Noland swallowed and shook his head. "The world has to

end eventually, Kaya."

Achaia swallowed hard, with no appetite left.

*** 

Shael strode into the arena with all of the arrogance of a baboon in pants. Most of the demons ignored him, as they carried on their speculations about who would win which matches. Shael however, marched straight up to the stand that Luc's seat was in, and through the crowd seated there, until he stood a few rows below Luc.

Luc looked down at him with poorly disguised curiosity. "So," Shael started, getting the attention of all of the demons seated between him and Luc. They all stopped talking, hissing, or whatever some of them were doing and stared. "What are the rules here exactly?" Shael asked. "Can I challenge anyone for rank?"

"Well, I would suggest challenging someone higher than you, but yes." Luc smiled, his eyes alight with intrigue. Shael knew he had Luc's attention. He also knew he needed to make this fun for him.

Shael pointed instantly at the nearest demon to his right, catching it off guard. "You." The demon looked startled. "Are you higher ranked than me?"

The demon, who was rather bulbous and unintimidating, looked at Luc, as if for help, then back to Shael before nodding. Shael smiled a fierce and crazy smile. "I challenge you." He jabbed his finger at the demon as if already triumphant.

The demon looked taken aback. He sat in his seat, and looked at the demons around him as if for intervention.

"Like, now." Shael said, to clarify, nodding toward the cage down on the floor.

The demon gulped, and again looked up to Luc, a question in his eyes, as if asking if Shael were serious.

"I'm confused," Shael said, though he clearly wasn't. "What's wrong with it?" He looked up at Luc with a look of mock befuddlement. "Is it scared?" Luc smiled and shrugged, staring at the demon. Shael lit up with facetiousness. "Are you scared?" He asked looking back over to the demon.

If the demon had eyebrows, they would have been raised on its flat gray wombat-like face. Its massive eyes were wide like terrified orbs.

Shael made a show of rolling his eyes, and caught a glimpse of Luc smiling. "You are a demon." Shael pointed out bluntly. "Eternally bound to Hell," he added. "Damned," he stated as if to put an exclamation mark on his point. "What in the hell do you have to lose?" Shael asked, as if it were the most ridiculous thing in the world.

The demon looked around at all of his fellow demons surrounding him and shrugged meekly. A demon somewhere in the back of the crowd called out "Rank!"

The wombat demon looked relieved that someone had generated a response, and nodded his agreement enthusiastically.

"Rank?" Shael asked exasperated. "Is that all you care about?" He asked looking around at the crowd of demonic faces.

They all looked at each other, shrugged, and nodded.

Shael squinted at them all in exaggerated disbelief. "Wow. This really is Hell isn't it?" Shael looked nonchalantly at Luc, and shrugged. "I am an island, in a sea of idiots," he sighed dramatically. "So are you done stalling?" he looked back to his opponent.

The wombat demon frowned. Shael didn't know that the corners of a mouth could go so far down without taking the rest of the mouth with it. He allowed himself to laugh.

Luc laughed, too. "Go on then!" he ordered.

Shael led the way down to the cage, and opened the door for the wombat demon.

"What's your name?" Shael asked, as the door was closed and locked behind them. "I feel like I probably should have asked that sooner." He said flippantly.

"Gaki," the demon answered, swallowing hard.

"Oh wow. That's an intimidating name." Shael shuddered.

"Really?" The demon asked.

"No." Shael winced and shook his head. "Actually, that's a really lame name. It's like, it's part of your punishment or something." Shael heard Luc laugh at his jab, and smiled. Shael went to a corner of the cage and warmed up with a few butterfly kicks.

When he looked back over to Gaki, the demon made a choking sound, wet himself, and promptly passed out. Shael was genuinely surprised and looked around in confusion. "Does that count?" He called to Luc.

Luc looked disappointed, and a little amused. He cocked an eyebrow and shrugged in a way that said 'I guess?'

"How far up did I just move?" Shael beamed.

Lucifer laughed.

\*\*\*

The rest of the group slowly trickled down to breakfast, at which point Achaia was completely filled in on the plan for the day. She and the guys told Amelia and Yellaina their sizes, and Achaia gave Yellaina a stern look as she told her specifically not to buy her anything pink. Amelia assured her, they would only buy her sweaters with unicorns on them, and the two girls set off.

Achaia had asked why Emile and Olivier didn't just purchase the train tickets online, or on an app, and Noland had explained to her that demons could trace the transaction too easily. They frequently possessed computer hackers, just to keep an eye on things. Which, Achaia silently thought, explained why her father had always gotten cash out of ATMs, instead of using a card.

Emile and Olivier left the hotel with Achaia and Noland, after they collected the bags from their rooms. They had tossed everything that was too worn to keep. What was left, Achaia and Noland packed into their own bags to take to the laundromat.

Achaia now sat staring at a dryer, watching the clothes spin in circles. A white sock had grabbed her focus, and her eyes followed it around and around amongst all the dark jeans, and t-shirts.

"What are you thinking about?" Noland asked, as he sat down next to her, after going to get more coins.

"Strangely, nothing. Except that I wear a lot of grey." Achaia smiled, cocking an eyebrow at the dryer contents. "It was actually kind of nice."

Noland huffed as he smiled. "You know, as a kid, I always wanted to get in the dryer."

Achaia looked up at him cocking her eyebrow again.

"My dad would never turn it on-- said I was bound to be concussed." He smiled, looking down at his hands, which lay in his lap, fingers twiddling. "It just looked like it would be so much fun. I was drawn to the heat too. I was always curling up in the laundry that my mom had gotten out to fold."

"I love that too." Achaia smiled. "There's nothing like warm sheets."

Noland smiled, still looking at his hands. "I always loved the jeans, the metal buttons were always so much hotter."

Achaia laughed as she nodded.

"She always used to say I made them warmer," he reminisced. "That I made everything warmer," he said quietly.

Achaia sat in silence, not wanting to interrupt whatever pleasant memories he was thinking of. "What was she like?" she asked after a few minutes.

Noland looked up at the dryer again. She could see the wheels of his mind spinning, as if his eyes were mirrors staring at the dryer. "Warm." He said plainly.

Achaia nodded. She had been hoping for a bit more, but she wasn't going to push it.

"I mean," Noland went on, to her surprise. "I remember she smelled like cinnamon. She loved that candy, like red hots. When she walked into a room, it was like Christmas."

"Because she smelled like cinnamon?" Achaia asked.

"Because everywhere she went, she brought joy. She had a gift for cheering people up, encouragement. She just made people happy."

"Was that her spiritual gift?" Achaia asked.

"Nah, that was fire, like me." Noland said, "but, the rest of it was God-given too." He smiled as the timer on the dryer went off. Noland checked the clothes, and added some more change to the machine, resetting the cycle.

"Do you remember anything about your mom?" Noland asked, sitting back down next to her.

Achaia thought for a moment. "I don't know." She had an image in her head. She was in a kitchen sink, and there was sun coming in through a window behind her. Her mother stood over her, bathing her. She was beautiful. A chunk of red curls, dangled down in her face; Achaia grabbed it and pulled. "I think I might, but I'm not even sure if it's real. Or if I made the memory up." She looked away from him. "You know, so I'd have something to hold on to." Achaia uncrossed her legs, and tapped the toes of her shoes under her chair.

"Yeah," Noland said, fiddling with his fingers again. "I don't even know if the memories I have are accurate. Sometimes, I think I may have romanticized them, so they are worth keeping. Like I created the company I wanted, so I wouldn't be alone."

Achaia looked up at him, and he looked back at her. "I can't imagine," she whispered.

Noland cocked a questioning eyebrow.

"I mean. I can't remember what it was like to have a mom. And I don't remember losing her. I've just never had her. And my dad—" Achaia broke off.

"He isn't gone," Noland finished. "Achaia, I don't want you to imagine it. But I really don't want you to experience it."

Achaia could feel the familiar soreness growing in the back of her throat, like she was trying really hard to swallow a boulder. "They hate him. They aren't going to help me, are they?" Achaia asked, her voice cracking and weak.

"I don't want to promise you something, if I can't keep it," Noland said sadly.

Achaia felt the hot, rebellious tears run silently down her cheeks.

"I'm not going to lie to you. It doesn't sound good. The silence in the Americas, the increase in the loss of Charges—" Noland swallowed hard, looking down at her. "It all started, when your dad disappeared."

"It's not him doing all of this!" Achaia said urgently, trying to keep her voice low. "He couldn't."

"Achaia, I don't think that he is. I think he was taken. But the council seems to think he went willingly, and—"

"And what?" Achaia asked, feeling a black hole opening up in her chest, threatening to swallow any ounce of hope she had left.

"These Nephilim have seen your father annihilate nations, entire armies. They wouldn't question whether or not he is capable of it. They know he is."

"So that's it then? I should just write him off?" Achaia asked on the edge of outrage.

"No. Not at all. I think we just have to look elsewhere for help," Noland said. He put a hand over hers on her lap.

They sat in silence for a minute as Achaia tried to steady her breathing. "How do you live after that? How do you do it all alone?" She asked.

"I'm not alone," Noland said, sounding a little choked. He put his arm tightly around her shoulders. "And I swear to you, you never will be, either."

***

After paying a small fortune to get the laundry done at the laverie, they took a long cab ride to the café to meet the others for lunch. The corner restaurant looked as French as Achaia could have hoped. It had checker-board tile floors, white subway tile covered walls, and long skinny booth seats with tiny café tables and chairs. She wished it was warm enough to eat out on the sidewalk, but being that it was the end of January, it was far too frigid.

The Saint-Regis, Achaia decided was worth its name. She thought there was something holy about it, and she would be happy to sing the cooks' praises. She decided not to mention that to the others.

They ate mostly in silence, since the food was so good. Achaia ordered the croque monsieur because Emile said she had to, and Olivier said she couldn't leave France without trying it. She wasn't disappointed. As far as sandwiches went, it was pretty much heaven in her mouth.

Noland had ordered the croque madame, and said it was the main reason he wanted to meet there for lunch. Apparently, he had fallen in love with the place the last time he had come with the Du-Bois siblings to visit their parents.

"This is one of mom and dad's favorite places. They are regulars here, when they're home," Emile said. He finished off his escargot, which Achaia thought looked especially disgusting since they were seasoned with something that made them green. Olivier ordered a hamburger and Achaia had made fun of him for it, since he was French, and in France, and that was the most American looking thing on the menu. Yellaina ate some sort of salad, and Amelia chose something that looked way too sophisticated for Achaia to guess at from the opposite end of the table.

Once they were done with lunch, they sat divvying up the clothes, cleaned and new, and packed their own bags. Achaia was pleased that not a single sweater had a unicorn on it. "She tried to buy you purple since you said no to pink," Amelia said, as they ordered crepes for desert, "But I thought it might have been too close. You usually wear grey, so I told her to stick to neutrals."

"But I did weasel this one in!" Yellaina said pulling out an emerald green sweater from a bag and yanking the tags off. "I thought it would look lovely with your hair!" She smiled wide as she passed it over Olivier to Achaia.

It was perhaps the softest sweater she had ever felt, though a little more colorful than she would have usually bought for herself. "Thank you," she said, folding it neatly before putting it in her bag.

"And we got layers," Yellaina said handing her a handful of white tank tops, and a few pairs of leggings that were lined with fleece.

"Goodness," Achaia said, struggling to fit anything more into her bag. "Are we never going home?" she joked.

Everyone went a little quiet.

Achaia looked up and around at all of their faces. "We are going home after all this, right?"

Silence.

"Guys?"

"It just all depends, doesn't it?" Yellaina said awkwardly.

"If we find your dad, and we get him back, then yeah. If you're in danger, then your best chance is to stay at the safe house," Emile said as comfortingly as he could.

"But there's a chance, if it comes down to it, and you need to join the Nephilim ranks on your own," Noland put tactfully, "you'll be assigned an institute where you'll go train."

"It just may not necessarily be in New York," Amelia put bluntly. "Nephilim try to break any excessive ties to family or home, and send you off. Hence, none of us are from America, and we are all stationed in New York."

"Who decides where I go? Do I have a say?" Achaia asked, trying to wrap her mind around all of this new information.

"The council will take your vote into account. But, if it isn't what they think is best, it won't count for much." Amelia said shrugging. "They are protectors by nature, ruthless, and efficient. Not many Nephilim are known for their kindness and compassion," she added, with a smile at her twin.

"Right, then…" Achaia nodded, thinking that for now, acceptance was better than dwelling on the uncertainty of what was to come.

The table fell silent again, until Yellaina gently broke it. "We got you this, too," She said handing over a thick wool peacoat, "and I made sure it was grey." She smiled pathetically. Achaia couldn't not smile at her face.

The train station was crowded, but it was eerily quiet, as the café had also been. Achaia could feel the city mourning the terrorist attacks they had suffered. The day itself seemed to be in mourning as the sky was cloaked in a thick layer of cloud cover.

Night fell early and cold, making Achaia dread the even colder temperatures they were heading to in Russia.

Achaia studied the crowds around her. Mothers impatiently shoved their progeny along the platforms toward the exit. Businessmen pushed through crowds, inadvertently knocking others aside on their way home from meetings that had gone poorly. Tourists gawked at maps as they looked around confused, asking in broken French for directions. Achaia took it all in as if it were happening in slow motion. There was so much hustle and bustle, but what she really saw was life.

All these people had lives, families, hopes, aspirations... some were excited, others stressed, and others bored out of their minds with the daily grind of it all. The scene struck her as beautiful and sad at the same time. She used to be one of them, a normal human being. Now, she wasn't sure how human she really was at all.

"It's going to leave with or without us," Noland said, turning around to look at her.

Achaia woke from her reverie and followed after him, not even getting annoyed with his impatience. She was getting used to it now. She followed the others onto a train car and down the narrow hall to find their cabins. Achaia, Noland, Yellaina, and Olivier were in a four bed share, and Emile and Amelia were in a two bed share.

Achaia knew this whole misadventure had been particularly hard on Amelia since the plane accident. She was still limping a little, and would wince if she moved wrong at times. And Achaia couldn't help but feel a little responsible for Emile's fatigue. He looked pale, and had bags under his eyes. She could tell he was wiped. This had been a stressful trip for all of them, but he had had to suffer under the weight of everyone's distress. She was glad they would have a nice long train ride, away from everything and everyone, and a chance to just rest.

***

Noland was on edge. His senses were running on the caffeine from the espresso he had had at the restaurant. He had insisted on getting to the station early to scope it out, and make sure that he didn't spot anyone suspicious scoping out the train. When the train arrived, he and Emile had walked the length of it, to see if Emile could feel anything hostile or out of place. Only when Emile had confirmed that everything seemed peaceful, aside from normal trav-eler's anxieties, did Noland finally take a seat.

They waited patiently until they were called to board. Noland led the way to their compartments, and checked them before allowing Achaia inside. He took the seat closest to the door, in case anyone attempted to come in. He knew he was acting paranoid, but the volume of people on and around the train was setting his teeth on edge.

"Hey man, we've got this." Olivier slapped him on the shoulder and smiled, reassuring him, before taking the seat opposite. The girls sat by the window, talking to each other.

"Yeah," Noland said, nodding. "I don't like this though."

Olivier cocked his head questioningly.

"It seems strange, doesn't it?" Noland said softly, hoping not to arouse Achaia's attention. He leaned forward, and Olivier did the same meeting him in the middle. "As soon as we move Achaia from the Vatican, all the static with the Americas, and the Charges being picked off left and right, terrorist attacks…"

"You think it's Shael?" Olivier whispered.

"No, I don't," Noland said, shaking his head. "It didn't start until after Achaia met with the council, and they ordered that we move her all the way from Rome to Moscow—." Noland shook his head, trying to make sense of it all. "Why not a closer safe house? Why Moscow?"

Olivier looked at Noland as if that was a good point, but one that utterly puzzled him as well.

Noland looked out of the window, past Achaia as the train began to rattle and shake as it set off.

A voice came on over the intercom making the usual, start of journey, announcements. Emile and Amelia were in a different car. Noland knew Emile needed the break and rest, but he was used to having Emile's senses around. Not having Emile to tell him something was off or about to happen, put Noland in a fixed state of hyper tension.

The girls were chatting lightly about Russia, and Yellaina was telling Achaia all about what Russia was like. Noland could tell, without Emile's senses, that she was excited to be going home.

Noland refocused on Achaia's face. She looked tired. Her eyes were heavy, a tiny bit bloodshot from crying, and she still had some bruises from the plane crash that hadn't completely healed. She never complained about any pain, though. She powered on. Noland thought about what it might be like from her perspective. He couldn't imagine never knowing about God, and Luc. About angels and demons, and the spiritual wars. He couldn't comprehend what it must have been like to be suddenly thrust into this world.

He knew he hadn't been the most compassionate or considerate. He hadn't been thinking about her feelings, but about her safety. He knew he might not be great at it, but he decided within himself to try to be a little more forgiving. She was so strong, and had been adapting so well, he forgot how hard it must be, to take all of this in.

"What?" Achaia asked, bringing his attention back to their cabin in the train where Olivier, Yellaina, and Achaia were all staring at him.

"What do you mean, 'what'?" he asked coolly, trying not to look embarrassed.

"You were staring at me like a creeper," Achaia said, smiling. Yellaina laughed.

"Dude, you were totally zoned out," Olivier joined in. "It's about time for dinner. We should probably go to the dining car."

"Right, yeah." Noland stood up, and checked both ways from their door before moving out into the narrow hall.

***

Emile and Amelia joined the others in the dining car for dinner. Emile sat with Noland at a tiny table for two on one side of the train, while the others sat together at a table for four, farther up the line.

"Okay, I know what this is going to sound like," Noland started, leaning forward with his forearms on the table. Emile could feel his conflict, confusion, urgency, and suspense. "Just hear me out, okay."

"Well I'm intrigued," Emile said, leaning forward, too, as Noland spoke more quietly.

"Okay. Before I start, I want you to tell me exactly what you felt in the council. Before Achaia walked into the room, and after."

Emile raised his eyebrows in surprise. That had not been what he had thought Noland was about to say, or request. "Okay." Emile thought back. The room had been dark, cold, and crowded. There was a lot going on. They had just announced that Shael had gone missing, but there was a lack of surprise for such an announcement. Emile had attributed this to the Nephilim believing that he had left voluntarily. There was anger in the room, and confusion, and relief. Emile had assumed there had been a great deal of Nephilim who had wanted Shael out of the picture entirely; they considered him a wildcard.

Then they had announced that his daughter had come to them, and that they were going to find out what she knew.

"Before Achaia came in, there was, I think, a normal and pretty expected reaction to the news of Shael's disappearance. Ya know, being that most of them hated the guy, or at the very least, didn't trust him. When Achaia came in, there was a sort of excited anxiety. I think people were curious about her. But they were also wary of her."

"Did anything or anyone stand out of all of that? Mainly," Noland looked over his shoulder and whispered, "Brother Joash. What was Joash feeling?"

Emile sat back, stunned. "Noland, what are you getting at?"

"The way he went at Achaia, it wasn't just for sport. He hates Shael, everyone knows that. But it would be unwise to assume the daughter is just like the father without ever even speaking to her. And yet, he immediately tried to discredit her in front of the council."

"I don't understand." Emile said, confused. "Noland, Joash has been a leader of the Nephilim for centuries—"

"I know." Noland said. "But he isn't God, Emile. He is fallible, biased, and in this instance, wrong. Achaia isn't Shael."

"What are you getting at though?" Emile asked, thoroughly confused.

"I think Joash knew Shael was gone. I think he was happy about it. I think he already knew more about Achaia than the rest of us, and he is hiding something. I think moving Achaia all the way to Moscow is Joash's way of hiding it." Noland's eyebrows were knit so tightly together Emile could hardly see his eyes beneath them. His face was dark with confused concentration.

"But Achaia doesn't know anything," Emile said, dumbstruck for any other reply.

"I know," Noland said, frustrated. "None of it makes sense." He took a deep breath as the wait staff put their dinner plates in front of them. Once they left, Noland spoke again, quietly. "Why Moscow? Why not a closer safe house? When we tried to get Achaia there by plane, God delayed us, and prevented us from being blown up. As soon as Shael goes missing, and Achaia goes off the map with our plane crash, these terrorist attacks start happening, and there's never been this many Charge casualties..." Noland looked down at his plate. "It all has to be linked."

"Hate." Emile said, looking straight at Noland.

Noland looked up at him, and cocked his head to the side.

"Joash. When Achaia walked into the room, he felt an overwhelming sense of hate."

# All Aboard

"Hell is empty
All the devils are here."
William Shakespeare, The Tempest

When they went back to the cabin after dinner, they found the seats turned into bunk beds, with the linens made up for the night. Achaia lingered outside the room after everyone else went in. She let the door close behind Olivier, and slipped her phone out of her pocket. She tried to call Naphtali using skype, but got no answer.

Noland cracked the door open to check on her, and she held up her index finger to ask for one more minute. He nodded and shut the door, back.

"Hey, it's me," she said to Naphtali's voicemail. "I was just wondering if you've found anything yet? Where you were? I'm on a train to Moscow now, with Noland and the others. It's been a crazy few weeks. Call me back." She hung up the phone, disappointment

274

flooding her, more than she anticipated.

She decided to text him. Maybe he couldn't talk, but he could text...

HEY. WRU?

BEEN TRYING TO CALL...

CALL ME!!!

...

Achaia watched the little dots that said Naphtali was typing, for three minutes before they stopped, and nothing came through.

\*\*\*

Naphtali pushed on the pearly bars in front of him, opening the gates, and pocketed his phone. The best part of Heaven was no cell service. There was no creak of wear, or rust; a silent smooth hinge admitted him in. He closed the gate behind him, feeling like a rebel. Somehow, looking for help for Shael outside of Heaven hadn't felt treacherous, but this... Naphtali prayed for forgiveness if what he was doing was wrong, but he also knew he couldn't stand by and do nothing; not as long as Achaia needed a father.

Red light reflected off of the golden bricks of the empty streets and the cathedral-like buildings lining them. The angels in Heaven usually stayed very busy, there was typically a lot of hustle and bustle. Naphtali was caught off guard by the city's silence.

The remaining Nephilim would be close to God, doing whatever important and high ranking tasks He saw fit. The Seraphim would be keeping an eye on the fallen Nephilim and their charges. With all the chaos below, Naphtali doubted if there was a single Seraphim left in Heaven, besides himself. Likewise, the Cherubim were probably busy keeping records of what all was happening below, and healing the wounded.

He imagined the lower two choirs were also deployed in response to all the terror on earth. Naphtali knew this was only the beginning, and yet it seemed like Heaven was already emptied, pouring out aid to the earth. He just prayed she was still here. Naphtali walked quickly and silently down the narrow golden streets, between buildings, clinging to the walls, in case someone were to appear and he needed to hide. When he reached her door, he knocked and prayed for an answer.

The door cracked open, and Naphtali slipped inside and shut the door behind him. Lailah stood before him looking only a little surprised. She was as beautiful as ever, though Naphtali hadn't seen her in thousands of years. Her thick brown hair curled down to her waist, strung through with gold. Her fair clear skin was touched with a natural blush of pink on her cheeks. Her green eyes held flecks of gold and were fixed curiously on Naphtali.

"Naph?" She smiled and lunged forward to hug him. They stood in a small entry hall. Lailah wore a long white gown with a belt of woven gold thread tied around her narrow waist. Her feet were fitted with sandals made of the same golden thread, laced up her calves.

"Lailah," Naphtali hugged her back and kissed the top of her head. "How do I find you?"

"As well as can be expected in such times." Lailah pulled away.

"What are you doing home? The streets are empty." Naphtali held her out at arm's reach, and took in the full sight of her. She really was a sight for sore eyes, he only hoped she was willing to help him.

"He knew you would come. I was ordered to be here when you came." Lailah said coolly, a sad smile played at her pomegranate lips. "But I know not why you come to me."

"Shael needs help." Naphtali said bluntly. He felt a twinge in his own heart as she flinched at the sound of Shael's name. She frowned and looked down. "I wouldn't ask you if I hadn't already exhausted every angel outside of Heaven. No one will help me." Naphtali heard the desperation in his own voice.

"Shael is prideful." Lailah said sadly, her green eyes flashed with more gold. "He cannot think beyond himself, and he never learns from his many mistakes, no matter who he hurts in the making of them." She frowned. Naphtali knew it hurt her to speak of him, especially to speak poorly of him, since she still did even that with love. "He sacrificed myself, Anna…"

Naphtali nodded that he understood. "But Achaia needs her father. If not for Shael, do this for his daughter." Naphtali pleaded.

Lailah looked heartbroken and torn. "I have spoken to Anna. Only once… It is painful to look at her."

Naphtali couldn't imagine how Lailah felt. She had been betrayed, and watched as her soul mate had replaced her, and with a human.

"I will not punish them for Shael's sins." Her voice was frustrated, yet resolved. "Lucifer," she spat the name, as if the sound of it were vile to her, "has taken him into the fourth circle."

"Thank you!" Naphtali took both of her hands into his, and kissed them. "Your heart is as beautiful as it has always been, and you have changed fate with your kindness."

"I only hope it is for the better," she said sadly. As Naphtali went to release her hands, she grabbed at his desperately. "This is a suicide mission for you." Her eyes pleaded with him. "Even I do not know what happens to angels who perish. Nathaniel…" Golden tears formed in her eyes, and Naphtali knew she still mourned the loss of her brother Nathaniel and his wife.

"I will not perish. I am going to fast and pray. I will be prepared. If I may go with your blessing?" Naphtali noticed how small her hands were in his.

Lailah kissed her thumb, and pressed it gently to Naphtali's forehead. "Be blessed, and go." She smiled sadly as Naphtali turned and left her, with what felt like small wings beating in his stomach.

***

"It can't be time for bed yet," Olivier said sitting on the left bottom bunk, checking his phone for the time. Yellaina sat back down next to him, where she'd been before, by the window. She dug in her bag for her toothbrush and folded up the table between the seats, to reveal a sink. Across from her, next to Noland, Achaia was also digging in her bag for the same purpose.

"Feels weird to be sitting here brushing my teeth at a sink." Achaia said, as she put the paste on her toothbrush.

"You've not done much train traveling then?" Yellaina asked.

"No, my dad always preferred planes." Achaia answered before putting her toothbrush in her mouth. That made sense to Yellaina. From what she'd heard, Shael seemed quick and efficient. Trains took too long, and had too many changeovers of passengers. They were more risky.

"I bet he misses flying," Olivier said sympathetically. Achaia looked over at him and shrugged. "I don't know what I'd do without my wings," Olivier said, now sounding really distressed about it.

"Well then," Yellaina said, after spitting into the sink, "don't sell the angelic half of your soul."

Achaia finished brushing her teeth and put her toothbrush away. "Switch me seats?" Noland asked, sliding closer next to her. Achaia stood, and Noland slipped behind her and took her seat next to the window. Achaia sat in the middle of the bed to avoid sitting on his pillow. Yellaina smiled as she watched them. She wondered if they even noticed how in sync their smallest movements were, when they just stopped overthinking them.

"I wish I could talk to him about it," Achaia said softly.

Yellaina swallowed hard, and regretted her tactlessness. She watched Noland's face drop as well, and knew the feeling resonated with him. Yellaina didn't get along with her father, but at least talking to him was always an option. One she knew she took for granted.

"I just... it'd be nice to know what he had been thinking." Achaia was looking at the floor.

"You can ask him," Olivier said confidently. "When we find him, you can ask." Olivier seemed so sure they would find him. Yellaina wasn't so positive. She had seen the faces of the Nephilim council members. She was sure they weren't going to back a search party. In this matter, they were on their own.

Yellaina looked back over at Noland who was finishing up brushing his teeth. Their eyes met for only a second, but she could tell he was thinking along the same lines.

Achaia was staring at the floor, when she spoke, "What's your God like?"

Yellaina couldn't hide her surprise. Achaia was looking back up, and around at each of them.

"I've seen your governing system, and I have to say, I don't like them." Achaia shook her head. "But I don't really know anything about your God. I've heard of a guy named Jesus, who was what? Like a prophet or something?" Achaia was looking a little confused.

Yellaina couldn't help feeling like this conversation was biting off more than one could chew, for bedtime conversation. "Well, Jesus is God." She said simply.

"But I thought Jesus was a dude?" Achaia said confused. "Or

was that Peter?"

"Well they were both dudes." Olivier smiled. "See, God really loves humans. Like, a lot. He knew things were going to get all screwed up when He gave them free will, so He came up with this plan when He made them: He would go down and be with them, to teach them and save them," Olivier explained.

"God isn't limited like us," Noland added. "He is God the creator, and He is also Jesus, the man, who is the Son of God. Then He is also the Holy Spirit, who is ever-present. Three in one. All of them are God, and God is each of the three separate beings."

Achaia was staring at him as if he'd lost her somewhere around the word "and".

"Yeah it's a bit confusing when you're used to mortal stuff. Trust me, the spiritual world is complicated. It's better if you just accept it. It doesn't make sense to human science. But, you'll see. It makes sense when you see Them. I mean, Him?" Olivier looked puzzled, then smiled. "He's awesome."

"Anyway," Noland picked back up. "It made a lot of angels angry. Why would God want to be like the humans? Why would He become one of them, and put so much into saving something that had been so disloyal? They didn't get it. But God loved humanity. He made all of this," Noland gestured out the train window, "and yet, it was humans He had made in His image."

"So, God looks like people?"

"Sort of. Yeah," Olivier said, still smiling.

"And yet, no. Not really," Yellaina had to add, squinting thoughtfully.

"So, God went through all this mess, and Jesus actually had to die. The humans killed Him," Noland went on.

"Well, He let them, because it needed to happen," Olivier

added. "One sacrifice to save them all," he added in his Mr. Moviephone voice.

Achaia laughed, but shook her head in obvious confusion. Yellaina knew it was a lot to take in, and felt like they were losing her. "Basically, humanity had screwed up a lot, and Jesus took the punishment for all of them, so that they could still get into Heaven to be with God, because He really wants them there," Yellaina tried to clarify.

"So why do so many people hate God?" Achaia asked, confused. "You make Him sound really generous."

"He is," Olivier said.

Yellaina cleared her throat. "I think every person who hates God probably has their own reason. And a lot of people just don't know Him, or can't understand Him, and so they give up, or get frustrated. But He is love. He isn't just loving, He is love." She looked over to Noland who was now leaning up against the wall, with one of his legs tucked up underneath him on the seat. He nodded at her encouragingly.

"That just sounds like some kind of fairy tale, He can't be that perfect," Achaia said, shaking her head. Noland looked at Achaia and frowned slightly.

"He is perfect," Yellaina said bluntly, turning her focus back to Achaia. "He is the only being who is. Even we angels are fallen, and messed up. Humanity, made in God's image doesn't even reflect just how perfect He is."

"Then why do bad things happen?" Achaia asked. "If He loved humanity so much, what about war, and all the crime?"

"Because God is love. He isn't a dictator. He gave people free will, to choose Him. Not to mindlessly follow Him because they had to. But unfortunately, a lot of people haven't chosen Him. People took their free will, and many have done terrible things with it. I mean just look at what Lucifer did when given just a little bit of wiggle room! He has punished thousands for the things they have done. But He promised to not flood the whole earth again. He won't destroy it again like He did with Noah. It hurt Him so deeply to do it. There has never been that much weeping in heaven. The angels closest to God are still in mourning. He wants everyone to have time to choose Him before He comes back to earth. So the humans have missionaries and preachers… They go around and try to tell as many other humans as possible," Yellaina said smiling. She could see the hope God had for people in that.

"But eventually He will come back, and the earth will be cleansed, and heaven will come down," Noland said plainly. "The world, the way it is, has to end eventually. This wasn't what God had in mind when He created everything. He didn't want crime and war. He wanted love, and peace."

"I don't know. That just all seems like—that's just a bit much for me," Achaia said honestly, shrugging. "I'm sorry," she said looking around at their faces.

"After seeing angels and demons, you have a hard time believing there's a God who loves?" Yellaina asked a little defensively, she couldn't help feeling disappointed. She couldn't understand how Achaia didn't get it.

"Yeah," Achaia said, as though it shouldn't be that hard to believe. "I've seen evil my entire life. Demons make sense. The angels I've seen, you guys excluded, didn't look that different from demons, not inside, if I'm being honest." Achaia shrugged again, her tone was genuine, and calm. "So yeah, believing there is an army of creatures out there who hate humanity, but are forced to protect it, and are at war with each other? Not a stretch. But a God who loves? And just loves, though the people He made are sick and twisted, and do nothing but spit in His face... And they are supposed to be made in His image? Yeah, it's a bit unbelievable." Achaia's face had gone pink, she took a breath.

"Hey." Noland put a hand on Achaia's knee, and one up, in Yellaina's direction, signaling for her to drop it.

Yellaina felt a little like a child being smacked on the wrist, and was embarrassed to feel even more deserving of it.

"It's a lot to take in." Noland said lowering his hand back down. "I don't blame you," he said looking directly at Achaia. "Our parents knew God face to face, were with Him for eternity and couldn't believe His love, and they betrayed Him, knowing Him." Noland looked at Yellaina, and she felt ashamed for not being more understanding and gracious. He looked back to Achaia and went on, "God is God. No one just understands Him, and gets it. Faith is that gap, between knowing and believing. Sometimes I think the fallen forget their place. They judge humanity so harshly for their sins, but they chose to betray God to His face. The Nephilim have less faith than men."

"So how do you get it?" Achaia asked, quietly, looking directly at Noland. "If it isn't from seeing Him?"

Yellaina wished she could just disappear into the back of her seat. Her stomach felt like someone had put it in a blender. She felt like she was burning, and knew it showed in the color on her cheeks.

Noland answered her, "You experience Him. It comes with getting to know what you can about Him. And with time." He smiled at Achaia encouragingly.

Olivier reached over and took Yellaina's hand. She flinched in surprise before looking back at him. He was smiling at her sympathetically. She squeezed his hand back but didn't smile. She resigned herself to stay quiet and just look out of the window, watching the dark silhouettes pass by outside. As much as she felt like they needed Achaia to pledge allegiance to God, she knew that pushing her wasn't the way to do it. She needed to have patience.

\*\*\*

Yellaina had climbed onto the bunk above Olivier's and gone to bed first. Olivier dosed off, not long after, still sitting up on his bed. Achaia sat on the bottom bed with Noland. "Why wouldn't my dad have told me about Him?" They were speaking softly about God, and Luc, and Achaia's father, so as not to wake the others.

"He probably didn't want you to affiliate," Noland whispered simply. "If you are completely ignorant of both sides, maybe he thought you stood a chance."

"Affiliate?" Achaia lowered her voice as Olivier slid down, and started snoring.

"In the spiritual realms, every being has to pledge allegiance to someone, to something. Most commonly God, or Lucifer. It's in our nature to serve something greater. Humans chase causes and that feeling of purpose. But fundamentally, we are created to worship God."

"What happens if you don't choose a side?" Achaia asked, looking down at her hands, which were wrung together in her lap.

"In Heaven the angels who wouldn't choose a side, during the war, slipped away. They disappeared into the abyss."

"They disappeared? Where'd they go?"

"Well, they aren't in the heavenly realms, they aren't in Hell, and they aren't on Earth. They say they ceased to exist. Their nature was dispersed."

Achaia swallowed. Her palms were sweating. She couldn't follow a God she didn't even really believe in, and she couldn't follow

Lucifer, could she? But was Lucifer really all that bad? He had been her father's best friend.

"It's choose or be chosen," Noland said softly. "I guess your father thought that if you didn't know either side, that you might be spared. But in the end, it's choose, or be chosen, or cease." Noland was looking at her with a sympathetic stare.

"How do you know if you're already chosen?" Achaia asked, worried.

"No one can take your will away. You're half human. You will always have a say. You choose when you're ready."

"What if I can't?" Achaia asked, looking back up from her hands into his face. "What if no one wants me on their side?"

Noland reached over and put a hand on her knee and smiled sympathetically. "Kaya, you're not all that bad."

Achaia huffed a laugh. The train came to a stop with a small jerk, and Achaia bumped Noland's hand with hers. He pulled his hand back away from her leg, his cheeks flushing slightly. More people were boarding, walking through the hall to their cabins. Glancing at Noland's watch, she was shocked to see it was almost eleven-thirty.

"It's not really like choosing teams in gym at school," Noland recovered, and smiled wider, "and thank God, because whose idea was it to let cruel, hormonal teenagers choose their own teams?" Noland looked utterly flummoxed. "Emile had a full time job consoling the cast-offs of high school society." Noland cocked an eyebrow at her and smirked.

Achaia laughed. "Yeah, I was always picked last. No one ever knew me."

Noland smiled at her. "I wasn't chosen at all."

Achaia was shocked. Noland was a huge athletic guy, he should have been the first any sane person would pick.

"But it was only because I didn't change out into gym clothes." Noland assured her with a phony air of arrogance.

Achaia laughed and smacked his leg playfully. She liked this Noland, laid back, relaxed, even funny.

"I didn't know humans did that. Your schools are so ill-equipped," he mocked.

Achaia rolled her eyes, and shook her head, smiling at him. She checked her phone quickly to see if Naphtali had responded, he hadn't.

Noland seemed to take this as her checking the time, and probably thought she was tired. "Anyway, we should get some sleep." The corner of his mouth twitched up in a sort of lip-shrug. "Off to bed, pip pip!" He tugged at the covers under her.

Achaia stood, smacking his hands. "Did you just 'pip pip', me?" She whispered. "Who says that in real life?"

"The same guy who kicks down doors in 'real life'." Noland smirked.

Achaia smiled, thinking back to the day he had kicked down the door to her apartment. The day her father had been taken. It felt like a lifetime had passed. And yet, she didn't want to think about how long it had been; how long her father had been held who-knew-where.

"Besides, sleep is lovely, and you look like you have Great Expectations."

"Great expectations of sleep?" she asked, climbing up onto her bunk. "You're weird."

"And you need to read more classic literature. So you can get my puns. It's my favorite thing about humans."

Achaia rolled her eyes, and pulled the covers down. "Puns? Or literature?"

Noland chuckled. "Yes."

Achaia giggled as she slid underneath her covers, and pulled them up to her chin. "You really just like their books?"

"More like their ability to create." Noland said seriously. "Made in the image of the Creator, they possess so much creativity."

Achaia hadn't ever really thought about it.

"Kaya," Noland whispered, after Achaia had gotten settled in her bunk.

"Yeah?" She whispered back.

"What is 'real life'?" Noland chortled.

"I don't know! Shut up!" Achaia whispered back giggling.

After a few minutes, Achaia could hear the deep breathing of all the others. She had just started wondering if Noland had fallen asleep yet, when he whispered her name again.

"Yeah?" She whispered back, rolling onto her side, facing the edge of the bed.

"I'd pick you first," Noland whispered, "for my team, I mean."

Achaia smiled, she felt her throat close up, and couldn't understand why her eyes were tearing. "Corny much?" She whispered back, trying to sound like she was laughing, and not choked up.

"I don't get the opportunity often. I had to make it count." She could hear the smile in his voice. "These other people actually take me for serious," Noland whispered with a laugh.

Achaia silently hoped he was serious and not making fun of her. She had never had friends like this. If she was honest, she wasn't picked last for teams, she wasn't picked at all and was always assigned to a team by default. Her last thought before falling asleep was that she wouldn't let that be the case this time. She would pick her own team. She would choose.

\*\*\*

Noland lay in bed, listening. He could hear everyone's breathing. He could tell Achaia had fallen asleep, but she was restless in the bunk above him. He wondered if she was having a nightmare…

He wasn't sure if she had been making fun of him, or not. She was a hard person to read. He made a mental note not to be vulnerable with her unless he could see her face. He turned over onto his side, facing the wall, prayed for Achaia to have sweeter dreams, and tried to sleep.

\*\*\*

*Achaia was in a vacuum of shadows. As she tried to fly away, the demons grabbed at her wings. Pain shot through her as, with the cracking of bones, they broke them. Achaia cried out, and fell to her knees. The shadows clawed at her and yanked her up to her feet, tying her to a pole. Achaia imagined the Salem witch trials, and wondered if they were going to burn her alive.*

*Another horde of demons advanced before her. They parted down the center, and out of the mass a man was dragged by his arms. Her father. He was beaten, and bloody. She couldn't tell if he was conscious, but they tied him to another pole, facing her. "Choose," a low booming voice yelled. "Choose!"*

\*\*\*

Shael walked with Luc down one of the many icy tunnels through the catacombs. They were on their way to the arena for more blood games. Shael had worked his way up to the higher ranking demons. However, the demons, out of fear of being challenged had stopped telling him what their rankings were. Shael had been forced to deduce who was higher than him, by weeding out the ones who with sighs of relief informed him they were beneath him. This had slightly slowed his progress. Prolonging Luc's entertainment, however, had worked toward getting Shael back into his good graces.

"It's nice to finally have some excitement around here." Luc said rubbing his hands together greedily. "I love a good bloodbath."

Shael was sore, and tired, and felt like he was dying, but he smiled and laughed, like he couldn't be enjoying himself more. "I've missed this," he lied.

Luc grinned from ear to ear, laughing with excitement.

Shael stopped in his tracks. At the end of the tunnel a cloud was forming. A breeze that came from nowhere, rushed passed them, making Shael's hair rise on the back of his neck. The mass neared, like a tide of ashes crashing over them. In the waves, Shael could hear whispered voices. He hated the shadows. The sheer mass of them. They were overwhelming. He caught snippets of what they were whispering to Luc. They were going somewhere, to someone. They wouldn't disappoint him.

Shael had a sinking feeling in his stomach. Who they were going after? When the tide of demons had washed out, and passed by them, Shael looked at Luc.

"They do have a flare for the dramatic," Luc said fixing his spiked black hair, which had been swept to the side. "But I kind of like that about them." Luc looked giddily excited.

"What are you up to?" Shael asked, trying to sound curious rather than suspicious.

Luc clapped him on the shoulder. "Just a little surprise. You'll have to wait and see!"

This didn't comfort Shael. He continued down the hall, following Luc. He silently prayed, that wherever that throng of demons was headed, it was nowhere near Achaia.

\*\*\*

The next morning at breakfast, Achaia noticed a lot of new faces in the dining car. She assumed they had gotten on at the stop they'd made during the night before. She picked at her plate of scrambled eggs and ate a bite of tomato. The others were all talking, but she wasn't following the conversation. She was thinking about everything they had talked about the night before.

Outside the window she watched towns and countryside fly by. She yawned, and set down her fork, picking up her coffee. She hadn't slept well at all. Her mind was racing, but it felt foggy and unfocused. She looked across the table at Emile, who was turned talking to Noland across the aisle of the train. She locked eyes with a little boy sitting at the table behind Emile. He stared at her without blinking.

Achaia, thinking the little boy was challenging her to a staring contest, leaned forward on the table and stared back at him. Then, the little boy's face went colder, and turned pale. Achaia squinted, thinking she must have imagined it. The little boy blinked, and blinked again, quickly, to relieve his eyes. This was perfectly normal. What was not, was that, between blinks, his eyes had been entirely black.

Achaia stared back more closely. But the boy looked perfectly normal. He stuck his tongue out at her and turned his attention back to his breakfast. His mother said something to him in what sounded like Russian. Probably fussing at him to eat. Achaia shook her head and took another sip of her coffee.

She told herself she must have imagined it. But she felt uneasy. She had that annoying feeling that someone behind her was watching her, and turned casually as if to look next to her at Amelia, to check the rest of the dining car.

Every person at the tables lining the train behind her was staring at her with eyes that were completely black. Achaia dropped her coffee mug with a loud clatter of china.

"Achaia?" Emile asked startled. "Why are you scared?" He asked in a low voice.

"Those people. They—" she turned to point behind her. Table upon table was full of families and travelers, talking quietly together, enjoying their breakfast. "Their eyes…" Achaia said, looking around confused. Only now, the only people looking at her, looked confused as to why she was staring at them.

"What's up?" Amelia asked, giving her a what's-wrong-with-you, look.

"They were…" Achaia looked back at the little boy. He was shoving something green around his plate with his fork, looking skeptical, but otherwise like a normal little boy. "Nothing," Achaia finished.

"You're probably tired. Olivier probably kept you up snoring," Noland said with a smile.

"I don't snore!" Olivier said defensively.

"Yes, you do." Noland, Achaia, Emile, and Amelia all said together. Everyone else laughed, but Noland gave Achaia a look of concern.

"I'm going to go take a shower. Maybe that will help me wake up." Achaia said squeezing past Amelia out of their table to leave the dining car.

"See you back in the room," Olivier said, recovering from his dismay.

After retrieving her bathroom bag from their cabin, Achaia went to the end of the train car where there was a small lavatory with a shower. She locked the door behind her and hopped in the shower, scrubbing her face with the soap Yellaina had given her. She breathed in the refreshing scent of lemon and oregano. It stung in the cuts still healing on her face, which definitely woke her up.

When she turned off the water, there was a knock on the door. "Just a few more minutes!" she called out.

Another knock.

"Um… Do you speak English?" Achaia said, more to herself than whoever was outside. "Un moment!" she recalled from her few French classes.

A thump on the door, as if someone had slumped against it, shook the room. "Um…"

Achaia dressed quickly and threw her things sloppily into her bag, and cracked the door. A man in a suit stood outside. "I'm done now," Achaia said opening the door further, to come out, and move past him.

"Achaia bat Shael?" The man said in a British sounding accent, his eyes turning black. His voice was hollow, and cold. Achaia barely had a chance to register her own surprise before the man was pushing her back into the bathroom, and closing the door behind him.

Achaia screamed for help, but the man covered her mouth. She bit his hand, and slapped his arm away from her. She felt the heat in her eyes, and knew they had turned red. The man raised both of his hands, his all-black eyes widening. "I am not here to harm you Miss Cohen," he said.

"Who are you?" Achaia said spitting the taste of his hand out of her mouth.

"A messenger," he lowered his hands, straightening his suit, "here to propose an offer." He smiled weakly, which only made him look more demonic. "Lucifer has a proposition for you."

"Noland!" Achaia called out.

"He can't hear you. Your friends are still in the dining car. Completely surrounded by demon possessed people. It would take them a while to get to you without killing any of them. We have the train covered." He smiled at her more widely. "A view of what could happen…" the man raised his hand up to cup her face.

His hand was cold against her cheek, and Achaia could no longer see what was right in front of her, but was back in the dining car. All the people in the car turned and looked at her, their eyes turning black and hungry. Their mouths opened wide to reveal needle like teeth, as they all stood as a horde and lashed out and pounced on Noland and the others.

Yellaina's throat was slashed in seconds, before Olivier could even get to her. Emile was swarmed. Amelia, was screaming in pain. Noland and Olivier were fighting to get to the others, but were themselves overrun.

Achaia blinked, and was once again standing in the bathroom with a strange man. "Now, are you prepared to listen?"

Achaia clenched her jaw, her mind racing with every possible scenario of how to get out of this. The least violent way, she figured, was to listen to the guy and see if he would let her leave afterwards. She cocked her head as a signal for him to continue.

"I'm sure you've become aware of the fact that your father has left you."

"Left? More like kidnapped," Achaia said outraged.

"Matter of opinion," the man brushed her comment away with his hand. "Lucifer would like to extend an invitation for you to join them, if you like." The man spoke formally, like some sort of butler.

"Satan is inviting me over for dinner?" Achaia asked in disbelief.

"It's Lucifer." The man said harshly, his features transforming into a sharper face, with thin translucent skin, laced with black veins.

He cleared his throat, and straightened his sports coat again, and his face relaxed into a human face once more. "And this isn't an invitation to dinner. It's an invitation to eternity. Join us, and you can be with your father forever." The man smiled.

"Where are they, anyway?" Achaia asked casually.

"Come with me and see." The man gestured toward the bathroom door, which shimmered around the edges and became some sort of a portal to the beyond. Achaia couldn't make out what was on the other side. She almost laughed, but she knew it was nerves. Nothing about this situation was actually funny. Not unless you found being stuck in a bathroom with a demon possessed business man talking conversationally about spending eternity in Hell, funny. But some people have a dark sense of humor.

Achaia thought for a minute, she needed to buy more time. Maybe the others would notice how long she'd taken by now. "What if I don't?"

"You'll never see him again."

Achaia went to open her mouth to respond, but the demon butler held up a hand to stop her. "Lucifer is willing to give you time to think this over. Those of us who got on in Strasbourg will get off in Warsaw, as a show of good faith. I'll be in touch." He slid aside, and let her out of the bathroom. "And if you should wish to reach me," he opened his mouth revealing rows of dagger-like teeth, and ripped one out from the back, "if you draw blood with this, it will foster a connection between us." He handed her the fang.

Achaia took it, looking down on it disgusted. It was big enough to span the palm of her hand. "I have to cut myself with your tooth? That is only a little intimately creepy... If that's the case, I think I should at least learn your name." She looked back up to his face.

"Kumbhakarna."

Achaia cocked an eyebrow.

"But you can call me John."

"John?" Achaia grinned. "An inspired alias!" Achaia complimented sarcastically, glancing at the toilet behind him.

"What's that?" The man asked.

"Nothing," Achaia said, raising her eyebrows and her hands in a mock-innocent dismissal of his question before turning around to walk away as John shook his head.

She walked back to the cabin slowly, putting John's tooth in her pocket and mulling over the whole conversation she'd had with him. Assuming John kept his word, and all the demons got off in Warsaw, Achaia thought she might keep the bathroom rendezvous to herself, at least for the time being. She knew Noland would be on high alert if he knew she'd been cornered by a demon in the shower. She'd never have a second's peace or privacy, and she didn't have much of that, now.

She also knew none of the others would be okay with her considering accepting the offer, even if it was under false pretenses. Achaia wondered if Hell was a place you could leave? Escape? But what if you couldn't, and she ended up trapped there forever with her dad— she had a lot to consider.

When she opened the door to the cabin, she found Noland standing at the door. "I was just coming to check on you."

"In the shower?" Achaia asked, cocking an eyebrow.

"You were gone for a long time." He said, going a little pink in the face. He sat back down on their seat, which was a seat again and no longer a bed.

"Girls take long showers." Achaia said putting her bathroom bag back into her book bag.

"Amen," Yellaina said in agreement. She smiled weakly at Achaia, and Achaia knew she was sorry about the night before. She smiled back, letting her know they were okay. She settled into the seat, leaning against the window.

"It looks like you could use some lavender on those." Yellaina said gesturing to the cuts on Achaia's face, and digging in her bag.

"Emile was worried about you at breakfast," Noland said, trying to sound casual.

"I think it's like you said. I just didn't get good sleep last night," Achaia brushed it off.

Noland gave her an appraising look. "You slept restlessly, I heard you." He said quietly, almost more to convince himself. She could tell he didn't believe her. She found herself really glad that Emile wasn't there now. She spent the rest of the train ride trying to figure out how to keep Emile from picking up on her dilemma.

## 14
## Bait

"Abandon all hope, ye who enter here."

-Dante Alighieri, Inferno

The lamp posts lining the street had flags of ice frozen mid-wave from where they had succumbed to the freezing wind. Walls of snow lined the streets, building trenches through which numbed pedestrians trudged. Even with her thick new clothes layered, and the snow boots Yellaina had picked out for her. Achaia couldn't feel her toes. Her nose, on the other hand, actually hurt, and her cheeks burned in the wind.

Noland had said it wasn't a long walk to the safe house from the station. Achaia followed him, bitterly watching the steam rise from his shoulders. She would have bet it didn't seem long, when you weren't getting frost bite.

As if feeling the knives she was stabbing through his back

with her eyes, he turned to look at her. She could tell he was doing a quick head count to make sure no one had fallen behind.

"It's just around the corner." He said reassuringly.

Achaia thought that even if they were walking through the doorway it wouldn't have been close enough. She didn't understand how the people in Russia could live like this.

Noland slowed his pace until he was next to her. Without a word he slipped his hand up her sleeve and under her glove to her wrist. The warmth spread through her arm and into her chest, then to the rest of her. Though she could breathe again, more easily, her feet were still unbearably heavy. The thought of a nice warm bed, in a quiet room, sounded beyond perfect; and yet the feeling that the place lay just out of reach, was torture. "It's just around the corner." He said flatly.

Achaia looked forward and saw the corner he was referring to. It was mostly hidden in the snow, and with the wind whipping that snow through the air, it was too far away to really make it out.

She remembered a day when she was a little girl and her father had taken her to the zoo. She had run from one exhibit to the next, thrilled at the sight of the animals. She could remember the smell, of earth and waste, of adventure. She had day-dreamed of safaris, and of living in a rainforest—yet, at the end of the day, she had grown so tired and fussy that her father had had to carry her back to the car. Before they had even reached it, she had fallen asleep.

Achaia remembered everything about that day, except the ride home. She remembered it more vividly now that the same exhaustion had taken hold. She had burnt through all of her sense of adventure long before, and now only felt the weary drain the adrenalin-rush-hangover had left behind. She almost wished someone would just pick her up and carry her the rest of the way. She couldn't bear anything else standing between her and heat.

Finally, Noland led them around the corner. Ahead, was one of the most magnificent buildings Achaia had ever seen. A cathedral composed of towers. Atop each tower was a dome which came to a point, each one painted ornately in an array of colors. They reminded her of Christmas ornaments. The walls were covered in arched windows, trimmed with yet more colors. She couldn't help but think it looked like an incredibly-intricate gingerbread house. Though undeniably beautiful, the building looked like a playhouse.

Noland marched up to the enormous front doors and knocked. The sound rang through, sounding like an empty tomb. The doors opened. The inside looked black, a stark contrast to its exuberant exterior.

Achaia squinted her eyes to adjust them from the brightness of the light reflecting off the ice and snow. Noland turned and waved the rest of them ahead, into the building. Achaia stuck close to Yellaina's side.

The large wooden doors clamored closed behind them, sending an echo through the immense hall, in which they now stood. Achaia took in the room. There was no bright colored paint here. The room was large and damp, cave-like. She was still incredibly cold. Going indoors had done little more than cut out the wind. As her eyes adjusted to the dim light, she noticed that the room was lit by candelabras mounted to the walls and ceiling. There was also a pair of large doors ahead of her, mirroring those through which they had just entered.

To her left, stood a single chair next to a small table, the only furniture in the room. On top of the table stood a half melted candle, flickering in the draft. Against the table, leaned a sword.

A man stood next to Noland, bolting the doors closed. Achaia had never seen so many locks and bolts. They ran the height of the man up the doors, and over his head as high as he could reach, reminding Achaia of a medieval castle.

The man had dark brown hair, long enough for him to have tucked it behind his ears and pulled it back into a short ponytail. It was a thick mess of curls. He had broad shoulders, made broader by the layers of winter clothes he wore. As he turned to face them, Achaia noticed he was whispering. Noland was speaking to him in hushed tones. She also noticed he was younger looking than she expected, which with Nephilim didn't mean much. Nephilim never looked older than forty. He wore a grey scarf, wrapped close to his face, but she could see that he had dark eyes, brown or hazel, she wasn't sure.

Then, the eyes she was appraising, started appraising her. She wasn't sure if she had become paranoid, or if there was a suspicion in his glance. Achaia looked away until the man redirected his attention to Noland.

Emile met her eye and gave her a reassuring nod, but his eyes were perturbed. She studied the man out of the corner of her eye, as he loosened his scarf. She glanced at him again to get a better read on him but was distracted by his mouth. There was something about his mouth when he spoke, something nice. She liked to watch it change as he shape his words.

"You just want to trust him don't you?" Yellaina said, her eyes also glued to his face. "It's because he is beautiful."

"Well he certainly isn't bad looking…" Amelia smirked.

Yellaina smiled and looked over at Achaia. "I meant his soul."

Amelia looked over at them. "Oh yeah, sure. That too…"

Emile chuckled, coming to stand next to them. "That's his gift."

"He's God's gift to women?" Olivier asked, staring the guy, sizing him up.

Yellaina and Amelia laughed. Achaia stared at the man as Emile went on.

"No," Emile smirked. "Trust."

"His gift is trust?" Olivier asked. Achaia and the rest looked at Emile.

"Care to expound on that?" Amelia said.

"Don't you know who that is?" Emile asked excitedly, looking star struck.

Achaia looked around at the others, who were all shaking their heads. She was thankful that for once, she wasn't the only clueless one in the room.

"Think about it." Emile looked alive, like the man was a celebrity he'd always wanted to meet. "You want to trust him without knowing him. Who, of the original generation, is trust worthy? Selfless...."

"Bale?" Amelia's eyes lit up.

Yellaina's eyes grew wide as she stared at Emile for confirmation.

Emile nodded.

"I always thought he'd be—" Olivier whispered, staring at the man. "Blond..."

"Who's Bale?" Achaia asked, but the man had turned to face them and was walking their way.

"Welcome to Russia." He said with a Russian accent. "I am Bale. I'll show you to your rooms."

Achaia thought that his eyes may have lingered on her a moment longer than the others as he met their eyes. But he had turned promptly and walked through the second set of doors that led into the safe house.

***

Inside, the walls were covered in murals that had not been maintained. They had grown dull in color and detail. Still, Noland could not take them all in. He had never seen anything like the intricacy of the safe house. The moldings were carved and etched, there was wainscoting, and what wasn't covered in murals was painted what once had surely been a rich blue.

The safe house's beauty was dulled by dust and neglect. "Do you live here alone?" Achaia asked.

"I, a healer, and a handful of servants are the only current occupants." Bale said in a flat tone that told them he wasn't the talkative type. He looked around at all of them admiring the ornate walls. "We don't frequent this part of the cathedral," he explained in way of an excuse.

He led them through hallways, each more beautiful than the last, until they came to the part of the cathedral that held the bed chambers. As they neared the heart of the house, Noland could smell clove and frankincense through the dust. The spicy scent of the place reminded him of Christmas.

One by one they were shown their rooms until Noland was left alone with Achaia following Bale through the halls.

"Very well," Bale said after depositing Emile into his room. "Achaia Connolly Cohen."

Noland saw Achaia's attention snap to.

"Your room—," Bale opened the door on the right and turned to them, blocking Achaia's entry with his arm. He spoke to Noland in a low his voice, "I know what she is. I sensed it the second she walked through that door."

Noland instinctively reached out a hand to Achaia, as if to

push her behind him. But he couldn't protect her from words.

"What I am?" Achaia asked.

Bale ignored her. "The council was audacious to send her here." He said to Noland. "Russia isn't safe. You'll bring Hell upon us."

Noland stepped halfway in front of Achaia. "What are you saying?" He struggled to regain his composure.

"I think you understand me."

Noland's mind was racing to comprehend if what Bale hinted at was true, or if he was simply wanting to trust him. She was her father's daughter...

"The council has sent orders for her," he said to Noland before turning to Achaia. "You'll have your studies, but no training." Bale had a tight expression on his face. Noland could tell, without Emile's abilities, that he was conflicted.

"No training?" Noland felt Achaia move away from him as he flushed in anger. Bale stared at him, eye to eye. "That is a violation—"

Bale studied his face appraisingly. Noland could see the sadness of agreement in his eyes. "Defense only." Bale said in compromise. "She won't be taught how to kill, here. We will discuss this more over lunch." He cocked his head, lowering his arm. Achaia followed his instruction, and entered the room.

Noland looked in past her. The room was sparse. It had stone walls, a small fireplace housing some dying embers, a single bed with a nightstand next to it with a short candle. The blanket on the bed looked old and worn thin. It looked like what you'd expect from an old monastery.

"What?" Noland asked. All of the other rooms had been lush, finely furnished, warm, and comfortable.

"Noland," Achaia said, putting a hand on his arm to stop him.

"It's okay."

Noland looked down to her pale resolute face.

She fixed Bale with a steady gaze. "Whatever you see fit to offer me is appreciated." Her face was stone cold and unreadable. Noland wished he were Emile so he could tell what she was feeling; if she had fallen for Bale's gift, and was just trusting that he was right to place her in a glorified cell.

Bale looked as if he didn't know what to make of her either. "You all must be hungry. Tell your friends, once you get settled, lunch will be served down in the dining room. You need only follow your nose to find it."

Achaia walked into the room, but before she shut the door, Noland winked at the fireplace. The fire roared back to life. Bale hadn't noticed, as he had started down the hall. Just before her door closed, Noland saw Achaia's lips spread into a smile.

Noland moved to catch up with Bale. "We will discuss the plan for Achaia's education while she is here. But, if she brings destruction upon this place, I will remove her myself," Bale said bluntly. "How do you know she is what you say?" Noland asked, unable to contain his curiosity.

"I am not limited like those who are fallen." Bale stopped and looked Noland in the eye, the way his father used to look at him when he was trying to teach him something. "I am a liaison. I still hold the glory of God, I can see her."

"What do you see?" Noland asked quietly.

"Death." Bale whispered. His eyes were weighed down by a deep sorrow, as if he had just witnessed the death of thousands, and fear.

"And," Noland began, taking a step nearer Bale, "what do you see in me?"

Bale studied him for a moment. "You are the fury of heaven." He turned and began walking back down the hall.

"Wait! What does that mean?" Noland asked, catching up to him quickly.

"Your room, Brother Amsel." Bale stopped outside of the next door. "Get some rest before lunch."

Noland entered the room, and went as if to close the door. As Bale rounded the corner, Noland doubled back to Emile's room. He knocked on the door, and only waited a second before it was opened. Noland pushed his way in, shutting the door behind him.

"Why Russia?" Noland said as he turned to face Emile, who looked incredibly confused. "If there was something going on, where would you send us?" Noland asked, looking at Emile's confused expression, waiting for him to see it.

It took a second before Emile's eyes lit with realization. "To the one Nephilim that you immediately and blindly trust."

Noland nodded curtly.

***

Shael entered the cage and looked up at the largest demon he had seen yet. In fact, the cage he had just entered had been expanded to fit it. The demon was easily twenty feet tall, if not taller. He had a dark blueish-grey skin that looked a bit like used coal that was cracked and ashy. He had broad muscular shoulders, and long sculpted arms. His torso was equally chiseled and on his head were massive horns. Now this is what humans pictured when they thought of demons, Shael mused. Unlike some of his previous opponents, this demon was not at all laughable.

Shael stretched his neck from side to side, cracked the knuckles in his hands, and shook out his arms, bracing himself for combat. The demon mimicked him, only the cracking sound of his bones, sounded like boulders crumbling from a rock face; like an avalanche of stone, instead of small pops. Shael could feel each one vibrate through his chest, and felt a little like throwing up. But he swallowed hard, and refused to "pull a Gaki".

"So," Shael started lightly, hoping to humanize the beast in front of him, "what's your name?"

"Orobas," the demon replied in a low rumbling voice, like thunder.

Shael nodded politely. When the demon spoke its name, the ground beneath Shael's feet shook violently. Around the room, the iced walls cracked and the demons in the stands cowered. Shael realized that Orobas must be the demon of "natural" disasters, but pretended not to be intimidated by any of these effects. How was he supposed to fight an earth quake?

Shael looked up at Luc, who looked anxious with excitement, but also a little like he didn't know what he wanted to see happen. More than ever, Shael wished he had his wings back. This was it, the last blood game he needed to win to get into Luc's inner circle. The fights had gotten progressively more violent and difficult. Shael's human strength was failing him. He was sore, and injured, and tired. He had hoped that Orobas would be dim witted, so that he could simply out strategize him. But with Orobas' size and ability, Shael didn't think that would work now.

Shael prayed silently, "Lord if You can hear me, here, I'm going to need Your help with this one. Forgive me my falling. Guard my Achaia. If I perish into the void, remember me as I was, when I lived love for You. Grant me the opportunity to go fighting for Your light in the darkness. May they see the spark of Your power in me, and tremble, knowing they will fail. If I am lost forever, Lord, let me perish for good."

Shael felt a peace wash over him, and with it warmth. The warmth turned into a heat in his chest that blossomed and spread throughout his body. He hadn't felt warmth in so long, he had forgotten the strength of it. The aches in his muscles eased, and his hands felt sure, and strong. He looked down at his arms, half expecting to see fire strung through his veins. (He thanked God there was no visible indication that anything had happened). Shael knew that God had heard his plea, and given him strength. He looked up, studying Orobas for weakness, and noticed a fracture in his left horn. Shael wondered how deep the fracture ran, and if it were enough to weaken the horn's integrity.

Luc stood, and held out his arms. The demons in the stands looked on with a hungry sort of anticipation. "Let the match commence!" He yelled, and the demons in the stands cheered loudly.

Shael side stepped as Orobas brought down his enormous fist to smash him. Though Orobas missed, the ground shook so violently, Shael lost his footing and fell to his side. As Orobas lifted his fist, Shael saw that the floor beneath it was cracked. Shael moved quickly, hoping that Orobas' size would make him slow or unsteady. He ran behind Orobas, hoping to get him to turn in circles and dizzy himself. Shael zigzagged, running between his feet and around him. Orobas shook his head, looking around and around, like someone trying to find an annoying fly.

Orobas yelled in frustration, and Shael stood frozen in place, shaken through with the vibration of every muscle in his body. His brain went fuzzy for a moment as if even his brain were shaking in his skull. Shael fell to his knees, dangerously close to one of Orobas' feet. Orobas lifted the foot to stomp. Shael rolled to the side, barely missing the impact, but was again shaken through his bones.

Shael took a deep breath to try and steady himself. He ran in circles again, and was pleased to notice that Orobas did in fact seem to be getting dizzy. Shael dogged between Orobas' legs and leapt up onto the cage, climbing as quickly as he could, looking over his shoulder to keep an eye on Orobas. The demon was looking around and around on the ground at his feet, dizzy and confused, unable to spot Shael. Once Shael was high enough he pushed off the cage, flipping backwards in the air, and landed on Orobas' shoulder.

Orobas roared, causing Shael to cling to his neck to avoid falling off, as he felt the quake through Orobas' body rush through his own. Shael's eyes rolled back in his head, and his hands were losing grip, when the demon finally took a breath in, affording Shael the silence to move once more.

Shael sprung from the neck, up off the demons shoulder, and grabbed hold of the fractured horn. He swung from it launching himself forward and pulling with all of his weight and might. The horn cracked, and the demon cried out, tilting his enormous head to the side. It took every ounce of Shael's strength and control not to release his grip of the horn.

Orobas shook his head violently, like someone trying to shake water out of their ears. Shael tucked into himself, bringing his legs up to wrap around the horn. He clung to it desperately, knowing this was his only chance at defeating Orobas.

As Orobas shook his head even more violently, the motion together with Shael's weight, finished the job, and the fracture deepened, severing the horn from Orobas' head. Shael, with the horn, hurtled toward the grown. He landed hard on his back. His arms and legs still wrapped around the horn.

Shael stood. Orobas wept loudly with his hands feeling frantically at his head where it now bled. He was disoriented and unbalanced, with his remaining horn causing him to lean heavily to his right side. Shael threw the horn up into the air, spinning it, and caught it point up. He ran as fast as he could, feeling like he was wielding a tree as a weapon, and launched himself up, pinging from leg to leg, up Orobas himself. The demon looked down just as Shael thrust the horn up, through Orobas' skull, just between his eyes.

The demon fell back, landing hard on the floor. Shael crouched to absorb the landing, then stood on Orobas' chest. He looked around. The stadium was silent. The demons looked shocked, appalled, and disturbed, as if Shael had just done something unspeakably wrong. Clearly, none of them had been expecting him to win. Shael realized that the chest he was standing on was still rising and falling slowly. Orobas was not dead, but was somehow only unconscious. However, Shael leapt gracefully down from his chest, knowing he had won. His muscles all seized, and were shaking from the quakes they had endured, but he managed to walk slowly to the door of the cage, and open it.

"I could really use a drink," Shael said exasperated, looking up to Luc, who was just as stunned into silence as all of the demons.

Luc huffed, and a weak fleeting smile crossed his lips, before his face fell back into shock. "Yeah," he shrugged. He looked to Orobas, unconscious still in the cage, and stood slowly. "I'm sure you could."

*\*\**

Achaia took in the small room around her. It looked like a cleaning closet converted into a minimalist Airbnb. There was a chair at a small table against the wall that she pulled over in front of the fire Noland had started for her before he left.

She removed her coat and draped it over the back to dry. She took off the sweat shirt she had on under it, and threw it over the back of the chair as well, before sitting down to take off her boots.

She wasn't surprised that Bale didn't trust her. After meeting the council, she hadn't been holding out much hope that the keeper of the safe house would be altogether welcoming. But she wondered what he had meant by "what she is". Wasn't she a Nephilim like the rest of them? Or was he offended by her humanity? She didn't fully understand what it meant for her mother to be a human, in this community. But it was obviously a big deal.

She put her frozen feet in front of the fire, and held her hands up to the flames with them. The more she thought about the council, the more she wasn't sure she liked Nephilim, her friends excluded. She could see why her father had chosen a sort of exile, and had chosen humanity, over his people. As she thought back to the questioning of the council, she realized her jaw hurt from clenching it. She didn't trust angels, not the majority of them.

Her father had sided with Luc, knowing everything. If the story everyone was telling was true, he had been willing to sell his soul to Luc… so, Luc couldn't be that bad. Her father wouldn't have agreed to leave her for a life of misery, would he? Maybe hell wasn't what people made it out to be… granted, she didn't know much about it at all, her father had seen to that.

Then Achaia thought back to the demons who attacked her in the woods, the horrible things they had whispered into her heart. If Hell was being constantly surrounded by them, then people weren't even close when they imagined Hell's darkness.

Her mind turned to Lussa, the demon who had taunted her with her mother's death. He had killed her mother, but he hadn't done it alone. Had her father really signed up to spend eternity with the demons who had taken her mother from them?

Achaia shook her head and ran her fingers through her hair. They got stuck in the damp knots tied by the wind. She twisted it all into a messy side braid, to get it out of her face.

As she sat, waiting for it to be time for lunch, she thought in circles about the demon's offer, and if there was any other way to find her father, because it didn't look like the Nephilim were going to help at all.

\*\*\*

Achaia opened her door when she started to smell something delicious wafting down the hallway. As she did, she saw she wasn't the only one; Emile was walking past her door as she entered the hall. "Smells good, doesn't it?" he said pausing for her to close her door and join him.

Noland was leaving his room as well, and walked with them toward the source of the smell. They followed their noses to a long narrow room lined on one side with windows. The room was lit by candles, but was still a little dark for it being the middle of the day. Achaia glanced outside to see the sky thick with snow clouds. She wondered absently if there would ever be an end to the cold.

Yellaina, Olivier, and Amelia were already sitting at the table as Achaia, Emile and Noland took their seats. They left the seats at either end of the table empty for Bale, as a sign of respect. Achaia was seated in the middle, between Emile and Noland. She felt a little more comfortable, flanked by the two of them, in an uncertain situation like this.

Bale entered the room and took the end chair at the far side of the room. He took his seat silently, and the rest of them spared glances at each other around the table. They followed Noland's lead, and remained silent. A servant entered, Achaia noticed she was a very thin girl, with fair skin, and plain features. She reached around them, expertly avoiding any physical contact as she removed the covers off the platters on the table.

Achaia couldn't help but salivate. Never before had she seen a feast like this. There was stroganoff, solyanka, pirozhki and borscht. There was also a dark looking drink in front of her plate, which was steaming. "Is that coffee?" she whispered, leaning closer to Noland.

"Sbiten," he whispered back. "It's spicy and sweet, you'll like it."

"You must be hungry after your journey. You may begin," Bale said not looking at them, as he began to ladle food into his own bowl, and onto his plate.

Achaia fearlessly sampled some of everything in front of her. Her eyes were bigger than her stomach though, and she was soon full, and sipping her sbiten.

"Logistics, then," Bale began, taking his napkin from his lap, and tossing it over his finished plate. "While you are here, please keep to your chamber save for your lessons, which will commence immediately following lunch," Bale said looking at Achaia for the first time since he had deposited her to her room. "Assignments for the rest of you are as follows. You are to continue the training regimen assigned each of you by Jocob. In addition to such, you will each take on the responsibility of educating Achaia bat Shael on the culture and customs of the Nephilim." Bale pushed his chair back away from the table, but stayed seated. "Yellaina, you will obviously take charge of teaching Achaia the different angelic languages. She will also need a working knowledge of Koine, Hebrew, and Latin."

Yellaina nodded, looking serious.

"Emile," Bale began, looking over at him in turn.

Emile perked up in his chair as if he were at attention. Achaia looked at him, then back to Bale.

"You are to educate Achaia on the history of the Nephilim, beginning pre-creation. She needs a perspective shift." Bale frowned, but did not look at Achaia. "There is much more at work here than she understands."

Achaia swallowed hard and tried to understand that he was right, without taking it personally. However, she wasn't really sure she could wrap her mind around a timeline that began with forever, and ended with never. Her human brain just couldn't comprehend that much.

"Olivier," Bale turned again, "You have the burden of teaching Achaia something of our duty as Nephilim, and our place in this world. Teach her the role and responsibility of what it is to be a Guardian, and how orders are given and received." There was a bitterness to his voice as he spoke of orders. Achaia wasn't sure if it was directed toward her, or the orders themselves. "Explain to her the Penance of Nephilim."

Olivier nodded then looked at Achaia with a small but encouraging smile.

"Amelia," a small smile played at the corner of Bale's lips. It left so quickly, Achaia questioned whether she had actually seen it at all. "You have the task of teaching Achaia our political structure and protocols. Especially when and where, and to whom she should speak."

Achaia got the strange feeling he had heard about what had happened in the council meeting. She swallowed again, but not with shame. She glanced sideways to see that Noland was looking at her. She raised her eyebrows and shrugged. The corner of Noland's mouth twitched upward in a smirk and she heard the tiniest little huff of a secret laugh catch on his breath.

"Brother Amsel," Bale called Noland's attention to himself. "You are assigned to Achaia's training."

Achaia noticed that Noland was completely still and reserved except for his hands under the table. Noland's fingers were fidgeting with the edges of the tablecloth, just ever so slightly, Achaia was sure she was the only one to notice.

"Teach her about Nephilim warfare. But she may only learn defensive tactics. To be clear," Bale leveled his gaze on Noland. Achaia noticed Noland's fingers go still. "You are strictly forbidden to train her. She is half human, we do not know entirely what this means, there is a chance that makes her too inferior to wield angelic blades."

"Inferior?" Yellaina said at the same time as Olivier spoke.

"How are we going to know unless she tries?" Olivier asked.

Bale glared at them for speaking, apparently out-of-turn. "You would risk her life to see?" Bale asked, not without an air of sarcasm, looking specifically at Olivier. "Be my guest." He waved his hand flippantly toward Achaia.

Olivier gulped.

"She still has Nephilim blood," Amelia argued in a reasonable tone. Bale softened when she spoke. "Surely she could at least try holding a blade to see."

"For the council, it is not only a matter of Achaia's safety that she remain ignorant," Bale said firmly. "The matter is not up for debate."

"What? Do they think Achaia would wage war on the council or something?" Olivier laughed. His laugher stopped when he was met with a serious look from Bale.

"They couldn't possibly," Emile gawked.

"She was not raised Nephilim. She has much to understand, and prove, before she can be trusted. In addition, she is unaffiliated, and half human…" Bale listed her transgressions, be them of her own doing or not, "as such, she is a liability," Bale said sternly. "This argument is finished." Bale laid his hand down on the table firmly, though not striking it.

Achaia sat back a little stunned. She met Olivier's eye across the table. His face screamed that this was unjust, but he remained silent. Emile was staring incredulously at Bale, Amelia was gesturing for Yellaina not to pursue the issue, as Yellaina looked like she was about to speak. Noland, however, was staring into his plate of leftover pirozhki, apparently submissive, but Achaia wondered if he wasn't just deep in thought. She remembered, too well, the way he had stood up for her in front of the council, to think he would cower before this one man. Unless, of course, he agreed with him… Achaia winced at the thought.

"If you are all full, you are dismissed. I trust you are capable enough of working out your own schedules." Bale stood abruptly and left the room without another word.

# 15

## Of Heritage and Hate

"Train yourself to let go of
everything you fear to lose."

-Yoda

They only sat in silence for a moment, staring at each other, when Amelia pushed back her chair and stood up, "follow me."

Without question, Achaia pushed her own chair back, threw her napkin on her plate and stood. The tiny servant girl from before entered the room to clear the table, as they were leaving. "Where is your library?" Amelia asked her.

The girl looked a little lost. Amelia looked to Yellaina, who repeated the question in Russian. The girl responded, and Yellaina gave them her directions in English. Achaia followed Amelia down several halls and flights of stairs into a grand and beautiful entrance hall, nothing similar to the way they had come. This room was bright, and airy with a dome shaped ceiling. The walls were ornately clad in gold, and the staircase they entered on was mirrored on the other side with one equally massive, which they climbed to exit.

The east wing was colder than the west wing, and obviously less lived in. After a few more haunted looking halls, they reached a set of heavy looking double doors that were engraved with angels, the way the servant had described. Amelia pushed the dusty doors open to reveal the most stunning and abandoned library Achaia had ever seen. The ceiling was higher here than even the entry hall. The walls were lined with books. The only spot of wall not covered with thousands of dusty old books was an enormous fireplace. Like the rest of the house, it was a work of art. A mosaic of tile, it looked like, buried under the dust and cobwebs. Achaia could stand in the fireplace, it was so large, without hitting her head.

"I'll have to ask the servants to clean this room if we are to use it for lessons," Amelia coughed on the dust. The room smelled musty like mildew. Aside from the walls, there were rows and rows of shelves holding even more books. There were also tables with ornate candle sticks, and yet more stacks of books. In front of the fire, and by the windows there were sets of overstuffed arm chairs. The windows themselves were so filthy, they hardly let in any light from outside. The room was cold, and felt a little like the set of a horror film.

Achaia laughed to herself and took out her phone. "Have you ever seen *The Blair Witch Project*?" Amelia shook her head, but when she looked over and saw the phone in Achaia's hand, she laughed. The two huddled together next to one of the book shelves and stared into Achaia's camera.

"We found the library," Achaia whispered, taking a few stuttering breaths. "I'm so scared." Achaia muffled her laugh in her hand, so it sounded like a scared sort of wine.

"I can't breathe. It's too… dusty." Amelia looked frantically around at the room, shaking the camera.

"And dark. It's…" Achaia shuddered, putting her face absurdly close to the camera. "It's really dark." She looked into the camera so that it was a close up of her eye, then her nose. She breathed heavily.

Amelia snickered, then grabbed Achaia's hand, holding the phone. "What's that?" Amelia shrieked, shaking the phone before stopping the recording.

Achaia laughed and sent the video to Olivier, who she knew would get a nerdy kick out of it.

Amelia chuckled as she walked over to the fire place and grabbed something from the mantel and knelt down. Within a few minutes there was a fire going, illuminating the room. With one of the foot-long, oversized matches, Amelia walked around the room lighting more candles.

Achaia could finally make the room out for what it was, rather than a series of shadows. She followed Amelia's lead and took a seat at one of the tables. The stacks of books piled before her looked like they lived inside teepees of dust and cobwebs.

Amelia crinkled her nose, and sat very still, trying not to touch more than was necessary. "Right…" she rolled her eyes. "I think before we start on the political structure of the Nephilim here on earth, you should probably understand where the Nephilim fit into the Heavenly infrastructure."

Achaia nodded and put her phone away. She didn't actually know what Amelia was talking about, but she assumed it made sense and was right, anyway.

"In Heaven, there is of course God. God is composed of the Father, the Son, and the Holy Spirit. Thank the Lord it isn't my job to explain that to you," Amelia sighed in relief.

"Yeah I already tried to take a bite out of that apple on the train. I think plain ol' acceptance might be best on that front." Achaia tossed up her hands in a show of surrender.

Amelia nodded. "Well, think of Him as the star on top of a Christmas tree. Beneath Him, in a sort of triangle structure, there are three, what we call Choirs. Closest to God is the Nephilim. Well, those still in Heaven," Amelia shrugged. "Just beneath them in rank are the Seraphim, like Naphtali, and beneath them are the Cherubim. Those three make up the first choir."

"Cherubim like Cupid?" Achaia asked.

Amelia shook her head violently. "No. No. No." She waved her hand in the air as if she could erase what had just come out of Achaia's mouth. "I see we have some unlearning to do first," Amelia smiled. "You're learning about Nephilim, so I'll leave that for now. Seraphim are warriors, like us. But they are a different breed. They are sometimes referred to as fiery serpents."

"And for good reason," Achaia said nodding.

"I take it Naphtali revealed himself to you?" Amelia asked.

Achaia raised her eyebrows and laughed.

"Not like that!" Amelia said swatting at Achaia's arm.

Achaia nodded and snickered.

"Okay then," Amelia laughed. "Cherubim are sphinx-like angels. They are full of wisdom. They are our historians, healers, and record keepers in Heaven. They keep the Lords annals. Yellaina's mother is actually a Cherubim, not a Nephilim. Which may be why she has a non-combative gift, and why she chooses not to train."

Achaia nodded, that would make sense.

"Beneath them are the three breeds that make up the second choir. The Thrones, they are governors and liaisons. The Dominions, managers…" Amelia waved a hand, "and the Virtues. The Virtues take care of creation. They nurture the earth. They are present in things like science…"

Achaia nodded. "Like gravity?"

Amelia huffed a laugh. "More like light."

"Right… another thing to just accept," Achaia made a big check in the air with her finger.

"And then there's the third choir which is made up of the Powers, who are like border patrol in the heavens. The Principalities, they are overseers. And then the bottom of the totem are the Archangels, they are influencers of man. They mix and mingle with humanity inspiring the Lords will, and occasionally bearing messages to them."

"We don't do that?" Achaia asked.

Amelia looked like she was tempted to be offended, but knew Achaia just didn't know any better. "No. We are more than messengers."

"That sounds like a band name," Achaia smiled.

Amelia rolled her eyes, but laughed.

\*\*\*

After about an hour of Achaia badgering Amelia with questions about all the breeds of angles, and Amelia finally breaking down and drawing a diagram (on a blank page ripped from the back of an ancient-looking book) for Achaia to study, the library doors opened.

Olivier walked in, and looked about the room, taking it all in. "Wow. It really is like the set of an exorcist movie."

"Well I guess I'm being relieved." Amelia stood, and brushed off her clothes, as if she felt like she had grown dusty sitting there.

"Yeah, Noland said you should report to the training room," Olivier said taking Amelia's seat. "He's waiting for you."

"When do I get to start training?" Achaia asked.

"Tomorrow," Olivier smiled. "I'm your last lesson for today. After this, we'll have some downtime before dinner."

Amelia left, closing the doors behind her.

Olivier looked at Achaia with a conspiring smile. "There's a book shop a couple blocks from here, I was thinking of going to check it out; see if they have any comic books!" Olivier looked so excited Achaia couldn't help but smile. "I would love a copy of The Green Arrow in Russian for my collection."

"Nerd," Achaia laughed, "That sounds awesome though! Do you think I'm allowed to leave? Bale told me to keep to my room."

"What Bale doesn't know won't hurt me," Olivier smirked.

Achaia laughed. "Okay then, how do we sneak out?"

"We'll figure out a way, for now, we speak of duty." Olivier put on his super serious (yet I'm not really that serious) face.

"Right, tell me Obi Wan, how does one become a Guardian of humanity," Achaia leaned forward on her elbows, as if truly intrigued.

"Well it's a bit like becoming a Guardian of the Galaxy, but we don't officially have an awesome soundtrack. Though, I myself have a pretty great playlist I train to…"

Achaia laughed. "Step one: Create training playlist." Achaia took notes on her phone.

Olivier nodded importantly. "Step two: Train hard."

Achaia nodded seriously. "Of course!"

"Step three: Get assigned a 'Charge.'"

"Okay, so a Charge is the person you are assigned to protect?

Who assigns those?" Achaia asked, seriously.

"Well, the order comes from God, only He knows who is going to play important roles, and need the extra security. We don't even get told why they are important or what they are meant to do, I guess it's like time travel, and knowing too much could change things?" Olivier shrugged. "We just get told who to protect, and are expected to follow orders and not ask questions." Olivier's mouth puckered in a way that made Achaia think that didn't sit so well with him.

"So is there, like, a designated person who talks to God, who divvies out orders? How is it decided which Nephilim gets assigned to which human?"

"The high elders of the council receive revelation from God and give specific Nephilim their designated Charges, God lays out who needs to go where. They usually receive messages through Archangels, or sometimes, dreams."

"So at some point some guy was told that Noland was supposed to protect me, and then he told Noland, and then Noland just tracked me down?" Achaia absentmindedly drug her finger through the dust on the table top as she processed, sketching stick figures.

"Actually it was my father. He had a dream, and knew that we needed to assimilate into the human school. So we did. It wasn't until a few weeks later that he called and said he had been visited by an Archangel who said that Noland had received his first charge, and that it was the daughter of Shael ben Yahweh. You can imagine how pleased the council was with that! I think they were all kind of hoping that Noland would screw things up, as a first-timer." A shadow of anger crossed Olivier's face. Achaia had never seen him so seriously angry. "Douches."

Achaia nodded in agreement.

"Right, so back to Guardians, and Charges…"

"Yes! Okay, so when you are assigned a Charge, you have to be careful. It is a bit like being a spy; you have to meet them seemingly naturally. The establishment of the relationship has to be organic, to earn their trust. You have to actually end up caring about your Charge, which is what motivates you to protect them."

"Like Noland puts so much effort into caring about me!" Achaia said sarcastically.

"Noland can be hard to read. But if you keep an eye on the subtleties, I think you'd be surprised." Olivier looked serious.

"For someone whose spiritual gift is fire, he isn't really the warm fuzzy type," Achaia said.

"I suspect he is the all-or-nothing, super passionate, type," Olivier said speculatively. "He is one of the very few Nephilim who has really experienced emotional pain on a deep level. He has learned to be more guarded than the rest of us. I've known him since I was ten, and I still can't ever tell what he is thinking. Makes him a little scary…" Olivier started talking more to himself than to Achaia.

Achaia noticed she was chewing on her bottom lip when she tasted salt. "So Charges. You spy your way into their lives, like a creeper, stalk them until you actually become friends, then what?"

Olivier smiled. "You protect them at all costs. Since we don't know what it is exactly they are supposed to do, we try to stay out of the way; just encourage them to really be themselves, the best version of themselves. Then someday, we are assigned a new Charge. We assume the current has fulfilled their purpose, and we leave."

"You just leave them?" Achaia asked.

"That's the hard part of the job, so I hear, and the best outcome," Olivier frowned. "The worst is, you lose them. Then you're assigned a new Charge."

"Lose them as in…"

"They die," Olivier said somberly. He looked down at his hands, fingers laced together on the table. He twiddled his thumbs, and Achaia lost herself just watching them. "On that note," Olivier chimed back in cheerfully. "Let's go in search of Russian comics!" Olivier stood, his chair screeching loudly as if in protest.

Achaia smiled weakly, but stood to follow him. "How are we going to get out?"

"Old buildings like this always have servant passages, where they could come and go without being seen… we find those, we find freedom." He smiled mischievously. "You with me Frenchy?"

A devilish smile spread across Achaia's lips. "Lead the way!"

\*\*\*

By the time Achaia got back to her room, she was freezing and exhausted. It had taken her and Olivier an hour to find the book-store, and then it hadn't even had any comic books. Though Olivier did buy a copy of *Harry Potter and the Philosopher's Stone* in Russian "to help with the language emersion."

Achaia was still full from lunch, and decided to skip dinner. Olivier said he would cover for her and create some excuse. Achaia wasn't sure if Bale would be happy to not have to see her, or if this would just give him more reason to be suspicious.

She spent the night in solitude and deep thought, trying to figure out if there was any way around the allegiance-pledging. She tried to come up with a way to find her father without the help of the council, or accepting the demon, John's offer. Her best bet was Naphtali, but she still hadn't heard back from him at all, and was starting to worry that something had happened to him.

She curled into herself in her bed, and pulled her covers up, shivering in the cold. She sighed before climbing out of her bed to mend the fire, jabbing at it with the iron poker. It faught nobly, but was still slowly dying out. She didn't have any spare wood to throw in, and didn't know where to find any.

Finally, she tugged the thin blankets off her bed, and curled up with them on the floor in front of the fire. It had to be at least one in the morning, she didn't want to wake anyone up, asking for help, like a child who had had a nightmare. Achaia determined to herself, that should she not be able to save her father, she would have to learn to start making it on her own.

*** 

Noland nocked on Achaia's door and waited, but there was no answer. He tried the handle, and found it was unlocked. He pushed it open a crack and saw that Achaia was not in her bed. "Achaia?"

He opened the door the rest of the way, peeking hesitantly in case she was dressing. "Achaia?" Noland looked down. There was a mound of sheets and tattered blankets on the floor in front of the smothered ashes in the fireplace. Noland felt a pang of sadness in his chest. No one should have to have slept like that. When he spoke to try and wake her, he forced his voice to sound casual, "Missed sleeping on the floor, did you?"

Achaia shifted, and pulled the blanket away from her face. There were black smudges on it from the ashes. "Oh, it's you."

"Good morning to you as well," Noland said smiling. "You'll want to wash up before breakfast." He pointed at her face. Her red hair was a rat's nest tangled at the back of her head. He suspected there was a hair tie in there somewhere, but he couldn't see one.

Noland offered Achaia a hand, which she took, and helped her to her feet. She twisted left and right, cracking her back and stretching.

"Why didn't you come get me to fix that for you?" Noland

asked pointing to the fire place.

"I can't always be asking you to fix everything for me," She said picking her blankets back up and making her bed. "It wasn't that bad."

"That's a stone floor. Not a wood one like the cabin," Noland said, pointing, as if there was a question as to which floor he was talking about. "You get changed, I'm going to get you a real blanket, and some firewood."

"Noland," Achaia called after him, but Noland shut the door a little too forcefully, showing his anger. This wasn't right, the way Achaia was being treated here. It wasn't just. He wondered why they would have ordered for her to be basically treated as a prisoner, and yet, begin a limited amount of training. None of it made sense.

Noland entered his own room, and ripped the blanket off his own bed. He balled it up under his arm, and with the other scooped up a few logs of wood from a pile next to his fireplace. He walked back out in the hall, daring Bale to see him, so he could tell him off, but no one was there.

Noland stood outside Achaia's door. "Achaia, are you decent?"

Achaia opened her door standing in the doorway with a damp towel in one hand, sponging her face clean. Her hair was pulled back into a slightly neater ponytail, and she was in jeans and a grey t-shirt. Noland smiled, she really did wear a lot of grey. She also smelled like lemon, and hyssop.

"Thank you," Achaia said taking the blanket from under his arm. As she threw it over her bed, and folded it in half to keep it from overflowing onto the floor, Noland went to work on the fire.

"Achaia," he said as he stood back up.

"Yeah?" Achaia turned to face him, putting one hand in her

back pocket. It was a casual enough stance, and yet she looked like she was braced for rebuke.

Noland smirked, before frowning. "Don't ever let pride keep you from asking for my help." Noland fixed Achaia with a serious look. "Ever."

"Are you calling me proud?" Achaia smirked without humor.

"Yes," Noland nodded.

"Gee, thanks," Achaia grabbed her sweat shirt and put it on quickly.

"Hey," Noland started.

"Breakfast, yeah?" Achaia said gesturing toward the door for them to go ahead through it.

***

Breakfast was dead silent. No one seemed to want to talk, for fear of starting an argument with Bale. Achaia wasn't sure what she had missed at dinner the night before, but everyone seemed to instinctively trust that even if they disagreed with him, Bale must be right; and his decisions to keep Achaia untrained were all for the best, even if they didn't understand it.

Achaia kept her thoughts to herself. She wasn't sure if it was her half-human nature that kept her from trusting Bale fully, or maybe just the fact that she was the object of his loathing… Part of her, though, wondered if he was right; maybe she was dangerous… She thought briefly of what she must look like from Bale's point of view. What was it like for him to meet her? What kind of first impression did she make?

***

The training room was dark, despite the ample windows lining the outer wall. Storm clouds were rolling in, and a foreboding darkness had commandeered the skies.

Noland had his head out the door, looking either way before closing it behind him. "I can't believe I'm doing this."

"Doing what?" Achaia asked more worried than confused. She had never seen him wear this expression. His brows were knit together, and his jaw set. He looked a little too resolute to just be preparing for a lesson. He looked as if he stood on the front line of a battle that was ready to commence.

"They have forbidden us to train you in anything but self-defense." Achaia knew this already, but Noland went on, "We are to teach you nothing of weapons," he started naming them on his fingers, "battle strategy, hand to hand combat, or aerial combat." His jaw was clenched as he spoke and his face was nearing an alarming shade of red.

"So I can only learn how to run away?" Achaia summarized. "These are going to be some fun lessons... I already know how to put one foot in front of the other in a rapid succession, thanks." She shook her head bitterly. "I mean, it kind of helps to have a weapon when you're defending yourself from enemies who get to have weapons."

"This is ludicrous!" Noland agreed. He shoved both of his hands through his hair, his elbows hanging down, and stared at the floor.

"I can't help but feel like they kind of want me to die." Achaia said not bothering to disguise the bitter sarcasm in her tone.

Noland remained still, staring down in thought. Unable to see his face, Achaia walked over to look out of the window. The sky was opaque with the ominous storm clouds. If she hadn't just finished breakfast, she would have sworn it were night.

She knew the reason behind their verdict. Joash, Bale, and probably a fair number of the others, saw her as a threat. You don't train your enemy... But if she were killed because she was prevented from learning to defend herself—she was still half human... they were obligated to at least halfheartedly protect her, perhaps. Would God care what happened to her? If she were compromised, would it count as a failure on the Nephilim's part, in His eyes? She was, after all, a Charge.

"What are you thinking about?" Noland joined her at the window.

Achaia looked up at him and cocked her eyebrow.

"Your face. That was a 'thinking face,'" he said sitting next to her on the wide windowsill.

"Why they wouldn't want me trained in combat." Achaia admitted, telling half the truth.

Noland seemed to be listing a few reasons silently in his mind. They sat quietly staring out the window at the mounting snow, and the flakes that fogged the view of the buildings across the street. After a few minutes, Noland spoke, "Achaia, you're my Charge." He looked down at her, searching her face, and studying her. "I have taken my place as an Elder, and I'm making my own verdict." He looked out of the window at the sky, again. Snow was packed tight along the city streets, and the wind howled. "I am going to turn you into the greatest warrior they've ever seen." He said hoarsely. He looked back down at her and smiled. "But, it's probably best if we don't tell anyone else about that."

"But—" Achaia looked at him in surprise.

Noland's expression of fixed resolution was back.

"When Emile—"

"This is different Achaia," Noland shook his head, a sadness filling his eyes, "the battlefield is different than yesterday. The lines are drawn up, and they've all turned grey."

Achaia sat for a moment in silence, rolling Noland's words over and over in her mind. She wondered what he meant by the lines being grey. Were the sides all shifting? For a fleeting second she thought of sharing the message from Lucifer, with his proposal, but quickly dismissed the idea. It was too risky. Instead, she simply asked, "So, where do we start?"

Noland smiled, and led her across the room. "Do you know what makes Nephilim weaponry so special?" he asked, coming to stand next to a large table covered with every type of weapon imaginable, from every time period Achaia had ever heard of. The table almost looked like a green flowing river with all of the weapons composed of the heavenly metal.

"Um, the fancy supernatural metal?"

Noland cocked an eyebrow and smirked. "Do you know what it's called?"

"Isn't it like, Diadamantium or something?"

"You've been spending way too much time with Olivier." Noland picked up a sword and spun it around in his hands like most high school boys would do with a pencil in class. He handled it with the ease that comes with years of practice. The blade was a continuation of his arms, his fingers... He manipulated it with his will, and it was almost like the blade was hearing his thoughts and acting, before his muscles had thus provoked it. "It's called Diemerilium." Noland looked from the blade to Achaia, and handed it out to her, presenting it flat, across his arms, with the handle free for her to grab.

The sword was heavier than it looked, and much more solid. It didn't feel anything like water, though it looked like it should. And instead of even being cool to the touch like metal, it was warm in her hand. "Is it warm from where you held it?" She asked.

"Actually, I'm glad you asked. That's perceptive of you." Noland smiled and picked up another, smaller blade. "No. Well, maybe a little. But Diemerilium isn't like other metals, it isn't going to be initially cool to the touch. Our blades are smithed with heavenly fire. They are heated and hammered repeatedly, to make the blades stronger. The more they are heated the stronger they get. Heavenly fire is the only force hot enough to melt the elements down to bond them. The core is steel, with the strongest iron. After the blade has been formed, that is only its core. The edges and point, the coating on the outside, that makes it look like water, is actually diamond and emerald."

"I get diamonds, I mean they are super strong, right? But why emerald?" Achaia asked, studying the greenish hue.

"Diamonds are strong yes, but they also symbolize innocence. Those we fight to protect. But the emerald is even more important. Emeralds not only symbolize love, and the preservation of it, it also symbolizes hope. The emerald also steadies your mind in battle. It gives the warrior bearing it wisdom, reason, and a connection to God. You'll never be closer to God than when you are fighting for his cause. Well, at least for as long as we are stuck here, paying for the sins of our fathers." Noland's mouth had moved into a straight line.

"So, you say these blades basically give you super fighting skills, just by holding them?" Achaia looked back down at the sword in her hand.

"Achaia, is it so hard to believe? I mean, you already have 'super fighting skills', you're a supernatural being, in a supernatural safe house, being punished for a supernatural father's supernatural transgression..."

"Well, when you put it that way..." Achaia tried to turn the sword in her hand the way Noland had done.

"No, wait," Noland said, coming beside her. "You want to hold it like this." He demonstrated the grip she should have, on the blade he held in his hand.

Achaia watched him and mimicked.

"Now, start slow, just get comfortable with it. Each blade is different, just like people. You have to get to know each one. The weight, where it settles in your hand, where it pulls... The blade will tell you where it wants to go. The wisdom of the blade comes when you listen."

Achaia mimicked Noland's movements, as he slowly moved the blade to and fro before him, stepping forward with a foot, and raising the blade, and withdrawing again. After a half hour or so, Achaia's arms were getting sore. Noland put his blade down on the table again.

"You're a quick learner. We should blast through these in no time." He smiled down at the table optimistically.

"Question," Achaia said, laying her sword next to Noland's.

"Answer," Noland said taking a sip of water from his bottle.

"You said that the blades get stronger the more times they are heated." Achaia cocked an eyebrow.

"With heavenly fire—" Noland nodded.

"So, can you make your sword stronger by heating it?" She felt her cheeks flush. "I'm sorry, I don't even know if that is considered, like, a personal question."

Noland smirked, as his cheeks warmed to a pink. "It is a little personal. But, I don't think it's weird that you should ask it. Most Nephilim would just already know the answer to that, and not have to ask. But, yes." Noland said very matter-of-factly, shrugging away the answer like it was nothing.

"Yes." Achaia nodded, waiting for more. Noland didn't speak.

"So do you just win all the time?" Achaia felt her eyes widen in wonder.

Noland laughed. "Okay, first, having the strongest weapon doesn't determine the winner. The person who knows how to use their weapon, usually wins. And the one who is the best at battle strategy, is cunning, focused..."

"I get it, there are lots of factors."

"Second, yes, I do win all the time." He smiled and started walking for the door.

"Well we'll just have to wait and see if that remains the case," Achaia said catching up to him.

Noland smiled sideways at her. "I guess we will."

***

Emile led Achaia up several flights of stairs and through a door leading out onto a flat section of roof surrounded by the pointed dome-like spears spiking the top of the safe house. The spears cut out most of the wind, but Achaia could still glance around them and take in the surrounding buildings and their architecture.

"Olivier and Yellaina are helping the servants clean the library," He said, sitting on a waist high ledge that surrounded the roof.

Achaia walked over to where he sat and glanced over the edge. It was quite a long way down, and there was quite a lot of architectural detail to hit on the way down.

At the look that must have crossed her face, Emile laughed. "We can fly, remember."

Achaia shook her head and perched herself on the ledge next to him.

"I think history is better absorbed when you have a broader perspective," Emile looked at the city around them, "rather than confined to a classroom."

Achaia nodded. Moscow was breathtaking. The buildings looked like massive intricate igloos. Snow and ice covered everything, painting the city white. Bright colors peeked out from under some of the ice, making Achaia wonder how colorful the city would be once it all melted, not that she cared to stay long enough to find out.

"Right, so history." Achaia turned her attention back to Emile.

"So I'll skip trying to explain that God was never created, and there was no beginning of time… We will start with when God decided to create angels; His first creation." Emile tugged on his scarf, bunching it up closer to his face. "When God was alone, His breath mixed with the atmosphere and formed clouds. One day, God took some of the cloud in His hand, and molded it into a form, as if shaping clay. He took His mold and breathed into it life, and the first Nephilim was created. Now the Nephilim were created from the essence of God, but were not God, so He called them His children. When the Nephilim brought Him joy, He decided to make for them brothers and sisters. So, He plucked a star from the heavens and He forged it with holy fire, and breathed into it life, and thus created Seraphim. Now the Seraphim were strong and brave, like the Nephilim, but they didn't contain the essence of God. When God saw that what He had created was different, and good, He desired those who would appreciate His work, and keep records of it, so He plucked a hair from the head of a Nephilim, and planted it with a tear from a Seraphim, and from the clouds grew Cherubim. Now the Cherubim not being quite as strong as the Nephilim or the Seraphim, but being born from the very mind of God were wise, and compassionate, they valued all that the Lord created, and wrote songs and poems about all they saw and heard."

"This sounds like a fairy tale," Achaia smiled as she pictured a universe of clouds.

Emile smiled, and kept talking, "That was the creation of the first choir. God knew His children needed shelter, so He set the Nephilim to building a city of gold, with streets laid in golden bricks. He set the Seraphim, with their fire, to smith gates of pearl and a pearly wall to surround the city. When the city was complete, and God saw that it was beautiful, He sought to fill it with more children, so He created six more breeds of angels whom He also called children."

"That's a lot of children," Achaia mused.

Emile nodded. "Heaven was radiantly beautiful, and all who lived inside it were loyal to the Lord."

"Then what happened?" Achaia asked, pulling her leg up under her to turn and face Emile.

"God, being a brilliant and wonderful creator, kept creating. He had created the heavens, and He moved on to create the earth and all that lives on the earth. For a time, all was splendor and beauty. But God was taken with this new creation, and loved it as He had loved the first. Some of the angels grew jealous of humans. See, they thought that the humans were lesser beings, and undeserving of God's affection. Some angels were infuriated to be equated with humans, and believed that they were superior and should be allowed to rule over humanity. When it was discovered that humans had been endowed with free will, a gift not bestowed upon angels, one angel in particular grew enraged, and sought to use that very gift to avenge God for this slight, and injustice."

"Lucifer," Achaia guessed.

"Yes. Lucifer was furious that these lowly lesser beings should have something that he was not allowed. He broke something inside of himself, and fractured his nature. His bond to the Lord was severed, and his spirit turned against the Lord. However, Lucifer was charming, and up to this point had been trusted, and worthy of that trust. So when he began to talk of equality, and doing what was best for all, the other angels listened to him. They thought that if they were all God's children, they should all be given equal privileges, and entrusted the same. They forgot that they each had their gifts that set them apart and made them different even from their own kind. Humanity's gift was free will.

"See the angels all worshiped God, day and night, but it was in their nature to do so, so they did. They did not think about it, or choose to worship, it was as natural and necessary as breathing. So God had fashioned a people who could choose Him, or deny Him. He wanted to be chosen. As He had chosen to create and to love, so He wished to be chosen and loved. But this gift, as the angels saw it, was also a curse, a weakness for humanity. Satan beguiled the humans, and turned them against God, hoping to see God hate them in return and spurn them."

"How manipulative and cruel!" Achaia spat. She found herself caught up in the story. She could see it all so clearly in her head, as she focused on the sound of Emile's voice.

"The very gift that God had granted to Lucifer was the one he was using to try to hurt God, and humanity. That is what happens when a nature is broken. It grows toxic, and vile."

"That's terrible," Achaia said softly.

"That is what makes the council so wary of you. You have free will. You have the ability to turn from God and manipulate others, without even breaking your nature. You can choose to be that way."

"But I wouldn't—"

"I know that," Emile assured her. "But the council has seen

many wars, and a lot of people choose deliberately to do terrible things. They may sometimes grow to care about their Charges on an individual basis, but humanity as a whole is not to be trusted."

"Emile," Achaia started, thinking of something.

"Yeah?"

"Are the Charges ever— well, are they ever bad?"

Emile frowned. "Olivier will get to that part eventually, but yes. Those who do great evil are sometimes necessary to shape history and change the hearts of men. We don't know what it is our Charges are bound for, only that they need to stay alive to do them."

Achaia shook her head, trying to process this. Could she protect the next Hitler? Achaia wasn't sure she wanted to be a Guardian if she was going to be assigned to protect a murderer to make sure he could murder. "That just doesn't seem right!"

"People are seldom, if ever, good or evil. They are all a civil war of both. Some days the light wins, and some days it's the darkness. But they all deserve the chance to fight."

Achaia tried to swallow this. Her brain, yet again, felt like it was going to explode.

"Maybe we should call that quits for today." Emile put a comforting hand on Achaia's shoulder and squeezed. "It's worth fighting."

"What is?" Achaia asked.

"That civil war."

# 16

# The Truth about Terror

"We cannot learn without pain"

-Aristotle

"Okay. Now, everyone has their favorite weapon that they are the most proficient with. But you need to be extremely comfortable with at least two, and capable of utilizing them all." Noland said, picking up the dagger and handing it back to Achaia, after disarming her.

Achaia nodded. She had learned a lot over the last few weeks, including which weapons she liked, and which ones she definitely needed to work on. "And if I am going to be the best, then I need to be proficient to the point that you can't tell which one is my favorite." She added, looking down at a diemerillium whip. It was covered in watery scales, and shaped like a snake with emerald eyes that glimmered up at her.

Noland cocked an eyebrow and looked impressed. "That'll do," he smirked. "Now, let's move on to something a little more long range." Noland eyed the table full of weaponry.

Achaia ran a finger along the whip's body, and it slithered toward her, affectionately nudging her back with its head. Noland looked down and smiled. "The weapon chooses the warrior Achaia, it is not always clear why."

Achaia looked up stunned. "Did you just make a *Harry Potter* reference?"

"I live in a church Achaia, not under a rock," Noland smiled, "but I'll deny any such geekery if you make mention of it to Olivier."

Achaia shook her head and laughed. She was taking her training very seriously. She had made it a ritual each night to sneak back to the training room once everyone else had gone to bed, and run the drills Noland had taught her each day, over again. Her arms were getting stronger, and her endurance longer. She could see a difference, and feel it with every training session.

"Now, when you're shooting a bow," Noland handed her a recurve bow that was surprisingly long, nearly the same height as her, "you don't want to hold it just straight up and down. Hold it at a forty-five or so degree angle, wherever you feel the most comfortable…"

"Gangster style?" Achaia asked turning the bow parallel to the ground.

"Achaia—" Noland shook his head.

Achaia released the arrow. It struck near the center of the target.

"Okay, not bad. But we want perfect. So, be serious." Noland came up behind her and adjusted the bow back to a forty-five degree angle and put his hand over hers on the string. "Use these fingers, and let the arrow just rest there." He reached around with his other hand to grab the bow over her hand. "Then draw it back—" Noland's thumb rested against her jaw as she leaned in to look down the sight. "Take a second to just focus." He took a breath, and let it out. "Forget about your dad. Forget about the council. Forget about Bale, training, all of us. Forget that I am here."

Achaia, feeling the heat of him surround her, thought that was a bit much to ask, but nodded that she understood what he meant.

"Just breathe," he sucked in a slow breath in her ear, and she followed, "and be." He let the breath out slowly and released the arrow. Bullseye.

Achaia jogged over to release the arrow and found it stuck through the target up to the cresting. She grabbed hold of the fletching and pulled. The shaft squeaked as it slid back through the target, she cringed at the sound. Everything had been so quiet, it felt like a violation to her ears.

"Again." Noland said as she came back to the line.

***

Lunch was served, and eaten, quickly. Achaia was always ravenous after her training sessions with Noland; and the cook, Dahlia, was a little too good at her job. The sky outside had brightened in the past weeks with the arrival of March, but the air outside was still frigid cold, and snow still covered the city.

Achaia sat at the table, sipping her tea (which she had been training just as hard to learn to like), looking out the windows.

"Have you heard anything back from Naphtali?" Yellaina asked, looking to both Achaia and Noland for response.

"Not a whisper," Noland said. Achaia nodded that her response was the same.

"What about any word from the council?" Olivier asked. "I mean, how long do they expect us to stay here?"

"Not a peep from them either," Noland said, and stopped short as Bale entered the room.

"And you're not likely to," Bale mumbled, walking across the room without looking at any of them to stand at the window.

Achaia looked around the table at each of her friend's faces. The mood always dimmed and became tense when Bale entered the room. If Bale had distrusted Achaia when she had first arrived, he flat-out couldn't stand the sight of her now. For the last few weeks, Bale had hardly spoken a word to her, and when he did, she'd wished that he hadn't. She had grown to appreciate being ignored.

"What do you mean?" Emile asked.

"You think they mean for us to stay here indefinitely?" Amelia added.

"You say that like Russia is terrible." Yellaina looked at Amelia sharply. Everyone else at the table turned to stare at Yellaina with cocked eyebrows. Yellaina looked at each of them, then shrugged and turned her attention back to her plate as Bale answered.

"This is where the Nephilim send their undesirables."

"Undesirables?" Olivier asked, sounding affronted.

"Not you," Achaia said reassuringly. "Me."

Olivier gave her a sad sort of smile to reassure her that it wasn't true to him at least.

"And me." Bale said curtly.

"You?" Emile asked. "But—"

"The Nephilim don't like being reminded of their transgressions. They don't appreciate instruction or correction. They are prideful. Which is why they are fallen."

"But you're—"

"Holy?" Bale turned around. "They don't like the constant reminder of what they forfeited." Bale said shortly. "I can go to Him, see Him whenever I please. *They* are forever separated." He shrugged, as if this were all obvious. "I am an inconvenient reminder they hide away, and try to forget."

"And what am I?" Achaia asked boldly. Noland shot her a look, which she ignored, keeping her eyes on Bale.

Bale turned to look at her, his expression full of sympathy merged with disgust. "You're something I can't blame them for hiding away."

Achaia recoiled as if she'd been hit. "Why?" she asked, fighting the urge to cower. She forced herself to retain eye-contact, but her voice came out weak and stunned.

"Because you're nothing good. I could feel it on you the second you walked through that door, shrouded in death. Nothing good will come from you. *They* hid you away, *I* would have you in a cage." He spat out the last part, as Noland stood to his feet, knocking his chair back in the process.

"That decision does not lie with you alone. The council has declared her safe." Noland's voice was like ice.

"The council has declared her inconsequential. They're wrong!" Bale looked at Noland as if he were rebuking a child who was having a temper tantrum. "Her blood runs with destruction—"

"She is Nephilim!" Noland rounded the table, approaching Bale, nearly yelling.

"She is an abomination! If I must keep her in a cell, I will!" Bale had lost all of his composure. The blood had rushed to his face, and his body pulsed with rage. Achaia couldn't wrap her mind around why it was such a big deal that she was half-human. She wished she could be absorbed into the chair in which she sat, or disappear altogether. "You think I don't know what she does at night?" Achaia snapped to, in surprise.

"You would keep us apart?" Noland asked, lowering his voice, seeming to read something in Bale's eyes the rest of them could not see. He managed to sound deadlier than ever with incredulity.

Olivier and Yellaina were staring at Achaia with wide, shocked eyes. Achaia, realizing what the conversation must have sounded like to them, shook her head violently, before staring back and forth between the Bale and Noland; who seemed to carry on their argument silently. Their eyes were locked onto one another, but their expressions shifted in response to what the other seemed to be relaying by thought alone. Finally Noland's stare narrowed, and when he spoke, he did so with finality. "You will not keep us apart. Not by any country, city, building, door, or cell. She is *mine*."

Emile who was sitting diagonally across from Achaia gasped. She looked over at him, as he stared away from her toward Bale and Noland. His face was drained of blood and ghostly white. Achaia feeling that something wasn't right, stood and rounded the table toward him. She saw his eyes were locked, not on Noland and Bale, but on the window.

"Emile?"

"No," he uttered in a breathy whisper, his eyes full of terror. Achaia was not the only one to turn her attention to Emile. Everyone in the room followed his gaze and looked to the window.

Not a second later, an explosion shook the city. Everyone was grabbing whoever, or whatever was nearest to them as the cathedral shook.

Bale flew to the window, staring out at the city beyond, Noland at his side. Achaia could just see smoke billowing up from the streets, past their silhouettes.

Emile gasped again, a more choked and guttural sound than before. He grasped his chest as he collapsed to the floor. He lay on his side, gasping for air.

Achaia dropped to her knees next to him, as Noland rushed over, and everyone else clamored around them. "Emile!" Noland said, grabbing hold of Emile's shoulder. "Emile?"

"Is he having a heart attack?" Achaia asked, looking up to Bale, who still stood at the window, but had turned to face them.

"No." Bale said flatly. His voice, losing all emotion, sounded unnatural. He approached them slowly, staring at Emile on the floor, through the crowd around him. "He has the shock and grief of thousands, their utter despair, falling on him." He met her eye with a look that turned her blood cold. "Look!" He yelled, closing the space between them and dragging her by the arm over to the window. "Look!"

Below, car alarms were sounding, debris was scattered all over. Glass, and bits of walls, littered the street. Cries were welling up like waves, and the smoke and ashes like recalled rain.

Achaia's arm throbbed where Bale squeezed his hand around it. "You brought this down on us, *death angel*," he spat venomously, yanking her closer to the window.

Achaia flinched back from the inflection in his voice, shocked. What was a death angel? She thought she was Nephilim... she had thought he had hated her for being human, but this confused her even more. How could she have caused any of this destruction? She blamed herself for many things, but how had she caused this?

"Remove your hand, before I detach it from your body." Bale let go with a shove, and Achaia turned to see Noland standing with his sword drawn, pointing it at Bale's neck.

The cries of the people down below flooded Achaia's ears;

cries of grief, but also cries for help. She turned again and looked out of the window. "They need help," Achaia said, looking over at Emile, who was curled, shaking and whimpering on the floor. No one was paying attention to her. All eyes were locked on Noland and his sword.

The window next to them exploded inward, glass flying like bullets through the air. Achaia, Noland and Bale, were thrust back from the window as it shattered. Chunks of the ceiling crumbled down into the room. Achaia covered her head on the floor. As the shaking stopped, she stood back to her feet. She glanced around the room to see that everyone was alright, then took off at a sprint toward the now-open window.

"Achaia NO!" She heard Noland's voice yell, as she dove through. Releasing her wings, she plummeted downward, and was bathed in ashes. She soared down in the thick of the smoke, following the screams, and landed on the street. It appeared as if a car had been blown through the front windows of a shop front. Achaia stepped over the blown in wall, cutting her leg on the shards of glass, still held in the frame.

The sight that met her eyes, was worse than any action or horror film she'd ever seen. The walls that remained were splattered with dust, and ash, and blood. She could hardly see through the billowing ash and smoke. A small fire was burning in the engine of the car. Achaia hoped the car didn't explode.

"Pomogi mne!" A small voice was crying in Russian. Achaia ran toward the sound, tripped over something, and fell hard, hitting her chin on the floor. She tasted blood as she turned and looked behind her to see what she had tripped over. It was an arm. Just an arm. She felt bile rising in her throat, and threw up on the floor in front of her. She took a few ragged breaths, and pushed forward to where the voice had come. "Pomogi mne!" It cried.

Beneath the wheel well of the car, was pinned a girl who looked like she couldn't be any older than twelve. "I'm here!" Achaia said, kneeling next to the girl.

"Achaia!" A voice called on the street outside. "Achaia where are you?"

"Olly!" Achaia called back. "In here! Quick I need your help!"

Olivier appeared through the ashes, his hair white with them. He saw the car, and the girl and his face blanched. "I'll try to lift it, you pull her." He said squatting down and getting a grip on the edge of the car. "Agh!" He yelled, letting go of it. "It's hot!" He said, gulping back his dread, and taking hold of it again. "One, two—" Olivier struggled, and tried to lift the car, yelling with the effort.

Achaia grabbed the girl from beneath the shoulders, and pulled her as quickly as she could. Her legs were very obviously broken, bone peeking through the skin.

More people were yelling, Achaia fought against an overwhelming sense of helplessness. She knew she couldn't get to all of them. "We have to split up." Achaia said.

Olivier looked at her and nodded. The ground shook again and the already broken building around them crumbled more. Another bomb had detonated.

"How many?" Achaia breathed. Olivier looked to be thinking the same. "Where are the others?" Achaia asked.

"Noland is looking for you, I was just faster. Yellaina and Amelia stayed back with Emile."

"Come on," Achaia said, "get her out of here." Olivier picked up the little girl and began carrying her out toward the street.

Achaia followed them out, and took off at a run, listening for survivors. There was devastation everywhere she looked. She couldn't tell what was a pile of bricks, or a body adorned in dust. There were alarms, sirens in the distance, wails and screams, and parts of buildings still raining down onto the streets.

She heard loud weeping coming from across the street. A woman sat hunched over a man, who was obviously dead. The woman was scratched up and bruised, but otherwise unharmed. "You should leave, there may be more explosions." Achaia said. The woman looked up at her with bloodshot, tear drenched, eyes. It was apparent she didn't speak much English. Achaia bitterly thought of her language lessons with Yellaina, where she'd been studying Latin and angelic tongues, which were all useless in Russia, where they spoke Russian... She gestured with her hands for her to get out of there. The woman, sobbing, got to her feet, and limped away as fast as she could, holding her chest in anguish.

Everywhere in the streets there were people laying wounded. Some were struggling to get up. Others were missing limbs. Achaia saw a light to her left and turned to see what it was. Her heart sank as she saw the clock counting down. Ten seconds.

"Everyone get out!" She yelled as she ran into the building. Those who could, ran out passed her.

"Achaia!" She heard her name but didn't have time to turn to see who it belonged to. She did the only thing she could think of and threw herself onto the bomb, trying to cover it as much as possible with her body. "NO!"

Then she was being pushed off of it, hard, and another body took her place. Achaia rolled across the floor and looked up just in time to see the bomb detonate.

It all seemed to happen in a time of its own. She watched as the body on top of the bomb was thrust up into the air. She saw the fire beneath it begin to spread out. And then the body came back down, and the fire vanished.

Achaia felt the burn on her skin. The fire had been so hot, and then it was just gone. She sat up on the ground, struggling to raise herself into a sitting position. She slid across the floor, trying to see who had pushed her out of the way. The body on the bomb was Noland's.

***

Shael was sitting alone in his room when he heard the commotion out in the passageways. It was either a fight or a celebration. With demons it was hard to tell. Like German, everything just sounded angry in the demonic languages.

Shael opened his door and stepped out looking left, then right. Clusters of demons were gathered around two or three who seemed to have just come back from assignment. "What is going on?" Shael asked grabbing the nearest demon's shoulder.

The beast turned, with a snarl, but then changed his tune when he saw who had spoken to him. "Many have fallen, and the gates are crowded. There was a terrorist attack at the Nephilim's safe house," he laughed, a deep growling sound.

"Where was this? Which safe house? Were any Nephilim killed?" Shael asked frantically. If the council had taken Achaia they certainly would have placed her in one of their institutions.

"Moscow," The demon answered. "But I don't know of any angel blood at the gates."

Shael pushed through the crowd trying to get to the center to hear first-hand, from the demons who had been present.

"Women and children!" The demon was shrieking with glee. It was a tiny little bat-like creature with a thick seventh circle accent. "The Nephilim were trying to save them, but there were more bombs, and then more!"

"The Nephilim?" Shael piped in, as if he had just arrived and this were new news. The demons went quiet, realizing who was in their midst. Shael had become like royalty to them, Lucifer's right hand man. "What did they look like?"

The demon's smile vanished. "The angels?" Shael nodded impatiently. "Did they perish in the explosions?"

"Angel blood was spilled, I smelt it." The demons winced as if the smell was something awful. "Two of them ran in and tried to stop a bomb from detonating. They were blown up! I heard it go off!"

The crowd of demons cheered at this.

"What did they look like!" Shael was losing his temper. The demon looked taken aback.

"I don't know, the one guy was tall, and big. He had blond hair..."

"What about the other one?" Shael tried not to relax yet.

"I don't know, she had red hair."

Shael's knees went out, and he collapsed onto them. The demons around him, backed away, staring cautiously. Shaking, Shael stood back on his feet, and somehow pushed through all the demon's blocking him from his room. Once inside he shut the door, and fell to his knees again, shaking uncontrollably.

"Don't let it be true."

\*\*\*

Bale looked out of the window through which Achaia had disappeared. Smoke was rising in billows from the streets, and cries of terror were still rising in wisps on the wind. He felt each one in his chest. Rage filled his heart. The wailing filled his ears, with the sirens that had started flooding in. He turned his attention back to those remaining in the room. Emile had gone unconscious. Yellaina and Amelia were hunched over him, whispering.

"Come," Bale said gathering their attention, "we will take him to his bed. He'll be more comfortable there. I'll have a healer come in and look at him." Bale stooped, and put one of Emile's arms around his shoulders while Amelia grasped the other. They carried him that way back to his room, and laid him in the bed. Amelia covered him with blankets and turned to look at Bale.

"What else can I do?" she asked.

Bale looked down at Emile's pale face. "When he wakes, he'll be needing comfort more than anything. Whatever will bring him that, and warm his soul. What are his favorite things?"

"Well he really loves jazz music?" Amelia offered. "And... hot chocolate?"

"That's a good start," he said, reassuring her that she was heading in the right direction. "Can you go into the library and see if we have any jazz albums?" Bale asked, looking to Yellaina who had followed them in.

Yellaina nodded. "I think I saw some when we were cleaning."

"I'll go fetch the healer, and have some hot chocolate sent from the kitchens," Bale said with a small bow. "I also need to inform the council that the Cohen girl has escaped."

Yellaina stopped in the doorway, where she'd been heading for the library.

"She'll come back," Amelia said calmly.

"What makes you think that?" Bale asked, failing to keep the contempt out of his voice.

"We know her," Yellaina said not bothering with trying to hide her disdain.

Bale nodded curtly, and turned back to Amelia. "You need only remain at his side," he said as he exited the room passing Yellaina, and receiving a glare as he did. He admired her loyalty to her friend, even if it was misplaced. Amelia was wiser, less emotional. He liked that she displayed a rationale behind her decisions and actions, and didn't just react. That was something he could respect… Bale shook his head clear of these sorts of thoughts, and focused on the task at hand.

As he walked the halls to the healer's quarters, he focused on his breathing, trying to calm himself. He knew what he needed to do. But he would see Emile taken care of first. Emile was, after all, under *his* protection.

***

Olivier was pulling a man out from under a collapsed column when the bomb exploded. He heard it as if from a distance, coming from across the street; in the building that Achaia had just gone into. "No," he whispered to himself, perching the man against the wall, and leaving him to catch his breath and assess the damage.

Olivier was across the street before the man could have blinked and noticed he was gone. "Achaia?" He called. The building looked to have been some kind of restaurant or café. There were busted up tables, and a counter. It looked like most of the people that had been there, had cleared out after the first explosion. There was, it seemed, only property damage. "Achaia?" Olivier called again.

He knew he had heard something happen here, but there was no fire, no fresh floating ash…

Then he heard whimpering.

"No, no, no, no, no."

Olivier rounded the counter.

Behind it, her red hair frosted with dust and ash, Achaia lay on the floor slumped over someone. "Please wake up. Don't be gone. Please." She was sobbing. Her body convulsing as she laid atop the body of a man.

Olivier came to kneel next to her. Her long curly hair was concealing the man's face. But Olivier knew those clothes. He felt as if his heart had fallen into his stomach and the air was wretched from his lungs. Olivier's knees hit the ground, hard. "No." He fell over Achaia, pulling her off of him. "Noland?" Olivier said, seeing, for himself, his face. "Achaia?" Olivier asked looking to her to explain what had happened.

Achaia's face was streaked black with grime and tears. Her eyes were bright with red and green. Olivier thought to himself unimportantly that he had always thought her eyes were blue…

"I saw the bomb. It was going to go off." She looked down at Noland. She tugged at his arm, pulling him over, to lay face up. "I dove for it." She said looking down at his face, "but he pushed me off, and covered it himself." She hesitated on the last part as she looked down to Noland's torso. His jacket and shirt had been burned away, and were still smoking; but his skin was clear and golden brown. "What?" She whispered, touching his stomach. She drew back her hand as if she'd touched a hot stove.

Olivier looked at her, hope on both of their faces. "Noland," Olivier said, looking to Noland's face.

"Noland." Achaia leaned across his chest, cupping his face in her hands. "Noland please wake up," she begged. Olivier had never heard her sound so scared, or determined.

Olivier knelt forward and began praying. It was a prayer his mother had taught him as a child, in Greek. It was a prayer that was meant to plead for wholeness and restoration, for redemption. Every Nephilim child learned it, for it was the prayer their parents had prayed to come up out of Hell, and to have the opportunity to pay their penance. They called it the Metanoia.

As they sat there, Achaia had stopped crying and gone stone still, her head laid on Noland's chest. Olivier kept mumbling his prayer quietly to himself, laying his hand over Noland's forehead.

"I can hear his heart beating." Achaia said numbly. "Why won't he wake?"

Then, Noland abruptly took in a deep breath, causing Achaia to jump back as Olivier snapped his hand away. Olivier stared in amazement as Noland sat up on his elbows and looked around him.

"You're alright?" he asked Achaia, unable to see Olivier, who was kneeling behind him.

"How did you know you could absorb the bomb?" Achaia asked. Olivier leaned around to the side, to see the side of Noland's face.

Noland was looking at Achaia in a way that Olivier had never seen him look at anyone before. "I didn't," he answered.

With a small squeak-like sound Achaia fell forward and tucked herself into Noland's chest. Noland sat up completely and wrapped his arms around her. Olivier felt a little awkward. He debated sneaking out, before Noland realized he was there.

"I thought you were gone." Achaia was crying again.

"I did too." Noland said putting his mouth to the top of Achaia's head.

Olivier cleared his throat. Noland turned. "Olivier!"

"Welcome back buddy." Olivier smiled. "I think we should get you to the infirmary and let the healer take a look at you."

Noland smiled, and let Achaia go. She stood, and helped Olivier get Noland to his feet. Olivier was amazed that Noland seemed mostly unharmed, perhaps a little sore, but he could walk on his own.

Out of the smoke and ash, and past the small fires on the

streets, the three of them walked around the arriving ambulances back up to the front steps of the safe house.

***

The healer was every bit as good at her job, as the cook was at her's. She had just finished tending to Emile when Noland, Achaia, and Olivier came hobbling up the stairs.

"What's all this?" she asked, taking in the sight of them. "You," She said pointing at Olivier, "ice bath," she pointed to one of the small rooms off of the infirmary that Noland suspected were private baths. "You," she pointed at Achaia, who startled. Noland smiled to himself. The healer was a tiny Russian Nephilim woman who, though little, was intimidating with her Russian accent and ability to be assertive. "Go in that room and take off those filthy clothes and burn them. They have death and filth all over them, I will be in to take a look at you in a minute. But this one," the healer took a closer look at Noland, coming over and placing her hands on his face, and looking into his eyes. "We nearly lost you, didn't we?" She swallowed hard, looking into his face. Lowering her voice she whispered, "we don't need you taking after your parents." She gave him a stern look, and then began appraising his torso, where his clothes had been blown up.

"I'm okay, just a little sore, please go tend to the others first."

"You lay on a bomb, and tell me to check your friends first?" The woman gave an eerie laugh. "That is what makes you a great leader." She patted him on the shoulder, and then pushed him down forcefully into a chair. "Now sit, and shut up."

Noland sat in silence, as she hummed to herself over him, bandaging his wounds with oils, and rubbing something cold over his stomach and chest.

"You need to rest." She ordered, shooing him away to his

room. "For several days, yes."

"Da, da." Noland responded in Russian, and left, looking over his shoulder as the woman entered the room Achaia had gone into.

\*\*\*

Achaia stood awkwardly in the middle of a small bathroom. There was a corner fireplace, in which she had thrown her clothes, a wooden chair, and a bathtub. Above the bath were several shelves each holding jars filled with what looked like dried flowers, and salt.

The angry-Russian-healer-lady came into the bathroom without knocking. Achaia frantically moved to cover herself.

"I am a healer, I have seen all of everybody. You have nothing special. Please, sit."

Trying not to feel offended, Achaia plopped down onto the wooden chair.

"You have many cuts and burns." She made a low whistle when she took in the gash on Achaia's leg. "This will need stitches."

Achaia nodded, she felt pretty much numb all over. Whether it was adrenaline, or shock, she wasn't sure.

The healer started mixing a concoction of things in the tub, and started running the water. Steam rose up from the surface, and Achaia could smell the dried herbs that had been added. Her head felt light, and fuzzy. "What is your name?" Achaia asked, as the woman prepared a needle for the stitching.

"Inessa," she said shortly. "Now sit still."

Achaia didn't even flinch as Inessa stitched up the gash in her leg, and wrapped gauze around it. "You will need fresh, when you get out. And the rest of these will have to be wrapped." She said gesturing at Achaia's entire self. As Achaia stepped hesitantly into the hot tub, her cuts stung. She lowered herself in tentatively.

"You stay in till water gets cold." Inessa said and shut the door behind her as she left.

***

When her bath had run cold, Achaia stood from the tub, and dried off with a crisp white towel, feeling for the first time like she was in a doctor's office. "Inessa!" Achaia called out her cracked door. "Inessa, I need clothes!" Achaia heard laughter in the room next to hers. Olivier cracked his door.

"Looks like we're locked in the same boat. Did she burn yours too?" he chuckled.

"Yeah, 'too much death,'" Achaia laughed, mimicking Inessa's accent.

"Ah, here she comes," Olivier said cheerfully, "little ray of sunshine."

Inessa had just walked in the door with a stern almost angry look on her face; which Achaia suspected was her face at rest. "Here," she threw a robe at Achaia, and one at Olivier through the cracks in their doors.

Once dressed, Achaia and Olivier left together. Out in the hall Achaia grinned, "You know for a healer she has an incurable case of RBF?"

"What's RBF?" Olivier asked, looking over at her, as they turned down the hall their rooms were on.

"Well, um..." Achaia started.

"I'm just kidding," Olivier said nudging Achaia with his elbow.

They had reached Olivier's door. Achaia caught his arm, as he opened it to go inside. Olivier turned to face her. "Hey," she started. Olivier looked down at her cocking an eyebrow, a smile still painted on his face. Achaia had grown to love his smile. Olivier smiled so often, and could always joke and make lighter of situations which would otherwise destroy her. "Thanks for coming after me." Achaia wasn't great at being sentimental. "I'm sorry if my jumping seemed reckless or selfish, but I couldn't do nothing. I've done nothing my entire life, and it hasn't worked out so well. I don't want to do that anymore. But I wasn't trying to be reck—"

"Shh," Olivier wrapped one of his arms around Achaia's shoulders and pulled her into a hug. "You're my best friend, of course I came after you."

Achaia pulled back, shocked. "I'm your what?"

"You're my best friend." Olivier repeated, looking as if he felt a little unsure or awkward saying it a second time. "Is that? I'm sorry..."

"No!" Achaia said squeezing him back tightly. "You're my best friend too, I've just never had one before."

Olivier hugged her tighter, and rubbed her back, "well, I'm not going anywhere."

Achaia smiled, and tried not to admit there were tears welling up in her eyes.

"Besides, no one else gets my comic jokes or movie references."

Achaia laughed as they separated, and nodded before continuing on to her own room.

"And hey!" Olivier called after her, coming back out into the hall.

"Yeah?" Achaia turned.

"Noland came after you, too."

Achaia sucked in a breath that felt like a punch in the chest, as the image of Noland's body laid across the bomb flashed in her head. "Yeah, yeah he did." She nodded.

"You have more friends than you think, Frenchy." Olivier

winked at her, then shut his door.

Achaia struggled to steady her breathing again. The mental image of Noland's motionless body took her breath away and made her head shake involuntarily, as if that would loosen the image from her mind. She flinched all over, but opening her eyes, couldn't get rid of that sight. As she entered her room and closed the door she leaned heavily against it, and rubbed her eyes. Then she slid down her door and cried.

# 17

## Rescue Mission

"You don't always need a plan.
Sometimes you just need to breathe,
Trust, let go, and see what happens."
-Mandy Hale

The gates had been crowded. Shael had watched with his stomach mangled in horror as all the humans at the gates were sorted and dragged to the circle of Hell where they would spend their eternity. He had only been able to stand a moment, before the sight made him sick. When he didn't see any sign of Achaia or any other Nephilim he retreated back to his room. Shael didn't know what happened to Nephilim when they died. He knew Nathaniel and his wife had been killed, but no one seemed to have seen or heard anything of them since. He also wasn't sure if Achaia would be treated as a Nephilim or as a human in death…

He hoped she would be judged as a human. She was a good person, though, without faith, Shael wasn't sure that would be enough. Now more than ever, he regretted his decision to keep her in the dark. In his mind, he had always had more time. He had always believed without question that she would have a long life, and time to choose. Shael tried to take comfort in the fact that she wasn't in the crowd at the gate. If she had been killed, she was in Heaven, with her mother.

Shael thought for a moment about what their reunion would look like, and smiled. Anna would be able to run her hands through her daughter's curly red hair, which looked just like her own. Achaia would be able to see where she got her eyes, and her complexion. Would Anna see Shael in Achaia's nose? In the determined set of Achaia's jaw? Shael swallowed hard, and felt a lump in his throat. As long as Achaia wasn't here, he could forgive himself eventually. As long as Achaia never had to step foot in Hell.

***

Achaia sat next to Emile's bed. He was sitting up against the pillows with a cup of hot Russian tea in his hand. "How're you feeling?" Achaia asked, looking at the dark circles that lined his eyes, she could tell he hadn't slept much the night before.

"Pretty good, considering," he said taking a slow sip from his cup.

Soft morning light flooded the room through the windows. It was still cloudy and cold as ever outside, but the sun was fighting to make an appearance. It was just bright enough to almost make Achaia forget how dark the day before had been. Almost, but not quite. "I thought you were having a heart attack."

"Felt like one." Emile readjusted himself on the pillows. The room smelled like tea and lemons. The fire burning at the foot of the bed, made the room warm and cozy, to help Emile relax.

"I can't imagine." Achaia looked at the pale skin of Emile's neck, she could see his pulse. "It all happened so fast. I thought you were gasping at the argument, but then those bombs went off—"

"How many were there?" Emile asked, setting his teacup on the night stand.

"Four."

"Four?" Emile gasped, looking heartbroken.

"They were placed up and down the entire street," Achaia stood, and perched on the side of Emile's bed. Amelia had gone to take a shower, and a nap, leaving Achaia on "duty".

"Only this street?" Emile asked. "Not exactly a political move then. Was it?"

"Depends on which political system you're after," Achaia hinted. Emile looked at her with piqued interest. "Bale thinks they were trying to hit the safe house. They just didn't know exactly which building it was. Guess they thought an old Cathedral would be too obvious."

"Always the mental chess game. Do you go for the unexpected? Or the obvious? Since it's assumed they're smart enough to go for the unexpected... but then—"

"Yeah. I guess," Achaia said with a weak smile. "They got part of the building. There's damage, just not that much."

Emile nodded. "They say you jumped out the window."

Achaia sighed. "Who told you that?"

"Who do you think?" Emile smiled.

"Olivier."

Emile nodded.

"There were just so many cries," Achaia thought back, involuntarily, still hearing the echo in her ears, "people needed help. Then

I looked at you and thought, if that's what they were all feeling—how could I do nothing?"

"You might just be Nephilim after all." Emile smiled at her.

"Hey," A voice said from the doorway, behind Achaia. She turned to see Noland walking gingerly into the room.

"You shouldn't be up yet!" Achaia said standing. "The healer told you to stay in bed."

Noland waved for her to sit back down, and sat on the other side of Emile's bed, leaning against the other set of pillows. "Had to make sure Emile was holding up." He winced a little as he adjusted his legs.

"I'm well," Emile said looking at Noland as if he needed the bedrest more. "Dude, you got blown up…"

"Well if someone was going to, might as well be me." Noland shrugged, and winced again.

Achaia winced internally at the memory of Noland's body lying motionless where the bomb had been. "Tea?" she asked.

"I hate that stuff." Noland shook his head, looking over at the samovar on the bureau. "Don't tell Yellaina that, though." He gave each of them a warning glance.

Achaia smiled. "I thought I was the only one."

Noland's eyes grew wide in sarcastic surprise as he shook his head, again. "I'm more of a black coffee sort of guy."

"Me too," Achaia said. "I mean… black coffee, not that I'm a guy."

Noland and Emile both laughed silently. "Thanks for clarifying," Noland nodded. "I was confused there for a bit, but it's nice to know for sure you're female. I mean, I didn't want to assume your gender."

"Shut up!" Achaia slapped his leg.

Noland winced.

"Oh I'm sorry!"

"Gotcha," Noland laughed again.

Achaia rolled her eyes. Emile was shaking his head at them.

"Okay, so I wanted to check on Emile, but I also wanted to talk to you." Noland said, looking to Achaia; his expression more serious.

"Am I in trouble?" Achaia frowned. "Dumb question. Of course I am."

"Why did you do it?" Noland asked.

"Which part?" Achaia shrugged. "The jumping out a window, the going into collapsing buildings, or laying on top of a bomb?"

"All of the above," Noland said, sitting up a little straighter.

"Well from all the history Emile has been teaching me, I guess I could sum it all up by saying, I am my father's daughter."

"I don't want your father's reasons. I want yours." Noland's mouth was a thin line. He had gone quite serious.

Achaia took a deep breath and looked down at her hands, twiddling her fingers. "Over the last two months I have lost everything." She looked up into Noland's face. "I lost my dad. I lost the pride I had in my name. I lost my home. I lost my sense of security. I lost all sense of normalcy. I lost hope that the Nephilim are ever going to help me find my dad... I lost Naphtali." Noland just listened. "I couldn't stand by and hear the cries of those people, when I'm screaming like that inside, and do nothing. The only thing I haven't lost, is my purpose. And I'm not going to let you take that from me. It's all I have left."

Noland looked as if he'd been smacked in the face. "The only thing?"

"Achaia..." Emile whispered at the same time.

"Not the only thing," A voice said in the doorway behind them.

Achaia felt a rock of guilt drop in her stomach, looking at Noland and Emile's faces, before she turned and saw Naphtali standing in the doorway. "Naph!" She squealed leaping off the foot of the bed, and plunging herself into his chest. He hugged her tightly.

"You're alright?" he asked, looking to her busted chin, bandaged leg, and all her scrapes and bruises.

"I'll live," Achaia smiled.

"What's going on here?" Naphtali demanded from Noland. "The council won't tell me anything. They wouldn't even tell me where Achaia had been sent, as if I couldn't find out other ways..." he rolled his eyes.

"Shut the door," Noland said.

Achaia shut it and re-took her seat on the foot of the bed. Naphtali stood next to her.

"I'm really glad you're here. Something isn't right," Noland started. "The council isn't exactly forthcoming with information. Even after taking my place as an Elder, I am not privy to their decisions. They basically exiled us. I thought, in sending us to Bale, they were attempting to force our trust and keep us blind... but I'm not so sure anymore. Bale seems to be exiled himself. Something is happening. I can feel it. For whatever reason, they want us out of the way. I really don't think it's for our safety."

Naphtali listened patiently, and nodded when Noland finished. "I would say you're right. I don't think it's a coincidence that all of these attacks started happening after Shael's abduction. And Achaia's exile," he agreed.

"What are you thinking?" Noland sat up to his full height.

"Shael was a powerful force, even as a human he had more

knowledge than anyone on...certain matters." Naphtali appeared to be choosing his words carefully. "He was, after all the angel who reaped the souls of Egypt, the one who conquered armies... when it comes to mass destruction, he can see it coming or implement it better than anyone."

Achaia was somewhat aware of her mouth hanging slightly open, but she remained silent.

"With Shael out of the way, and his daughter ignorant and contained, as they hope, not necessarily the case I presume..." Naphtali looked between Noland and Achaia, Noland nodded the affirmative. "This opens the door wide for other players to step in and take up their aims."

"What do you mean?" Achaia asked.

"Achaia, in a way this opened up the battle field for all-out war between angels and demons. Humanity is getting caught in the crossfire. This is a war for territory. You haven't declared a side. You're a liability to both sides, until you pledge allegiance to one or the other. Your father was the one who negotiated the Nephilim's release from Hell, and sought out a covenant with God. He was the one keeping them in check, making sure humanity was protected. When he defected— The Nephilim don't know how you fit into this picture. They don't like your ties to humanity, but your father isn't trusted either."

"On that note," Achaia swallowed hard. "There's something I have to tell you." Achaia glanced guiltily at Noland and Emile, but turned her attention back to Naphtali. "On our way here I was contacted by Lucifer."

"WHAT?" Noland shouted.

"I'm sorry," Achaia said, feeling truly saddened that she had never told him. "The entire train was full of demons. I'm pretty sure that every passenger on the train was possessed. But they didn't want to show themselves, so they didn't make a move. They were there for insurance. A demon in the body of a businessman came to me while I was in the shower."

"Kaya." Noland looked stunned and nauseous.

"I was done showering, and dressed," she clarified. "He wanted to deliver a message. Luc was sending me an invitation. I could get to my father." Her throat contracted as she mentioned the opportunity to be reunited with her dad, and she had to swallow hard feeling the lump in her throat.

"Did this demon have a name?" Naphtali asked.

"It was something long and weird, I can't remember. But he told me to call him John."

"Did he say he'd be in touch? Have you heard from him since?"

"I haven't. But I haven't been alone since, except briefly during the explosions. He gave me this," Achaia pulled the razor sharp tooth from her pocket, and held it out in her palm, "said if I cut myself with it, he would be able to speak to me."

"If the demons were responsible, it's possible they were using the bombs to draw you out and get you alone. They just never had long enough to make contact. Olivier went right out after you," Noland said.

"Two birds with one stone," Emile said in agreement.

"What do you mean 'if it was the demons'?" Achaia cocked her head in interest. "You think human terrorists would have picked this street randomly?"

"I don't think the humans were responsible either." Noland said diplomatically.

"You think the council orchestrated the attack?" Emile only

looked a little shocked. Achaia, on the other hand, stared at Noland as if he'd grown a second head.

"I'm just saying, we need to consider all the possibilities," Noland shrugged.

"I mean, don't get me wrong, the council sucks. But you really think they would attack their own safe house?" Achaia asked.

"If they are looking for an excuse to start a war and go on offense instead of just playing defense with their Charges? Yeah, I could see it happening," Noland said bluntly.

Emile nodded as he listened.

"It's possible," Naphtali granted, "But back to the matter at hand, Achaia," Naphtali said, gathering her attention back to himself. "I want you to do something very brave."

"Anything."

"I want you to go with John."

"What?" Noland asked outraged. "No. Out of the question. What if that thing is poisoned? Are you insane?"

"No," Naphtali said annoyed. "But, I was the partner of one of the greatest battle strategists, and one of the most messed-up angels you've ever heard of, for millennia. I picked up a thing or two. We are to use what we've got. What we've got is an angel who has no allegiance. She can go where we cannot. We are forbidden to enter Hell. Shael has been removed to its depths. I cannot enter its inner circles. Achaia can. If she goes on her own. Then you, as her Guardian, are able to go in after her to save her. As a younger generation, you will not be denied reinforcements." Naphtali said this all very calmly as if it were obvious. "Achaia will go down first. We will follow with a rescue party. We will go in after Achaia, but we will save Shael in the process."

"You think that will work?" Achaia asked, closing her hand

tightly around the fang.

Emile was shaking his head. "This is madness. You're talking about going into Hell. This isn't like breaking into a prison, this is Hell we are talking about. Do you even know what the circles look like?" Emile asked.

"I do not," Naphtali confessed. "Only the fallen know."

"What if they don't help?" Noland asked. "We can't do this alone."

"There is only one who has ever gone through Hell to see Heaven again."

Emile and Noland's faces lit with recognition. "You think He will come?" Noland asked in awe.

"Achaia is half human." Naphtali said. "He will come."

"But how will you find me, once I'm there? None of you know your way around." Achaia pointed out.

"You remember how you found Noland in the woods, when that hunter was possessed?" Emile asked.

"Is that something Nephilim can always do?" Achaia asked.

"Not all Nephilim," Emile said delicately. He was looking at Noland to take over explanation.

"Is it like a Guardian, and Charge connection?" Achaia asked confused.

"No. Every other Charge has been only human," Noland said, his voice tight and quiet. He was giving Emile a look that Achaia couldn't read.

"It is the connection fostered between mates, Achaia," Naphtali said bluntly.

"Mates?" Achaia said laughing, and looking to Noland, whose face had gone sickly white. "Mates?" She asked again, looking at him more seriously.

Noland met her eyes and nodded.

"You knew?" Achaia asked, turning and looking at Emile.

Emile and Noland both nodded again.

"You've known, for… for over a month?" Achaia felt her stomach tie itself into knots. "Why didn't you tell me?" she asked, sounding angrier than she intended, looking back to Noland.

"Because you would have known when your time was right."

"If you thought I was pissed about the wings, you—"

"You're half human. You might have more say in it than I do," Noland said looking away from her. "And you might not have—"

"Chosen him," Emile finished.

Achaia glanced at a million thoughts as they each flew through her mind. Was Noland insecure? Did she have a choice? "When do I leave?" She said, finally, looking back at Naphtali.

Noland and Emile looked taken aback by her sudden change of subject.

Naphtali, who knew Achaia since she was born, was not shocked. "It is only right to discuss all of this with Bale. You are under his watch. As soon as we've talked with him, you'll need to get in contact with John," he said practically.

Noland was pale, and his jaw was clinched. "I don't like this at all."

"Well, I'm going to need you to get on board with this really quickly Noland. Without you, we have no chance of success."

"What if I say no?" Noland asked.

Achaia looked at him, feeling betrayed. This was the first glance at hope she'd had when it came to finding and saving her father.

"I don't know much about Hell. I imagine it's awful, and I hate asking you to do this, but please, Noland. Even if all I get is the chance to say goodbye. Help me see my father again. I can't look at an opportunity to save him and do nothing."

"This was his choice Achaia. He chose this. No matter what we do now, this is how it will end." Noland's voice was growing louder, out of his control.

"I'm going with or without you." Achaia felt like fire was flowing through her veins. She felt the heat rising in her face. "I don't need you to save me," she said icily. "I don't need anything from you." She stood, and left the room leading Naphtali to Bale's quarters.

"I'll work on him," Naphtali promised her quietly as they walked. Achaia felt pathetic for fighting back tears. She cursed herself for being stupid enough to trust Noland. He was Nephilim after-all. Maybe they really were all the same. She limped on her leg that had been sliced in the back by the glass.

"Have you seen the healer for that?" Naphtali asked.

"Yes," Achaia answered. "What if you can't find me?" Achaia asked, stopping in the hall outside of Bale's door.

"If we don't show up, and you get into danger, Noland will have no choice but to act. He won't be able to feel your need and do nothing."

"That's pretty manipulative," Achaia said disdainfully.

"He'll chose to follow you before it comes to that, I assure you. He cares too much for you to wait for that."

"Could have fooled me," Achaia said in a grumble.

"Achaia, he does not fear Hell for himself," Naphtali said as if it were obvious. "I've never known Noland to fear anything for himself. He fears what it will mean for you. You'll come back different from this."

"I don't need him to fear for me," Achaia said bitterly, shaking away the image of Noland pushing her off the bomb.

"Somebody has to," Naphtali said, simply. "A little fear and a sense of self-preservation is not cowardly, Achaia. It is healthy."

\*\*\*

"That is a terrible idea," Bale said as Naphtali finished speaking. "And what do you plan to do if the demons attack you before the rest of them arrive?" Bale asked looking to Achaia.

Achaia shrugged. "Use those fine defense tactics Noland has been teaching me and run away?" She answered sarcastically.

"And what do you plan to do if Noland is less than compliant?" Bale asked looking to Naphtali.

"Improvise?" Naphtali answered. "We don't need a plan that's laid in stone. We can plan all we want, as soon as we enter Hell that all goes out the window, anyway. None of us know what we're facing, only that we need to face it."

Bale looked down. "If you had come to me yesterday, I would have promptly refused. But in light of all the terror that has unleashed upon Shael's disappearance, I am inclined to believe it is no coincidence. This will continue getting worse before it gets better." Bale stood in silence for a moment. "And you know what she is?" He asked looking to Naphtali for confirmation.

"What she is," Naphtali said smiling, "is our greatest asset."

Bale looked down at Achaia, apparently in deep thought. "You don't think we are giving Hell what it most desires? A weapon that can be used against us?"

Achaia wanted to ask him to explain to her what she was. What had made him hate her before ever speaking to her... She could see his internal conflict through his eyes, which she met, pleadingly.

"What woe has fallen on you..." He said softly. "What blood that curses your veins... and what destruction you will bring on us all."

"Even the greatest builders must demolish to build," Naphtali said reassuringly to Bale.

Achaia couldn't take it anymore, she heard herself speak as if it were someone else's voice, instead of her own. "Is anyone ever going to fill me in on what the hell all this means?"

Bale cocked his head, studying her. "No."

Achaia stared boldly into his face. "Right then," she said, sarcastically. "Moving on. Will you help me, or not?"

"Against my better judgement, I will," Bale said finally. "The council should have gotten more involved long before now, but their ignorance knows no bounds. As always, it is left to us to clean up the mess of the fallen." Bale said looking to Naphtali.

Naphtali smiled, and reached out a hand, to shake Bale's.

"What preparation do you need?" Bale asked Achaia.

"Time alone and a little blood." Achaia fidgeted with the demon tooth in her fingers.

"Demons need little more than opportunity," Bale said disgustedly, looking at what she held. "You need only to be open."

"Right. Well I'll go be alone then. And hopefully I'll see you guys soon." Achaia smiled tightly. "And if not," Achaia turned to Naphtali and hugged him.

"Be brave, little firecracker." Naphtali kissed the top of Achaia's head. "We will come for you."

"I know." Achaia smiled.

*** 

Achaia sat on a frozen park bench, feeling quite alone. She had gone to the training room and grabbed her favorite weapons that could be easily carried and concealed; the whip that had caught her attention from the start, and a dagger with a feathered handle, that wrapped her hand like a friend. She tried to silence the torrent of thoughts and emotions coursing through her.

There was no denying she was afraid. She wasn't just shaking from the cold. The tooth protruded from her pocket, and she pulled it out and ran her thumb over it. She wasn't exactly sure what to expect, or what would happen when she drew blood with it. She wasn't sure where John would take her, what state her father would be in when she got there...

Achaia closed her eyes, took a deep breath and tried to steady herself. She welcomed adrenaline to help her power through and do what was necessary. She looked back down at the tip of the tooth, so sharp she could barely see the tip of its point. She grabbed it in her right hand, and dragged it across her left wrist, a thin line of blood trailing its wake. She felt as if ice had entered her veins through the cut and traveled up her arm. The blood veins that marked its trail turned black under her pale white skin.

Achaia tensed watching the blood flowing back toward her heart, carrying the venom directly to it. She knew there was nothing she could do now to stop it from doing whatever damage it could. As the venom reached her heart, Achaia felt like she'd been hit hard in the chest; it rocked her back. She squeezed her eyes shut as her head was thrown backwards with the force.

When Achaia opened her eyes again, she was blind. She couldn't see anything. She blinked rapidly, but her vision didn't clear.

"Achaia," a voice whispered in her mind.

Achaia shook her head violently, as if trying to shake water out of her ears.

"Achaia," it drawled out in an almost hiss.

Achaia couldn't see if there was anyone around to see her talk to herself, she answered back in her mind. "Yes, I'm here."

"Come to me," the voice hissed.

"I don't know where you are," Achaia thought.

"Follow my voice." At that, whispers seemed to erupt around her. Achaia turned her head in every direction, trying to discern where they were coming from. She blinked her eyes, trying desperately to see, but couldn't. She covered her ears, and tucked her head between her knees, fighting back a scream. She couldn't focus, she couldn't tell where the whispers were coming from.

Shakily, Achaia tried standing. Her balance was off, but she started walking, following the loudest whispers into the dark.

\*\*\*

"What do you mean she's gone?" Noland yelled murderously.

Bale's quarters were lit only by the grand fireplace behind his desk, making the room smell of wood and smoke. Its illumination painted shadows over the rest of the minimal furniture in the room; a couple of chairs, and a bureau. It was however enough light for Noland to see Bale and Naphtali's faces clearly.

"She's left. She is most likely making contact with the demon at this very moment," Naphtali said calmly.

"You didn't put a stop to this?" Noland stared at Bale incredulously; steam was rising from his skin, making his shirt damp with it.

"I believe it, unfortunately, to be necessary," Bale said coolly with a less than apologetic tone.

Noland turned on his heel, bound for the armory. He stopped at the door with his hand clenching the door frame, the heat of it charring the wood, and looked back at Bale, "If anything happens to her, I'll make Hell look like paradise to you." Noland said through clenched teeth, his eyes mirroring the flames in the fire.

# 18

# The Descent

"The path to paradise
Begins in Hell."
-Dante Alighieri, Inferno

Shael sat leaning against the arm of one of the ice sofas, with a glass of something amber colored in his hand. Luc sat across from him on the other sofa. "You've been low lately."

Shael looked up. "Your demons are tedious," Shael responded.

Luc shrugged. "I am working on a surprise for you," he smiled in a way that made Shael cringe inside, Luc's smile wasn't a comforting sight. However, Shael forced himself to return it, at least in part; a sort of shrug of the mouth. "I think it will cheer you right up."

"What are you up to?" Shael asked, setting his glass down on the arm of the sofa.

"If I revealed my endeavors it would hardly be a surprise anymore, now, would it?"

Shael shrugged. He wasn't sure what Luc could possibly do which would actually cheer him up. Any gift Luc gave always had a bite that made the receiver regret ever accepting anything given in the first place.

"You'll see very soon, brother." Luc smiled again.

***

Achaia stood next to a young man with a scruffy, unshaven face and pale blue eyes at the mouth of a cavern. The air around them had gone dead still, and there wasn't a sound to be heard ahead or behind, save for their breath. Achaia blinked, her eyes adjusting to the light. She took in her surroundings. She definitely was not in Moscow anymore.

"Where am I? How did I get here?" Achaia asked.

"Welcome home, Achaia. I'm afraid it won't be a warm welcome, but you are welcome none the less. We are happy to have you." The man smiled.

"Are you the new John?" Achaia asked, shaking her head in confusion, struggling to adjust to her new surroundings.

"Shall we?" He smiled in confirmation and gestured for her to go on ahead of him over the threshold.

Achaia stepped tentatively through the mouth of the cavern. As she did, all the air was pushed from her lungs. She had thought Russia was cold. She had never felt a cold like this. It was as if every cell and molecule in her body had forgotten what warmth was. She couldn't remember the feel of the sun on her skin, or a mug of hot coffee in her hand. She forgot the flush of embarrassment and happiness. She forgot the heat of anger. That which filled her was a death-like indifference. All she knew was cold, the empty cavernous depth of the ice penetrating deep into her soul.

"I'd like to tell you, you get used to it," John said frowning down at her, "but you really don't."

Achaia shivered, holding her arms around herself.

"You're lucky we are only going into the fourth circle." John said gesturing for her to walk on.

\*\*\*

"Wait! What?" Yellaina yelled as Emile and Noland filled the others in on what had transpired with Naphtali's arrival.

"She's gone?" Amelia asked. "Like, to Hell?"

"Yes, Emile said. He could feel their worry, their anger, and their fear.

"But we're going after her right?" Olivier asked. "Why haven't we left yet?"

"We have to wait for her to be in danger before Noland is going to be able to find her," Emile said.

"But we need to be ready. We need to grab weapons, we need to—"

"Olivier, we will," Noland said.

"And by 'we' I mean, not you." Olivier said looking over to Yellaina.

"What?" Yellaina said angrily.

"You're not well trained in combat. I don't want you getting hurt." Olivier said plainly.

"And none of you are fluent in every demonic dialect!" Emile felt the anger that was blooming in Yellaina's chest.

"We don't need to be able to talk to demons to kill them." Olivier argued. "You're not going."

"And we aren't married! You can't tell me to stay. She's my

friend, too!" Yellaina's face was flushed.

"Olivier's right," Noland said loudly, stopping the argument once and for all. Emile could feel his frustration, his annoyance. "You'd be a liability. I'm sorry," Noland said looking to Yellaina and Amelia.

"What? Me?" Amelia asked outraged. "I'm trained!"

"And you'll feel everything that happens to all of us. You'll be useless before we even reach her. Let alone getting her out." Noland raised his eyebrows as if asking her to argue that he wasn't right.

Amelia was furious. Emile felt like every ounce of blood in his body was boiling.

"Okay," he said putting his hands up in the air. "I need everyone to calm down. Yes, this sucks. Yes, Noland could have worded that better. No, you're not useless," he said looking at the girls. "Yes, he can be a prick," he added looking at Noland, "but they're right." He said standing between the girls and Olivier and Noland.

"We love you. And we aren't going to let you go into a dangerous situation where the odds are stacked against us, and where it would potentially cause more problems and decrease our odds of getting everyone out alive," Emile said sadly. "It's nothing personal."

"It doesn't get any more personal," Amelia said venomously before storming out of the library.

Yellaina stared them down with bloodshot eyes. Emile could tell she was trying not to cry. "If anything happens to her, and I have to live with the guilt that I did nothing to prevent it, I will never forgive you," she said looking directly into Olivier's eyes.

Emile felt the hit to the gut that it had been for Olivier. Yellaina followed Amelia out of the room. "It's for her own good," Olivier said quietly, more to himself than anyone else.

"So what's the plan?" Emile asked, looking at Noland.

He felt his rush of anxiety.

"We don't really have one."

***

Achaia spent hours following John through legions of demons. Any shred of hope she had that Noland and Naphtali could get to her, was gone. Even if they were to find her location, they would be outnumbered beyond belief. Coming after her would be suicide.

Hell was designed like a never ending cavernous catacomb. The iced over walls occasionally granting glimpses of bone, of skulls. It trailed on in a round spiral with archways branching off into what John explained were the various circles of Hell, where humans with no Godly allegiance were sorted based on the severity of the actions of their lives. Beyond the arches, Achaia could hear the occupants' cries of misery. The first circles started as moans and weeping. The further they descended, the more desperate and horrible the sounds of their agony became.

Finally, they came to an opening. She could see in the distance what looked like a grand room coming into view. As they drew closer, the ceiling rose into a high vault. It was an icy room with a stalactite strewn ceiling. Stalagmites rose from the ground like ice pillars and columns. The room was blindingly white, with the reflection off the ice hitting her from every angle. She blinked in an effort to adjust her eyes from the dark tunnel to this vast, white room.

"Welcome to the fourth circle, the home of those damned for greed." John bowed his head as he gestured for her to go on into the grand hall.

"Achaia!" A voice called happily. A man in a floor length leather coat walked briskly toward her from beyond the pillars. His arms were spread in welcome.

She'd never seen this man in her life, but he greeted her like a long lost friend. A perfect smile shown at her from behind his perfectly symmetrical and shapely lips. His blue eyes were as deep as the Caspian Sea. His features were flawless, save for where he was obviously frozen. His face, as he came closer, had translucent fractures, and was chipped with frost bite. He looked like a living ice sculpture who had been chiseled out by the world's most talented artist, and had endured years of use and abuse, but was still, undeniably, a masterpiece of beauty.

"Lucifer?" Achaia asked, as the man finally closed the remaining space between them.

"At your service, Love." He smiled so brightly at her, she couldn't help but want to smile back.

Somewhere in the back of her mind she wondered if his gift was the same as Bale's. How could someone so beautiful be as tainted as everyone made him out to be?

"Come in! Come in!" Lucifer turned and led her into the room, around pillars, and down some steps into what looked like a formal sitting room. The icy floor was covered with an ancient, expensive looking rug. There were sofas carved out of the ice, which were covered with thick furs. On one of them, sat her father.

"Dad!" Achaia ran to him, throwing herself onto the sofa, and hugging him fiercely.

"Achaia," her father's voice sounded stunned and sad in her ear. "What are you doing here? You shouldn't be here." He said, his eyes full of fear. Achaia pulled back and looked up into his face.

"I had to see you." Her eyes were filling with tears, but instead of warm salty tears gliding down her cheeks, they froze in her lashes. She hugged her father again.

"One big happy family!" Lucifer said throwing himself on the sofa across from them.

"She can't stay here," Shael said with finality.

"Dad?" Achaia said sitting back up and looking into her father's face. His once brown skin was pale. His vivid brown eyes were dull. His once fierce face was without hope.

"I thought this would cheer you up!" Lucifer said looking at Shael, confused. "Didn't you miss her?"

"Of course I missed her," Shael said grasping Achaia's hand over her knee. He squeezed it firmly. "But this isn't the future I wanted for her. I want her to have warmth, and love."

"You want her to have Him." Lucifer's voice was full of contempt.

"Luc, please. All of this mess was created out of your jealousy of Him. Of course I want her to have Him."

"Then why did you keep her unaffiliated?" Lucifer sat up straight on the edge of his seat.

"I wanted her to have a choice, when the time came."

"The time did come, and she did choose!" Lucifer's face would have been flushed by now, if there was any blood in him to make it to his cheeks. Achaia, however, was beginning to believe he was made entirely of ice, inside and out. "And now she has joined us forever."

"What did you promise him?" Shael asked turning to look Achaia in the eye.

"Nothing." Achaia said.

"False." Lucifer said triumphantly. "It was made perfectly clear that the offer was for you to join us for eternity."

"But I didn't accept the offer." Achaia said looking from her father to Lucifer.

"You came with John, that was acceptance." Luc said, looking over to John, who was standing in the distance.

"You did ask her?" Luc said, a tinge of doubt in his voice.

"I asked her if she considered the offer, yes."

Luc looked back at Achaia triumphantly.

"I said 'yes' I had considered it. Not ''yes' that I agreed or accepted it." Achaia said, hoping this counted as a loophole. "I did consider it, and I decided I didn't like it. But that I'd really like to see my dad."

Lucifer's smile fled his face. "Pledge allegiance to me, and you'll have him forever," Luc said coming to stand before Achaia. "There's no need to ever say goodbye."

"No." Achaia looked into his eyes, and no longer saw the beauty in them, only the coldness. She thought of Noland, and tried to remember what warmth felt like. She couldn't.

Shael was on his feet. "Leave her, Luc."

"Shut up, Shael," Luc said pushing Shael in the chest. "You always were the weak one." Luc spat. "You and your feelings."

"Oh, stop it," Achaia said rising to her feet. "Everyone talks about you as if you're someone to fear."

Luc's attention snapped back to Achaia, giving her a look to use extreme caution. "Tread carefully," He growled.

"Or what?" Achaia asked.

"Achaia," Shael warned.

"What? You'll kill me?" Achaia asked. "So I'll just still be stuck here? Or miraculously I'll go to Heaven I suppose. I'm not sure how that works really. But either that changes nothing, or I escape?" Achaia cocked an eyebrow. "You still wouldn't win…"

"There are worse fates than death," Luc spat.

"I can't imagine anything worse than being stuck in this conversation," Achaia said sarcastically.

Luc laughed without mirth. "If you're trying to bait me Cohen, you'll have to avoid my favorite languages. Hate, sarcasm, bit-terness… I eat it up. I *like* this side of you."

"Then shall I discuss love?" Achaia asked, lowering her voice. "And how you'll never know it?"

Luc's face, if possible, carved itself into sharper features. His jaw protruding in a scowl, his eyes sharp and menacing. "I'll make this very clear." His voice hardly sounded human. There was an animalistic growl to his tone that rose from the depths of his loathing. "Pledge allegiance to me, or you will never see your father again." His voice grew even lower. "The last glimpse you get of him, I will be torturing him. You will have that image forever fixed in your mind. You can live with the knowledge that his eternal torment was not due to his decision to join me, but yours to leave me."

Achaia stood frozen. She felt a huge weight drop in the pit of her stomach that made her nauseous. She couldn't pledge. But she couldn't leave her father under those conditions. She stood in a staring contest, locked eye to eye with Luc, and her brain turned over endless scenarios, none of them working in her favor. She needed to be in danger. She needed Noland to find her. She needed back up. If it could even make it to her.

Luc stepped closer to her. His face inches from hers. "Choose. Or be chosen. I will not hesitate to kill you and let fate decide."

\*\*\*

Noland, Olivier and Emile were holed up in the study with Bale and Naphtali. All of them armed to the teeth, and pacing.

"The eve of battle is scarcely less dreadful than the battle itself," Bale said, clasping Noland on the shoulder.

Noland nodded, but said nothing.

He had just passed by the fireplace when he felt a tugging in his chest. He stopped in his tracks.

"What was that?" Emile asked. "It was—"

"Fear?" Noland asked, looking at Emile. "But it wasn't…"

Noland looked into the fire focusing all of his attention on that spot in his chest. "Could the distance affect the connection?" Noland asked turning to Bale.

"Well, it would be stronger if you were united," Bale said, "but I don't know. Perhaps it is the separation of Hell itself."

"We need to start moving. Maybe if we got closer?" Noland suggested.

"We will go," Naphtali said. "Bale will remain. When we are gone," Naphtali turned to Bale, "contact the council, they won't refuse aid to the underage Nephilim. They will send reinforcements."

Bale nodded, then turned to face Noland. "We follow you, Amsel," Bale said, his eyes steady on Noland's. "Wherever this leads. God go before you."

\*\*\*

Shael stood, studying Luc's face. He could see that twitch at the left of his mouth. His temper wouldn't hold for long. He was scared for Achaia. What was she doing? What did she mean by following him here? "Achaia," he said in warning.

"I'm not going to pledge allegiance to you," Achaia said firmly, not taking her eyes off Luc's.

"Achaia," Shael said stepping forward.

"No," Achaia said putting out her arm, stopping her father. "If he wants to take his chances, and test the odds, let him." She kept her eyes fixed on Luc's.

Shael heard the daring tone in her voice, but her eyes were trying to tell him something else. She wasn't just trying to goad Luc for no reason. But what was she doing? Shael stepped back, dumbfounded. Her look was telling him to let this happen, but why?

"So, are you all talk or what?" Achaia asked stepping even closer to Luc. Shael was fighting every impulse in his body. Everything in him was screaming to protect her. To stand between them, to attack Luc; to do anything but stand and watch her die like her mother.

Something in Luc snapped, his eyes flashed as he reached forward grabbing Achaia by the neck. "I will not be manipulated. I am the father of lies. You cannot fool me, Achaia Connolly Cohen. Who sent you?"

Achaia didn't answer.

"WHO?" Luc yelled, throwing her backwards against a pillar of ice. "The council?"

Shael, unable to stand still any longer leapt over the sofa and landed in front of where Achaia lay on the ground. She was smiling, drawing her hand away from her head, where it had hit the ice. It was covered in blood.

"Touch her again, and I will magnify your suffering in this place for eternity," Shael said rounding on Luc.

"What is all this?" Luc asked, staring at Achaia with all the disdain in the world in his glare.

"I've heard you have no virtue. But have you heard of patience?" Achaia said, wavering dizzily on her arm. She blinked her eyes, which were unfocused, but she refused to admit weakness. Shael knelt next to her. "Wait and see, Love," she spat mockingly.

\*\*\*

Bale slammed the phone down. He had explained as much of what had happened to Joash, leaving out the part that it had all been planned and intentional. However, the council had "regrettably had to decline" any aid or assistance. What were a few children in the scheme of the greater good?

Bale was shaking with rage at the council's cold indifference to the lives of their own offspring. Their legalism was a mask for blind ignorance. Bale pulled a cell phone from his pocket and dialed Naphtali. "The council has denied the request for aid. Where are you? Wait for me."

"We seem to be heading to the Ukraine." Naphtali said, Bale could hear wind in the phone, and knew they were still flying.

"Stay on the line, I'm right behind you," Bale said, running from his office and taking the stairs to the roof three at a time.

\*\*\*

Noland had felt the shock in his chest, like paddles of a defibrillator reviving him. He had flown and led the others to the mouth of the cavern, where they now stood.

"Forsaken are the souls who enter here," Naphtali said, looking at the rock face as if reading a sign.

"Whatever happens," Noland said looking over at Emile.

"I'm with you brother," Emile said, drawing his bow, and readying an arrow.

Bale landed behind them, reading the sign overhead as well. He nodded at Noland, as he finished it.

Noland drew his long sword, and Naphtali and Bale drew their weapons as well.

"Shall I scout it out?" Olivier asked.

Noland nodded, and Olivier disappeared in a blur into the cave. A minute later he returned. His face was white, and his breath was like smoke. But the color had not drained from him from the cold, alone. "I've never seen so many demons," he said, his voice shaking. "I'd have better luck counting the sand on the beach."

"We are not our own," Noland said, resolutely. "His will be done."

"Shall we wage war on Hell then?" Emile asked.

Noland smiled, nodded, and stepped forward. They hadn't made it five yards before the demons fell upon them. Emile stayed back, and shot those that advanced from behind Noland, Bale, and Naphtali, as they plunged forward into the horde. Olivier ran through the masses, slicing the throats of demons who never saw him coming, clearing a path. Noland slashed and spun, hitting everything in reach as he spread out from the others to divide and conquer. He glanced up and saw a humanoid demon with long, skeletally thin arms and legs, making him almost spider-like, grab Emile from behind, lowering its needle-like teeth toward his neck.

"Emile!" Noland said, slinging a throwing knife from his belt, he hit the demon just between its glassy black eyes, as Emile stabbed it in the neck with the arrow in his hand. As it fell, Emile pulled either end of his bow, unsheathing two feathered daggers.

The tunnel seemed to catch fire, and Noland turned to see Naphtali in all of his angelic glory, a walking torch of a being, his sword moving more like a flaming wind tunnel.

Bale seemed to move on the air, without wings. Noland had never seen anyone so light on their feet. He seemed to not be affected at all by gravity or mass. His technique was perfect, and his fighting looked more like a dance of death, than actual effort. Noland turned his attention back to the advancing demons. He surged forward, summoning all the strength he could to produce his own fire in this warmth forsaken place.

\*\*\*

Emile couldn't feel anything over how cold he was. There were demons as far as he could see, and no sign of a reprieve. He wasn't sure how far they would make it, or how far they needed to. Demons had closed in behind them, so there was no turning back, either.

Emile was fighting with everything he had in him, and from the glimpses he caught of the others through the horde, they were doing the same. He wasn't entirely convinced they were gaining ground or moving forward at all, but all they could do now was keep fighting, and not give in to death.

There was no telling how long they had been fighting, there was an infinity to the scene. Emile had lost count of how many demons he had killed, how many blows he had taken, or cuts he had received. Both of his forearms were sliced and bleeding, and there was blood dripping into his left eye from a wound somewhere on his head that he didn't remember getting.

Emile spun with his daggers outstretched, slicing the throats of three demons that had tried to surround him; he was kicked back in the chest, hard, by a fourth demon. He staggered back, slamming against the icy wall of the catacomb. Over his shoulder he saw a face, and turned to stab at it, but it was frozen into the icy wall, the mouth and eyes contorted into an endless scream.

"Emile!" Noland's voice called out from somewhere ahead.

Emile was falling behind. The demon that had kicked him was before him now, reaching for his throat, with his mouth open in a roar. Emile threw up his hands, one holding a dagger to the front of the demon's throat, and the other to the back of his neck; as the demon leaned in to tear Emile apart with his teeth, Emile pushed out with one, and pulled in with the other, beheading the demon, and cutting his roar off with a sickening gurgle. Its head fell onto Emile's shoulder before falling with a thick thud to the ground.

"Okay, stop focusing on killing demons, and just fight like hell to get around them." Emile said to himself. He took a deep breath and plunged forward into the crowd before him with renewed speed and agility. He kicked up from the lunging leg of one demon, and stepped off the shoulder of another, leaping over the heads, stepping on any demon that came at him. He landed in a clearing next to Noland.

"I don't know how much longer we can keep this up!" He yelled over the growls of their opponents, backing up to Noland. They turned back to back, taking a count of the demons surrounding them. "Where are the others?"

"Bale and Naphtali are ahead of us, and Olivier is scouting out if there is an end to this multitude."

At that moment there was a blindingly bright light that reflected off the ice, catching them all off guard. The demons flinched back covering their eyes and squinting around to see where the light was coming from. Down the tunnel from where they had entered, an angel dressed in all white robes was striding toward them.

At the sight of Him, the demons crouched or fled. He walked forward, the crowd of demons, parting before Him. He passed by them without speaking, but the demons clung to the wall as He did. Emile hit Noland's arm to see if he was thinking the same thing Emile was.

Noland didn't turn to look at him, but followed the angel. They caught up to Bale and Naphtali, who looked shocked and relieved, and fell into step next to the cloaked figure.

"Is this…"

"I think it must be, don't you." Emile answered before Noland could even finish his question.

Some demons came from behind, as if trying to claw and scratch at them without being noticed by their leader, but Emile and Noland slashed out, and the demons were either dispatched, or cringed away into the shadows once more away from them.

"We have to be at about, what? The third circle?" Emile asked.

Noland nodded. "How far down do you think she is? She feels close."

"The fourth circle is just ahead," Olivier said appearing beside them in a blur. He was out of breath and covered in sweat and blood, he looked as exhausted as Emile felt. Adrenaline was the only thing keeping them on their feet. "I saw the light, and fell back," Olivier said looking awe struck. "He came."

\*\*\*

"I'm not going to kill you Achaia," Luc said, lounging on the couch across from her.

Her father was sitting over her, he had moved the fur from over the arm of the couch and had rested her bleeding head against it.

"What are you doing?" Shael whispered.

"I'm saving you," she whispered back.

Luc was going on a self-important tangent, laying with his eyes closed. Shael and Achaia were using this as an opportunity to talk.

"How exactly is nearly getting yourself knocked out, saving me?" Shael asked, in a firm fatherly whisper.

Achaia smiled. "I missed you."

"I missed you too, but you shouldn't be here," Shael said shaking his head.

"I'm not ready to say goodbye," Achaia said, her head aching, as her blood froze to the ice as it ran down the arm of the sofa.

"I know," Shael said sadly.

"Lucifer." A new voice spoke from outside of Achaia's line of vision.

She looked over as Luc stopped talking and slowly opened his eyes. His body stiffened, and his face had an expression of disbelief. Luc raised himself up into a sitting position, then to a stand almost robotically. "You? What are you doing here?" he asked, sounding less formidable.

"I have conquered this place. I can come and go as I please. Today, I felt like coming." The man walked into view. He was a dark skinned man of average height, and looks. He had long dark curling hair, with dark eyes, either brown or hazel, Achaia couldn't tell. His smile was warm. She could feel its warmth. He was such a contrast to his surroundings, that he seemed cut out of them, and entirely separate. As if someone had done a terrible photoshop job of adding him into their presence.

"Brother!" Shael stood, Achaia had never seen his face so lit with pure joy.

"Dad?" Achaia asked sitting up. "Who is that?"

"Achaia," The man clasped her father in a firm embrace, and spoke over his shoulder to her. "I've been watching you."

"Because, that's not creepy," Achaia said, before she could stop herself.

Shael turned to look at her, and seemed incapable of containing his enthusiasm. "Is he my uncle?" Achaia asked her father.

"In a manner of speaking. Perhaps that is the easiest way for you to think of me in human terms. Brother also works." The man walked over, and sat on the sofa at her feet.

"We never lived in West Virginia." Achaia said looking up at her father, clearly confused.

The man put his hand on one of her feet, and immediately all the pain left her body. Her head was clear, her headache, gone.

"Are you a healer?" She asked.

"He is The Healer, Achaia," her father said, coming to sit behind her.

Achaia sat up looking back and forth from her father on her right, to this new stranger on her left. "You look familiar," Achaia said staring at the man.

"Never have I left you," He said smiling.

"Again, not creepy at all...Mr. Brother-Uncle," she said cocking an eyebrow, though there was nothing about the man that made her feel uncomfortable. In fact, everything about him gave her a feeling of reassurance.

"Achaia this is I Am." Her father said in way of introduction, though it made no sense to her.

"His name is you are?"

"I am."

"That's what I said..."

Shael laughed. "No."

"You can call me Iesou."

"Like, Jesus? Jesus?" Achaia asked.

"The very same." The man smiled kindly.

"Holy crap! You're real?" Achaia asked.

"You're surprised? After all you've encountered and survived?" The man laughed. "You are all so slow to understand." He added, not without affection. "As are you," Iesou said looking to Luc. "Even after all this time. Did you really not realize that I would come? You know the things that are yet to come. You know how it will occur."

"What is he talking about?" Achaia asked leaning over to her father.

Her dad hushed her. His focus absorbed in watching the conversation between Iesou and Luc.

"You are a manipulator of truth. You really didn't expect me to not-come and set paths straight?" Iesou went on. Achaia tried to follow as best she could, along with her father. "I am not ignorant of the bargain you struck with Shael. However, I believe you may need a reminder of the terms."

"I created the terms, I am well aware of their implications." Luc's anger flared again.

"Are you? What of their context?" Iesou's voice was calm, but it wasn't without impact.

"What are you getting at?" Luc spat.

"You agreed that once Achaia was a woman, once she had come of age Shael would fulfill the rest of his commitment." Iesou explained. "You are no stranger to shifting culture Lucifer, you've played a part in its development."

Achaia was staring at Iesou. Was there a loophole in her father's agreement?

"In this day's culture a girl is not necessarily considered a woman at puberty, nor is she of age. This bargain was made under the terms of the modern cultural context. As such, she is still in need of a father for several more years. When she is no longer a daughter in need of her father, you may collect Shael. I can do nothing to prevent that, it was his choice." Iesou looked at her father sadly. "However, I will not permit you to collect early on a deal that was made with the intent to deceive."

Achaia felt like a balloon had lifted her from her chest.

"You're saying he can just leave?" Achaia asked?

"He can," Iesou said. "He is free to leave. Lucifer is also free to attempt to stop him."

Luc smiled. "You'll never make it out of here. There is but one route, and it is blocked by thousands." Luc laughed.

"Was." Iesou said.

"What?" Luc stopped laughing and stared at him.

"I think you'll find there are a few less than there were." Iesou smiled politely. "Ah, here we are." He raised a hand, and gestured toward the entrance.

Achaia heard running feet, and turned to look. Around the columns of ice ran Noland, Emile, Olivier, Naphtali and Bale. They were all covered in blood, both black and red.

"Iesou!" Bale fell to his knees, as did the others.

"Oops, was I supposed to bow?" Achaia asked her father.

"Next time. You'll know next time," he smiled.

Noland was the first to stand. He ran over to Achaia, kneeling before her, and studied her face. "Are you alright?"

"Nathaniel?" Shael was looking at Noland as if he had seen a ghost. He shook his head, as if realizing his mistake. "Who are you?" Shael asked sternly.

"Noland ben Nathaniel," Noland said bowing to her father.

"What are you doing?" Achaia asked somewhat embarrassed. "Stand up."

"And?" Shael looked from Noland to Iesou. "You've got to be joking me—" Shael said sounding exasperated. "She is definitely a girl in need of a father," Shael said standing, shooting Noland an evil glare. "And I'll take my chances with the rest."

Noland handed Shael a long sword.

"A long sword, eh?" He said, taking it. "And what's wrong with a dagger? Too afraid to get close to your enemies?" Shael asked, looking Noland dead in the face.

"No, sir." Noland said, sounding oddly formal. "I have one, if it's what you prefer." Noland said, offering him one from his belt.

"Don't be a people pleaser, it's obnoxious," Shael said shortly, taking the dagger anyway, and handing the long sword back to Noland.

After Shael had looked away, Noland looked to the ceiling and blew out his breath.

"I'm right here." Iesou said smiling, and patting Noland on the back as he stood.

"Right…" Noland said, smiling.

"Achaia will be needing a weapon." Shael said, turning his back on Luc, who was fuming with rage.

"I'm sure she has several," Noland said, looking at Achaia for confirmation. "Sir," he added, looking at Shael, who didn't seem impressed.

Shael looked at Achaia for her to confirm or deny. Noland however was throwing a guilty look toward Bale, who was staring on in disbelief, as Achaia pulled up her left sleeve. Around her wrist was the beautiful diemerilium snake that looked like a bracelet wrapped up her arm. It glimmered with watery looking emerald silver scales, and emerald eyes. Achaia grabbed the head of the snake and yanked. It uncoiled from around her wrist and lashed out in a wide arch with a loud crack.

"I'm ready."

"You're a slave driver like your mother," Shael said rolling his eyes at her whip.

"But I am my father's daughter," Achaia said, pulling her feather dagger from her belt with her left hand.

Shael smiled at her proudly.

"Can I catch my breath first?" Emile asked, looking exhausted.

"By all means," Iesou said, gesturing to the sofas. "You have nothing to fear here, for the moment."

Luc was fuming, he had remained silent for too long. "You

will rue this day. Mark my words. You will wish you had chosen eternity with me when this is over." Achaia looked at him, expecting him to be talking to her father, only to find him staring into her eyes.

She only took a moment to recover. "I can't imagine what I would have to go through, to prefer an eternity with you in its place."

"I can." Luc growled.

***

Luc had retreated to the other side of the hall while waiting for Iesou to leave. Achaia watched him huddle together whispering with his demons by the bar. She finally took a good look at her father and chronicled a list of his apparent injuries.

"Did they torture you?" Achaia asked him under her breath, as the others checked each other over for any serious damage.

"No," her father shook his head. "This is all from sport."

"Are you okay?"

"Are you?" Shael leveled his gaze demanding an honest response.

"I haven't had a chance to think about it. Ask me again when we get out of this place." Achaia absentmindedly rubbed a finger over the cut on her wrist from the demon tooth. She felt violated not being able to remember how she had gotten to where John wanted her.

"Iesou left," Noland said coming up next to Achaia. "We're on our own from here on out."

Shael nodded and looked over at Luc appraisingly. "He won't make it easy."

As if that was his cue, Luc sauntered over, a devilish grin on his face. "Your welcome here has expired." He was looking at Noland. Emile, and the others came to stand behind him. Achaia found herself taking an involuntary step toward him herself, and her father followed. They stood grouped together, bracing themselves for whatever Luc might have in store for them.

Luc turned and nodded at two demons that were still next to the bar; one of them promptly left the room, and the other came and stood next to him. The demon that joined them was a short squat demon that looked something like a wombat.

Achaia heard her father snort, and looked up to see him grinning.

"This is your second?" Shael laughed. "Surprisingly anticlimactic choice, there." Shael nodded toward the pathetic looking creature. "Hello again, Gaki."

Luc's brow flinched with contempt. "He is not my only second." At that, Achaia heard a scratching scuttling sound. She turned her attention to the archways around the room, the only exits, and saw to her horror that they were swarmed. Dozens of demons, like massive insects were scaling the walls, and climbing up to the ceiling. Others were approaching from the ground. They were being surrounded. Ice chips fell from the ceiling as the demons' claws, like massive icepicks, dislodged chunks of the ceiling as they moved along its surface.

"Holy sh—"

Luc grabbed Gaki and covered his ears. "Watch your language!" He spat. "They are no such thing!" He patted Gaki consolingly on the back, as he released his huge ears. He mumbled something about no sane person being able to mistake them for holy, and turned his attention back to Achaia with a frown. "You have a vile temper, a biting sarcasm, and a coldness about you Achaia."

Achaia stepped back as if she had been smacked, but recovered quickly.

"I feel we would have done quite well together." Luc smiled. "Who knows, maybe we'll still get our chance."

Achaia cringed and felt like something slimy had dripped down her spine at the word 'our'.

"As nice as this visit has been, I'm beyond ready to get out of here," Shael said, looking at the others to make sure they were all ready.

Luc sneered. "As you wish, brother." Luc whistled loudly, it echoed through the hall, and the demons on the ceiling rose like an upside down tide as the ones on the floor advanced.

"Two up!" Shael yelled looking to Noland and Naphtali.

Achaia had no idea what he was talking about, but they seemed to get the message. Naphtali and Noland unleashed their wings and rose like torches into the air, burning and slashing the demons from the ceiling. Noland was using the fire coming from Naphtali to create tornados of fire that he used to lash out at the masses of demons. They fell from the ceiling, landing on their comrades on the ground with sickening, bone-crunching thuds.

Achaia stood with her whip in one hand and her dagger in the other. She slashed one demon across the eye as he approached, and while he was distracted, she jumped on his front and slit his throat with the dagger.

"That's my girl!" Her father yelled. "Like an angry spider monkey." He laughed, joyfully.

Achaia smiled, but didn't turn to look at him. She leapt from the chest of the demon as he fell, and lunged for the one coming from behind him. One step, and one demon, closer to the exit.

Bale and Olivier were thinning the path in front of them, and she knew without looking that Emile was behind her with his bow; arrows were soaring over her head, impaling demons that were coming up on her.

Achaia looked up, and saw a demon like a large-man-sized

lizard stalking her. She swung her whip around her head like a lasso and aimed for the demon, her whip wrapping around its waist. She pulled him down from the ceiling hard, and was happy to see one of Emile's arrows hit him in the abdomen on the way down. He landed on the arrow so that it pierced him through as his head collided with the floor. She jumped up, and landed in a straddle over him as he squirmed, and jammed her dagger down into his temple.

They had all made it to the archway. Achaia hoped that if they made it into the narrowness of the tunnel, they could make faster progress. The crowds of demons would have a harder time following them if they were tripping over themselves.

Achaia heard her father's voice, and knew he was shouting instruction. Noland and Naphtali took up the lead, clearing the path with fire, torching all the demons that came before them, but Achaia noticed that Noland was already looking exhausted. She wondered how long the fight had been for him to get to her, and he had hardly had a chance to rest.

Emile took up the rear, shooting all the demons that tried to follow them. Olivier helped by darting around quickly retrieving arrows from the fallen demons and returning them to his brother's quiver.

Achaia, Bale, and Shael fought off all the demons not vanquished by fire, or who broke passed Emile's line of fire.

Achaia was feeling hopeful, until she remembered just how long the tunnel had been when she had walked through it peacefully with John. A wave of dread washed over her, as she looked down the tunnel, and saw nothing but demons, and no light.

# 19

# The Difference Between Battle and War.

"Know thyself, know thy enemy.
A thousand battles, a thousand victories."

-Sun Tzu

The tunnel was crowded with humanoid demons that looked wolfish and reptilian. They reminded Achaia of horrible looking werewolves in a sci-fi movie. Their scales were a dark green, and black, but their muscles were thick and bulky like the beasts of fantasy.

Achaia slung her whip through the air, catching one of the beasts around the neck, as it went for Olivier. The demon scratched at the whip around its neck as it tightened. Olivier dug his dagger into the side of the beast's head, and it slumped over.

Achaia recalled her whip, just as another demon charged her as if to tackle her to the ground. As its head barreled under her arm, she wrapped the thick of her whip around its neck. Instead of falling backward onto the ground, Achaia flung herself around the side of the demon landing on its back, and pulled on the whip, choking it. The creature fell to its knees, gagging. Another demon came up behind her. She kept one hand pulling hard on the whip, while stabbing blindly behind her with the other. She could hear the demon growling, but it had not released her.

The demon had grabbed her around the neck, and lifted her into the air from behind. She kicked backward, her feet making contact with it repeatedly, but again, to no apparent avail. Achaia recalled her whip from the demon in front of her, and lashed out backwards. She couldn't tell if she was hitting the demon holding her, or something else, but it choked her harder.

White lights were flashing before her eyes, and she started losing the ability to focus.

"Achaia!" She heard someone call her name, but she couldn't tell who it had been. Then she was falling. She hit the ground hard, her legs didn't catch her. Feet were rushing in every direction, most of them were gigantic, clawed and paw-like.

She took a couple deep breaths which caused her to cough, and sat up still disoriented. A demon, on all fours, hunched over her, roaring with its jaws open wide, and coming toward her face. She stared into the vast mouth beyond, and seemed to snap to. As the jaw loomed over her, she jammed her arm quickly into its mouth and grabbed the back of the beast's tongue. Its breath smelled like iron. The demon coughed and gagged, its mouth opening wider in reflex. Then she pushed with her other hand against its trap, and yanked on its tongue. It roared with anger and pain, and Achaia felt the resistance give, and then give *way completely as she pulled the demon's tongue from its mouth. As it writhed in pain, she looked quickly around for a weapon. A few feet away, she saw her dagger laying on the ground, and crawled toward it.*

*Demons were all over them. As she grabbed her dagger and turned back Achaia couldn't see any of her companions in the mass hysteria.*

Achaia woke up sweating and gasping for air. She sat up straight, holding her dagger out in front of her. Checking her wrist quickly, she saw that her whip was still coiled up her arm, the head of the snake looking as if it were napping on her hand. She also saw the thin line from where she had cut herself with the demon tooth.

Achaia lowered her dagger and fought to keep her eyes open. She stared around the room, knowing the second she closed her eyes she would see them again; even if it was just to blink. She lit the candle on the nightstand and sat all the way up, leaning against her headboard.

Giving up on getting anymore sleep, she wrapped the blanket Noland had given her around her shoulders, her fire had gone out, and her room was drafty. She grabbed the candle and decided to go and sit by the fire in the library and read until everyone else woke up.

She walked the quiet and empty halls of the safe house until she reached the library double doors. The door creaked loudly as she opened it. She flinched at the contrast it posed to the silence. She picked up the book that was left next to one of the arm chairs and almost laughed. It was Dante's *Inferno*. She curled up in the chair in front of the fire and started reading.

She had made it through the first canto and had started the second when she heard footsteps. A figure appeared in the door. She saw the shadow of the figure move into the room, and as it rounded one of the bookshelves, she saw that it was Noland.

"Oh," he said as he saw her. "I didn't think anyone else would be here," he said honestly.

Achaia shrugged.

"Couldn't sleep?" he asked.

Achaia shook her head. There was a long moment of silence as Noland selected a book and sat in the chair across from her.

"I—," Achaia started but stopped when she realized that she had no idea what she had been meaning to say, only that she felt like she should say something.

"We don't have to talk about it," Noland said quietly. There was a numb sort of sadness to his voice that Achaia felt in her chest when she heard it, like a push against her ribs.

"Ever?" She asked.

Noland looked across at her. More than ever Achaia wished for even just a hint of Emile's gift, that she could have an idea of Noland's thoughts and what he was feeling. He said nothing, though, just looked back down at his book and started reading. Achaia felt as if a wall had been built between them. She wasn't sure when or how it had gone up, or if it could ever come back down. But something was broken.

\*\*\*

The sun had come up at some point, and had finally reached the point of coming over the surrounding buildings to filter in through the windows of the library.

Noland had fallen asleep with his book in his lap, and his head leaning against the wing of the armchair. With a loud bang, the doors of the library were thrust open, and Yellaina came running in looking around frantically. Noland startled awake, holding up his book as if prepared to use it as a weapon against the intruder.

Yellaina stepped back, looking relieved and alarmed. "I've

been looking everywhere for you two!"

Noland looked over to see Achaia was still sitting in her arm chair, looking as though sleep had evaded her once and for all the night before. Her eyes were red, and had dark circles under them, her hair was a tangled mess, from where, he guessed, she had tossed and turned whenever she *had* slept. He hadn't noticed in the dim firelight, the night before, how rough she looked.

"What's up?" Noland asked, standing and stretching.

"Joash is here." Yellaina said, urgently.

Noland stopped mid-stretch and stared at her. "What?"

"He isn't alone. A lot of the elders are here, including Olivier's parents. They really aren't happy."

Noland nodded and looked over at Achaia. He had known there would be repercussions for their actions, but their transgressions were unprecedented. He had no idea how severe the punishment would be. He sighed, and set his book down on the seat of his chair. He searched his mind for any kind of words of encouragement for Achaia, but found nothing. He wouldn't lie to her. This was bad. So he didn't say anything. He looked over at her and saw her set her book down, and square her shoulders.

Noland followed Yellaina, Achaia walking behind them, to Bales quarters.

The room was crowded with four council elders, Shael, Naphtali, and Bale all surrounding the desk. Olivier and Emile entered behind them, and Yellaina exited the room, closing the door behind her.

"Do you care to explain why on earth you would decide to enter the domain of Lucifer?" Emile's father asked, in a stern, fatherly tone, looking mainly at Noland and Emile and Olivier.

"It was my fault." Achaia said, before anyone else could think to speak. "I went to save my father. Your council didn't seem inclined to help me, so I took matters into my own hands. As you're well aware, I'm not one of you. Your rules don't apply to me. Your rules do however mandate that Noland, as my Guardian, do everything in his power to protect me. Needless to say, in the fulfillment of his duty, he and the others, came after me." Achaia looked at the elders not only as if she were absolutely fearless, but as if she were livid. "So I ask you, why, in defiance of your own laws, you denied underage Nephilim back up and support in a dangerous situation?"

Mr. Dubois looked thunderstruck. Mrs. Dubois was trying to hide a smile, and Noland wondered if she had already asked them this question herself. Elders Joash and Zion however looked as if they would burn Achaia alive for her audacity.

"You do not get to pose questions to us, Achaia bat Shael."

"Then you can not pose questions to me. And as I have already explained, the incident was entirely of my making. So I am left to wonder why you wasted the trip." She was staring Joash down with a look of such loathing, Noland was tempted to cringe, but he didn't.

"You will never be one of us." It seemed that Joash for once, was at a loss of anything else to say. Noland had never seen him look so angry.

"You think very highly of yourself. I think we both know, you don't really have a say in that matter. I think you also assume too much in thinking I want anything to do with your council. I have yet to see your worth."

Noland looked over to see a very distinct look of pride on Shael's face.

"So let me make this clear. My allegiance will not be pledged to *you*. That is not to say that I have or ever will pledge allegiance to Lucifer. It is my business and not yours who I pledge myself to. And you can keep your nose and the rest of your vile self out of my endeavors."

Noland was surprised to look over and see Bale hiding a smile and perhaps even a laugh. Noland, Emile, and Olivier were watching in shock and horror, knowing that if any of them had ever spoken in such a way the ramifications would have been severe. And yet, Achaia was baring all.

There was a tense and awkward moment of silence where everyone in the room was watching Achaia and Joash stare each other down, bright green eyes against unfeeling blue ones.

"You're free to leave." Achaia said coolly.

Joash looked as if he had been smacked, and that was the last straw. "You do not dismiss me, you—"

"No, but I do." Bale said cutting him off. "You forget that I am not fallen, I am not of your council, and you are trespassing on my hospitality. The young lady is right. You neglected your own, and as far as I am concerned, and I am a delegate from heaven," he reminded them, "you have forfeited your right to punish them. The battle they faced, bravely," he looked at Noland then, and smiled, "was punishment enough. You are dismissed."

Joash and Zion looked outraged and stormed out of the room. Emile's parents followed, pausing only for a moment for Mrs. Dubois to caress each of her son's faces. A motherly look of relief washed over her face.

"Did you just call me a young lady?" Achaia asked, once the council members were gone.

Bale rolled his eyes, but smiled. "Whatever is coming, and something is coming, you have an ally in me, Achaia bat Shael."

Noland smiled.

***

Back in New York, the warmth of spring was thawing winter. Achaia sat in the bedroom of her apartment with the windows open to the fire escape outside. It had been a week since they had come home from Russia. Conversation between her and her father had been strained, awkward.

Upon arriving home, she was given the option of going back to mortal school or training full time with the others under the tutelage of Yallaina's father Jacob. Achaia had been so focused on figuring out the spiritual world, and finding her father, she'd never given a second's thought toward what day to day life as a Nephilim would look like.

She knew she couldn't take it all back. There was no denying what she was now. The council had been less than enthusiastic about her venture into Hell to find her father. They distrusted her and her father now more than ever.

She couldn't help feeling that she didn't belong in their world any more than the mortal world. Could she train, grow up to be a Guardian and protector of humanity? It sounded nice, helping people, serving a greater purpose… but would the council ever really allow it? Or would she be more of a vigilante? That wouldn't pay the bills, but she had a hard time considering joining the mortal workforce… Her father seemed to make both work… kind of.

Achaia laid back on her bed, and stared at the ceiling fan, turning around and around. She hadn't seen any of the others since they'd gotten back. Yellaina and Amelia had been so happy to see her, but she was worried that she had tainted the reputations of Olivier, Emile, Noland and Bale. Bale didn't even like her, yet had gone into Hell for her, and he was going to pay for it, she was sure.

There was a knock on her door and she jumped up.

"Sorry," her father said in the doorway. "You're probably going to be jumpy for a while. But you'll get used to it all." He smiled sadly. "This isn't what I wanted for you." He came into her room and sat on the bed next to her.

"What did you want exactly?" Achaia asked. She was happy to have her father back, but after the relief had worn off, it was quite evident that she was very angry with him. She felt guilty for not acting happier to have him back. She knew she wasn't making much of a homecoming for him, but she was so angry. "There were just so many lies… I don't know what to believe." She said honestly.

"I know," Shael said. "I expected this. I don't expect it to be okay overnight, but I need you to understand, that I wanted you to be saved from all of this."

"From what I am?" Achaia asked standing and pacing the floor in front of her windows.

"Look," he said, "we will have plenty of time to talk about all of this, but you have a visitor."

"Who?" Achaia asked.

"I believe his name is Olivier?" Shael said.

"Olivier?" Achaia asked, her anger subsiding. She walked quickly out of her room and down the short hall. Sure enough, Olivier was standing in front of the fireplace, his hands clasped behind his back. "Hey," Achaia said coming into the room.

"Your dad?" Olivier started.

Achaia glanced down the hall just as her father's bedroom door closed. "You're good," Achaia smiled.

"Dang, he is intimidating!" Olivier said letting out a sigh of relief. "I forgot your name when he answered the door. I asked to see Sheila."

"Who's Sheila?" Achaia laughed.

"I've never even actually met a Sheila!" Olivier said throwing his hands up and collapsing on the couch.

Achaia laughed and sat down next to him. "How are you?"

"I'm alright. Yellaina is still mad at me for not letting her come to help you." Achaia nodded her sympathy.

"I'm glad you didn't though. That tunnel out was rough." She winced remembering it. "What about Amelia?"

"She came around. She understands. She knows her gift can also be a liability." He shrugged. "How are you?"

Achaia felt her face fall.

"Do you have nightmares, too?" Olivier asked.

"You have nightmares?" Achaia asked.

Olivier nodded. "That tunnel was bad."

"What about the others?" Achaia asked.

"Well Noland doesn't really show anything, does he?" Olivier said shrugging. "And Emile has had to put up with everyone's anger, resentment, anxiety, blah blah blah," Olivier said rolling his hand through the air to symbolize the apparently never-ending list. "But they all miss you."

"I've just needed some space," Achaia said, feeling guilty.

"I get that, I do. Processing room, it's important. I just wanted to remind you that you're not alone in all of this, and that we love you."

Achaia couldn't keep from startling at those last words.

Olivier smiled. "We do," he said seriously. "You're our family now." He reached over and wrapped an arm around her and pulled her into a side hug. Achaia laid her head on his chest, and Olivier tucked it in under his chin. "Frenchy, we're not just going to let you disappear. It's time to come back."

"Do you think I can do it?" Achaia asked. "Be a Guardian?"

"I think you can do whatever you want to, and there's not a

soul alive who could prevent it," Olivier smirked. "Not after the way you talked to Joash! You really gave him a—" Olivier boxed the air with his fists.

Achaia laughed, sitting back up. "You have so much more confidence in me than I do."

"You'll get there. And we're going to need you to. I heard what Luc said to you down there." Olivier looked very solemn all of a sudden. "He's got it out for you now, for sure. This isn't over."

Achaia nodded, she knew it was true. She felt the truth of it every time an unforeseen noise sounded, or someone appeared unexpectedly. She was constantly on edge.

"You won a battle, but it may have started an entirely new war," Olivier said bleakly.

"Well," Achaia said, tucking up a knee to her chest, "when he comes I want to be ready."

"So you'll train with us?" Olivier asked excitedly.

Achaia looked back at her father's closed bedroom door. "I want to make sure I know exactly how to fight him. I am going to be trained by the best." Achaia said turning back to Olivier, "Wether he likes it or not."

Olivier smiled down at her, looking at the whip wrapped around her wrist. "Have you named it yet?" He asked, looking back up to her face.

"I think so," Achaia said, smiling. "I'm going to call him Aka-kios."

"Innocence?" Olivier smirked.

Achaia smiled mischievously. "With what other weapon would you fight the father of lies?" She laughed and rubbed the scales of the snake with her index finger, as if he were a living pet. In some ways, she felt like he was. Noland had taught her that weapons each had their own personality.

"I was actually coming over to see if you wanted to go to the Farmacy?" Olivier smiled at her, hopefully. "Everyone has been a mess since we got back. I just want to talk to someone sane who isn't mad at me, and appreciates the dynamic between Wolverine and Magneto."

Achaia laughed and grabbed her sweat shirt off the coat rack. "I could use a float."

"We're going to need our strength if there is a war brewing," Olivier half-joked.

Achaia opened the door, "Luc can come after me if he wants. I'm going to make sure we're ready."

# About the Author

Brandy Ange is the YA author of The Kingdom Come Series. A published author of essays, poetry, and short stories since 2004, Transgression is her debut novel. With a BA in Bible, her fiction explores age old mysteries of the spiritual world, and mortal world alike. She currently resides on the barrier islands of North Carolina where she mentors at risk youth. For more information or to contact the author you can visit her website brandyange.me

# Notes from the Author

The Brooklyn Farmacy and Soda Fountain is a real place! It is one of my favorite spots in Brooklyn and I highly suggest you all try it out if you're ever in the neighborhood.

Brooklyn Farmacy
513 Henry Street
Brooklyn New York 11231

http://www.brooklynfarmacyandsodafountain.com/

## RAPHA❋HOUSE
## [LOVE-RESCUE-HEAL]

Rapha House is an organization that I have admired and supported for years. They serve an important purpose in our world today, helping those who often cannot help themselves. For more details, and to see where a portion of the proceeds of this book have gone, visit their website.

https://raphahouse.org/